Praise for the Novels of Martha Grimes

The Blue Last
A *New York Times* Bestseller

"Grimes's best Jury novel since *The Case Has Altered*. She excels at creating a haunting atmosphere and characters both poignant and preposterous." —*USA Today*

"A diverting, chilling mystery of the past. . . . [Grimes] is at the top of her form. . . . Profoundly affecting and hauntingly sad . . . [an] explosive, cliffhanger ending." —*Richmond Times-Dispatch*

"[Grimes's] gift for evoking mood and emotion is as keen as her talent for inventing a demanding puzzle and solving it." —*The Wall Street Journal*

"*The Blue Last* checks in as the pinnacle of her popular series . . . a more solid, cohesive plot and darker tones elevate this seventeenth Jury novel. . . . It is not the villian who is as important in *The Blue Last* as it is this intense visit with Jury." —*South Florida Sun-Sentinel*

"Vintage Grimes, atmospheric, humorous, and hauntingly sad."—*News & Record* (Greensboro, NC)

continued . . .

"Combines all the essentials for a good read between and under the covers . . . full of twists and turns and told in Grimes's tantalizingly literate style—it's fun; it's filling; it's literature."
—*The State* (Columbia, SC)

"The author is so skilled in creating plot and character that the reader will feel plunked down in the midst of modern London and will be grateful for being made privy to Jury's uncommon insights rendered through Grimes's affecting prose."
—*Chattanooga Times Free Press*

"This is vintage Jury: a historic pub, a crew of well fleshed out characters, and the inspector himself, sensitive and caustic as ever, an old-time seer able to explain the unexplainable."   —*Booklist*

"[A] surprising but logical solution . . . ingenious. . . . Grimes's delicious people portraits and elegant prose are as entertaining as ever."   —*Kirkus Reviews*

"[A] literate tale of loss tempered with wit . . . enigmatic . . . a bittersweet end."
—*The Orlando Sentinel*

The Lamorna Wink
A *New York Times* Bestseller

"Atmospheric . . . an elegantly styled series."
— *The New York Times Book Review*

"Swift and satisfying . . . grafts the old-fashioned
'Golden Age' amateur-detective story to the
contemporary police procedural . . . real charm."
— *The Wall Street Journal*

"Fans . . . will not be disappointed." — *USA Today*

"As consuming as its fifteen predecessors."
— *Publishers Weekly* (starred review)

"Charming, delightful. . . . Grimes fleshes out her
characters with witty dialogue. Long may she write
Richard Jury mysteries." — *Chicago Tribune*

The Stargazey
A *New York Times* Bestseller

"Wondrously eccentric characters. . . . The details are
divine." — *The New York Times Book Review*

"The literary equivalent of a box of Godiva
truffles. . . . Wonderful." — *Los Angeles Times*

"*The Stargazey* is well worth setting your sights on."
— *USA Today*

"A delightfully entertaining blend of irony, danger,
and intrigue, liberally laced with wit and charm. . . .
A must-have from one of today's most gifted and
intelligent writers." — *Booklist* (starred review)

continued . . .

The Case Has Altered

"Richly textured."
> —*The New York Times Book Review*

"Grimes is dazzling in this deftly plotted Richard Jury mystery." —*Publishers Weekly*

"A delicious ebb and flow of tension. . . . Twists and turns. . . . Beautifully rendered atmosphere. . . . Vintage Grimes." —*Library Journal*

"Provocative entertainment." —*The Orlando Sentinel*

"Brilliant . . . [an] outstanding story from one of today's most talented writers." —*Booklist*

I Am the Only Running Footman

"Everything about Miss Grimes's new novel shows her at her best. . . . [She] gets our immediate attention. . . . She holds it, however, with something more than mere suspense." —*The New Yorker*

"Literate, witty, and stylishly crafted."
> —*The Washington Post*

"One of the most fascinating mystery writers today."
> —*Houston Chronicle*

"A superior writer."
> —*The New York Times Book Review*

"A gem of a mystery writer."
> —*The Christian Science Monitor*

Martha Grimes

The Blue Last

A RICHARD JURY MYSTERY

AN ONYX BOOK

ONYX
Published by New American Library, a division of
Penguin Putnam Inc., 375 Hudson Street,
New York, New York 10014, U.S.A.
Penguin Books Ltd, 80 Strand,
London WC2R 0RL, England
Penguin Books Australia Ltd, Ringwood,
Victoria, Australia
Penguin Books Canada Ltd, 10 Alcorn Avenue,
Toronto, Ontario, Canada M4V 3B2
Penguin Books (N.Z.) Ltd, 182–190 Wairau Road,
Auckland 10, New Zealand

Penguin Books Ltd, Registered Offices:
Harmondsworth, Middlesex, England

Published by Onyx, an imprint of New American Library,
a division of Penguin Putnam Inc. Previously published in a Viking edition.

First Onyx Printing, September 2002
10 9 8 7 6 5 4 3 2 1

Good-bye, Blue

Dark hills at evening, in the west
Where sunset hovers like a sound
Of golden horns that sang to rest
Old bones of warriors underground,

Far now from all the bannered ways
Where flash the legions of the sun,
You fade—as if the last of days
Were fading, and all wars were done.

"The Dark Hills"
E. A. Robinson

I

Remembrance Mile

ONE

" 'Poet,' it says, 'died from stab of rose.' Must be a thorn that stabbed him. Who do you suppose that is?"

Richard Jury looked up and across at Sergeant Wiggins. "Rilke. What is that, the crossword? Rilke, if memory serves me." Memory served up entirely too much. Jury sat reading a forensics report while Detective Sergeant Wiggins, seated at a desk across the room, was stirring up ever more esoteric means of dying. Wiggins was really into death, Jury remarked not for the first time. Or at least into the ills that flesh is heir to. Wiggins was heir to the lot, to hear him talk.

"Rilke?" said Wiggins. He counted the spaces. "That'd fit all right. You'd be a whiz at crosswords, knowing things like that." He poured out the tea.

"That's the only thing I know like that."

Wiggins was spooning in sugar, and, having dumped four teaspoonfuls into his own tea, started in on Jury's.

"One," said Jury, not even looking up from his folder. Tea making in this office had achieved the status of ritual, one so long undertaken that Jury knew where Sergeant Wiggins was at every step. Perhaps it was the spoon clicking against the cup with each teaspoonful that sent out a signal.

"Was he hemophiliac, then, this Rilke?"

"Beats me." Trust Wiggins to put it down to a disorder of blood or bone. A lengthy silence followed, during which Jury did look up to see Wiggins sitting with his hands wrapped around both mugs as he stared out of the window. "Is my mug going to grow little mug legs and walk over here on its own?"

Wiggins jumped. "Oh, sorry." He rose and took Jury's tea to him, saying, when he'd returned to his own desk, "I just can't think of other blood conditions that would result in death from a rose-thorn prick."

Lines of a poem came unbidden to Jury's mind:

> *O Rose, thou ar't sick.*
> *The invisible worm . . .*

William Blake. He wouldn't mention this to Wiggins. One rose death was enough for one morning.

Wiggins persisted. "A prick could cause that much blood to flow? I mean, the guy could hardly bleed out from it." He frowned, drank his tea, kept on frowning. "I should know the answer to that."

"Why? That's what police doctors are for. Call forensics if you're desperate."

> *That flies in the night*
> *In the howling storm . . .*

Jury closed the file on skeletal remains and watched the slow-falling snow. Hardly enough to dampen the pavement, much less a ski slope. Well, had he planned on skiing in Islington? He could go to High Wycombe; they had all-season skiing around there. How depressing. In two weeks, Christmas would be here. More depressing. "You going to Manchester for Christmas, Wiggins?"

"To my sister and her brood, yes. You, sir?"

"You mean am I going to Newcastle? No." That he would not go to his cousin (and *her* brood) filled him with such a delicious ease that he wondered if happiness lay not in doing but in not doing.

Wiggins appeared to be waiting for Jury to fill him in on his Christmas plans. If Newcastle was out, what then? When Jury didn't supply something better, Wiggins didn't delve. He just returned to death and its antidotes, a few bottles and vials of which were arranged on his desk. Wiggins looked them over, hit on the viscous pink liquid and squeezed several drops into a half glass of water, which he then swirled into thinner viscosity.

He said, "But we're on rota for Christmas, at least Christmas morning. I won't get to Manchester until dinnertime, probably."

"Hell, just go ahead. I'll cover for you."

Wiggins shook his head. "No, that wouldn't be fair, sir. No, I'll be here. Christmas can be hell on wheels for people deciding to bloody up other people. Just give some guy a holiday and he goes for a gun."

Jury laughed. "True. Maybe we'll have time for a bang-up lunch at Danny Wu's on Christmas Day. He never closes on holidays." Ruiyi was the best restaurant in Soho.

Then came silence and snow. Jury thought about a present for Wiggins. Some medical book, one that might define Rilke's "disease of the blood," if that's what it was. A thorn prick. *O Rose, thou ar't sick.* He tried to remember the last four lines of this short poem, but couldn't.

Wiggins had gone back to the newspaper. "They're starting to clear the old Greenwich gasworks. To put up the dome, that millennium dome they're talking about."

Jury didn't want to hear about it or talk about it. Wiggins loved the subject. "That's years away, Wiggins. Let's wait and be surprised."

Wiggins regarded him narrowly, not knowing what to make of that runic comment.

Jury got up, pulled on his coat and picked up the folder which held Haggerty's report. "I'm going to the

City; if you need me I'll be at Snow Hill police station with Mickey Haggerty."

"All right." Wiggins drank his pink stuff and turned toward the window. He said, as Jury was going out the door, "It sounds like something out of a fairy tale, almost."

"What does? The millennium dome?"

"No, no, no. It's this Rilke fellow. It's like the princess who pricked her finger spinning, falling asleep forever. Dying from the prick of a rose thorn." He looked at Jury. "It's sort of a breathtaking death, isn't it?"

"I guess I don't want to be breathtaken, Wiggins. See you."

TWO

The City of London, that square mile which was London's commercial and financial heart, had never been a hive of industry at the weekend. At the weekend, it was quaintly dead.

Jury left Tower Hill underground station and stood looking across Lower Thames Street. He couldn't remember the last time he'd been this close to the Tower of London. The tourists were snapping pictures, a few with disposable cameras, others with more sophisticated ones. Christmas was in two weeks, a popular time for tourists. He passed an Indian restaurant on Fenchurch Street, and if that was closed he could pretty well bet that everything was.

But not the Snow Hill station, of course. An unhappy-looking constable was on duty behind the information desk and looked almost grateful that Jury wanted nothing more than a direction to Haggerty's office. Detective Chief Inspector Haggerty? Through there, down there, his door there. Jury thanked him.

Haggerty was sitting at his desk, looking at police photographs when Jury walked in. Mickey Haggerty got up and walked around the desk to take Jury's hand and punch him on the shoulder a couple of times, making it more than a handshake, less than an embrace. Jury hadn't seen Mickey Haggerty, or his wife Liza, in several years and felt guilty for allowing the friendship to languish. But that wasn't entirely down to him, was it? Mickey must bear some of the brunt.

No cop (thought Jury) was more "in place" than Mickey Haggerty. He fit the Job as snugly as a paving stone in a new-laid path. "Hello, Mickey. It's been a long time."

"Too damned long," said Mickey, who indicated a chair for Jury before reseating himself. "How're you keeping, Rich?"

"Fine." This sort of exchange would have been banal between most people, but not with Mickey on the other end of it. He genuinely wanted to know. They talked for a minute about Liza and the kids, and then Jury slid the file he'd brought across the desk to Mickey. "Looks like a dig. This is a case you're working on? Was I supposed to come up with some helpful response? I don't know much about forensic anthropology—"

Mickey was shaking his head. "I only wanted you to see the file so you'd have a better idea of what I'm talking about. Yes, it's a case I'm working on. Me, personally. Say it's unofficial business. Or say I don't really want anyone to know about it. It's personal." He turned one photograph around. In the center of the rubble were two skeletons.

At least, Jury made out what he thought were two. "What is this, then, Mickey?"

"Skeletons recovered from a bomb site."

"Bomb site? Where?"

"Here. In the City. Near Ludgate Circus. If you want to see it, it's not far from St. Paul's, on a street called Blackfriars Lane." Mickey drew a little map and passed it over. "The last bomb site in London."

Jury's eyebrows went up a notch higher, in question.

"The war. You know. The Second World War?"

Jury's smile did not reach his eyes. "I've heard of it, yes."

Mickey picked up a cigar that had been smoldering in a large blue ashtray to his right. When Mickey exhaled,

Jury tracked the smoke. He hadn't had a cigarette in nearly two years, but his need for one hadn't abated. It infuriated him. He smiled. "So go on."

From another folder, Mickey took another report. "Two skeletons recovered at the site."

"What are you reading?"

"From the anthropology people at the University of London. They took the skeletons to do a study. They were, naturally, interested. For all they knew, these remains could have been ancient remains."

"But they weren't?"

Mickey shook his head. "Skeletons of a female, early twenties, a baby not more than a few months, probably two or three."

"They can fix it that closely? In a baby? But the bones are still forming."

"Teeth. They can even fix the development of a fetus by teeth. The teeth form underneath the gums. These were the only skeletons recovered. The bomb site was where a pub once stood; it was demolished in the blitz. That was back in 1940. Specifically, December 29, 1940. The site's been bought up by a developer. There's construction going on now."

Jury sat back and said nothing. He had never been able to reflect upon the war without considerable pain. But his intense feelings about that time made it, ironically and uncomfortably enough, magnetic.

Mickey picked up the cigar from the ashtray and smoked. And thought.

It was one of the things Jury liked about him: he was a meditative man. Like Jury himself, he did not jump to conclusions; yet at the same time, he acted on instinct. Jury knew it was difficult to do both. He recalled sitting in a pub with Mickey when they were working a case nine or ten years ago and not a word passed between them for ten minutes. Mickey reminded Jury of Brian Macalvie; they both drove their crime scene people mad with their extended silences.

The station house was oddly quiet. They might have been visiting a memorial. "Who found the remains?"

"Construction crew. They didn't disturb them." Mickey turned the photograph of the two skeletons around so Jury could see it. "What's your off-the-wall guess?"

"It looks as if the baby's skeleton was lying close to the adult's—the mother?"

"I'll tell you a little story." Mickey had opened his desk drawer and taken out a handful of snapshots, old ones in black and white. He took the one off the top and shoved it toward Jury. "This was taken in Dagenham. It was at the beginning of the evacuation, in 1939. Children who were taken by boat to one of the trains bound for the country." Mickey pushed over two more snapshots. "These were taken in Stepney. Evacuation again. My dad used to talk about the unearthly quiet. All those children and hardly a peep out of them."

Jury looked at the band of children, at the gray, unsmiling faces of the mothers.

"That was the exodus in forty, during the so-called phony war, when London prepared for war, but nothing really happened."

Jury hated talking about the war. And what were all of these pictures in aid of? What was the point?

Mickey was pushing yet another snapshot toward Jury. "Right here, I think, are the woman and the child who ended up in the rubble. Alexandra Tynedale, twenty-one or -two, and a baby of maybe four months. Not, however, her *own* baby. The nanny had taken Alexandra's baby out to get some air." Mickey spun another photo to Jury's side of the desk. "This is that baby now: Maisie Tynedale."

Jury looked at the photo. She was attractive, early fifties, he guessed, but from calculating the passing years rather than her looks. She could have been forty, judging by the picture. This was a better picture than the others, taken by a camera superior to the one that had taken the snaps. Jury set it down. He now had five pictures lined up before him. "These two of the evacuation—what about them? What's the story?"

In answer, Mickey pushed over another snapshot. It showed a young woman, back to the camera, face turned to smile down at a baby whose round little chin was propped on the woman's shoulder, arm and hand flat against the woman's back. Jury lined that up in the row, number six, and simply looked the question at Mickey.

"Kitty, the nanny. Katherine Riordin and baby Erin."

Like a card dealer, Mickey flicked another snapshot over. A shot of demolished buildings, red brick blown to bits. A few people were making their way through the rubble. Jury said, "I expect scenes like this must have duplicated themselves thousands of times all over London. I really hate this, Mickey. Both my parents died in this war."

"Sorry, Rich. There is something—"

Jury looked at him thoughtfully. "Something wrong, Mickey?" He thought he actually saw tears forming in the other man's eyes. Maybe not. "Listen, I'm in no hurry. But where is this?" He held up the shot of the blasted building, the all-but-leveled street.

"What I was telling you before. That's the pub—was the pub—owned by Francis Croft. Here's one taken while it was still standing. The Blue Last, it was called. Those two in front of it are Alexandra Tynedale Herrick and Francis Croft. Christmas lights around the door, so it must have been a very short time either before or after this picture was taken. Francis Croft was the business partner and best friend of a man named Oliver Tynedale, Alexandra's father. They'd been friends since childhood. Francis is dead, but Oliver is still alive. Amazing, since he must be ninety. They were like brothers, he and Croft.

"The nanny's—Kitty Riordin's—baby was killed, too; her name was Erin. Kitty was an Irish girl, came over here, as did thousands of poor Irish girls, looking for work *and* her husband. He'd just walked out on her, apparently. Alexandra took her on as a child keeper for Maisie. Kitty's baby, Erin, was the same age as Alexandra's, a few months old." He sighed and ran his hand across his hair, roughing it up, as if that would improve the thought process.

Jury sat back. "Tynedale. Of Tynedale Brewery? One of the biggest in the country?"

"Both of them actually owned it. Tynedale and Croft."

"Francis Croft must have been pretty down to earth if he was part of the Tynedale empire and was still landlord of a pub."

Smiling, Mickey leaned back in his swivel chair, hands folded on his chest. "He was. He was great, a great person. My dad was a close friend of Francis's. When I was growing up, Dad talked about him a lot." Mickey passed over another snapshot.

Jury found himself looking at an airfield, at what appeared to be a fighter plane, Spitfire or maybe a Hawker Hurricane. The pilot, getting into or out of the cockpit, squinted into the sun. "Ralph Herrick, Alexandra's husband. They'd only been married a little over a year when she died. Ralph died soon after."

Jury wanted to look away, but looking away would make him feel weak. He thought he expended a lot of energy in pulling back from feelings of weakness. "Active duty? His plane was shot down?"

"No, as a matter of fact, he drowned. He was out of the RAF, doing some sort of work in the Orkney Islands, when it happened. He got the V.C., incidentally. A real hero, that's what my father told me."

His head bent over the pictures—seven of them now and showing some anomalous progression of events. Jury studied each in turn. He felt somehow his and his mother's house in Fulham should have been one of them. Mickey had asked him a question which he only half heard.

"I'm sorry, Mickey. I was—" Jury shrugged. Then he asked, "But how can you remember all this?"

"Some of it I remember because it was told me so convincingly and in such detail by my dad. Dad talked about Francis Croft a lot. I know Francis's son, Simon, a little; I haven't seen Oliver Tynedale since I was a kid, though. These snapshots I found among other things in a desk of his. I was going through some papers recently and came across the pictures." He was back to the snapshots again, pulling out of Jury's lineup the ones of Alexandra and the baby Maisie and the one of the nursemaid, Kitty Riordin, and her baby, Erin. The poses were very similar, might have been the same adult and same child. He directed Jury to study the arm and hand of each child bending around the neck or down the back of the mothers.

"Look at the faces. They're both girls, or did I tell you that?"

Jury held the snapshots, one in each hand. He let his eyes travel back and forth. "At this age it's hard to tell the difference, isn't it? Are you going to tell me they shared the father? Something like that?"

"No, no. Look at the hands, the fingers." Mickey handed him a magnifying glass.

Jury did so, carefully. "The Herrick baby's hand looks deformed. A couple of the fingers look disjointed or broken. The Riordin infant's hand is normal, from what I can see."

"You see correctly. Here's another picture, taken *after* the bombing." He shoved it across. "Kitty Riordin holding the baby Maisie."

"The hand's bandaged. Why?"

Mickey sat back in his swivel chair, hands locked behind his head, rocking slightly.

Enjoying this, thought Jury, with a smile. *About to administer the coup de grâce.* Mickey loved mysteries.

"According to Kitty, they'd had an accident that night. Part of a bombed wall had given way, some of the bricks hit them. Kitty wasn't hurt, but the baby Maisie's hand was. Broken in a couple of places. That's interesting. My point being: Maisie Tynedale isn't Maisie Tynedale. She's Erin Riordin. Before you ask why the nanny would try to pass off her own daughter as the Tynedale baby, Maisie is heiress to the Tynedale millions. She goes by Tynedale, incidentally, not Herrick. Again, before you ask why, if I was heir to millions, I'd go by Mickey Mouse, if I thought it would help."

Jury sat back, shocked that this was the end of the story, or at least Mickey's end. "But Mickey, it *could* have happened. And even if the baby's mother was killed, surely others could have identified the baby. I mean, they might look much the same to us, but to a mother—but the mother is dead; to the grandfather, then, to Oliver Tynedale?"

Mickey shook his head. "Imagine you're the granddad. Do you really *want* to dispute the identity? Or do you want to believe, yes, this is your granddaughter? To say nothing of the fact that Kitty Riordin would be denying her own baby is still alive?"

"But others—"

Mickey shrugged. "What others? No one on Kitty Riordin's side, there wasn't anyone. Francis Croft? He's dead. Brother and sisters? All little kids. There was one Croft girl who was Alexandra's age, Emily Croft. I expect she *could* have recognized that the baby wasn't Maisie, but as she didn't say anything about it, I assume she didn't know either." He shrugged again.

"Kitty Riordin took advantage of the bombing and told whoever made any inquiries her own baby was killed in that bombing and she'd had the Tynedale child with her."

Mickey nodded, rubbed his hands through his hair. "That's what I'm saying."

"You haven't enough to go on here. What about your forensics report?"

"Couldn't confirm because the bones were just too

small. I need a forensic anthropologist. I'm sure I'm right."

Shaking his head, Jury sat back and was silent. They were both silent while the longcase clock ticked and the gray day grew a darker gray. Jury said, "This is fascinating, Mickey, but why me? Why did you want to tell it to me? Did you want something from us, I mean the Yard?"

"Yes. I want you to prove it."

Jury's laugh was abrupt, less a laugh than a sound of disbelief. "Me? Are you kidding? Even if it could be proven, you're as good a cop as I am, better probably."

Mickey's smile was thin. "Maybe, but I'm a dead cop. Will be in a couple of months, anyway."

Jury felt as if he'd taken a hard blow to the stomach. "What? Jesus, what's wrong?"

"Leukemia. Specifically, chronic myelogenous leukemia, or in its cozier abbreviation, CML. It's not all that common, but it hits people my age—another version of the midlife crisis, perhaps? Unfortunately, there are no symptoms early on; I found out when it was already pretty much too late. It's very aggressive, very."

Jury's mouth was too dry for him to speak, as if words were liquid, a balm denied him at the moment.

"I've done the chemo crap, but not the bone marrow transplant, assuming even if I could find a donor. The evidence, shall we say, does not stand up to intense scrutiny. Survival rate is almost nil. Two or three months, the doctors give me, which means around one or two, since they always lie. The thing is, Richie, even if I could find the answer to this in a few weeks, I'm just too bloody tired to do it and my other work as well."

Irrationally, as people will out of a sense of hopelessness get angry with the person who is making them feel that way, Jury got angry. "Why in hell aren't you taking the time off? Spend it with Liza and the kids?"

Mickey looked a little disappointed with Jury. "Because I don't want all that spare time to think about it, that's why." He leaned forward across his desk, earnest. "Listen, will you do this? Will you try to find out? It means a lot to me; it sure as hell would to my dad if he were still here."

Jury tapped the pictures together. "Yes. You don't want to see the Crofts and Tynedales swindled. May I keep these for a while?" Jury held up the pictures. Mickey nodded and Jury said, "On the other hand"—he paused, wondering if his taking some high moral tone would sound as priggish as he already had—"this woman Maisie, or Erin, has been part of the family for so long and thought to be the man's granddaughter—"

"You mean wouldn't it be better to let sleeping dogs lie?"

"Something like that. Imagine finding out Maisie isn't Maisie after over a half century." Jury paused. "Anyway, I'll do what I can." He stuffed the pictures into an inside coat pocket and rose and so did Mickey. Jury walked around the desk and embraced him. "Anything, any time, Mickey, day or night. I mean it."

"Thanks, Rich." Tears stood in Mickey's eyes. "It means a lot."

Mickey dying. Mickey dead.

Jury studied the paving stones at his feet as he walked up Ludgate Hill. He walked slowly, almost hesitatingly, thinking it must be like the unsure gait of an aging man. He was too young for this, still, to start thinking of himself as aging, for God's sake.

No one occupied these buildings on the weekend except for the City's caretakers—police, fire brigade, hospital—and the emptiness was partly responsible for this mood.

Then he realized what it reminded him of: a no-man's-land. Though he had no firsthand knowledge of that area in battle of neutral territory which marked neither advance nor retreat and was claimed by neither side. His father had known, though; his father had talked about it. No, it had been his mother's account, such a vivid account it seemed to have been his father's.

I thought it was the work of my own memory. Mickey had said that.

Near St. Paul's Churchyard he looked for Blackfriars Lane and the construction site. He came upon it almost by chance, given the convolutions of the narrow streets. Material hadn't been thrown up yet to shroud it, and the cranes and bulldozers and other equipment sat about in the cratered ground like prehistoric Tinkertoys.

He felt he wanted to gather his few memories about him like a coat or a blanket. He wondered how reliable his memory was, or anyone's memory, come to that.

You could never get what dying was like across to someone else, no matter how intimate the relationship or how sensitive the couple—no matter how able, how willing, how articulate—the sick person is the only one who could possibly know, who could take the measure of it, limn the page, see the borderland.

Maybe it was like walking a beat at two A.M. in a depopulated City. Maybe it was like this and maybe it wasn't. How would he know? The only one who knew was Mickey himself. No wonder the man looked ill.

And what was the admission to this museum of ravaged portraiture? Nothing. Until dying yourself, you couldn't get in. Nothing, nada, nil.

He looked down at the place where the Blue Last had once stood and tried to reconstruct it as he did with any crime scene. The customers in the pub, the extra pints bolstering them, Dutch courage, camaraderie.

Jury had no trouble envisioning a building collapsing around him; what he couldn't imagine is how it had missed him and yet buried his mother. Yet it happened all the time.

And the girl Kitty, stumbling past the matchstick remains of buildings. Half a house sheared off here, another one there, so that you could see in the odd still-standing other half, doorless rooms, a staircase open to view as if it were a dollhouse. But also, at any corner turning, there would be a building left untouched, undamaged as if for pure spite. This would lend the girl hope that the pub had been lucky and had also escaped.

Only it hadn't, and Kitty set about making her own luck.

THREE

On Ludgate Hill, Jury stopped in front of a restaurant that advertised its cappuccino bar. He stood outside dumbly looking in, thinking about Mickey. Would finding out what had happened and to whom, whether the Tynedale granddaughter was who she claimed to be, make Mickey feel connected to earth again?

He walked into the restaurant, deserted except for the help and one woman with dark hair and cold eyes sitting at a table by the window. Jury took a seat at the counter—or bar, he supposed, depending on what you'd come in for. In front of the huge mirror were glass shelves with as good an assortment of liquor as he'd find at any pub.

A pretty waitress with large, dark, soulful-looking eyes came to where he was sitting and took his order for coffee, plain and black. Who did she remind him of? Someone, some actress? Who? She brought the coffee and he sipped it, strong as lye and black as sin, and thought about the morning again. Had it been anyone but Mickey—no. If it had been asked of him in different circumstances by Mickey or anyone else he would have said no. He did not want to dwell on the war again.

"Coffee too strong?" asked the soulful waitress, as if it were all her fault.

"A little, yes." He broke out a smile to replace what must have been his black-coffee expression.

"It hasn't been sitting. I mean, it's fresh, just made." She shrugged slightly. "Our coffee, it's just that way." She gazed at the miscreant cup. "I could put in some hot water." Her expression picked up a smidgen of hope.

"No. I'll tell you what, though. Get me a shot of that." He pointed to a shelf holding the liquor bottles. "That Glen Grant."

She took the bottle from the shelf and pulled a shot glass from beneath the bar and poured. "That should liven it up," she said, pushing the shot glass toward him.

Jury poured it in the cup, sipped, and declared it much improved. Then he asked, "Is it always as empty as this at the weekends?" The only other customer was the icy-eyed brunette. She was smoking what Jury fancied to be the last cigarette in the world.

"Yes, it's because people don't live around here, you know. I mean, except for Docklands, but that's not really the City."

"If it isn't, it's becoming so. All those new condos."

The brunette made a sign and the waitress moved off toward her table.

Jury took the envelope out of his pocket and spread the pictures, one by one, on the bar. He positioned them as nearly as he could in chronological order: the pub, the au pair, Kitty Riordin, the young woman Alex. He smiled. *That* was who the waitress reminded him of! He looked at Alexandra Herrick with her baby, Maisie, then at the fighter plane and the sun-blinded young pilot. He stopped, thinking about his father. He had also been RAF, could have piloted that Spitfire, could have been a friend of Ralph Herrick. The faces themselves meant nothing; Jury could not recall his father's face—how old had he been? But the plane, he could always see the plane spinning toward earth. He had not actually seen it, of course; but in his mind he saw it thus, and there was no one or nothing to correct this vision.

After his mother died, there was the Social, always eager to swoop down and claim another kid. It must have claimed him some time for there was that period in the orphanage. Good Hope, it was called. Funny he'd remember that detail and have lost so many others. First, a kindly uncle had taken him in. He had died and then came Good Hope. Somehow, he had got in his head he was there for five or six years, but now when he tried to call up that period, he wasn't at all sure—five or six months, it could have been. He saw a row of single beds, the sheets so taut a kid could bounce on them. But he wasn't bouncing, only sitting on his own bed in a corner. He tried to remember if his feet had reached to the floor; that might have told him how old he was. How long had he been there?

He thought of his cousin in Newcastle, the daughter of the pleasant aunt and uncle, a girl who hadn't liked him coming into the household. Could his cousin, a bitter woman now, a bitter child then, have put the six years in his head? He could call her and ask; he could even go to Newcastle to try to get some information from her. The husband, a Tyne-and-Wear man, had fallen victim to the North's unspeakable unemployment rate (the "joke shop" is what they called the employment office), and his cousin had for some obscure reason thought it was in part Jury's fault, he being a superintendent at New Scotland Yard. Why should Richard be successful and her Bert not?

He signed to the waitress by making a circle over the shot glass with his finger, then over the coffee cup. The coffee was surprisingly good with a jigger of whiskey, but then what wasn't?

His cousin had four kids, a toddler and the others teenagers by now, he guessed; it had been years since he'd seen her. The last time, that had been Christmas, too. He had not wanted to see her, and not because she herself would heap her troubles on his shoulders, but because she was the last relation he had on earth and he hated being reminded of that fact. He envied Wiggins his sister in Manchester.

The waitress came along the bar with fresh coffee and fresh whiskey. She seemed pleased that Jury was stopping here, that her ministrations had succeeded in some small way. Jury smiled at her, wanting her to think so. When actually the whiskey, as whiskey usually does, merely opened him up to sadder ruminations, to cold little scenes of childhood.

He saw himself seated at a large dinner table with eight or ten other children and the old lady from Oxfordshire (or was it Devon?) at its head, admonishing all of them to eat like little ladies and gentlemen. She had just said grace and while hearing it, Jury had stared down at a plate of pale sausage and sauerkraut which made the bile rise in his throat as it always did when he looked at this once-a-week meal. He would be sick if he ate it.

"Richard's not eating, Richard's not eating, missus—"
Who was taunting him?

"Not eating, not eating," the voice went on fluting, and then the whole table picked it up—*"Richard's not eating, not eating."* And a violent rapping of spoons grew in volume before the old lady brought her hand down to silence them (and it had taken her a long time to do it) and she herself commanded him to eat. Who was she? Not the aunt, who with his uncle had taken him in after his mother was killed when their block was bombed. . . . No . . . Jury's head and shoulders had barely cleared the table at the old lady's. So he must have been very young.

His eye fell on the middle snapshot of the evacuation. All of those children. He saw his child's face there, looking over the shoulder of an unknown woman, carting him away.

It was he and two or three other boys and a girl—he recalled her vivid hair—she was older than the others, nine or ten perhaps, and she seemed to be the leader. They were trooping across a field. He could not read the signs posted all around but the skull and crossbones on one of them told him the place was dangerous. The girl had told them all the signs were danger signs, DANGER was what they said. The field was full of unexploded bombs, she said.

"We're going to the sea!" she said.

It was there, in the distance, the grim gray sea and low cliffs. So it couldn't have been Oxfordshire, it must have been the West Country—Devon or Dorset, Cornwall maybe. He hung back, stopped on the inside of a listing fence made of wire and wood, fallen down in one long section. It was meant to keep people out of this danger zone, but they had walked right over it. He stood there, small and stocky as they yelled back: *"Richard's a scaredy cat!"*

He wondered why his mother had left him in such a place. Everywhere was dangerous—the stubbly fields, the sea, the long table where they ate, the gray sausages, the games. The redheaded girl.

Secretly he must have envied her. She did not seem afraid of anything, not the field of bombs, not the old lady whose house it was. *"Dried up old prune!"* was what she had called the old lady. The redheaded girl filled him with dread. Dread.

So did the old lady's parlor, for there were photographs of dead servicemen all around. He knew some of them were dead for around two of the frames she had draped black velvet and in front of a few had placed little candles. He spent long times studying the faces of these men, who were all in uniform, all young. Of the others, the ones who must have still been alive, he wondered if one was his father. There was at least one who could have been, for he wore the uniform of an RAF pilot. Maybe his mother had brought it here to be placed where Richard could see it whenever he wanted.

The hellion, the redheaded girl, had told them about the photographs, making them sit as she picked up one after the other and told them who the subject was.

When she came to the one who might have been his father, he slid from his chair and told them all who the fighter pilot was. They laughed and laughed.

"Then he's dead! Pilots die a lot more because it's more dangerous!"

Richard shouted that he was not. He still flew his plane.

"It went down—" Her hand made a spiral toward the floor.

Richard was beside himself. He could no more have controlled the spasms of rage that overtook him than he could have manned that Hurricane. He went for her. The old lady was summoned by shouting voices. The girl was screaming and the old lady came diving at the two tangled bodies, ripping Richard away and all but flinging him into the cold fireplace.

"What's going on here? What's going on?"

"Nothing," the redheaded girl had said. *"Playing is all."*

At least, he thought now (for he could not then, probably), there had been some code of honor at work. They might have warred among themselves, but it was still them against the old lady. He had lain in bed heaving with sobs and anger. Later, he had crept down to the parlor, grabbed up the photograph of the flier that might have been his father and carried it up to his small room. He had stood looking out of his dormer window at the black sky, littered with stars that he imagined exploding and turning to silver rubble and wondered if his father's plane was up there now. He remembered that spiral motion of the redheaded girl's hand, diving toward the floor. But that wouldn't happen to his father. God holds certain people up by strings and he was sure his father was one.

Jury had not thought of all this in a long time. It was Mickey and his pictures bringing it to mind again; it was the mystery. He picked up the snapshot of the fighter squadron and remembered that downward spiral of her hand. He wondered what had happened to her, the girl with the hellfire hair.

He felt a feathery touch on his cheek and looked up. The waitress had touched his face with a napkin or perhaps her own handkerchief.

"It's just the one tear." She held out the handkerchief, smiling uncertainly.

He smiled back. "I'm not crying, am I?"

She raised the bottle of Glen Grant she'd brought with the coffeepot, and he nodded and held up the shot glass, then pushed over his cup. "Thanks."

Inclining her head slightly toward the counter, she said, "I guess it's the sad pictures. They look like old ones, those snapshots."

"They are." He turned the one of Alexandra Tynedale and her baby so that the waitress could see it. "I was trying to think who you reminded me of." He tapped the snapshot. "Her."

The waitress smiled. "People are always telling me I look like Vivien Leigh. She was that actress a long time ago. I've only seen pictures of her; I never saw her movies. Do you remember her? Was she that beautiful?" She was blushing because she hadn't meant to say she herself was beautiful.

"Oh, I remember her. And, yes, she was that beautiful. Like you."

The girl's color deepened even more. "Oh . . ." She flapped her hand, waving the compliment away. Then she asked, "Was she a friend of yours?" She nodded toward the snapshots.

"No. They're not my pictures."

The hell they're not.

Jury drained the coffee cup in one go, put more than enough money on the counter and turned to leave. The cold-eyed brunette was still there, putting another cigarette between her lips. So the one before had been the next-to-the-last cigarette in the world.

This one was the last.

FOUR

The dog Stone preceded Carole-anne Palutski into Jury's room and lay down in front of Jury's easy chair and fell asleep. Dogs amazed Jury.

Not as much as Carole-anne Palutski amazed him, though. She stood in the doorway, dressed in a short dress of burning blue. Standing in her vibrant rays, Jury thought he ought to be wearing sunscreen. Wordlessly, he held the door wider. She entered.

He did not know why she had hesitated on his doorsill, since she immediately plopped herself down on his sofa. Invisible strings seemed to pull and tug Carole-anne from place to place, as if even space wanted a taste of her.

"It's Saturday night and I don't expect you'd like to go down to the Nine-One-Nine?"

This was Stan Keeler's regular gig when he was home. The flat directly overhead was home. "Don't be so defeatist. When did Stan come back?"

"Last night. You weren't here," she added, accusingly.

The second-floor flat had been empty for years as a result of Carole-anne's managerial skills. She had convinced the landlord that he should put its letting in her hands in order to keep out the riffraff, the riffraff being females, married couples and all men who failed to meet her standards. So there was silence overhead until Stan Keeler had come along with his guitar and his dog

Stone, a caramel-colored Labrador now draped across Jury's feet, dreaming of empty fields—

Which brought Jury back to the present, or, rather, to the past. Carole-anne reminded him a little of the red-headed girl, though Carole-anne's hair had more gold mixed in with the red. And she hadn't a mean bone in her gorgeous body.

She put her feet up on the paper- and magazine-strewn coffee table. Picking up a copy of *Time Out,* she started flicking through it and yawned as she said, "Am I to take 'I-shouldn't-be-defeatist' as a yes?"

He loved her feigned indifference. "Yes."

"Good. Elevenish?" The Nine-One-Nine never really got going until just before midnight. Then she was frowning over *Time Out.* "I don't see why you buy this, seeing you never go anywhere."

"But I do. I go many wheres. You just don't happen to be with me when I go." Resting his head against the back of his chair, he was aware of her narrow scrutiny. *A secret life?* she'd be thinking. That's what worried her.

"Like where?"

"To the City, for example, which is where I was today. To visit an old friend, hit the pubs, the coffee shops. All over. Found a nice waitress, really pretty." She was looking at him avidly. Jury smiled. Carole-anne sometimes seemed unsure but what Jury might just vanish before her turquoise eyes. "You'd be surprised at some of the things I get up to. Even though you see no life beyond these four walls for me"—Carole-anne had a job at the Starrdust in Covent Garden, telling fortunes. Costumes like a chorus girl—"I do have quite an eventful life." He went on to tell her some wild tale about a case he'd just wrapped up, exaggerating his own Scarlet Pimpernel role in the proceedings. From the wide-eyed way she was looking at him, he wouldn't be surprised if he was becoming to her more myth than man.

"What waitress?" she said.

FIVE

Sunday and Jury could not shake off the depression over Mickey Haggerty's fate. Fate, doom. Terminal disease. Interminable sorrow. He tried to put himself in Mickey's shoes, but he couldn't. He lacked the imagination.

At the moment it was his own shoe, dangling from his hand, that he was now putting on as he sat on the edge of his sofa, its worn material resplendent in the slant of sunlight coming through his window.

Above him, Stone barked once. Stone was not profligate with his barks. That meant Stan was up and in a few minutes the guitar would start warming up. This was not an unpleasant prospect for Stan was careful to tailor his tunes to the time of day. Nothing raucous on a late Sunday morning.

Music. Carole-anne was sure to follow.

There came a *rat-a-tat-tat* on his door. He opened it. Carole-anne said good morning and entered, wearing a blindingly bright coral-colored dress that, together with the sunlight, set her red hair and the room afire. She plunked herself down on the sofa from which he had just risen and removed one of her sandals.

Jury was holding his other shoe and wondered if in this symmetry there was some oblique, symbolic message. No. Carole-anne had a pedicure in mind. She was unscrewing a bottle of hot-pink nail polish.

"You look like the coral reef off Key West, an endangered species."

"Is that a compliment, then? Or are you saying I look like crumbled rocks?"

Jury had seated himself in his easy chair and said, "I don't think any of our conservationists would call a coral reef or you crumbled rocks."

Her toes planted against the edge of his coffee table, she applied the nail polish in little dabs to her toes, observed Jury's shoe lacing up and asked, "You going out? It's Sunday."

"Sunday is a going-out day. Maybe the most of the entire week. People veritably live in pubs from noon to night."

Her chin on her upraised knee, she asked, "You going to the Angel, then?"

"Nope."

"Then where?"

Jury stopped his lacing to take in the mellow music coming through the ceiling. He sighed. "He's great."

"Stan? We're going to the Angel." She had taken down one foot and put up the other. "Where're you going?"

"Oh, I don't know."

"Well, you were looking pretty hangdog yesterday when you came home."

"No kidding?" Jury wondered if there was any breakfast stuff in his fridge and wished for the zillionth time he had a cigarette.

"So where were you? I mean besides where the waitress was?"

He smiled. "Around."

She paused in her polish application and looked at him. "Then you need a little hair of the dog like."

He gave a short laugh. "I'm not hung over, though I admit I tried hard enough to wind up with one last night."

"I don't mean booze." Her head bent again, she

worked on her little toenail. "I mean you should go back around."

"Back around?"

"Back around the City, back where you were yesterday." She examined her bare foot, the freshly painted nails. "Except," she added, "that coffee place. Too much caffeine is bad for a person."

Plus other things, Jury thought, with a smile.

SIX

Perhaps she was right, even though it was strange advice coming from Carole-anne, who usually saved her prognostications, anything that hinted of Jury's future, for the Starrdust, where she told fortunes by way of a crystal ball. Or rather by way of her blue-green eyes. Andrew Starr loved it; it was unusual to have men patronize the Starrdust, given its main purpose was the casting of astrological charts, and men didn't want to be seen as believing in astrology. But now there were men aplenty.

Sunday was a good day for an undisturbed walk about the City. He wondered if Mickey was in his office, if he spent weekends there instead of at home where his mortality would be constantly mirrored in the faces of his family. Even if Mickey could forget for five minutes, they couldn't, at least not for the same five minutes.

Jury supposed it was another price, ironic in being exacted, that the seriously ill had to pay: people didn't really want to be around them and for precisely the same reason they should. They were afraid of their own dying; they didn't want to be reminded. Beneath that obvious cowardice, though, were other, more complicated reasons. He would probably see enough of Mickey, anyway; there would be questions, problems, things to report.

Jury had left the train at Holborn underground and walked along High Holborn, stopping to regard Lincoln's Inn Fields. He called to mind the poet Chidiock Tichbourne, who was trapped in the net of a conspiracy to murder Queen Elizabeth. Though utterly innocent of anything, he was executed. Jury had always thought that poem he composed had one of the saddest refrains he'd ever come across. *"And now I live and now my life is done."* Chidiock Tichbourne had been seventeen when he wrote that, seventeen when he was executed. Seventeen.

He had brought Mickey's snapshots with him. He did not know why. Occasionally, he would take out one or the other, stare at it for a few moments and wonder if Mickey was right. And wonder also why the solving of this puzzle meant so much to him. *"There's not enough time."* There never is, thought Jury. Of course he knew why he'd brought the pictures along; the mystery was locked inside them.

He walked along Holborn Viaduct into Newgate Street, past St. Paul's and into Cheapside, which he had always liked and which he would have liked to traverse back in the seventeenth century when it was a huge, bustling market. He loved it for its Londonness. He liked the way that each guild had its own area: bakers in Bread Street, fishmongers in Friday Street, dairymen in Milk Street, which is where he had stopped now. He thought he might fancy a drink in the pub before him called the Hole in the Wall. On this bit of land had once been one of those prisons called counters, where the poor wretches could acquire "accommodation" according to their ability to pay. Since some weren't poor, they got the best. But the poorest were stuck in the darkest dungeon, where the fetid air could turn to fresh only by the admission of fresh air entering through a hole in the wall. It was here also that the prisoners begged food of passersby. If there had ever been a more corrupt system than the prison system, Jury was hard put to think of one. He decided he didn't fancy a drink after all but to go into Bread Street.

He stopped again near the corner of Cheapside. Here, if his modicum of geography served him right, was almost hallowed ground for here had stood the Mermaid Tavern until the Great Fire of 1666. He stood looking at the building here now and envisioning what had gone before, until the one peeled away and the Mermaid emerged (not, perhaps true to itself, but wasn't the shell of one public house pretty much like another?). In his mind's eye he entered to find it smokier, rowdier and filled with more raucous laughter and louder screams for beer than could be witnessed at his pub in Islington, the Angel. There were no women, nary a one, except for the barmaid, her breasts spilling out of her loosely laced shift.

And since his imaginings landed him in the first part of the seventeenth century—there they sat, ranged around a table, men more sagacious, less bemused than any others he could name: Ben Jonson, Shakespeare, Donne, Beaumont and Fletcher, John Webster, Walter Raleigh (who had founded this "club") and in a shadowy corner Dr. Johnson, the only one standing in case he wanted to make a quick exit and the only one as yet unborn.

Jury thought it remarkable that all of these icons of literature could be gathered in the same room, sitting around the same table. He wanted to know what they thought. So he told them the story in the photos. None of them but only half attended to him for they laughed and quipped all the while (Webster asking, *"Is this, then, what the Peelers have come to? If you lit all the lamps in London could this man find his feet?"*).

"You know what it sounds like?" said Webster.

"I do indeed, Mr. Webster," said Beaumont. *"Sounds like someone's stolen my plot of* The Changeling.*"*

"Don't be ridiculous," said Shakespeare. *"It's a tale told by an idiot, et cetera, et cetera."* He banged his tankard on the table and yelled for ale through the smoke and coal-dusted air.

Ben Jonson called for *"a cup o' Canary wine, now, Megs!"*

The buxom barmaid waved her hand.

"My point is," said Jury, "should I believe it?"

All seven of them sat transfixed by the idiocy of this question. Then they found it wonderfully risible.

Megs had come, laces dancing, and answered him: *"If it's belief as concerns you, sir, you just step across the street to St. Mary-le-Bow."*

"Ah, but they might come along and burn him for high treason," yelled Fletcher.

Jury stuck to his guns, for here was more sagacity than he would meet in his lifetime: "Is it true?"

Unborn or not, Samuel Johnson couldn't keep still. *"The man's dying, you fool; why would he waste his time talking about this impersonation if it hadn't occurred or something else occurred enough like it to ribbon the tale round with such finery as would secure your aid. He needs your help, man, though I must say, help from you is about as necessary as t'was Chesterton's."*

Jury did not know what he meant; Dr. Johnson did not enlighten him, but faded back into the shadows again.

Jury thought: yet there's something in the advice he should pay attention to but, in the way of elusive clues, he could not see what.

"You're all intuitionists."

They regarded one another with a raised eyebrow, a questioning glance, a finger pointed in Jury's direction.

Refusing to give up, Jury said, "Intuit. Go on."

Donne, who had joined less in the raillery around the table, cleared his throat and said, *"You undertake to help this man because you feel his story is yours."*

"Yes. No. I wasn't posing as someone else. Not that part of the story."

Donne waved this away, saying, *"That's merely the pièce de résistance to engage your interest; it's merely a corner turned in the real mystery and is insignificant."*

"But it's the *whole* mystery. It's the one question to be answered."

"It is crucial only if you're not looking around."

"Looking around? Looking around for *what*? Pardon me, but you're talking in riddles."

"Riddles!" said Beaumont. *"It's* you *who're hearing them; he's not talking them."*

"You're too insistent, Mr. Jury," said Webster, *"on your own notion of mystery. Probably because you're one of these detective types such as our so-called writers in Grubb Street write about, composers of temporary poems and bad detective novels,"* said Fletcher.

"The thing is, Mr. Jury, you already know that part of it. What you'd call the solution, the answer, the conclusion, call it what you will. But that's the chaff; that's what's left behind in the dust. A kills B. You strive to discover A's identity. You do and bring him in."

"It's not that simple—"

"Of course it is," said Webster. *"A hundred hacks in Grubb Street right this moment are writing their detective tales–"*

"Century! Century!" bellowed Dr. Johnson. *"There are no detective stories until E. A. Poe!"*

"You're past it, mate," said Fletcher to Jury.

"Can't see the woods for the trees," said Beaumont, adding, *"who said that, anyway?"*

Fuck you two, Jury thought. Couple of pricks. "Thank you, Mr. Donne and Dr. Johnson. I know you're trying to help. Unlike some others I could name." He cast a baleful look at Beaumont and Fletcher, then asked, "Just what *did* you guys write?" Jury was pleased to see the pink flush across their faces.

"T'is Pity She's a Whore," called out Ben Jonson. *"Megs, Megs! We're talking about you! More wine! An excellent play! Ran six months in the Duchess."*

Dr. Johnson turned to bang his head against one of the tavern's stout beams. *"Century, you idiot! That theater wasn't even built for several hundred years!"*

Ben Jonson was engaged in tweaking the good Megs's bottom, and said, *"Yes, you're right."*

"Of course," said Shakespeare, *"one wonders about Sam back there. You're not the one to talk, Sam, for what are you doing here?"*

Only silence inhabited the shadows for some moments. Then Samuel Johnson said, *"Patrolling. One has to patrol. One has to oversee the literary scene. I wouldn't mind it except for this blockhead who keeps following me."*

Then Jury watched the scene dissolve and turned his feet in the direction of Ludgate Hill. Could one feel both elated and deflated simultaneously? Apparently one could, he told himself, ruefully. It was only minutes to Ludgate and then to the cramped little streets that hemmed in the construction site. He stood looking at the blank face of it for some moments before taking out Mickey's picture of the Blue Last.

It showed a three-storied building, much like the houses around it, gabled, dormer-windowed and with a door painted darker than the rest of the structure. It was the Christmas four or five days before the bombs fell. The Christmas decorations—the strings of lights that ran across the edge of the roof and around the downstairs windows—struck Jury as awfully sad. In front of the pub stood a man, Francis Croft, and Oliver Tynedale's daughter, Alexandra. They stood smiling and slightly blinded by the winter sunlight. In just a few days their lives, and the lives of all the families of whoever was unlucky enough to be in the pub—all would be horribly and irrevocably changed.

Alexandra Herrick, even in this faint and awkward likeness, could be seen to be beautiful, though you had to imagine her coloring, which Jury had no trouble doing. The baby would probably be beautiful also. Here, she was wrapped in a blanket. Then he looked at the one of the baby looking over Alexandra's shoulder.

Jury studied the picture of Kitty Riordin holding her own baby, Erin, wearing a little cap also looking over her mother's shoulder. How could what Mickey believed be possible? How could one child be substituted for another and no one know? If he himself had seen both children and then had been asked to identify one or the other—? He doubted if he could. But the mothers would know. That, of course, was Mickey's point. If Kitty said the baby she had taken out in the stroller was Maisie Tynedale Herrick, who would contradict her? Who would want to? In Maisie's case there was a grandfather, uncles, aunts— an entire roster of people who would want Maisie alive far more than they'd care if Erin was. It would take the most hardened cynic—this was war, after all—to pose such a devastating question to Kitty Riordin, a woman whose own child had very probably died inside the Blue Last, buried under the debris— no. Mickey was right to be suspicious; it could well have been, still could be, an imposture.

But the alternative was equally possible: Alexandra's baby, Maisie, really was Maisie, and Mickey was wrong. Jury stood looking at the blank face of an office building before him, which served as a kind of screen on which he could project his thoughts.

London in the dreadful last months of 1940. He had heard people who'd been here then say that if you could hear that searing whistle, the bomb had already missed you and gone down somewhere else. In the spring of that year, people were calling it the phoney war. Men and women in their seventies now, talking about the blackouts, how you couldn't go anywhere after dark because you couldn't see. "Always stumbling over the goddamned sandbags, picking your way through the dark, in a block of terraced houses, going up a path and trying to open the wrong door." One man said he almost welcomed a storm so people could navigate by lightning flashes. No light, no torches, no headlamps—the blackness was like a cave, "like wandering about in a bloody *cave,* it was." Jury thought he heard his uncle's voice saying this. It's what he himself must have felt in the months after their own flat in the Fulham Road had taken a direct hit. Seeing his mum lying under a ton of rubble.

But had it happened? Had he been there? Was this the reason he hadn't wanted to be forced back in time, was it that he had begun to question his own memory?

Despite his earlier thoughts about his cousin, he now had the urge to ring her in Newcastle, see what she remembered. Better yet, he would go there. Only, he warned himself, she would not treat memory kindly; she was likely to remember what would make him unhappy, what sad, and even embellish on the sadness of it.

For he knew, if he knew anything, it had been and would be sad.

SEVEN

Benny Keegan and his dog Sparky climbed the cement steps and crossed to the other side of the Embankment to get the bus to take them across Waterloo Bridge to the South Bank.

Benny made deliveries for several small merchants in Southwark. He knew he couldn't compete with the swift, helmeted bicycle messengers, but then speed wasn't everything (he'd told his prospective employers). "Sparky adds a bit of fun to your customers' day." Benny (and Sparky) had been hired by the five shops he'd solicited, three of them because Sparky did indeed put a bit of fun in the day. The other two, newsagent and butcher, had agreed to give him a try because Benny (and Sparky) worked cheap. That had been a year ago.

So there were Mr. Siptick, the newsagent; the butcher, Mr. Gyp; the two young men at Delphinium, the flower shop, who reminded Benny of flowers themselves, tall, thin, pastel-colored flowers; the greengrocer, Mr. Smith; and Miss Penforwarden, who owned the Moonraker Bookshop.

These five shops were all handily within a few blocks so that Benny could go from one to the other, making out a schedule for deliveries as he went. He would do this once in the morning and again in the afternoon, to see if any other deliveries had been added. He was very efficient and his way of handling his business worked quite smoothly.

He wouldn't have exchanged his day of irregular work for a regular job for anything (not that he had the opportunity to, as he was only twelve). During the time between deliveries, and there was always some time, he could stop and have a rest and a look around the shops he served. His favorite was the Moonraker. Waiting for Miss Penforwarden to make up her delivery orders, he could take down a book and read. Sparky would sit and not bother anything, not even the Moonraker's cat, who tried everything in its power to get Sparky to chase it. Sparky didn't. Benny did not know where Sparky had learned such discipline, unless he'd been part of a circus or magic act before Benny had found him that day, nosing through a dustbin. All Benny had ever taught Sparky was how to carry things in his mouth. Newspapers and magazines were easy. But Sparky could even be trusted by the Delphinium owners to carry flowers. To the cone of vibrantly pink paper wrapped around the flowers, they would attach a string handle by which Sparky could carry the bouquet remarkably ably. Sparky loved flowers. Whenever they stopped at Delphinium, Sparky would make a circuit of the wide, cool room, stopping to sniff each kind of flower, bunched in its tall metal holder. The bluebells were his favorite, even though they made him sneeze sometimes. The Delphinium owners would often give Benny, at the end of the day, whatever flowers they thought wouldn't sit well overnight. They said for him to take them to his mum. Benny said he would and thanked them and went off.

He only wished he didn't have to make up so many stories about his mum and her daily dealings. How she was really an actress, but had to do waitress work to make money until she got her big break. The trouble with making up a story was that you had to remember to stick with it and flesh it out with all kinds of detail, such as where his mum waited on tables. *Lyon's*

Corner House, oh that closed, did it? Well, I meant when it was still open. Right now she waits tables in the food hall at Harrods; no, I know they don't have tables, just counter work, I mean. It was such a strain.

When there was time in the Moonraker, Benny would sit on the library ladder and read *David Copperfield*, his favorite book. It was because David was worse off than Benny that he liked it. Benny felt lucky there was no Mr. Murdstone in his own life to make him miserable. Of course, the other side of that was there was no Peggotty to help Benny over a misery, so maybe life evened itself out pretty much, the same terms for him and for David.

But it still made him sit there thinking, his chin in his cupped hand, elbow on knee, for long periods. Was it better to have no enemies, even if it meant no friends, or have both? This was not an easy question. Anyway, he really couldn't say he had no friends for there were the people he lived with, and the people he delivered to, who were very friendly toward Benny and Sparky. As for his employers, it was only Mr. Siptick and Mr. Gyp who could stand in for Mr. Murdstone. Mr. Siptick was forever going on about the things he did wrong and Mr. Gyp was always asking pointed questions about Benny's mum (his dad being dead, which was true) and ending up with asking *"You sure you got a mum, Benny Keegan?"*—he'd ask with his wheezing kind of laughter—*"or should I go call the Social?"*

This froze Benny's insides, not only for himself, but also for Sparky. And Sparky even took a couple of steps backward when Mr. Gyp mentioned the Social. But for all the icy fear that replaced the blood running through his veins, Benny was canny enough to keep his expression noncommittal when he answered, *"Well, you could do, but when they came to the house to take me away, Mum, she'd be pretty mad and I wouldn't work here no more. Anymore,"* he'd corrected himself. A lot of reading in the Moonraker had vastly improved his speech.

The thing was, Mr. Siptick and Mr. Gyp, neither of them wanted to lose Benny, for Benny worked for much less—and did a better job—than anyone else they could have found.

This morning Mr. Siptick, wearing his same old green jacket with his name, SIPTICK, on the pocket, rolled up a copy of *Gardener's World* and handed it to Benny. "Just you mind that mutt don't slobber all over it." Mr. Siptick said this every day.

"His name's Sparky and did anyone ever complain about slobbering?" Benny also answered this way every day. Sparky could carry two papers at once, since Benny put them in a thin, brown bag to make it easier for him to keep them together.

Mr. Siptick waved a dismissive hand and settled down on his stool to count his money out for the day. "Well, go on, *go* on!"

"You forgot the Toblerone for old Mrs. Ely."

"For pity's sake, boy, just pick one up, candy's right in front of you!"

Benny took a Toblerone from one of the candy boxes lined up on a rack. "Okay, I'm off."

Mr. Siptick made no answer.

On Monday morning, which this was, his usual deliveries were one, *Daily Telegraph* to the butcher, Mr. Gyp; two, sausages and racing form to Brian Ely; three, *Telegraph, Times* and *Guardian* to the boys at Delphinium (Benny thought they used all these papers to cut flowers over); four, *Times* to the Moonraker; and five, if Miss Penforwarden was sending books along, Benny's favorite stop was a big house called Tynedale Lodge.

It was convenient to go next to the butcher's for that way he could pick up the sausages for Brian Ely when he dropped off Mr. Gyp's paper. Sparky always knew when they were going to Mr. Gyp's for he seemed to droop. Sparky was some kind of terrier, Sealyham, maybe. Sparky looked just like Snowy, the white dog in *Tin-Tin*, with his oblong white-tufted face. Neither of them could stand Mr. Gyp. In his usual sharp-tongued way, he started complaining about lateness when Benny and Sparky were hardly in the door.

"I can't help it if Mr. Siptick makes me late."

"You just mind your tongue, Master Keegan. And that there dog, too. I don't want him gettin' his teeth into these sausages for the Elys."

As if Sparky didn't know better. Benny handed Sparky two more papers he'd been carrying under his arm, and he himself carried the sausage. He said the same thing and got the same reply.

"Well, I'm off."

Nothing.

Brian Ely was a stocky man with a head like a bullet, which was close to his shoulders, so that he seemed to be perpetually shrugging. He wore loud suits with wide lapels.

"Ah! Sausages! Have these for our tea, we will. Paper's here, Mum!" he shouted back over his shoulder. Benny couldn't decipher the tremulous reply. He wondered why old Mrs. Ely didn't die. She always seemed in the process, what with her lack of breath and always having to hang on to things—chair backs, stair rails, coatracks, people—to keep herself upright. She was worn down to nothing but a bag of bones. It was a wonder.

Brian Ely exclaimed over the racing form as if he didn't get it nearly every morning. "The form! Good lad." He took the brown bag from Sparky's mouth, removed the racing form. He shook it open. "What d'you like in the ninth at Doncaster?" He looked down at Sparky, who seemed to be thinking it over.

"See you, Mr. Ely. Oh, and here's your mum's Toblerone." He handed that over and then raised his voice. "'Bye, Mrs. Ely!" he shouted. He wished he'd just gone ahead and left, for now he saw Mrs. Ely making her breathless way toward them from the rear parlor.

"C'm on, Ma, no need to exert yourself."

There was a wooden rod all along the wall of the hall-

way, attached there just so old Mrs. Ely could hold herself up. "Just . . . wan' . . . pa . . ." she said, or tried to.
The rest was lost in her gathering in enough breath even
to get that across. She stopped, holding on with both
hands and breathed asthmatically. Her face was blood-
less, but that appeared to be its natural color. Benny
wondered if she would drop dead there and then, but he
supposed not, as she'd done this many times before. She
was always falling down, too.

Brian Ely just shook his head and heaved a sigh as he
refolded the racing form. He went a few paces down the
hall to where his mum was gasping for breath, handed
her the racing form and she then turned to make her
breathless way back.

"Got no patience, has Mum. No, she's got to have that
form first thing and don't even like me reading it first."

Benny asked, "Why don't I bring two, then? You
could each have your own copy."

Brian Ely laughed. "Oh, I thought of that. But she'd
just think I was hiding something. Ever so suspicious.
Well, she's a good old mum fer all that. I'll say it if I
must—she can really pick 'em. Would 'ave made a good
tout, she would."

After the door closed on them, Benny just stood
there until Sparky gave him a nudge. They both trotted
on to the Moonraker.

It was four steps down, each step bearing a gold-
painted moon in its different phases. Sybil Penforwarden had hired a painter to do that. Inside the walls were
brownish-red brick. On two sides of the room were
arched openings, forming what looked like four separate chambers filled with shelves of books.

The bell rasped at the opening of the door and
brought Miss Penforwarden from the shadows of the
back shelves into the shadows of the front ones. Benny
looked around, then called, "Morning, Miss Penforwarden." The little shop was ill lit, but that was one of the
reasons Benny liked it. There were dim wall sconces

against the brick and an old metal shade hung from the ceiling, throwing a swooning kind of yellow light over the books. This light made his eyelids heavy. He always thought there was something stranded about the shop, something alien and other-worldly. Maybe it was just the name.

Miss Penforwarden came out from the rear of the shop, cheerful as ever. "Benny, I'm so glad you came round this morning. I'm getting up a parcel of books to go to the Lodge. Can you take them?"

Of course he could, as she well knew. Yet she always acted as if Benny's appearances here were a stroke of wonderful luck, something that happened erratically, even though he'd been coming for a year like clockwork. She liked to allude to his "larger" life, as if there were important things going on in it and the Moonraker was merely a blip on the screen.

"You just find a seat and I'll be back in two shakes."

"Okay," he said. She'd be back in many more shakes than just two. He headed toward the shelf of books nearest the window, Sparky at his heels. He loved the room and the alcoves in which were floor lamps situated over easy chairs, in case a customer needed more light to have a quiet read. The chintz slipcovers were faded and threadbare, which made them all that much more comfortable and less apt to bother Miss Penforwarden, the bother of children's sticky hands or dirty shoes. There was the children's corner in the back that held a table and small chairs, stuffed animals, blocks, puzzles. Yet Benny had never seen a child back there; the few who came gravitated to the front room.

Miss Penforwarden had told Benny the room originally must have been a wine cellar for the house (now sectioned off into small flats). Benny said the only other purpose it could have served was as a dungeon. He liked this dungeon notion. He had never been to the Tower of London or any of the great houses and castles that might have harbored a dungeon, so dungeon life was fair game. What he really had to worry about more than being thrown in a dungeon was thinking up explanations of why he wasn't in school. First, he considered illness, like a heart murmur he'd had since a baby, but then somebody had said working the way he did, wouldn't that put more strain on a heart than just sitting in a schoolroom? Then he had said it was his asthma and had given a few voluntary wheezy coughs to demonstrate. But it was mostly Mr. Gyp who bothered him this way and he tried to ignore it.

Benny pulled down *David Copperfield* and looked for the place he'd marked with a toothpick. He didn't think Miss Penforwarden would mind.

But his thoughts trailed across the page. He was thinking of that "larger" life Miss Penforwarden liked to refer to, the one he didn't have. He wasn't sure he even wanted one. For he liked routine, the sort of action that would go with a "smaller" life: the blue dawn over Waterloo Bridge, his morning tea and thick bread and making his deliveries. But a "larger" life was the kind of life he imagined for the inhabitants of Tynedale Lodge, though he couldn't clothe it in any particular activity. Tennis, perhaps? Dancing? Swordplay with masks on? A mysterious life. He was curious about it, but as he never went anywhere except for the garden and kitchen when he delivered things, he supposed he would never know. Certainly, it would include countless relations and friends. He hadn't any relations and the nearest he had to friends were the people within his delivery route and his mates where he lived.

David Copperfield still open in his hands, he leaned his head against the other Dickens books and thought about his mum. She had liked her routines, too. Selfridges had been on Thursdays. Harrods, Monday; Harvey Nick's, Tuesday. He had argued that people knew right away they were Irish, for that's what so many of the Irishwomen did, keeping a baby with them or a child. And these people didn't like the Irish. Begging

mortified Benny. Whenever some passerby dropped
coins in his upturned cap, Benny looked away. But at
least his mother didn't walk on the pavement holding
his hand and stopping first one woman, then another.
That's what so many of them did. His mum would tell
him, when he asked about their present awful state, that
she was so sorry things had gone to the bad for them.

Da died, he would say, as if he were explaining things
to her. But she didn't seem to like to speak of his father
because it pained her so much.

She'd talk about their old home in County Clare. *Ah,
beautiful it was! But never mind; we'll get back there
when things improve, so.*

Benny looked down at the pages of *David Copperfield.* It was something about Steerforth. Benny thought
about David's mum, how pretty she was. And so had his
own been. Prettier, he bet. Images of County Clare
floated in his mind: the rough coast and the sea, the
great smooth rocks worn down by the waves' onslaught,
and fierce weather, the kind that met Steerforth and
David when they went to visit Peggotty.

Good books, his mum had said, will always keep you
in good stead. *Good books, Bernie, are important. Read
as much as you can.*

His name was really Bernard, but he had so much
trouble getting his tongue around that *r* when he was
tiny, it came out "Benny." As names you start out with
will stick, so had his.

"Here we are, dear," said Miss Penforwarden, who
had come with the tied-up parcel. There was also a small
book, which she tied with string so Sparky could carry
it. "It's for young Gemma," said Miss Penforwarden.

It wasn't wrapped, so Benny could see the title: *Name
Your Cat.* "She's not even got a cat."

Benny and Sparky left with the books.

EIGHT

Gemma was already at the back gate when Benny and Sparky got there, as usual holding the doll dressed in its "baptismal clothes"(Gemma called them), a bonnet and a biscuit-colored and dingy dress, its length covering the feet and trailing down. This doll remained nameless; she could not decide. Last time, she had been through the Qs and must now be up to the Rs.

The gate creaked back and he entered the rear garden of the Lodge. The top of the gate was higher than Gemma's head. She was nine and the butler, Barkins, was always telling her she was too old for dolls. Benny had said that's ridiculous, you can never be too old for something you really liked.

Benny asked, "What'd you want this cat book for?" Sparky had dropped it at her feet and himself trotted off, over to the pond, which he seemed partial to. Probably to watch the big goldfish.

"I mean," Benny continued, as she leafed through it, "the only cat around here is Snowball and she's got a name. And she's Mrs. Riordin's cat, anyway."

"It's what she had at the Moonraker. It's the only book on names. I'm into the Rs. There's Ruth, Renee, Rita, Renata—"

"Renata? That's not a name."

"It is, too. I saw it on a book cover. It's the person who wrote the book. Then there's Roberta, which I don't like at all—"

"You don't like any of them; you never do. Next comes the *S*s. You could name her Sparky."

Gemma looked at him, shaking her head. "I'm not naming her after a *dog*."

Benny was practical; Gemma wasn't; she seemed to live in Never-Never Land, or at least went straight there the minute she saw Benny. That was actually what she called the great gray pile of stone that was Tynedale Lodge: Neverland.

"Let's go sit in the tree."

They were still by the gate. Benny said, "Mr. Barkins doesn't like me hanging around."

Gemma sighed. She was always being put out by Benny. "Well, this doll—" she thrust the doll in its grimy, trailing dress toward him "—doesn't like being unbaptized, but it is."

Benny tried to make a connection between the two things but couldn't. "Miss Penforwarden sent some more books."

"I know. Let's open them."

"No." He followed her to the beech tree, which was her favorite place to sit. It was enormous, sending out roots that themselves looked prehistoric. Gemma had wedged a board in between the trunk and a thick branch. It was roomy enough for both of them and near the ground. If they straddled the board, they could each lean against the trunk and the branch.

She set the doll between them and reached for the parcel. "Let's see."

"Gemma!" He wheeled the parcel upward.

"I need to see if they're about poisoning."

He forgot and let the parcel down. She grabbed it.

"What are you talking about?"

"I told you somebody tried to poison me." Humming a scrap of a song, she carefully undid the string. She looked at him out of eyes like agate. The green swam in them.

Benny fell back against the trunk. "Not *that* again! Why'd anyone want to?"

Matter-of-factly, she said, "For my money." She had removed the brown paper and picked up one of the books.

"What money? You don't have any money! I tried to borrow fifty P from you a couple weeks ago and you said you didn't even have that."

"Not to loan out, I didn't." She was looking through one of the books.

Benny gave up and looked across the lawn at the "baptismal pool"; Sparky was still there, peering over the edge.

Gemma said, "There's nothing much in this one except a lot of rubbishy gardens."

Benny leaned forward and she turned the book so he could see it. He was looking at queerly sculpted garden topiaries. He frowned. "That's Italy somewhere."

"Italy. Oh." She looked around, thinking. "Wasn't that where this family kept poisoning each other?"

Benny reflected. "I don't know. Med-something? It's like 'medicine.' Gemma, why do you always think somebody's trying to murder you? First it was shooting. You thought you were being shot at."

"I was being. They missed." She turned a page. Another garden.

"Then after that, it was somebody trying to smother you."

"Yes." She opened the second book. "Look." Holding the book open in front of her face so that only her eyes were visible peering over the brown calfskin binding, she tapped at the page.

Benny leaned closer. The illustration was an outline of a human form showing a map of arteries and veins. The direction of the blood flow was indicated by arrows. He frowned. "So?"

"It could show a person how the poison gets in your blood and travels around and where it travels."

Benny took it and looked at the spine. "It's just a medical book."

She looked up at the sky, as if the cloud formations held an answer. "But it's got poisons in it. A list of them. Look and see."

"No. Gemma, be sensible. You're too young to have somebody want to kill you. And don't tell me again it's your money."

Incensed, she said, "I am *not* too young. Even babies get murdered."

"But that's different. That's because—" For the life of him he couldn't think of one good reason. Then he hit on one. "They make too much noise or they're always crying and the parents go daft listening to them. And it's—ah—*impulse,* that's what. It's not—" What was the word? She was looking at him as if maybe he'd finally come up with something that would save her. It made Benny feel terrible; she really believed what she was telling him. If no amount of reasoning could dislodge this notion from her mind, Benny thought he would go at it from a different angle. "We'll have to narrow down who's doing this. It's only one person we're looking for, isn't it? I mean, you don't think it's more than one?"

She scratched her ear and said, "I guess not. Only—" She put her thumbs on the eyes of her doll as if to shut them against the sight of something awful.

"Only what?"

"I don't know. It could be two people working together."

"But why would you think that instead of just one?"

She shrugged. "I don't know. I'm only saying you should keep an open mind."

His mind was so open talking about this you could have landed a plane on it. "Let's just take them one by one. For a start."

"Well, all I know is, it's somebody there." She glanced around at the Lodge and stuck out her tongue.

Benny knew Gemma didn't much like the inside of the place, or some of the people who lived in it. Most of her time was spent outside—in the gardens and the greenhouse, or with the gardener, Mr. Murphy, as he was tending the beds and the hedges. Benny thought he was a bit sharpish.

"Let's start with the ones you don't like."

"I don't like any of them except Mr. Tynedale, but he's sick. He stays in bed."

"You like Rachael."

"Well, I'm not talking about staff, like Mrs. MacLeish and Rachael. They're all *right,* I guess."

Benny wondered how much that was a part of all this murder business. None of the people in the Lodge, except for Mr. Tynedale, seemed to care about Gemma.

"What about Mrs. Riordin?" She occupied the small gatehouse.

The mere mention of the name made Gemma hug herself and fake retching noises. Then she wiped at the doll's skirt as if vomit had dirtied it. "No, she doesn't want me dead, exactly. She needs me alive to torture." Katherine Riordin occupied what was once a gatehouse called Keeper's Cottage.

Oliver Tynedale was the one person Gemma did like; she spent time with him every day, carrying up cups of tea and reading to him. They told each other stories, his true, hers invented. Gemma was imaginative (the murder plots being proof of that) and good at making up stories. She remembered these stories, too, and told them to Benny sometimes. She had a remarkable memory, the kind of memory that might be thought of as "inconvenient" by some people who preferred forgetting.

Benny had picked up this term from Mr. Siptick, who was talking about a customer who had claimed to have paid his bill when (Mr. Siptick said) he hadn't, as a man with a "convenient" memory.

Sparky moved from the pool over to where the gardener, Angus Murphy, had just come around the side of the house, shearing the hawthorn hedge. Mr. Murphy (as far as Sparky was concerned), although not himself a flower, partook of their scents and possibly even their colors and contours, as if embedded in Mr. Murphy's physical self.

At least, that's how Sparky smelled it.

Flower vapor drifted out and around Mr. Murphy, and at his ankles, where Sparky stopped, were the smell of peat and moss, snail, worm, grub.

"Hi, Mr. Murphy!" Gemma called across the garden. Mr. Murphy turned, raised his shears and waved them in reply. No one fit the category of old middle age as well as Mr. Murphy with his faded ginger hair fast going gray, blue eyes also faded and a back slightly twisted with arthritis that prevented him reaching any higher than the top of the hawthorn hedge, which left the quarter mile of privet and yew hedges unshorn. Or had, that is, until Mr. Tynedale had hired an assistant to do such work as required a strong back and tall enough to do this shearing. There were also the two swan-shaped topiaries on either side of the big front gate. Mr. Murphy could not stand his new assistant, who hadn't lasted long. Mr. Murphy was always complaining about his "trendy" ways.

Here now he's one that's always talking "design" and keeps wanting to pull up my dahlias and phlox to plant red kinpholias and some electric blue. Wants to pull up my roses and put in something "shaggier." If you can believe it. Shaggy, that's the new thing and I says to 'im, just you leave my roses alone, m'lad. And he says at least let's get in some driftwood. Driftwood? Are you daft? I says to 'im. Don't tell me he ain't a little Nellie, way he floats around here with his Hermès secateurs. Cost him over two hundred quid, he says. He's plain daft. Hermès, no less.

That undergardener had been replaced by a girl

whom Mr. Murphy had liked better, but only fractionally, as he found her too young and "summat silly." She
had left, too, but of her own accord. She had simply
stopped showing up. So Mr. Murphy was on his own
again and might have preferred it that way.

"Maybe," said Benny, watching Sparky move along
the hedge with Mr. Murphy, "maybe it was that girl gardener. She left all of a sudden."

Gemma fell back against the tree trunk. "Jenny? Why
would she want to murder me?"

Benny sighed. She was so illogical. "I don't think *anyone* wants to murder you—"

"There's Maisie Tynedale. She hates me."

Maisie was Mr. Tynedale's granddaughter. She had
never married, had always lived in Tynedale Lodge.
"What reason would she have?"

"If I'm not allowed to say 'money,' I don't know. She
was in an air raid when she was a baby, Mrs. MacLeish
said. A bomb hit the building and exploded it to bits.
Mrs. Riordin's baby got blown up." Gemma expanded.
"Everybody got blown up. Everything was dust and all
these body parts. Bodies were all in pieces. Hands stick-
ing up through the rubble you could pull one out and no
body was attached to it."

"I don't think Mrs. MacLeish told you all that."

"Yes, she did. I can't get it out of my system. It was a
pub and there were eyeballs in beer glasses."

"That's ridiculous. How could an eyeball fly out of
your face and land on its own inside a pint glass?"

She lay her doll down again and leaned back against
her branch and swung her feet. "I'm only saying what
she told me."

"She didn't tell you that. Anyway, let's not talk about
it; it's nothing to do with the family wanting you dead."
He watched Gemma wipe her doll's face with a white
tissue. "Mr. Tynedale, he'll probably leave you a trust,
maybe." Benny's knowledge of trusts was a little thin, as
it was about most things financially elaborate. "Aren't

you glad for that? It might pay you back for having to put up with someone like Mrs. Riordin."

"I know what I'd do with some money if I had it right now."

"What?"

"Hire a detective." She looked at her name-starved doll for a moment, and held it up so Benny could see it. "Rhonda?"

NINE

"I don't know what you expect me to do about it," said Fiona Clingmore, trying unsuccessfully to pull down a black skirt that had too far to stretch to cover her knees.

"I expect you to take a *hatchet* to him, Miss Clingmore." Racer was standing, still looking stupidly around his office for the cat Cyril, who had pawed a sapphire shirt stud from the little velvet box on the desk and made off with it.

Jury sat on the sidelines with the file Racer had told him to bring: Danny Wu, with whom, Jury thought, Chief Superintendent Racer was obsessed. The obsession paid off royally for Jury and Wiggins, as it gave them a good excuse to eat at his Soho restaurant.

"You should never have left that velvet box there and gone off for lunch," said Fiona, in that annoying hindsight way people had.

Racer was attending some black-tie function and needed his shirt studs ("all of them," he'd said).

"Sapphires? Don't you think that to be a bit, well, showy?" This unpopular opinion was offered (precisely because it was unpopular) by the human equivalent (in Racer's eyes) of the cat Cyril; that is, the police detective Jury. "You don't want to outshine the chief constable, do you?"

Chief Superintendent Racer's face reddened to an alarming degree, and he, near desperate with rage, as if he feared there wasn't enough to be portioned out among the three of them (Cyril, Fiona, Jury), seemed to swell like a balloon.

The ladder which Racer was climbing had been furnished by one of the maintenance crew who had asked if he wanted a picture hung and would he like maintenance to do it?

"No!" Racer said, as if he meant to nullify the entire visible world in the manner of John Ruskin. Abashed, the maintenance man had left. (Jury had missed this opening chapter in the cat fracas; Fiona had reported it in fulsome detail.)

Racer had been positioning the ladder against the wall, climbing up and looking in the small well made to accommodate the recessed lighting, a well that could also accommodate cat-sized objects. There was a row of tiny lights just beneath the ceiling around all the walls. The lights were hidden by a strip of molding (cat height, if the cat was lying down).

As Racer looked right and left up there, Jury did not bother telling him that Cyril could easily slip right round the corner and be hidden by the recess on the other wall that Racer had given the all-clear to. Enjoying life immensely on this Monday morning, relieved of his Sunday depression for a while, Jury looked up, not at the recessed lighting but at the ceiling fixture, an iron rod ending in two light bulbs which were covered by a chic copper shade, inverted like a large bowl. This was a perfect place for a catnap, as Jury was bearing witness to, if that bit of paw over the edge was any proof.

Racer descended the ladder, disgusted. His back was to the paw. "I'm setting the trap again." He dusted his hands. "The next time that bloody ball of mange appears will be the *last time, do you hear me, Miss Clingmore*?"

The caramel-colored paw drew in. Nap disturbed. Jury sighed, envious of such sangfroid.

Dragging the ladder, Racer went to the outer office, picked up the phone when it rang on Fiona's desk and barked into it. Cyril sat up in the copper shade, measuring distances. He was so fast and so agile that had he been a villain, police never would have caught him. As if auditioning for the Royal Ballet, Cyril leaped, a graceful curve in air to make a four-point landing on Racer's desk. While Racer barked, Cyril washed. Then hearing the phone slam down, and other microscopic moves and sounds that announced the chief superintendent's return, Cyril streaked off the desk and oozed underneath it.

"The hell with it," said Racer. "Here. Open this and set that trap." Racer sent a tin of sardines sailing to his desk in an arc. Then, in a matador move Cyril would have appreciated, Racer swirled his coat from the rack and around his shoulders. "Oh, Wiggins wants you," he said to Jury, tilting his head toward the phone. "That was him." He walked out, calling "lunch" over his shoulder.

Cyril squirmed out from beneath the desk, and, from a sitting position, made another four-point landing atop the desk. He moved over to the can of sardines.

Lunch?

Jury walked through the door of his own office, laughing.

"Sir—" Wiggins began.

"You missed it, Wiggins, too bad."

"Sir, you just got a call—"

Wiping a few tears of laughter away, he said, "A call about what?"

"A shooting. It was from that DCI Haggerty you went to see." Wiggins looked at his tablet. "The name will be familiar to you, he said. A Simon Croft. He's been shot; he's dead."

A cold breeze fought its way past the shuddering windowpanes and touched Jury's face. He felt thrust into the midst of events he could not control. What the source of this feeling was he didn't know.

"You know him, sir? I mean this Croft person, the victim?"

Jury nodded. It was easier than explaining. "Where did he call from?"

"Croft's house. It's in the City, big house on the Thames. Here." Wiggins ripped the page from his notebook. "He said he'd like you to come if you possibly can."

Jury looked at the notes. "There's a problem I'm helping him with. I'll go. You have the number so that you can reach me?"

Wiggins nodded. Jury left.

TEN

A few people were still hanging about, wide-eyed
and thrilled, on the other side of the yellow crime
scene tape, watching the police van slide out of
the forecourt of the Croft house and make its way, signals flashing, along the Embankment.

Jury thought Simon Croft must have had quite a bit
of money to live in this large house backing onto the
Thames. Behind the house was a short pier jutting out
over the river; fifty or sixty feet beyond it was a boat,
anchored. How had the owner ever got the London
Port Authority to permit a private boat to anchor
there? The Thames was still a working river, after all.
The boat looked as if it were drifting there in a gray
mist.

Mickey Haggerty waited in what Jury supposed was
the library, considering the books and the dark wood
paneling. Bookshelves lined the walls, except for the
wall behind the table, in which a bow window looked
out over the river. Jury could see the boat through this
window. There was a large walnut writing table inset
with dark green leather. Simon Croft's body had fallen
forward across this green leather. Blood had pooled on
the desk, dripped down onto the floor beside his chair.
His left arm was reaching out and beside his hand lay a
9mm automatic.

"It was the cook who found Croft when she came this morning—" Mickey had come up beside him and was flipping over a page in his notebook "—at ten A.M. I'll tell you . . ."

But whatever it was remained untold; Mickey just shook his head. Jury said, "You look tired out, Mickey."

"It's the bloody medication."

Jury put his hand on Mickey's shoulder; he looked pale and exhausted.

Mickey shoved the handkerchief he'd used to wipe his forehead back in his pocket. "I got the call an hour ago. His cook rang the station. Mrs. MacLeish."

"Where is she now?"

"At the station, answering some questions. She wanted to get away from here. She's really the Tynedale cook, but comes over here to cook for Croft a couple of days each week."

"Croft lived here alone?"

Mickey nodded. "He was a broker, very successful. Had his own small—what's called boutique—firm. One of the few that didn't get swallowed up by the banks in the eighties. Croft stayed independent. Smart man. He was writing a book about the Second World War. I think he was using the Blue Last as a symbol for the loss of the real Britain, which 'real' I think he equated with ale and beer. A slow erosion of the British spirit."

Jury smiled. "That's always been the sentimental view."

"How cynical. Listen, I want a word with the doctor."

This person had been talking to one of the crime scene officers. Mickey asked him how soon he could do the autopsy.

"Late this afternoon or tomorrow morning, early."

"Early? I'd appreciate that."

The doctor smiled fractionally. What Jury remembered about the way Mickey worked was that he never pushed people already pushed to the limit for favors. He often got favors as a consequence.

"It's pretty straightforward," said the doctor. "He died somewhere between midnight and four or five A.M.; the rigor's fairly well established. Body temp and room temp don't suggest anything delayed or sped up the decomposition. Still, you know how hard it is to fix the time of death. I'll know better when I do the autopsy. And of course you know it's no suicide. Whoever tried to make it look like one knows sod all about ballistics."

"I figured. Thanks." He nodded to the doctor. Then he said to Jury, "According to this Mrs. MacLeish, Croft was working on a book. He had a laptop and a manuscript and also a card index, notes for the book, which she said was always sitting on the desk. The manuscript sat on that table by the printer." He paused. "Don't printers have memory? Anyway, someone, presumably the shooter, nicked all that stuff. At the moment, that's all I know that was taken."

"You said before you knew him a little."

"That's right—I've got to sit down for a minute." They moved to an armchair in front of an elaborate stereo system. "Not well," Mickey repeated, again taking out his handkerchief and wiping what looked like cold perspiration from his forehead. "Croft knew me because—you remember? I told you his father, Francis, and my dad were such good friends. Simon there—" Mickey nodded toward the body of Simon Croft "—knew I was in the Job, so asked me if I'd just come by once in a while because he thought someone was trying to get at him. That's how he put it, 'get at me.' But he couldn't or wouldn't say who or why. To tell the truth, he struck me as more than a little paranoid. Anyway, I did it; I've come by here maybe five or six times." Mickey shook his head. "Obviously, I was wrong. Someone *was* trying to get at him. Someone did. It makes me feel bad, Rich, really bad. I should've taken it more seriously." He shook his head. "Look over here."

Mickey rose and Jury moved with him to the raised

window behind the desk where Mickey pointed out chipped paint along the sill and obvious gashes on the outside that looked made by a knife. "Whoever did this is a real amateur. We're supposed to think it was a break-in. But look at the way the marks go. It was done from inside, not out. Like I said, a real amateur." Mickey moved to talk to the police photographer, and Jury looked at the CDs spread out across the table on which the stereo sat. Without touching them, he let his eyes stray over them. Simon Croft was not so careful about their arrangement as he was about his books. There must have been a dozen or more CDs out of their cases. Jury smiled. Vera Lynn, Jo Stafford, Tommy Dorsey's band. All of the music was popular in the Second World War. "We'll Meet Again," "A Nightingale Sang in Berkeley Square." He'd been too little to take them in when they first came out, but later, yes, he remembered. "Yesterday," yes, he certainly recalled that. But wasn't that song much later? In his mind's eye he saw again Elicia Deauville dancing by herself in her white nightgown. She was eight years old. Eight or nine? Given all the activity behind him in the room, it surprised him how well he could mute the sounds to an incomprehensible cloud of talk, and hear "Yesterday." And see Elicia Deauville through that hole in the wall. It was her hair that was so astonishing. It was tawny, but several shades of it—taffy to gold to copper, amazing hair. He thought she had lived next door to them on the Fulham Road, but now he wasn't so sure.

Had it happened? Was he there?

Mickey was beside him. "It's meant to look like a robbery—" Mickey shoved at the glass slivers with the toe of his shoe "—yet the only thing of any value missing is a Sony laptop. The watch he was wearing was worth more than that. Not a Rolex, that other one that costs as much as a small car. You know?"

"Piaget?"

"That's the guy. See those pictures?" Mickey pointed

out a small painting propped against the books on one shelf. "Bonnard. That one—" he indicated another on the top shelf, ultramarine water, yellow so heavy it looked like the weight of the sun "—Hopper, no not Hopper—the other one—Hockney, that's it. David Hockney. Those two paintings are easily transported. Who in hell would rob the room and leave those behind?"

"Did they take *anything* besides the computer? Computer-related stuff? Diskettes?"

Mickey called to one of the crime scene officers. "Johnny? Did you find any computer diskettes?"

"No," said Johnny. "Not used, but there were some new ones, that's all, sealed."

Jury scanned the desk, the shelves. "No manuscript? No notes? Didn't you say he was writing a book about the Second World War?"

"You think he turned up something someone didn't want turned up?"

"Don't you? Everything associated with the writing of it appears to be gone. And that's all that's gone. The man must have had hard copy, some, at least. A historical event calls for research; research calls for notes. You saw him—when? A couple of weeks ago?"

"The computer was on; I didn't pay much attention to whether he was writing from notes." Mickey looked around the room as if either determined or desperate. "Maybe when they go over the house—"

"The killer could have done that, easily, at his leisure. Assuming this was someone who knew Simon Croft lived here alone, no staff except for the Tynedale cook, who didn't, in any case, live here. The last time you saw him, you said—are you okay? Mickey?"

Haggerty had grown very pale. He swayed slightly. "Let me just sit for a minute." As he sat in one of the wing chairs, he took out his handkerchief, damp by now, and wiped his forehead, beaded with cold perspiration. "I've got to go over to talk to the family." He said that and folded the handkerchief.

"Uh-uh," said Jury. "You go the hell home. Leave the family to me."

"I can't—"

"The hell you can't. I'll get the initial stuff out of the way; you can talk to them later."

Sotto voce, Mickey said, "Look, keep this under your hat, Rich, will you? I mean, me being sick."

Jury said, "Of course, I will. You know I will. Does the family know about Simon Croft yet?"

Mickey nodded. "Two of my people went over there, sergeant and WPC. They told them I'd be talking to them this morning." Mickey checked his watch, shook his wrist. "Damn thing."

"Get yourself a Piaget. Give me the details and I'll go over there now."

Mickey did so.

ELEVEN

Ian Tynedale was an intelligent, good-looking man in his late fifties or early sixties. At least Jury assumed that age, given he was a young child when his sister Alexandra was killed. He sat forward on the dining-room chair, elbows on knees. His eyes were red rimmed.

"It wasn't suicide, if that's what the gun being there implies," Ian said. Pulling himself together, he sat back and took out a cigar case and dragged a pewter ashtray closer.

"You're sure of that?" said Jury.

"Never been surer. Not Simon." He thought for a moment. "Was it robbery? Were any of the paintings missing?"

"I don't think so, but of course we couldn't be sure. You're familiar with his paintings?"

"Yes, I got a few of them for him at auction. Art's my life. Italian Renaissance art, to be specific. I'm pretty passionate about that. There was one painting worth a quarter of a million on the wall behind the desk."

"I think I recall seeing that." Jury paused. "Mr. Croft was actually no relation, was he?"

"No. The two families have always been exceptionally close. Simon's father, Francis, and mine knew each other from a very early age. They were boyhood friends, then they were business partners. They were quite remarkable, really. They were every bit as close as blood brothers. Maybe you could say the same for Simon and me. It's a very close family. Living out of each other's pockets, you could say."

"Francis Croft owned a pub in the forties called the Blue Last?"

That surprised Ian. "Yes. How'd you know that?"

Jury smiled. "I'm a policeman."

"Funny old thing to bring up, though. That pub's been gone for more than half a century. Bombed during the war. Maisie—that's Alexandra's daughter—was a baby then. They were at the Blue Last when it happened. Rather, Alex was; Maisie, fortunately for her, was out with the au pair, Katherine Riordin. Kitty, we call her. She survived because Kitty had taken her out in a stroller. Not the best time for a stroll, you might say, but there were long, long lulls between the bombings and it was pretty safe for the most part. The bombings, of course, were mostly at night. You can't keep yourself cooped up all of the time, can you? It was a pity, and perhaps ironic that Kitty's own baby was killed in the blast that took out the Blue Last."

"I understand she lives here with the family."

Ian motioned with his head. "That's right. In the gatehouse. Keeper's Cottage we call it. You passed it in the drive. 'Gatehouse' seems a bit pretentious."

"And she's lived here ever since that time?" If Ian was curious about this interest in Kitty Riordin, he didn't show it.

Ian nodded. "You can imagine how grateful my father was that the baby was all right. Her own baby—Kitty's—was in the pub at the time. The wrong time. So was Alex." Turning his cigar around and around as if it aided thought, he said, "That was a terrible loss, you know."

"Your sister, you mean?"

He nodded. "Alex was . . . there was something about her . . ." He paused, as if searching for the right word and sighed, as if he couldn't find it. "She was young when she married a chap in the RAF named Ralph Herrick. She was only twenty or twenty-one, I think, when Maisie was born."

Jury changed the subject. "Was Simon Croft wealthy? He was a banker, wasn't he?"

"Broker. There's a difference. He was very well off. He inherited a great deal of money when his father died."

"He himself had done well?"

"Absolutely. He was a brilliant broker. Thing is, though, the whole climate of banking and brokering changed in the eighties. Until fifteen years ago, the City was run on—you could say—gentlemanly standards. I don't mean more honest, more scrupulous, or nicer, I mean clubbier—you know, much like a gentlemen's club. They simply weren't up to American and international methods of management. It was as if the City was run by Old Etonians. So when things changed, most of these people were left out in the smoke. Not Simon, though. He was one of those with a boutique sort of business and he saw it coming. He stayed independent and afterward was heavily courted by the big banks— God, why am I going on about money? He's dead. I can't really take it in."

"Who will inherit this money?"

"Inherit? Oh, all of us, probably. More, of course, to Emily and Marie-France. They're Simon's sisters. Emily lives in Brighton in one of those 'assisted-living' homes. She has a bit of heart trouble, I think. Simon was married years ago but it lasted only a few years. No children, sad to say. Haven't seen her in twenty years. I think she went off to Australia or Africa with a new husband." He tapped ash from his cigar into the ashtray and looked up at Jury as he did it, smiling slightly. "You think one of us did it, is that it? For the swag?"

"The thought had crossed my mind. That's the way it

so often plays out. For the record, where were you in the early hours of the morning?"

"Asleep in bed. Alone, no one to vouch for me." Ian smiled as if the notion of his shooting Simon Croft were so unlikely it hardly bore discussing.

"Mr. Croft had no enemies you know of? Any fellow brokers? Bankers? Businessmen? Anyone holding a grudge?"

Ian shook his head. "Nary a one, Superintendent, not to my knowledge. Christ . . ." Turning in the dining-room chair, he looked away.

"Yes?" Jury prompted him.

Ian shook his head. "Nothing, nothing. It's still sinking in." He put the heels of his palms against his eyes and pressed.

Jury said nothing for a few moments, and then decided on something that might not be so volatile a subject. "Apparently, Mr. Croft was writing a book. What do you know about that?"

Ian turned to face Jury, looking a little surprised. "That's important?"

"Given that all traces of it seem to have vanished, yes, I expect it is important. His computer was taken along with the manuscript and ostensibly any notes he'd made. That's why we're wondering about it."

Ian frowned, looked at the cigar turned to ash that he'd left in the ashtray. "He didn't say much about it. Might have talked to Dad about it, though. Dad's been keeping to his bed lately. He's taking this very hard, Superintendent. Simon was like a son to him. Trite sounding, but it's true. I hope you don't have to question him today."

"Not if you think I shouldn't. I can come back."

"I appreciate that; it's so tough for him—" He knocked the worm of ash into the tray.

Marie-France Muir, Simon's sister, sat at the head of the table in the chair Ian Tynedale had just vacated. Jury was on her right. The romance of her name was almost borne out by the melancholy air, the pale, nearly translucent complexion, the fine, forlorn gray eyes.

For Marie-France, the appearance, he was fairly sure, was the reality. That what one saw was what one got. So, looked at that way—her unmade-up face, her literal answers—it might be honesty at its most banal, but honesty nonetheless. He should at least be as direct in his questions.

"Have you any idea why this happened to your brother?"

She was silent, as if she were trying to formulate a difficult answer. "No."

Jury waited a moment, but saw she wasn't about to embroider on this no. "Did he have enemies or was he in financial straits? Anything like that?"

"Financial straits? I think not." Her smile was sad and her voice sounded as if it had been scoured, raspy and uneven. "Enemies? I didn't know all of my brother's acquaintances, but I don't see why he should have had. He was quite a decent person."

"Your father used to run a pub during the war called the Blue Last—"

He surprised a real smile from her. "Oh, yes, I remember it. I remember it well. The Blue Last. Simon and I used to love playing there. Heavens—" She rested her forehead in her hand as if she might be going to weep, but she didn't. "It's been over fifty years." She pushed a strand of hair back into a rather careless chignon with a slightly flushed cheek and a bashful look, as if flirting with memory. "We had so much fun back then. Simon was around ten and I was two years older and Em—Emily, my sister—must have been in her teens." Her eyebrows drew together in puzzlement. "Actually, Emily was much nearer Alex's age than she was mine. Yes, she must have been seventeen or eighteen when Alex died." She went on, smiling once more, saying, "We always thought the pub a great adventure.

Alexandra always loved it, too. But that was in the years before the war came and ruined it all. Yes, my father Francis had the Blue Last for—it must have been fifteen years. He didn't, of course, need to run it, I mean, he had no financial need of it. Tynedale Brewery owned several."

"Your father was killed in the blast, also?"

"Yes. And our mother had died two years before that. Had it not been for Oliver, we would have been—well, orphans." She smiled slightly, as if the thought of their being orphans almost amused her. "The Blue Last. It was a lark, such a lark before the war." Her voice seemed to unwind with these words and, like the clock on the mantel, stop. She was looking out of the window, as if on the other side of it she saw larks flighting. She looked profoundly sad.

Jury felt a little ashamed of himself for thinking she was all surface.

She went on. "I really loved that pub. It was endlessly exciting. The people, the talk, the 'crack,' as they say. That we owned it, that was part of it, like the scullery maid finding she owns the castle."

The metaphor surprised Jury, both that she had drawn it and that it had been drawn at all. He smiled. "Scullery maid. Is that how you saw yourself at home?"

Her answer was oblique. "But the Blue Last *was* home. I mean, of course, we had another house. The one that Simon occupies—I mean, occupied—" She turned away.

Jury was silent.

Looking down at her hands, she said, "It sounds awful, but—" A flush spread upward from her neck. Again she took refuge in the light beyond the window.

He waited for more, but she remained silent, as if, done with memories of the Blue Last, there was nothing to speak of, not even her brother's murder. It was as if the loss of the Blue Last had enervated her.

Why was this hard to understand? There was a sense

of a particular place that haunted us all, wasn't there? A place to which we ascribed the power to confer happiness. An image deeply etched in the mind that had fled and taken something of us with it. Strange we should put so much stock in childhood, a time when we were vulnerable, unprotected and at the mercy of those we hoped would have mercy. Yet that time, that childhood seemed to rise above the lurking danger and present itself as the most seductive, longed-for, unassailable thing in our lives.

"You said you got on so well then."

"What?" Marie-France turned blank, gray eyes to him.

"You said you and your brother and sister got on so well back then."

"We did, yes. Sometimes we got to stay all night at the pub, as there was a large flat above. Alexandra and Ian did, too. And Alexandra did after she was married. She seemed to like it even more than Tynedale Lodge. I think I was jealous of her; she was so beautiful. And then she married this dashing RAF pilot—did you ever see the film *Waterloo Bridge*?"

"Yes." Jury smiled. "One of the great romances in film history." (*That's* who it was, he thought, Vivien Leigh; *that's* who Alexandra looked like, and the waitress in the cappuccino bar.)

"Kitty used to say that's just how they were, that Alexandra and Ralph were like Myra and Roy. Kitty—she was the au pair, or nanny, I suppose. I remember how it irritated me that Alex really *did* resemble Vivien Leigh with her smooth dark hair and ivory complexion and dark eyes. And the cheekbones." She shook her head. "'A silly comparison,' I once heard Alex tell her. 'Vivien was a prostitute and that's why she *didn't* marry Robert Taylor. And that's why she jumped from the bridge. I don't think I'll have to do that,' Alex said."

Jury said, "Alexandra doesn't sound like an incurable romantic." He smiled. "She sounds more the practical type." He drew the envelope from an inside pocket where he carried Mickey's snapshots. He removed the one of Alexandra and Francis Croft and set it before Marie-France.

Surprised, she picked it up "Where did you ever . . . it's the Blue Last. That's my father and Alexandra. Where did you get it?"

Jury noticed she identified the pub before she did the people. "One of the CID men in the City." He found the one of Katherine Riordin and her baby.

"It's Kitty and Erin . . . wait, no, it's Maisie." She drew the snapshot close to her eyes. "No, it is Erin. All babies tend to look alike, don't you think?"

Jury smiled again. "I'm sure the mothers would disagree with you. So Kitty Riordin stayed on with the Tynedales here."

"Oliver kept her on after Alex was killed. And Erin, poor thing. God, but that was awful. *Awful.* Both Oliver and Kitty lost their child. I don't know who was more heartbroken."

"And Alexandra's husband?"

It was as though Marie-France were trying to recollect him. "Oh, of course. Ralph was devastated."

Had he really been, or was she simply mouthing a platitude? Ralph Herrick didn't seem to be a person remembered for anything but his looks and the RAF. But, then, they'd been married such a little while.

Marie-France went on: "Ralph was killed in the war." She dredged up memory. "Yes, that's right. During the war. He'd left the RAF. Actually, he was awarded the Victoria Cross. Yes. How could I have forgotten that? He had something to do with those code breakers. . . . Anyway, he drowned. Somewhere in Scotland."

"You live exactly where, Mrs. Muir?"

"In Belgravia, in Chapel Street."

"Is that where you were early this morning?"

"Mm?" She seemed distracted by the past. "Oh. Yes, of course, I'm always there mornings. I live alone."

"No maid? Cook?"

"No, none. It's quite a small house and I prefer not to have to be bumping into other people."

Jury pushed back his chair and Marie-France rose as he did. "Thanks very much, Mrs. Muir. And if you could just give me your sister's address—?"

They were standing at the door and she nodded, sadly. *Must have been a beauty back then,* he thought. *Another one I completely misjudged.* So much for police intuition.

When Maisie Tynedale entered the room elegantly suited in black, and sat down, Jury felt a sense of disquietude and thought it had been very poor judgment on his part to talk to the others first, but, then, Mickey had already planted an idea in his mind which had neither been reinforced nor dispelled by the others.

His eye traveled to the portrait and back to her, trying to limn in the features of Alexandra Tynedale on Maisie. Maisie followed his line of vision. "Yes, I know," she said. "Disappointingly unbeautiful." She smiled.

So did Jury. "Not at all. I was merely wondering if you looked like your mother."

Maisie looked again at the portrait. "Her coloring, her hair, possibly her mouth, but definitely not the eyes; the eyes are what count."

In this case it was the coloring that did it. Black hair, falling straight just below the ears; ivory skin, a heightened color on the lips and cheekbones. A person who had no reason to suspect she wasn't Alexandra Herrick's daughter would think straightaway Maisie was her daughter.

The thing was, though, hair and coloring could always be altered, and hers had been. The black hair was not her natural color, and rouge had been artfully applied. But even so, she could still be Alexandra's daughter, wanting to look more like her.

"What about your father? Is there a picture of him?"

"He's around." Her eyes turned to the serving table and the photographs there. "My grandfather might have him. He shifts photographs around—have you spoken to him?"

Jury shook his head. "No. He's quite ill, I understand."

"He'll be crippled by Simon's death. You know, we might as well all be brothers, sisters, sons, daughters. The two families are that close. Simon might as well have been Oliver's son. I know Ian always thought of him as a brother."

"I've got the impression all of you find the friendship of Francis Croft and Oliver Tynedale rather astonishing."

"Unusual, at least. How it could go on like that, how it could go on since they were boys. Yes, perhaps 'astonishing' is the right word."

"Your relationship with—" Jury consulted his notebook as if searching for the name which he perfectly well knew "—Katherine Riordin goes back a long way, too."

"Kitty. Yes, I suppose you know about that night the Blue Last was bombed."

Jury nodded.

"Well, Kitty just stayed on."

And stayed. But, then, a lot of old nannies, family retainers, stayed on with their employers for a long time. And never having met the woman, Jury decided to drop that particular line of inquiry.

But Maisie continued. "Granddad gave her the cottage so she would feel more independent—"

"Which she isn't; she's completely dependent upon your family."

Maisie grew somewhat defensive. "That sounds a little hostile."

Jury raised his eyebrows. "I don't mean it to. I'm stating facts, at least, as I know them. The source of Mrs. Riordin's income could be important."

"What are you hinting—?"

"Noth—"

"—that she murdered Simon for an inheritance?"

"That hadn't crossed my mind. Why would Simon Croft leave money to your old nursemaid?"

Angry, she started to rise.

"No—" Jury put out his hand. "Please stay seated. I have more questions."

Reluctantly and with mouth compressed, she sat back, arms folded in a somewhat combative stance. He noticed the deformity of the hand, then, a skewing of the index and middle fingers, a dislocation of the thumb. He recalled the snapshot of the baby Maisie, her tiny hand on her mother's neck.

"You appear to be protective of Katherine Riordin."

"She saved my *life;* yes, I suppose I am."

Jury doodled on a fresh page of his small notebook. Doodles were the only thing in the notebook aside from a few telephone numbers and addresses. Wiggins saw to notes; he was the most thorough note taker around. Jury himself was afraid of impeding, muffling, the flow of speech. He didn't like tapes either.

"Why is it," he asked, eyes on his notebook, "everyone I've talked to makes it sound as if Mrs. Riordin rushed into that bombed building and pulled you out? Coincidence saved your life, not Katherine Riordin. She happened to have taken you out in a pram. That hardly makes her a heroine. It was also coincidence—of the worst kind, I imagine, to her—that she had taken you and not her own child."

Maisie sat back, looking stunned, almost despairing that someone would not see Kitty Riordin as a heroine. Why, he wondered, was this so important to her? He could understand it if Maisie was really Erin Riordin and Kitty was indeed Erin's real mother. Or could it be that the story of that night of the Blue Last's destruction had taken on mythic proportions of salvation, self-sacrifice and heroism? Maisie caught up in that period of her life, the baby who had lost mother and father and could have lost her own life without Kitty Riordin's intervention. Jury wondered if Oliver Tynedale was caught up in the same myth.

"Where were you between midnight and eight A.M.?"

"Across the river shooting Simon, perhaps?"

He smiled. "We have to ask everyone that question."

"We're all suspects? I'm a suspect? What on earth would be my reason? I don't stand to gain by his death. I've got enough right now for a dozen people."

Jury closed up his notebook and pocketed it. "I doubt the motive had to do with money. I expect everyone here has enough for a dozen people."

"Then why? Why did someone shoot Simon?"

Jury just looked at her and repeated it: "Where were you early this morning?"

TWELVE

He wanted, after all of this sitting-still talk, to move about and told the butler, Barkins, that he was going to have a walk in the garden and that that was where he was to be found in case Detective Chief Inspector Haggerty called.

It was early afternoon. He left the dining room through a set of French doors to a terrace and a walk that stretched along the side of the house, the house being much deeper than it looked from the front. The walk was flanked on its outer side by a series of columns. It was, actually, a covered colonnade, along the length of which these white pillars caught the mellow light of the sun. Jury had never been of the peripatetic school; he was very poor at thinking while he walked; what he was good at was smoking and he was dying for a cigarette. *A year and nine months and two weeks— Good Lord, and you're still dying for a smoke.*

Across the grass at a distance of some twenty feet stood a line of cypresses along a garden path inside the high stone wall. This tree-lined path ran parallel to the white columns, and between them was the statue of a child reaching her hand down to a duck. He heard voices and saw, between the pillars and the trees, somebody walking there, as he was doing. No, just the one voice was what he heard. He could not make out the words. The cypress trees, themselves like gray columns, were set in counterpoint to these white pillars, so that they appeared, as he walked, in the space between the pillars. Thus between cypresses and pillars, he caught the barest glimpse of the person he had determined was a little girl.

Perhaps it was talk of *Waterloo Bridge* that caused Jury to keep walking and looking over at the child between the line of trees, enjoying the cinematic effect of all this. It was as if he were watching a shuttle weaving a tapestry, a picture of a garden. All of its discrete elements—the white columns, the cypresses, the girl, the statue, himself—coming together, locking into one another to form this picture. Jury liked this; it was something like the feeling he got when a solution to what had seemed an impenetrable mystery finally locked into place.

He had come to the end of the covered walk marked by two wide, shallow steps, going down to a pool or pond, in the center of which a maiden was pouring water from a jug. When he saw the little girl (why had no one mentioned her? A grandchild? A great-grandchild?) emerge from the line of trees, Jury crouched down and pretended to be tying his shoelace. He did not want her intimidated by six feet two of police. His head was down, examining this shoe as if it were as fascinating as the tapestry he had just woven in his mind.

She stopped and was watching.

Raising his head and, in a taken-by-surprise tone, he called to her, "Oh, hullo. I'm just trying to get this lace—do yours ever break?"

In response, she took a few steps closer and raised her shoe, which was a buckled sandal, and shook her head. Her sandals were not winterproof, but she did wear white socks with them. The rest of her was covered in a sprigged muslin dress (too long) and a heavy green coat-sweater the color of her eyes.

Pretending finally to have fixed the lace, he said,

"You're smart to wear shoes without laces." He saw now that what she had been talking to all along in her walk was a doll, oddly clothed in a lace-fringed bonnet and a dress also too long, which flowed over the doll's feet. When she stepped even closer (though not within hand-shaking distance) he took in her burnished black hair, pearlescent skin, dark green eyes. He did not know if Vivien Leigh had green eyes. If she didn't, poor Vivien.

"This garden is lovely, even in winter. I imagine you spend a lot of time here."

She nodded. Solemn and beautiful. Who did she belong to? With her black hair and translucent skin, of course she resembled Alexandra Tynedale. "My name's Richard Jury, incidentally." There was no name response from her. He said, "Your doll is all covered up. Is she cold?"

The little girl shook her head. "She always wears this; it's her baptismal clothes. I saw one once." Her look at Jury was slightly challenging as if he might contest the kind of clothes worn to a baptism.

He assumed she meant she'd seen a baptism. "I never have."

This was a comfort as now he couldn't dispute the details she offered. "They pour water on your head. It's like they do in beauty shops except in baptisms they don't have soap and you don't wash your hair. It just gets rinsed."

This was a place of metaphor, certainly. Jury smiled. "So is your doll baptized, then?"

"Not until I find a name. I've been looking for a long time. I'm all the way to the *R*s right now. I just can't decide. I'm thinking about Rebecca." She glanced at him to see if he was thinking about that, too.

Jury said, "Could we sit down over there?" He motioned to a white bench enclosed on two sides by vine-covered lattice.

"Okay."

They settled on the bench—the three of them, the

doll sitting between—and Jury said, "Are you sure your doll is a girl?"

Gemma looked at him wide-eyed. "What?" It had been wearing this dress when she found it. No matter what she told others, she believed the dress meant it was a girl.

Jury shrugged. "I was just wondering why you're having a hard time finding a girl's name. Maybe it's really a boy and doesn't want to walk around with a girl's name. I wouldn't either."

She had often wondered on this subject, but never knew whom to ask. Turning away a little, she lifted the doll's christening dress and looked. Then she turned it so Jury could see. But said nothing.

Jury said, "Oh, you're in luck. It could be either a boy or girl, you have your choice. Not many people do. You've got the evidence right there in case anyone disputes it."

Gemma thought this wondrous.

"Speaking of names, you haven't told me yours."

"Gemma Trimm."

"You live here, Gemma?"

"I'm Mr. Tynedale's ward. A ward is different from being adopted. I'm not related to anybody; I'm kind of left over. Mr. Tynedale's sick, and he likes me to read to him. I do that every day, nearly. I read *The Old Curiosity Shop* and I'm a lot like Little Nell, he says. But I don't think so. She's kind of sappy."

"You're young to be reading complicated books like that. Even adults sometimes find it hard to read Charles Dickens."

"I'm nine." She seemed pleased with herself, being able to read what adults couldn't. "I skip the hard parts, but it doesn't hurt because he wrote so many pages about everything."

"He did, that's true." After a few moments' contemplation of Gemma and Dickens, Jury said, "I'm here because of Simon Croft. Did you hear what happened to him?"

"Yes. He's dead. He got shot." She pulled the bonnet down over the doll's head, hiding the eyes. "What did he do? It must've been bad to make somebody shoot him."

"We don't know yet. I'm a detective, incidentally, and I intend to find out."

Her look was one of utter astonishment. "*You* are? Did Benny send you?"

"Benny? No, he didn't. Is he a friend?"

"My best one. He argues a lot, though. If you're a detective, you should work out who's trying to kill *me*."

"*Kill* you? Why do you think that?"

"Because they already tried a bunch of times. Once was in the greenhouse." She pointed to it. "They tried to shoot me when I was thinking about planting something in a pot. Mr. Murphy takes care of the garden. Next time when I was asleep in my room somebody tried to choke me and smother me. *Next* time it was trying to poison me and Mrs. MacLeish nearly quit because she was afraid they blamed her cooking."

Jury did not shock easily. But this compendium of crime, delivered by such a small person, in such a matter-of-fact tone, shocked him, although he doubted it had all happened. He could appreciate the melodrama in all of this. Take a child with apparently no family and put her down in the midst of one who wasn't hers and perhaps indifferent (except for the elderly Oliver), and it would not be surprising that she might concoct this story of these attempts on her life. Still . . . "Tell me more about these incidents, Gemma. I mean, give me more details."

"I was in the greenhouse, like I said. I was looking at the cuttings Mr. Murphy had in there. I was wondering when he'd plant the snowdrop bulbs. Those over there." She pointed at the drift of snowdrops he'd noticed before, white petals with a green spot positioned with such regularity in each petal they looked painted. "They're called Tryms. Like my name, only it's spelled different. They're very unusual. I planted one in a pot and looked around for the Day-Gro. I was holding my doll in my other hand. That's when I heard the glass shatter and felt something whiz by me. I thought maybe somebody threw a rock. That's *that* time.

"The second time I was in bed asleep so I can't tell you more than I did. Something woke me up; I guess it was because I couldn't breathe. I yanked open a window and stuck my head out. They got a doctor and they called the police again. I saw a film with a murderer in it who used to put pillows over his victims' faces." Gemma stopped to move her doll to a sitting position and then went on for a fascinated Jury.

"The *third* time I was eating spotted Dick that Mrs. MacLeish made with custard sauce. I got really sick and the doctor had to come again and said I was lucky I threw up and got rid of it. I said it was poisoned, but he didn't think it was. That's all." She sat back and picked up the doll again.

Jury was winded, as if he'd been doing all the talking. "That must have been terribly frightening."

Her silence as she looked at him suggested any fool could see that.

"The police came, did they?"

She nodded energetically.

"And did they find any bullet casings?"

"I guess that's what you call it. It was outside on the ground. Or maybe stuck in a tree."

"Are you sure the shooter was aiming at *you*, though?"

"You mean maybe they were trying to shoot the Trym bulbs?" This was said with more acidity than a nine-year-old could usually muster.

"No. I mean, what about the gardener?"

"He wasn't there. Anyway, why would anybody want to kill *him*?"

"Why would anybody want to kill *you*?"

THIRTEEN

"I just don't know, Mickey," Jury said. "I certainly think it's possible."

They were in Mickey's office and Mickey wanted to get out of it. He was up and pulling on his coat. "Pub?"

"Liberty Bounds?"

"Nah. Too far. Let's walk, then, find a coffee."

Jury said, "I know the perfect place. I've got kind of a crush on a waitress there." It would give him more material to irritate Carole-anne with, too.

Mickey smiled. "Okay, we're out of here."

The cappuccino-bar-restaurant was barely three blocks from headquarters. There were more customers this morning than there had been at the weekend, but the place was large and still two-thirds empty.

The pretty waitress had taken their order, lattè for Jury, house coffee and a fruit Danish for Mickey; she had been sincerely glad to see Jury again, almost as if she'd worried about his getting safely home on Saturday.

Mickey watched her walk away and smiled. "You've got good taste, Richie; if I weren't a happily married man—" He held his hands out, palm upward. Then he said, "When I felt better yesterday afternoon I sent Johnny and a uniform over to pick up Kitty Riordin. Just for some friendly questioning. I didn't want to go to Tynedale Lodge; I thought the two of us might be too much 'police presence,' if you know what I mean."

"You've talked to her before, haven't you?"

"Oh, yeah. Anyway, she didn't overdo it as far as Simon Croft was concerned. She found it 'regrettable.' She'd known him for a long time, ever since he was a kid, but at the same time felt she didn't *really* know him. 'He was never terribly outgoing. He had his secrets.'"

Jury told Mickey what he'd learned yesterday from his talk with family members. "Marie-France Muir and her memories of the Blue Last—she seems to feel it was home. She loved the place. I got the feeling she thought of that pub as a living, breathing organism. But I suppose you can never attach too much importance to a place. It filled you up when you had it, left you empty when it was gone. We're all orphans when it comes to that." He thought of Gemma. *Left over.*

"We're all orphans anyway. You are, I am, so's Liza," Mickey mused. "I was lucky when it came to foster parents. It's hard to remember they weren't my own flesh and blood. Liza was lucky, too." He looked at Jury. "You weren't." He sighed. "Had a good time, though, the three of us, didn't we?"

"We did indeed." Jury had forgotten that—that all of them were orphans. He wondered if that was one thing they had in common.

Mickey raised his coffee cup, half in salute and half to summon the waitress.

"Did anyone mention Gemma Trimm?"

"I don't remember anyone named Trimm," said Mickey, puzzled.

"I guess that's the point, Mickey. No one said a word about her. She's old Oliver Tynedale's ward. She's nine. I found her walking in the garden." Jury told Mickey Gemma's story.

"She was making it up, I hope."

"Not all of it, anyway. Police found a bullet casing after it had gone through the greenhouse."

"Thanks," Mickey said to the waitress who refilled his cup and set down his pastry. She asked Jury if he'd like another lattè.

"Just pour me some of that, thanks."

She did, and smiled at him, and walked away.

"I'd say she's the one that's got the crush," Mickey said, absently. He leaned across the table, over his folded arms. "We can't clutter this case up with threats that don't exist, Rich."

"Every case is cluttered until you sort it. And stuff like this girl has to be sorted. You're much too meticulous a cop to ignore Gemma's story."

Mickey took a bite of the pastry and said, around a mouthful of crumbs, "Okay, okay. I guess I'm just in a hurry. What could the motive be for killing this little girl? Who is she? She's a ward, which keeps the Social at just beyond breathing distance. What's her history?"

"I don't know because I haven't talked to Oliver Tynedale. I expect he might be the only one who does."

Mickey frowned over his cup. "You don't think she's actually related to Oliver Tynedale, do you?"

"I thought about that. She could be. Her resemblance to Alexandra Tynedale is marked."

"But not to Maisie. It couldn't be."

Jury laughed. "You're pretty certain of that. But I tend to agree. There's something about Maisie—"

"Hell, yeah, there's something about her. Like not being Alexandra and Ralph Herrick's daughter. That's something."

"Odd, how she's got the black hair, the dark eyes . . . and yet. She doesn't look like Vivien Leigh. Gemma does, in miniature."

"Like Liza."

"What?"

"Don't you remember you used to tell her that? People think she looks like Vivien Leigh or else Claire Bloom."

Jury frowned. "Vivien Leigh and Claire Bloom don't look *anything* alike. Our waitress looks like Vivien Leigh, in case you didn't notice."

Mickey turned around and looked at her. From across the room, she smiled at him. Or them. "She looks like Claire Bloom."

"Hell, she does."

This bickering went on.

Finally, Mickey asked, "When will you talk to dear old nanny Kitty? A.k.a. Maisie's real mother?"

"Today. You talked to her. How did she strike you?"

"As the mother of an impostor."

"That was your objective assessment, was it?"

Mickey's hand squeezed Jury's shoulder. "That's what you're here for—objectivity." He removed his hand and shrugged. "You'll see."

A laugh caught in Jury's throat. "I'll *see?* You mean I'll agree that Maisie is really Erin Riordin and that Kitty Riordin is her mother? Mickey, all you've got to go on are those old snapshots—"

"And instinct. You said yourself my instincts are good."

"I did? I'll bet the instinct here is just a by-product of those pictures. Mickey, what if I don't agree with you? What if I find out Maisie Tynedale really is who she says she is?"

"Then I'll drop it."

Jury flinched, surprised. It was true he wanted Mickey to be open to this possibility, but he wasn't sure he wanted Mickey to put so much faith in his, Jury's, ability.

"Look, Rich, you're the best cop I know. You're certainly the best with witnesses. Look at how much you got out of these people that I didn't. I didn't know this little Gemma Trimm even existed, for Christ's sake."

"I only found her by chance, by luck. I was outside, walking."

"Still . . ." Mickey sighed.

"How *is* Liza?" She was Mickey's wife when Jury met her. Liza had been with the Met herself, detective sergeant, and a very good one. She'd gotten pregnant and given up the Job.

"Wonderful. Liza knows what it is, what it's like. She *knows.* It's almost like she can read my mind; her intuition is almost magical. She knows what this is like, too." Mickey fisted his hand and made light hammering blows against his chest. "And she doesn't go on about my smoking. People do, my mates do, as if stopping the fags would save my life. They've given me a new painkiller which is an improvement on the other."

Jury would have thought the doctors at least could eliminate pain, if nothing else. "Do you get a lot of pain?"

"Some." Mickey swirled the dregs of his coffee.

Some, of course, meant a lot. As if, as if.

"Nothing's gonna stop this. It's everywhere now, in blood and bone."

"I'm sorry, Mickey. I really am." Jury felt it, too. What a loss it was going to be. What on earth would Liza and the children do without him? "How are the kids with all this?"

"They're great. I'm proud of them, too."

One of Mickey's children was grown and married and gone to another country. Then there were the twins, a boy and a girl who'd lived after a car crash had killed both their parents, Mickey and Liza's daughter and son-in-law. That had happened two years ago. Jury supposed the twins were no more than six or seven now. In addition, there were two others, one in her late teens, a boy readying himself for university. Mickey had too many responsibilities.

"Peter is going to Oxford next year. I'm really happy about that."

Although you couldn't easily tell it, Mickey had read literature there. He loved poetry, was always pulling out a line here and there.

"Beth, she's already talking about London University. Clara and Toby—the twins—are in public school." He moved his gaze from whatever lay outside the window to Jury. "Liza will probably go back to the Met; well, she'll have to do something because my bloody pension sure won't do it. Not as far as Oxford goes, that's certain. I don't like being forced to think about all this, know what I mean? Of course, I'd think about it anyway, but in the abstract, kind of. I'd think but I wouldn't have to feel everything ending." He pushed his cup away. "I really need a drink." He barked out a laugh. "Well, at least I can stop worrying about whether I have a drinking problem. 'Drinking problem.' I love that euphemism. That last round I did with the chemo they thought might have stopped it. I went into remission for a while. I thought I might even have it licked. I didn't.

"There's a chilling side effect to this cancer. People don't want to be around it; they feel they should do something but don't know what the something is. They steer clear; they cross the street, metaphorically, and maybe even literally. It amazes me that my mates, my colleagues, who've seen every form of violent death, who walk with it every day—they can't take this."

"Because it's a lot closer to home, Mickey. Because they're your mates, your friends."

Mickey looked at him, smiling. "You're my friend, too, Rich, but you're here. I love this fragment:

The world and his mother go reeling and jiggling forever
In answer to something that troubles the blood and the bone.

Written on the wall of an Irish pub, that was. The three of us should've been there together."

The expression in Mickey's eyes when he said this was so utterly confident of Jury's friendship, Jury knew he would do whatever it took to help him.

FOURTEEN

Keeper's Cottage was small but comfortable. Jury was standing in the living room beyond which he saw a kitchen; upstairs (he guessed) would be one large bedroom and a bath, not en suite.

Kitty Riordin invited him to sit down and offered to get him tea. He thanked her but declined.

A table at Jury's elbow held several silver-framed pictures, together with a few pieces of milky blue glass. The pictures were of the Tynedale family, the largest of Maisie herself.

"You're here about Simon Croft." It wasn't a question. Her expression went from soft to sober. "I was . . . I couldn't quite take it in." Her hand clenched and pressed against her breast in a gesture that was very much like Mickey's had been. As if she were in mourning, she was dressed in black; around the collar of the dress was a bit of ocher ruffle, which softened the effect. The dress was old-fashioned, as was she herself, a cameo of a person.

She said, "It's unbelievable that anyone could have murdered him."

"Then you know of no one he'd had a falling out with?"

With an impatient gesture, she waved this away. "I've been with the family for over fifty years, Superintendent. Of course, I don't know everything about their private lives—well, obviously I don't."

"How often did you see Simon Croft?"

"Not often. When he came here, sometimes."

"And did he come regularly?"

"Hm. He's very fond of Oliver Tynedale."

"Who would inherit Mr. Croft's money?"

Almost before the words were out, she laughed. "Oh, good Lord, Superintendent. I hope you're not looking for the murderer there?"

Jury smiled. "I often do. Nothing speaks louder than money, certainly not conscience."

"In this case, you'd be wasting your time. Everyone in the family has money."

"What about Maisie?"

Somehow she hadn't expected this, Jury thought. She flinched. "Maisie has money from her mother. She inherited also from Francis Croft."

"Does it work that way with these two families? The Tynedales and the Crofts bequeath money not only to the immediate family, but to the other family, too?"

"Yes. After all, they don't think of themselves as 'other.'"

"Then Simon Croft would have left Maisie and Ian money?"

Exasperated with his seeming obtuseness, she shook her head. "Francis Croft left Alexandra a small fortune, which of course went to Maisie upon her mother's death. He was as fond of Alexandra as her own father was. I expect my point is, again, that if Simon Croft were murdered for money, it wouldn't be a member of the family who did it."

"But upon the death of Oliver Tynedale, Maisie will be a wealthy woman—"

"She's *already* a wealthy woman, Superintendent. That's what I'm saying."

"Ah, yes. So you indicated. What about you, Mrs. Riordin?"

Kitty Riordin cocked her head. "Did I murder him, do you mean?"

Jury shrugged. "Not to put too fine a point on it, yes. Would Simon Croft have left you any money?"

"I seriously doubt it. But I expect we'll know one way or the other when his will is read and you can come and arrest me."

Jury smiled. "Bargain. Actually, what I really meant was, how about your own history? Your husband?"

"My husband, Aiden, was a very silly man. He walked out on me—us—so that he could cavort with the Black-shirts. Oswald Mosley's followers. How utterly absurd."

"A lot of people don't think so. If Hitler had indeed invaded Britain, he would have wanted someone here in place. Who better as a puppet dictator than Mosley?"

"Perhaps you're right. Anyway, I came over to look for Aiden, found him, took what little money he had with an absolutely clean conscience and never heard from him again."

"You don't like foolish people, do you?"

"Do you?"

Jury laughed. "I expect not. I think I'm just trying to make a point about you, Mrs. Riordin. You're a very competent person. When you came back with Maisie after the bombing and found the Blue Last was smoking rubble, did you search for them? Erin and Alexandra. And Francis Croft?" Jury sat forward, closer to her.

"Of course I did, as well as I could, as well as they'd let me. But the wardens kept me back. I went back, though; I went back."

Jury regarded her, her look of determination. Then his eyes shifted to the photographs on the small table, to a small one of, he presumed, the baby Erin and Kitty. Then to a larger one of Alexandra and baby Maisie. How beautiful Alexandra was! But also, how pretty Kitty Riordin had been. He was surprised that another man hadn't snapped her up. But it was wartime and a lot of things that should otherwise have happened, didn't.

Over the corner of Maisie's silver frame, a little silver bracelet dangled. Jury picked it up.

"Identity bracelets," said Kitty, smiling. "A bit of a lark, that was. The two were scarcely a week or two apart in age—of course you can't see that in the photographs. Alexandra had the bracelets made up. The other one's upstairs." She picked up the small photograph of Erin, wiped the glass with her sleeve, smiled down at it, returned it to the table.

Jury found the smile extremely disconcerting. Someone kinder than he might have simply described what prompted it as "bittersweet." What he had trouble with was that she could have smiled at all. She then picked up the one of Maisie and Alexandra, moving the bracelet to the table. "She was beautiful, so. Maisie looks like her, don't you think?"

It wasn't really a question put to Jury. He said nothing. But, yes, Alexandra was beautiful. No one would deny that. Jury wondered.

"She was bowled over by that flier of hers—handsome and a hero. Poor boy. They'd only been married a little over a year when he died."

"How did he die?" Jury knew one answer to this. He wondered if it would be confirmed.

"Drowned, I think. He'd been out of the RAF for a bit. Got the Victoria Cross. He was somewhere in Scotland, I don't know why."

"Did you know him?"

"I met him. It was just that one time when he was at the Lodge."

"Did you go back and forth with Alexandra? It sounds as if she lived in both places."

"She did, so. I would sometimes go with her to the pub. Of course, I had my own place here. Mr. Tynedale is that generous." She shook her head as if in awe of such generosity. She picked up the small photograph of Erin. "Both our daughters were sweet as lambs."

But only one, thought Jury, was filthy rich.

FIFTEEN

Marshall Trueblood gave the saintly figure depicted in the painting an affectionate pat. The painting was propped on the fourth chair at the table in the window embrasure of the Jack and Hammer, the other two chairs taken up by Melrose Plant and Diane Demorney. The pub and all of Long Piddleton were in the festive mood occasioned by this pre-Christmas week. Up and down the High Street, shops and houses were festooned with wreaths and ribbons. Outside Jurvis the Butcher's, the plaster pig wore a red stocking cap and a spray of holly. The mechanical Jack above the pub wore a tunic of red velvet and little bells around the wrist holding the hammer that made simulated strikes at the big clock. A scraggly pine sat beside the fireplace; winking white lights dripped from its branches.

"You came across it where?" asked Melrose.

"That antique shop, Jasperson's, in Swinton Barrow. You know, the town that's awash in antiques and art."

Diane Demorney ran her lacquered nail around her martini glass and looked at Trueblood as if he'd just spilled the last gin in the bottle—in other words, with horrified disbelief. "Marshall, you're telling us that you paid two thousand for this painting and it's only *part* of a—what'd you call it?"

"A polyptych."

"It's from some church in Pizza, did you say?"

"Pisa," said Melrose, who had rested his chin on his fists and was studying the red-cloaked figure in the painting. The panel was quite high, but also quite narrow, giving credence to the belief that there might originally have been another figure beside this one, which is what the dealer had told Trueblood, apparently. "This is St. Who?"

Trueblood pursed his lips and gave the picture a squint-eyed look, as if such facial exertion were needed to pin down St. Who's identity. "Julian. Or Nicholas? Jerome? Perhaps St. John the Baptist. Nicholas, I think. Nicholas is one of the missing pieces. Or panels, I should say."

"Marshall," said Melrose, patiently, "just what are the chances that this panel was actually painted by Masaccio? One million to one, maybe? And if it is, no one in his right mind would be selling it for two thousand quid."

"I like the red cloak," said Diane. "I saw one just like it in Sloane Street. Givenchy, I think. But I still don't understand. You're telling us that this piece is only *part* of a poly something. Why would you bother with only part of it? It's like buying the Mona Lisa's ear, or something."

"It isn't at all. Triptychs and polyptychs were common back then. We're talking about the Italian Renaissance, remember—"

Diane looked as if she'd as soon be talking about how many hamsters would fit in a vodka bottle.

"—They served as altarpieces, which the Pisa one undoubtedly is. Sometimes they were taken apart for one reason or another and carted about and the various parts went missing," he explained, rather lamely. "Well, it was a lot of information to process, see. I have to study up on Masaccio."

"If you had all the panels or whatever they are, it

would make a nice fire screen, wouldn't it?" said Diane as she signaled Dick Scroggs for another martini.

"How does this dealer know parts are missing if he's never seen the entire polyptych?"

"Vasari says so."

"Who?" asked Diane.

"Vasari, Vasari. He chronicled fifteenth-century painters and sculptors."

Diane screwed a fresh cigarette into her ebony holder, saying, "So you spend two thousand on *part* of a painting, on the say-so of some Italian we don't even *know*? Two thousand would buy a perfectly service-able Lacroix." She tapped the front of her black suit jacket to indicate one of these perfectly serviceable Lacroix.

"Life is not all Lacroix, Lacroix, Lacroix, Diane."

"No, part of it's Armani, Armani, Armani." Here she reached over and tapped Trueblood's silk wool jacket. "What d'you think, Melrose? Have you ever heard of any of these people and their paintings?"

"Mm . . . I've heard of Vasari and Masaccio. I don't know much about Italian Renaissance art, to tell the truth." He leaned back against the window. He had the window seat today, so sat on cushions. They took turns with this seat as it was quite comfortable and you could see people coming along the street whom you wanted to avoid, such as his aunt, Lady Ardry. "What I can't work out is, if this is really a Masaccio, why would this Swinton gallery be selling it? You'd think they'd be shopping it about to the Tate or the National Gallery. It would be a museum piece."

Diane blew out a ribbon of smoke. "Aren't there tests they do on paintings that tell if the paint and so forth were actually in use at the time—what century did you say this was?"

"The 1420s, to be exact."

Melrose said, "I assume the owner of the gallery would have done that, surely."

"He did. But there are more sophisticated tests yet, she said—"

"Who's 'she'?"

"A woman named Eccleston. She manages the place when Jasperson's not there. She's very knowledgeable."

Melrose frowned. "Jasperson. I think I dealt with him once. Seemed honest enough. But then the man's been in business a long time. He wouldn't be hawking forgeries." Melrose had been holding the painting up. "Tell Jury to get the fraud squad on it."

"Don't be ridiculous. There's no fraud here; the gallery isn't guaranteeing it's a Masaccio. If it was I think I'd assume it was a fake."

"Can you show it to somebody else? I mean some expert on that period?"

"Of course. There's one in London, and we can go there tomorrow."

Melrose raised an eyebrow. "'We?'"

"You and I."

"What makes you think I'm going to London?"

"Oh, come on, Melrose. You'll want to go to London before we go to Florence."

"Florence?" Both eyebrows shot up.

SIXTEEN

enny Keegan was sweeping out the Moonraker
Bookshop as a favor he sometimes did for Miss
Penforwarden when the arthritis which had
started to deform her hands made them painfully stiff.

Benny was whistling when the bell rang and a tall
man, a stranger, entered. He had to stoop to clear the
lintel. He smiled at Benny, a really nice, friendly smile
that had not seemed pulled out and put on just because
Benny was a kid. Benny returned the smile and opened
his mouth to say he'd go fetch Miss Penforwarden, when
the tall man asked him if he was Benny Keegan.

Benny frowned. Why would anyone want him,
Benny? Mother o' God, the Social! He turned around
and called to the back room, "Hey, Ben, someone t' see
ya."

Also interested in the stranger, the dog Sparky left its
cushioned bench in a window and hurried over to stand
by Benny. Then Benny turned back, hoping he was giving the impression of not caring tuppence for this man's
presence. He said, "'Course, he coulda gone down the
shops." He took a duster from his hip pocket and applied it to Miss Penforwarden's desk. A stack of books
sat there, the topmost being *Interpretation of Dreams,*
which Benny didn't think he'd like, but maybe Gemma
would.

"Okay," said the man, "suppose we start with your name, then."

"Me? Well—" a glance at the books "—it's, ah, Sigmund— Sid, for short." Another glance at the books. "—Austen."

"Sid Austen. It's nice to meet you. Tell me, the dog— is he yours or Benny's?"

Sparky was looking from the man to his master as if seeking some lesson in what they were saying. Sparky gave one of his barely discernible barks.

"Oh, him. He's just the shop dog. Always have 'em in bookshops, them or cats, if you never noticed."

The voice of Miss Penforwarden preceded her into the main room. "Benny, would you just—oh!"

Benny shut his eyes. *Cover blown, fuck it.* He went to help her with the stack of books she was carrying.

"Thank you, dear." Then she said to the tall man, "May I help you?"

"No, thanks. I was just speaking to young Sid, here."

Miss Penforwarden looked confused. "Benny?"

Jury held out his warrant card. "I'm Richard Jury. Detective superintendent, New Scotland Yard."

"Here, let me see that, then," said Benny, trying to cover up his embarrassment. "I didn't know you was— were—a copper, ah, policeman. Should 'ave showed me this." He handed it back to Jury.

Jury had known this was Benny; he'd been described—so had the dog—by the owners of Delphinium, the flower shop. The two young men, gay as a couple of maypoles and just as thin, one in a pale yellow shirt and the other in pale pink reminded Jury of calla lilies.

"Benny? Why on earth . . ." The one named Tommy Peake had pressed his long fingers against his mouth, like the image on the old war poster enjoining everyone to avoid any talk of troop activities.

Basil Rice (in the yellow shirt) had said, "Why, Benny'll be at Smith's, won't he?"

"No. Benny goes to the Moonraker about this time. That's a bookshop just along the street," he said to Jury.

"I take it the Keegan boy does a lot of odd jobs?"

Basil nodded. "And very good he is at them. Everyone says so."

"Where does he live?" asked Jury.

This question seemed to bring Basil and Tommy up short. Tommy said, "Now you mention it, why, I don't think we've ever known, have we?"

Basil shook his head, frowning, as if they should have known.

"The newsagent didn't know either. No one seems to know where he lives or what his phone number is, if he has one."

"No, Benny's not on the phone. Look, I do hope our Benny isn't in trouble."

Jury shook his head. "No. Thanks." He turned toward the door.

Happily, Tommy said, "Just you remember, Benny's clever. He's shifty."

"I'm shiftier. Good day, gentlemen."

When Benny asked to see Jury's ID again, Miss Penforwarden said, "Benny, he's a Scotland Yard *superintendent.*"

"You can't be too careful, Miss Penforwarden, not these days. The thing is, why would a detective want to talk to me?" His eyes widened, not with awe, but anxiety. *They've found out, that's what. They found our place, mine and Sparky's.* Benny looked down at Sparky, who was looking up at him as if absorbing this bad news and wanting to show support. He banged his tail on the floor several times.

"Maybe we could talk somewhere, Benny."

Miss Penforwarden, eyes fixed on Jury as if he were a rock star, made no move to leave.

Looking for means of controlling this situation, Benny said to her, "I think maybe he needs to talk to me in private, Miss Penforwarden."

"Oh, yes. Oh, I'm so sorry. Yes, well, you go right ahead. I'll just pop back to my room and if you need anything . . . perhaps, Superintendent, you'd care for tea?"

Jury said, "That's kind of you, but I've had my quota."

"Then I'll just go along to wrap some books." She left.

"There's a couple chairs right back here." Benny led Jury to the armchair by the window and pulled up a straight-backed chair for himself. "It's okay that Sparky's here, I guess?"

Soberly, Jury nodded. "He looks as if he can be trusted."

"Hear that, Sparky?"

Sparky made no sound; he was concentrating on Jury.

Jury said, "I've talked to several people you work for—the florists, the newsagent—I mean, in trying to find you. They all know your schedule, so you must be very dependable."

"I am. It's what you gotta be, right? I mean I guess you're dependable or you'd never catch anybody."

Jury could tell Benny was pleased and trying not to look it. When he, Jury, was this age, he remembered how important it was to appear cool and detached. When you were on your own, you needed to seem in control, otherwise things could start coming apart fast. The glue that held them together could too easily dissolve. And Jury was pretty certain this boy was on his own and didn't want people knowing it. He thus skirted the issue of where Benny lived. Jury felt a moment of melancholy. He remembered what being alone was like. He had never had the courage to strike out on his own, at least not until he was older—sixteen, maybe. But there hadn't been much choice, had there? The only relation remaining then was his cousin, the one who lived up in Newcastle now. She had grudgingly offered to have him come live with her when he was young, and he had refused, with thanks that he felt she never deserved.

What lay beneath this calm exterior was desolation. It

was an emotion no kid should have to feel—not Benny, not Gemma, not himself back then. Yet he wondered if it wasn't the legacy of childhood. At some point in the game, you would come to it, no matter how you were raised, no matter if you had a big family around you, desolation was inevitable, it ran beneath everything, the always-available unbearably adult emotion that clung to one's still-breathing body like drowned clothes.

A curtain shifted, spinning light across the window-pane and the faded blue of the rolled arms of the easy chair where Benny sat, his light blue eyes fixing Jury with unchildlike patience.

"Benny, you make deliveries for Miss Penforwarden sometimes to Tynedale Lodge?"

"That's right—hey, wait a tic. *That's* why you're here! It's about that Mr. Croft that got murdered!" How stupid he'd been, thought Benny, thinking this police superintendent came about *him*. "He was shot to death over in his house on the Thames. I saw it a few times, me and Sparky delivered some books to him. And Sparky likes to have a look round there at night . . ." Benny stopped, looked off.

"He does? But then you must live near the river, right?"

"Oh, not too far, I guess. Sparky, he just likes a bit of a wander nights."

Sparky looked from one to the other, seeming ready to contravene any unfavorable account.

Jury didn't push for the address. Benny didn't want to give it out, clearly.

"Had you been to Simon Croft's lately? Within, say, the last month or two?"

Benny shook his head. "The last time I think was September."

"Was he, well, friendly?"

"Him? Sure. Why?"

"Nothing. Listen: tell me about Gemma Trimm. I just met her yesterday and she mentioned you."

"Oh, aye." Benny sat up straighter. "Talked about me, did she?"

Jury smiled. "She did, yes. She thought that you'd sent me."

His mouth gaped. He seemed at a loss for words. "*Me* send you?"

"She needed a policeman, she said. She said somebody was trying to kill her."

Dramatically, Benny slapped his hand to his forehead. "Gem's not going on about that with you, is she?"

"I thought you might know something about all of this. Do you?"

"Yeah, I do: I know it's her imagination, is what I know."

"What else do you know about her?"

Jury thought from the way the boy wouldn't meet his eyes that Benny was a little ashamed of not knowing more about Gemma.

"All I know about Gem is, she's what you call a ward of old Mr. Tynedale. Kind of like being adopted, only it isn't. Mr. Tynedale really likes Gemma."

"The others don't?"

"It's more that they don't pay any attention to her. Like she's invisible."

"You don't think that's her imagination, too?"

Benny shook his head. "No, because that's even what Mr. Murphy says. He's head gardener. 'Like she's invisible, pore gurl.' That's what he said. Cook likes her; so does the maid. And Mr. Murphy, of course. Gem goes up to Mr. Tynedale's room—he's sick, see, and keeps pretty much to his bed. She reads to him, reads a lot. Gem's only nine, but she's a good reader. She could read this stuff—" he extended his arms to take in the bookshelves "—as good as I could, and I'm pretty good."

"Does she ever talk about her parents?"

Benny shook his head. "No, never. Sad, that."

Benny, thought Jury, probably knew a lot about sadness. "None of them so much as mentioned her." Jury looked around at the shadowy walls, the dull yellow of the wall sconces. This was a very restful little place.

Benny spread his hands. "Like I said, because she's invisible."

"I hope not." Jury sat back, thinking, resting his eyes on the dog Sparky, who had been lying motionless beside Benny's chair. Sparky, feeling eyes on him, looked up at Jury. Jury thought of the cat Cyril and wondered, not for the first time, if animals weren't really the superior species.

Benny looked down at Sparky, too, and then at Jury. "I don't know where she ever got this harebrained idea."

"Your dog?"

"*No,* of course not. And he's not a she."

"Sorry."

"I mean Gem. About somebody trying to kill her. She even has them doing it different ways."

"I know: shooting, smothering, poisoning."

"Well, it's daft. I mean, I *guess* she could be, a little. Then I wonder if maybe it's something she saw or maybe something that *did* happen to someone and she made all this up from scraps."

Jury thought "Sigmund" mightn't have been a bad name, after all, for Benny.

"Or maybe," Benny went on, "being ignored or being *invisible,* well, being shot at or poisoned is just the opposite. You know, the most attention getting."

"That's a very smart diagnosis, Benny, except you're forgetting another possibility."

"What?"

"Maybe it's true."

SEVENTEEN

He wanted to talk to Mickey and thought they must be on the same wavelength when Mickey called and suggested a drink and maybe dinner.

"Liza and I were kicking around the idea of drinks and a meal at the Liberty Bounds, you've been there; it's near the Tower Hill tube station. They've got good food."

Liza. Back then, years ago, he'd had feelings for Liza that crossed the borders of friendship. But she was married to Mickey, so . . . Jury said, "I haven't seen her in years, Mickey. As I remember, she was very indulgent when it came to cop talk."

"Hell, yes. You've forgotten she was one? Let's meet at seven, seven-fifteen? That sound all right?"

"Definitely."

Jury left the Tower Hill station and arrived at the Liberty Bounds at twenty to seven. He had a pint at the bar, drank that down, then ordered another and carried it over to a table in a window. It was the table in the window that made him think of the Jack and Hammer, though this pub was ten times larger. He pictured them there in Long Pidd: Melrose, Trueblood, Diane, Vivian—

It was while he was thinking of Vivian that he had

raised his eyes to the door and seen them walk in—
Mickey and Liza Haggerty.

He had forgotten how Liza Haggerty looked. He
waved them over and thought his expression must have
been rather sappy for Mickey laughed.

"What's wrong, Richie? You drunk? Or have you forgotten Liza?"

"No way I could forget Liza." Jury smiled. He also
blushed.

So did Liza.

"Waterloo Bridge," said Jury.

Liza laughed. "What?"

"Ever since someone brought that film up, I've been
seeing that actress everywhere."

"Richard." She laughed and shrugged her coat off.

Jury shook his head. "I'd forgotten how pretty you
were, Liza."

"Oh, don't let that worry you. He forgets all the
time." She tilted her head in Mickey's direction. "I'll
have a martini, straight up, with a twist. And tell them I
don't want watered gin, either." This last she called to
Mickey's departing back.

"Lord, but it's good to see you both again," said Jury.

"Yes." That was all she said, but there was conviction
in the word. "Friends shouldn't lose touch, should
they?" Liza's smile stopped just short of glorious. It
must have taken a hell of a lot of courage to smile like
that. Serious now, she said, "Mickey told you?"

He nodded. "I'm—" Looking at her, he simply
couldn't say more.

Liza gave him the most sorrowful look he'd ever seen.
"I try not to think about it. Having been on the Job once
makes it a little easier. I mean, we deal with death so
much. We haven't spent so much time ignoring it; we've
had to come to grips with it—" It was hollow talk and
she knew it.

Mickey was back with the round of drinks.

Liza raised hers as if she were going to toast them,

and said, "Don't they know what a martini glass is?" She shook the stubby whiskey glass. "And there's ice in it. *Mick*ey? Now why'd you let him do that?"

Mickey threw up his hands in surrender. "I told him, baby, I really did. Just be glad he didn't use the sweet stuff."

She took a sip. "I'd say this was three parts vermouth to one part vermouth."

Jury laughed. "You should have drinks with a friend of mine in Northamptonshire; she was born with a bottle of vodka in one hand and two olives on a stick in the other."

Mickey said, "Not to change the subject—"

"But you will."

Mickey smiled and looked at Jury. "You talked to Kitty Riordin. What do you think? Am I right?"

"I agree she could've done it." Jury still hadn't gotten over the way the woman had smiled, looking at her baby's picture.

"What I wonder is, does Erin know about all this?"

"You mean Maisie. I don't know." Suddenly, he looked at Mickey and laughed. "Hell, Mickey, you sound more interested in this alleged imposture than in the murder itself."

"Forget 'alleged.' You don't see any connection?"

"With the murder of Simon Croft? Not at the moment."

"Then maybe money wasn't the motive."

"That kind of money? Moneyed money? I'd say it's always a motive. Few other motives could touch it. The Tynedale inheritance would be one hell of a motive."

Liza said, "Mickey told me about this case. She would have to be the Medea of all mothers to carry this off for half a century. Now, would someone get me a *real* martini?" She pushed her glass toward them.

Jury smiled and took her glass and went to the bar, where he stood as the bartender poured a frugal measure of gin. He thought about his walk on Sunday. It had taken him past the site of the old Bridewell Prison, supposedly a "house of correction" for beggars, thieves and harlots. He tried to imagine the hopeless horrible life there. Bridewell was a scandal. The Bridewell orphans—what a way to begin a life. Orphans. He looked back at the table. Then the drinks came.

"Here we go," Jury said, setting down the drinks. "Is this my fourth? Or my fifth?"

"Well, it's only my second, so hand it over." She took a sip, got up.

"What's wrong?"

"I'll be right back."

"Croft found out," said Mickey.

Jury laughed. "You don't even speculate, do you?"

"Of course I speculate. Sometimes."

Liza was back holding a stemmed glass. "It just took a little bit of convincing. It's a trick I picked up in my former line of work. I offered to shoot him." She tossed a couple of bags of crisps on the table.

Mickey, Jury thought, was obsessing. Jury tried to get him off the subject, but Mickey managed to slide back to it. Jury wondered if being obsessed with Kitty Riordin kept him from obsession with his own condition.

Liza, though, knew how to get him off the tangent: she brought up some old cases either he or she or both had worked. Fairly soon all three of them were laughing and ordering up more drinks. "Remember—" Liza began "—that bank job?"

"I didn't do bank jobs, babe."

"No, no, no. That bank job where the perp ran out with a satchel of money right into several cops and surrendered and it turned out to be the cast of *The Bill*?" The three laughed until they choked.

Remember? Remember? They swapped stories for nearly an hour, drank and ate vinegar crisps. Mickey laughed so hard he got one up his nose. Liza sat between them with a hand on each of their arms and once, laughing, got her head down so low a strand of black hair trailed through her martini.

Jury thought how much alike Liza and Mickey were, and yet they weren't in any way competitive.

Liza went on about the time Mickey thought she was the perp in a theft and locked her outside.

Jury was laughing. "Liza, if you're ever available, remember—" He realized what he'd said, and could not unsay it. They both sat smiling but the smiles were wooden. It was only a moment, and Jury got up, nearly toppling his chair in the process. He moved between tables, heading in the direction of the men's room. He did not go in. Instead he leaned against the wall opposite, giving himself a mental lashing. Poor Mickey, poor Liza. He felt as if he'd poured the black night, like ink, across their table. He held this position for a century or two, then he felt a light hand on his arm.

"Richard," said Liza. "Never mind. Come on back."

He looked at her and saw her smile was real and bright. She tugged. "Come on!"

Jury followed her back to the table, where they resumed their stories and laughter and got pleasantly, wittily, winningly drunk.

EIGHTEEN

"**Y**ou've got to come with us, Superintendent."

It was Marshall Trueblood's voice coming over the wire to Jury, who was sitting in his office at New Scotland Yard, chucking a memo from DCS Racer into his OUT box and pulling out the file on Danny Wu. When Marshall Trueblood was talking, you could do things like this, for listening only to every other word in Trueblood's conversation sometimes made more sense than paying close attention.

"Why," asked Jury, "do I 'got to'? I seem to recall that trip you and Plant took to Venice, where you also said I'd 'got to.' But why you need my actual physical presence is a total mystery to me since you have no trouble at all making me up. For example, how I intended once to marry an alcoholic woman with four crazy kids, two in Borstal."

There was a pause, then Trueblood said, "Not Borstal—"

Jury brought his feet off his desk with a frustrated thud. "Trueblood, these were not real people. And you made up that sob story to keep Vivian from marrying Franco Gioppino. Well, Vivian's *left* Count Dracula, or he left her and marched right out of Long Pidd with some transparent story about his mum getting sick."

"Yes, yes, yes, but she still hasn't broken it off officially."

"Meaning what the hell? That still doesn't explain Florence."

Jury took one of the papers from the Wu file. Danny Wu had never been indicted, much less convicted, for any of the various things he was charged with. He held the page up to the light as if looking for a watermark. He could scarcely believe it: Danny Wu was being investigated in a case involving some stolen art. That was as hard to believe as this phone call. "Is Melrose Plant part of this scheme? Where are you calling from?"

"The Jack and Hammer. It's Diane's new cell phone we're using."

"The real reason," said Melrose Plant, who was now in possession of the cell phone, "he's going to Florence is to get a painting authenticated. I think he wants you along as security. A goon."

"He's got that right, but why in hell does he have to go to Italy? Aren't there people here in England who do that sort of thing? Sotheby's? Christie's?"

"Oh, he's going to one in London, yes. I told him to call the fraud squad. Heh heh."

"The Fine Arts and Antiques Division, you mean." He heard a scuffle at the Long Pidd end, or at least a scuffle of voices. Trueblood returned. "I see no point in advertising this picture. It could easily be stolen."

Jury was reading the details of the alleged art theft. "I know just the man for the job."

"What?"

"Never mind. So what's this painting, anyway?"

"A Masaccio."

"Never heard of him."

"He was a famous Florentine painter, a pupil of Masolino."

"That's two down; want to go for three?" Jury put the Wu file on his desk and leaned over it.

"The Renaissance."

"Yes, I have heard of that."

"We have to—" There was another scuffle around the

telephone in Long Piddleton, then a female voice said: "Superintendent, I'm glad I caught you before you engaged in any idiotic plan that involves travel *abroad*." Diane Demorney warned him off. "Your stars are in direct opposition to one another. Scorpios have to be careful when this happens."

"I'm not a Scorpio." Jury didn't really know this. But neither did Diane. Direct opposition?

One-beat pause on Diane's part. "Yes, I *know*. What I meant was that a Scorpio is going to figure prominently in your horoscope."

Diane Demorney could make the quickest recoveries of anyone Jury knew. "I'll bear that in mind. Now put Plant back on, love."

She didn't. She said, "You know what they say, 'See Florence and die.'"

"Actually, what they say is, 'See *Rome* and die.'"

"Well, it makes no difference, since you'd be dead, anyway."

Jury heard the rasp of a cigarette lighter. "True."

Plant came on. Jury asked, "What in hell is this call? One of those family round-robin things we used to get when we were away at school?"

Melrose Plant's voice seemed to shrug. "I never got one. Of course, that might have been because—"

Jury squeezed his eyes shut and gave his head a few soft blows with the receiver. "Has there been an epidemic of the literalism virus there?"

"Huh?"

Jury slapped another page of the Wu file over. "I can't go to Florence."

"When did you last have a vacation?"

Jury's eyes strayed to several travel brochures Wiggins had left on his desk. "Last week. I hopped over to Vegas to perform with the Cirque du Soleil. I was diving from the rafters onto a water-covered stage."

A real silence ensued this time. They seemed to be passing the phone around again. When Melrose came on again, Jury asked, "Do you remember being evacuated during the war?"

"Good Lord, that's a bit of a change of subject. Evacuated to *where*? This is the kind of place people got evacuated *to*. Anyway, no. I wasn't born yet," said Melrose.

"So you don't remember?"

"That generally is the case with the unborn. Why?"

Jury was looking at the snapshot of Kitty Riordin holding the baby Maisie (if she was Maisie). "I'm just trying to sort the identity of someone born then. Whether the mother of this baby is one woman or another."

"Offer to cut it in half. It worked for Solomon."

"I knew you'd help." Jury was looking now at the snapshot of Alexandra and Francis Croft. "Do you know what a screen memory is?"

"Yes, a recollection of Agatha walking through the door as she did just now. That's a scream memory if ever there was one."

"Not 'scream,' 'screen.'"

"Screen? Oh. Isn't that a Freudian concept? The idea being one throws up an image to mask another image too painful to be let into consciousness. Is this about the women and the unfortunate babe?"

"No, not really." *It's more about me.* "Look, I've got to be going—"

"You picked just the time. Agatha is heading for the telephone."

"Right. Are you really going to Florence?"

"Yes, of course. As Diane says, see Florence and die."

"Right. 'Bye."

"Richard! Richard! Come away from there, love; it's too dangerous!"

The street was barely recognizable, almost leveled, flattened, not a building remaining. Small fires burned all across this expanse of concrete and rubble, as if fallen stars had ignited.

"Richard!"

His mother's voice. He should have left. But there were too many fascinating things out here, the dusk festooned with tiny winking lights. She still called. He still stayed, rooting through broken concrete, through rubble . . .

His mother called again . . .

Had that street, that building, that voice been a screen memory? But for what? The memory of finding his mother under all of that rubble, that was what should have been screened, shouldn't it?

"Sir?"

Jury looked up from the snapshots and the file at Wiggins, who was setting newspapers down on his desk.

"You all right? You look kind of squiffy."

"Squiffy? What's that? Where've you been all morning, anyway?"

"Collecting these old newspapers you asked for." Wiggins's frown suggested his superior might be totally out of it.

"Oh. Sorry. I forgot." He sorted through Danny Wu's file again, closed it and tapped his chin. "Want some lunch? I mean something beyond that row of black biscuits, oat cakes, rye crisp and whatever liquid refreshment you added eye of newt to?" Jury nodded toward a glass of dark green stuff.

Wiggins looked hurt.

Jury smiled. "I was thinking of lunch at Ruiyi."

The frown disappeared and Wiggins's face lit up. There were few places he'd want to visit more than Danny Wu's restaurant, an idea shared with a great many Londoners. Ruiyi was the best Chinese restaurant in Soho, and generally one of the best in London. There was always a line. For all of his health nuttiness, Wiggins really perked right up in the presence of MSG, at least Danny's MSG.

While Jury was up and donning his coat, Wiggins crumbled half a black biscuit into his thickish, green, anodyne drink.

Telling himself not to ask, Jury asked, "What's that?"

"Kava Kava, very good for relaxation, calming down. I should take some along to Ruiyi." He shook his arms into his coat. "Danny Wu might like it. You know how these Asian gentlemen are about calm, peace, that sort of thing."

"And tiger bone. This particular Asian gentleman would jettison calm, peace of mind and levitation for a Michelin two-star and a fast car any day."

"Oh, I wouldn't say that, sir." Wiggins laughed and followed Jury out the door.

"You don't have to. I just did."

Struck by the literalism virus.

Wiggins drove smooth as foam on a Guinness, turning from Victoria Street into Grosvenor Place toward Piccadilly. He asked Jury about Mickey Haggerty, whom Wiggins knew, too. Jury told him.

"My God, chronic myelogenous, that's the worst kind of leukemia. It's so aggressive, gets into the bones. There must be *something* they can do."

"Mickey says not . . ."

"But—his wife, his kids. He's got five, hasn't he? How will they ever manage? I hope he has insurance. With five children—"

"Four. His oldest daughter died in that car crash, if you remember. And I have an idea he doesn't have much insurance; I think he probably had to spend everything he made. One son's supposed to be going to Oxford; there's also a teenage daughter *and* two grandchildren they've been taking care of since their parents were killed in the crash."

"That's a hell of a lot to have on your platter in any circumstances, but in these . . ." Wiggins could only shake his head. He added, "Wasn't his wife with City police too?"

"No, with the Met. Detective sergeant, I think."

"Move!" Wiggins shouted. Driving exerted a nonsalu-brious effect on Wiggins. In front of them, an old-age pensioner whose gray head barely cleared the driver's seat (so that the Volvo appeared unoccupied) was dither-ing about trying to decide on which exit to take from Pic-cadilly Circus. The ordinarily sanguine Sergeant Wiggins showed hidden springs of aggressiveness and hostility be-hind the wheel.

Finally, the Volvo turned off toward Leicester Square and proceeded to gum things up there, nearly plowing into a wave of pedestrians who (to do the old driver jus-tice) couldn't care less about the flashing red NO WALK indicator up there attempting to stop them. Wiggins turned off into Shaftesbury Avenue.

Ruiyi was on a heavily trafficked corner in Soho. Wig-gins pulled into a handicapped parking spot, switched off the engine and rooted through the glove compart-ment. He pulled out a handicapped sign and stuck it on the rearview mirror.

"Where'd you get that?" Jury asked as they got out of the car.

Wiggins sniggered. "I *am* a policeman, after all."

"Yes, and as one, you can pretty much park wherever you want to, anyway."

The line was long and out the door of the restaurant. "Bugger all," muttered Wiggins.

Jury shoved around Ruiyi's patrons, followed by Wig-gins, catching a few black looks, a few snarls and a tem-per tantrum from a man (who'd had the benefit of several pints before lunch) who had "a mind to signal that copper right across the street." Upon which, Jury broke out his ID and shoved it up to the fellow's face, saying, "I *am* the copper right across the street, mate."

Through the door, Wiggins said, "We shouldn't be doing this, sir, stealing a march on all of these people—"

Jury bestowed his own black look on the sergeant as they moved up undeterred.

The elderly waiter who always showed them to a table

had been about to seat the couple at the head of the line. But seeing Jury and Wiggins, he held out one arm to bar the couple from stepping up and with the other arm hastened Jury and Wiggins to the only vacant table.

Jury sniggered (as had Wiggins, a few minutes ago) when he heard the couple demand to see the manager. As the manager was Danny Wu, a precious lot of good it would do them to complain about "those two" getting the table they should have had.

Wiggins opened the menu and sighed. It was the same copious list of offerings as always. It was tall and narrow and eight pages long. Wiggins always read it with the reverence a Hasidic Jew might read the Talmud. He listened to the specials the elderly waiter recited and couldn't make up his mind. The waiter shuffled off to get the tea.

"Is this business or pleasure, sir? Is Danny Wu in more trouble?"

Jury shook out his red napkin and said, "Danny's always in the same amount of trouble: up to his chest, but not his chin, leaving him plenty of room to maneuver. Haven't you taken a look at his file?"

"Not since he came under suspicion when that murder occurred in Limehouse. D'ya think he might have Mafia connections?"

"He's got connections to the Triads, to Whitehall, to Downing Street and most *certainly* to Victoria Street. I'm not suggesting he *belongs* to the Mafia or that he freelances for them."

"You said Victoria Street: but that's us."

"'Us' is right. Not specifically you and me, but someone."

"How do you—?"

A brown little nut of an old waitress set down tea in a burnt sienna clay pot and two little cups, into which she poured out molten amber.

"How do you work that out, sir?" Wiggins spooned two well-rounded teaspoons of sugar into his tiny cup.

"Have you ever seen this restaurant closed? I mean closed down?"

Wiggins's brow furrowed as he sipped his tea. "Never, to my knowledge."

"All anyone would have to do is shriek because a mouse skittered over her shoe and Public Health would come along and slap a CLOSED sign on the door. The obvious way to get Danny to 'help with our inquiries' would be to put him out of business. You wouldn't even need the mouse; all you'd need is a bent Public Health inspector. Cheers." Jury drank his tea.

Danny Wu was suddenly, almost magically, at their table, dressed with the usual elegance.

"Stegna?" asked Wiggins.

"Right," said Danny. "How is it you are so conversant with Italian design?"

"From observing mine," said Jury. "Oxfam."

Danny laughed and said, "You're a man clothes do not make, Superintendent."

"Is that a compliment?" Jury smiled, remembering that this was a Carole-anne question: *Is that one of your compliments, then?*

Wiggins said, "I like to have a walk along Upper Sloane Street, pop into Harvey Nick's occasionally."

With a raised eyebrow, Jury said, "Harvey Nick's, is it? Well, you've certainly picked up the Upper Sloane Street lingo, even if you haven't picked up Hugo Boss or Ferragamo."

Danny made his recommendations from that day's specials—Crispy Fish with brown sauce and Jeweled Duck. Wiggins took one, Jury the other. Danny relayed the order in rapid-fire Cantonese to the little woman who'd brought the tea. To Jury exchanges in that language always suggested a show-down, as if the participants had whipped out Uzis and fired away. Danny turned back to them, asked, "Is this visit business or pleasure?"

"Both, you could say. I'm interested in the alleged theft of paintings in the Duncan collection. Formerly, I should say, in his collection. And the consequent murder of the chauffeur driving the limo used to transport the paintings. This occurred in Wapping near the Town of Ramsgate. Wapping Old Stairs is where the chauffeur was found by Thames police."

"How do you know whoever stopped this limousine was after the paintings?"

"For the simple reason that they were gone."

Danny shrugged, the barest movement of his Stegna-clad shoulders. "That could have been a mere cover. Maybe they were after the chauffeur."

At that point steaming, silver-domed dishes were delivered to the table. Danny quickly lifted each dome and checked the contents, then, in another dialect blitz, sent back the duck.

"Is it time for me to complain about police harassment?" asked Danny, in his impeccable English.

"It's been time for a long time. Trouble is, my guv'nor likes you for the murder of that pimp in Limehouse last year."

"Ah! So he's the mastermind behind all this."

"Not all. But some. What did you send the Jeweled Duck back for?"

"Diamonds were paste. You'll pardon me?"

He was off across the room to the couple who'd complained when Jury and Wiggins had preempted their table. Even though they had by now been seated and were tucking into an array of dishes, they were still angry. After Danny said a few words, they smiled and went back to their dinners. Danny had no doubt said their meal was on the house.

NINETEEN

The last time Jury had been to Newcastle was several years before (he hated to think how many) when he'd worked a case in Durham. Old Washington. Jerusalem Inn. *Stop while you're ahead.* Each name hit him with its little hammer blow as he stepped from the train down to the platform. Today there weren't many passengers. He thought he would go in the station buffet and have a drink. He knew he was fortifying himself and disliked the idea. But he did it anyway.

For years he had been sending his cousin sums of money, which did little to endear him to her. She would hate to be in some way dependent upon him; he, after all, had once been the interloper; he had been the charity case.

Brendan, her husband, really did exert himself to get a job. And it wasn't his fault he hadn't had work in over a year. Jury knew this. Jury had gone with him once to the joke shop to look at their scant offerings. Brendan told him he was always checking with the agencies, too, never passed one, with its job "opportunities," the cards taped up in the window announcing jobs that seemed to dissolve once you put your foot across the sill. Brendan had worked for maybe one year out of the last five. He was a nice bloke, Brendan was, who managed to hold on to a sense of humor. He loved Jury to visit for it was someone to go to the pub with, someone with money. Jury was glad to pay for the drinks for he knew Brendan genuinely liked him. Jury, after all, was "family," which meant he was someone Brendan could be honest with.

In the station buffet, Jury got his pint refilled.

Even leaving off how high ranking he was in the police, the ones sitting in this buffet would envy him every day of their bloody lives. Imagine that one at the bar eating a sausage roll, think how he would like having digs in London where he could come and go as he wanted, not a wife who keeps letting him know what a failure he is, and no screaming kids. Imagine being able to lock the door, or go down to the pub, money and then some, to come back on his own or with someone . . .

Jury smiled (*sure*), finished his pint and left.

His cousin's flat was located in a big redbrick house. Above the landing outside the front door were affixed six mailboxes, one for each of the flats the renovation had squeezed from its formerly spacious interior. Brendan and Sarah occupied one of the two flats on the top floor, three flights up. There was no lift. The stairs were dark except for the landing between the first and second. Every time Jury had been here, he had replaced one or more burned-out bulbs that were supposed to light the landings. It was dangerous, he'd told her, for she could make a misstep, fall and break something.

"*I live by missteps,*" she'd replied. It had made Jury smile, that way of putting it.

He had hoped it would be Brendan answering the door, but Brendan was out. "Looking," Sarah said. "Come on in."

"At least be glad he's looking. Most aren't." Jury removed his coat and let it fall on a nubby-textured dark green chair.

Sarah had picked up a pale blue pillow from a blue

armchair. The pillow was embroidered iris and she stood clutching it to her breasts as if some attack were imminent. But she was always like this with him. Sarah was full of these defensive gestures. She was a tightly wound woman who must be by now in her early sixties, yet for all of the strain and stress life caused her, not looking that old. If time, like acid, had scored deep grooves around her nose and mouth, she was still blessed with a sort of silky hair that even in turning gray was the soft color of autumn smoke.

"Want a beer?"

It was what she was drinking, but Jury had had too much already. His stomach was sour, more from stress than beer, he thought, but he still didn't want any. "I'd really love some tea."

Rising, she said (in that baiting way of hers), "My, my. You're turning down a beer?" as if drink were a particular problem with him. Then she turned toward the kitchen, a bit of which he could spy from where he sat: the white countertop, the Aga cooker of which she was very proud.

It always began that way, some deprecating remark made in her attempt to undermine him. Though he wondered if it wasn't really Brendan she was addressing, Brendan whose drinking was the problem. Jury sat down in the blue armchair, one of a pair and both the worse for wear. He retrieved the embroidered pillow she had tossed down and ran his thumb over its delicate embroidery and wondered if she'd done it.

He leaned back, feeling absurdly weary and knew the cause lay in coming here. But it wasn't Sarah herself, no, it was how she stirred up a host of complex emotions about his past. His discomfort was fueled by fear. Sarah had had the upper hand—she had held every hand—when they were kids: she was older, and she belonged. That he was afraid of her struck him as ludicrous; he was ashamed of the feeling. But the fear was very old, as old as childhood.

He was being handed a mug of tea. He sat up (feeling much like an invalid). "Thanks."

Inexplicably, she shrugged, perhaps saying, *So what? I'd do it for the dustbin men.* Then she sat down on the matching blue armchair with a bottle of Adnams and a cigarette. When Jury didn't drag out his own pack, she offered him her Silk Cut. When he shook his head, she said, "Don't tell me! You've stopped!"

"Right."

Throwing back her head, she said, "Please, God, not another one. I hope you're not about to go self-righteous on me and start lecturing."

Jury half smiled. "Hardly. I'm in much too weak a position to do that. I could start back any day."

There was a moment of silence as she languidly smoked, drawing in deeply, exhaling tiny smoke rings, smoking in silence. Jury would bet that Newcastle had one of the highest smoking rates in the country.

"Where are the kids?"

"Birthday party. Except the little one, Georgie. My niece's boy, Ruth's? You remember her? When he wakes up you can see him. You never have. And he's eighteen months." Her mouth tight, she shook her head as if Jury were himself eighteen months old and more hopeless than Ruth's Georgie. "So, Richard. To what do I owe the honor of this visit?"

Sarah seemed unable to say anything to him without that bite, that begrudging air.

"Had to come here on police business," he lied, "and just wanted to see you. I'm sorry it's been so long. No excuse except the same old thing: busy on the Job." He paused, wondering how to commence. He knew that what made all of this so painful was that he would be trying to get information from someone who wouldn't want to give it to him, who wouldn't want to help him remember. Being able to fill in gaps in Jury's memory would be a source of power for her, to give or to withhold. It was hard to believe she could still resent his childhood self. But, he reminded himself, it was also himself now, the life he had examined in the station buffet.

"Remember when we were kids?"

She raised her eyebrows in question. "Remember what?"

"Oh, I guess just . . . you know. Nothing specific." When she offered nothing, just sat there smoking and drinking, he didn't know how to go on. His chair faced a west-looking window and the sun in its descent edged the clouds in white gold. "I was just thinking about my mother. And the war. You remember the house in the Fulham Road was demolished. I can still hear the bombs; I can still hear the one that hit the house."

She frowned. "The house was hit by a bomb but you weren't there. This was one of those 'nuisance' raids, in 1944, I think. Well, that's life, you get through the blitz, through the worst of it and then get killed in the last one that never even made a difference." She shook her head at the irony of it.

Jury was stunned. "But I always thought I was there. I mean I *remember* . . . you know, being there." The blackout, his mother buried under rubble. He couldn't process this new information.

"You really are bloody fucked up, Richard. Maybe you need a shrink." She smiled slightly, as if finding an inroad into Jury's mind, a place where she might play about, play with facts, with memories, pleased her.

"The house in Fulham. I keep seeing Mum . . . under all that plaster and boards." And he couldn't do anything about it.

Inconceivably, she started laughing.

He was furious. "What in the bloody hell's so funny, Sarah?"

The laughter was for the most part faked. "It's just so . . . dramatic, the way you see it. Like a film." She liked this analysis. "Really, it is. Just like a war film. *Mrs. Miniver* or one of those."

He could scarcely believe all of this. How could he

walk around all of his life, these few memories indelibly fixed in his head, and discover they were false, bogus, his own invention? How? But then he'd been free to make them up; no one had ever said anything to contradict them. If he had asked his uncle, a very kind man, then he would have told him. But of course most adults would steer clear of bringing up such a subject involuntarily.

She stubbed out her cigarette, finished off her Adnams and got up. "You wait just a minute." She left the room and he could hear her moving about and swearing, as if someone were in the other room with her.

He half rose to see if she was all right, but she was back now with a white shoe box. Between the dark brown sofa and the blue armchairs was a round table which she hauled over to stand between them. She pulled her chair around to face his across the table.

Pictures, thought Jury. *More pictures.* She slid the top from the box and he felt a surge of adrenaline clamp him to his chair with a hard swift hand. If they were different, these pictures, from what he remembered, he didn't want to know. He just didn't. He had lived for too many years with these images of life and death in the Fulham Road. "She was wearing black."

Sarah was sorting through snapshots, pulling out one here and there. Either he hadn't said it aloud or she hadn't heard him say it: *she was wearing black.*

She put down the pictures, fanned out like a poker hand, and tapped one snapshot, square and poorly lit, taken perhaps with one of those boxy Brownie cameras. "This is all of us, except your dad. He was in Germany."

Jury saw a group of four adults, a toddler and a girl of perhaps seven or eight. "This is you, isn't it? Am I in this?"

"Don't be daft, of course you are; you're the little one. Here's your dad." She handed him a picture of a man in uniform, a flier. "You know he was RAF?"

"Yes, of course." He felt defensive because she knew

more than he. And how had she come to be the depository for memories? "Wasn't his plane—a Spitfire—shot down?"

"You got that right, at least."

As if memory's fallibility were all down to him. "I remember being evacuated; I remember being in Devon or Dorset somewhere as a kid with a lot of other kids."

"That wasn't the war. You weren't evacuated; you were in foster care with some others."

Jury looked at her, frowning. "Foster care?"

"You don't recall that woman, that awful Mrs. Simkin? Wasn't she the one, though? Jesus, it must've been half a dozen she was getting a government stipend for. They took two away from her, and you were one of them." Her fingers rooted in the shoe box again. "Look." She pulled another snapshot from the box and handed it to Jury.

He looked at the awkward lineup of children. It was a relief to see that they were here as he remembered them even if he'd been mistaken about why he was among them. There he was, standing next to the tallest girl. Even though the picture was in black and white, he still knew the tall girl was the one with hair like a torch. It looked unconfined, as if not even the stillness of a photograph could still it. Jury smiled at her, the bane of his small existence. She had turned out to be a still point, this horrific child who teased and taunted him, still had the power to help or hinder. For some reason Jury liked that idea.

"Now, this one's the best. It's you and your mum."

It was not a snapshot, but looked to be more a photographer's work. It was larger, too. Her arm extended along the back of a settee, the back rising higher on one end. He looked about three or four and was sitting on her left, her left arm encircling him. He looked pleased as punch.

Sarah was talking but her voice seemed to come from a distance, as a sound trying to make its way around some obstruction. He did not comment on this picture. It was quite beautiful, he thought. "May I have this one of the foster care kids? And the one of mum and me?"

She shrugged, falling back to her original pose of indifference. "You can have the lot if you want." Having produced this revisionist childhood, she was no longer concerned for its proofs.

Jury was tired and was ready to go; he would be relieved to get out. He said he'd a train to catch.

"You're not stopping for tea? Brendan'll be back—"

And as if her voice could call up spirits, the door opened just then and Brendan walked in.

"Speak of the devil," Sarah said.

Brendan brought with him the memory of more than one John Jamison. He was happy as a lark when he saw Jury. "Richard! Where in hell did you drop from?" He gave Jury a comradely punch on the shoulder.

Sarah asked, querulously, "Where're Jasmine and Christabel? You were to collect them from Raffertys."

"I went by. They wanted to go to Burger King with the others."

Jasmine. Christabel. The names she had chosen (certainly Brendan hadn't) for her children. You could always tell the parents with no confidence. They went for the exotic names, afraid that just plain Mary or Alice wouldn't set their own kids apart.

"You spent the giro already at Noonan's, I expect."

"Oh, leave off, woman." Brendan drew a folded, grimy bit of paper from his breast pocket and handed it to her. "It ain't even cashed, lovely. Speaking of Noonan's, Rich, how about it?"

Jury didn't much want to go, but this would probably be the least awkward way of making an exit. "Thanks, I could do with a pint."

Brendan did a little jig—never had Jury known a more ingrained Irishman than Brendan—and washed his hands in air. "Let's go, then."

Jury gave Sarah a look, inviting her along, though he knew she wouldn't take them up on the invitation.

"Me? Me go? Then who'd look after the baby, I want to know? You haven't even seen him," she said to Jury.

"Maybe when we come back." Jury was not coming back.

"Why does she dislike me so much?" Jury asked Brendan as they stood at the bar of Noonan's, a noisy pub. There were, of course, some men in here who had jobs, whom the Job Center had actually lined up with employment. For them the pub was the way to escape the tedium of work as it was the way to escape the tedium of not working for the others.

Brendan raised his pint and said, "Hell, man, she doesn't dislike you, at least not when your back's turned." He wiped his handkerchief under his nose. "She's always bragging on you to friends." He went on in fluting tones, "'A detective *superintendent*, that's right, Scotland Yard, no less.'"

Jury smiled. "We were talking about childhood. It seems all my memories were wrong."

Brendan waved his hand in a gesture of dismissal. "Hell, she was windin' you up, man, she was takin' the piss out. She does it to me, does it to the kids. Don't take it to heart."

Jury drank his beer and went back over the afternoon. He wondered. He patted the pocket of his coat that held the two pictures.

When Jury walked up the steps of the terraced house in Islington, Mrs. Wassermann, who had the so-called garden flat, came up the stone steps outside her door, hurrying as much as she could. Jury had helped Mrs. Wassermann over the years with "security," installing locks, inspecting windows and any other way of entering, and anything else that would make her feel more secure. She had been a young girl in the prison camp; she had watched her family die before her eyes, first one, then another. And worse.

"Mrs. Wassermann," Jury said, retracing his steps, going back down, "is something the matter? It's late for you to be still up."

She clutched her bathrobe more closely about her throat. "No, no, many times I'm up till morning. Such a hard time sleeping. Could you come in just a minute, Mr. Jury? One minute and I won't keep you."

Jury smiled. "I can make it more than a minute." He followed her down the steps and into her flat. It was a comfortable flat with good old armchairs and a chintz-covered sofa. A breakfront, some side chairs and tables.

"Would you like something? Whiskey? Coffee? Chai?"

"What?"

"Carole-anne got me some. She says it's much healthier than other drinks. It's kind of a mixture of tea and spice."

"In matters of health, I wouldn't look to Carole-anne, queen of the breakfast fry-up."

"Well, what she told me was to drink it for a week and tell her if I felt better. It's supposed to do wonders, but the taste, Mr. Jury! It's awful."

"That explains Nurse Carole-anne's motive. She wants you to test it so she won't have to. A cup of plain old English black tea would be fine."

She left the living room. Jury saw there were a couple of old photograph albums on the coffee table, one of them open. Sitting down on the sofa, he sighed. Pictures, more pictures, old ones.

Mrs. Wassermann returned with two mugs of tea that Jury knew would be sweeter than he liked, but would drink. When she saw Jury turning the pages of the photograph album, she said, "They have been making me feel . . . well . . ."

Jury waited for her to continue. When she didn't, he asked, "Are these of your family, Mrs. Wassermann?" He knew they must be and was a little surprised he had never seen them before. But she still stood there by the sofa, holding her cup of tea and looking anxiously at the photographs. He said, carefully, "Mrs. Wassermann?"

Hesitating, she said, "Yes. And yet—"

She appeared very distraught. He looked more closely at one picture of a girl of perhaps thirteen or fourteen, flanked by a middle-aged man and woman who must surely be her mother and father. It was not that he recognized the child as Mrs. Wassermann, but the older woman who looked so much like his Mrs. Wassermann, looks that weren't yet delineated in the face of the teenage girl.

"This is you as a girl, isn't it?" He tapped that picture.

Mrs. Wassermann laughed a little and without humor. It was a nervous laugh, an anxious one. "Yes. My mother, the woman must be. The man is my father?"

What she seemed to be doing was asking for Jury's assurance. "You certainly look like your mother." He studied the picture, the background, the building in front of which they stood. On the right-hand border he saw the heel of a shoe and a tiny patch of leg. It was a public street and someone had just passed by. He imagined others, not wanting to block the picture taker, were no doubt waiting in the wings to pass. Behind the little family was a sign, the first half obscured by their bodies. It said ANIST and Jury wondered if it was the end of the word *tobaccanist*. To the right, a couple of stiles of postcards sat alongside a rack of newspapers. Jury squinted.

"Mrs. Wassermann, do you have a magnifying glass?"

Now that somebody was doing something about her problem (whatever that might be, Jury wasn't sure yet) she was eager to do what she could. "Yes, yes." She hurried over to the breakfront, opened a drawer, took out a large glass. This she handed to Jury.

Jury held it close to the picture. What he wanted to

see was the date on the name of the newspaper. It looked like *"Berlin"* something. He could even see the date: November 9, 1938. The date had a familiar ring. Unfortunately, the headline of the paper was obscured.

Looking abstracted, she sat down on the edge of a chair with a rosewood frame.

"You lived in Berlin, didn't you? Your father—" And then he remembered, her father had died as a result of one of those terrifying and random sweeps of the SS.

She frowned and looked away. "Yes, for a while. It must have been then." She nodded toward the photograph, the snapshot. Yet the snapshot apparently wasn't nudging memory further and perhaps that's what bothered her.

He took out the snapshot of the children in the charge of the awful Mrs. Simkin and handed it to her.

She put her spectacles back on, looked and smiled. "But is this you, Mr. Jury? And your friends?"

"I think so, Mrs. Wassermann." He wanted her to know that a failure of memory wasn't hers alone. "Some things we can never be sure of, I guess." Jury rose and said good night.

Walking upstairs, he thought of it: November 9, 1938. *Kristallnacht.* That was it. That was when her father was taken away, never to be seen again.

The loss of memory, he thought, can be fortuitous.

Later, in bed, hands folded behind his head, the pictures of his mother and the foster-care children tilted against the bedside lamp, Jury thought: *it never ends.* It might stretch around a corner or across the country or into death, but it never ended, this bond between parents and children.

TWENTY

All the way from Northampton to the M1, and off at Newport Pagnel for a ploughman's and a beer, then back to the M1 and around road works that kept them crawling at fifteen miles per hour, to Toddington and another stop at a Trusthouse Forte, and back on the M1 again, past the Luton exits and the suggestion (quickly shot down) that they get off at Haysendon to see the wild fowl park, and on to St. Alban's, finally hitting the North Circular road and the A41 that would take them to the center of London, or would have done if they hadn't got off onto the A-nothing and taken a wrong turn at Hornsley and wandered all around Finchley and Hornsley and Crouch End—all this way Melrose had listened to Trueblood's lecture on the Italian Renaissance and art—not only the art of Masaccio, but also all of Masaccio's friends and teachers and trainers—Masolino, Donatello, Brunelleschi, and branching off (much as they had at Toddington) onto side trips to Siena, Pisa and Lucca, and back to Florence and Michaelangelo and Mannerism, to Brunelleschi's dome for the cathedral (and was that after or before he'd lost the competition for the Baptistery doors?), and the Baptistery's south doors, done by Pisano in panels depicting the eight cardinal virtues (none of which were being catered for during this trip) through the ridiculous conflicts of Guelphs and Ghibellines, to the Palazzo Vecchio and the Uffizi and Leonardo, back through Giotto and the invention of space in perspective to that witty little restaurant just off the Ponte Vecchio, whose name he had forgotten (unfortunately, forgetting nothing else)—

—So that when Trueblood at last squealed to a stop in front of Boring's, Melrose felt he'd been hit by a stun gun.

"I'm off to Ellie Ickley's. We're dining at Fisole. She *adores* Florence, she lived there for ten years and all but ate it alive! You're absolutely welcome to join."

"Thanks, but I'm dining with Jury."

Trueblood revved up the engine, gave him a wave and shot off down the street.

Melrose entered Boring's with his brain churned to butter. Even so, he reckoned that what he'd been given was the larger picture, brush stroke by heavy brush stroke. Imagine the *two* of them, Trueblood and Ickley, able to dole out *details* of Brunelleschi's construction of the dome, tile after tile, brick after brick, herringboned in place to be self-supporting. Melrose felt anything but self-supporting. Dinner, bookended by Florence enthusiasts, by Firenze fanatics. He'd be squashed to pesto sauce, stuffed into tortellini, grated with pecorino. At least if Trueblood was running around Florence on his own, Melrose would be spared an hour or two of the contribution of Giorgio Vasari to art (Giorgio Armani being quite another matter).

Boring's, Melrose was happy to see, had recovered from the shock of the murder of one of its members a year ago and had returned to its usual state of somnolence. Even the fly on the parchment lampshade, whose subdued golden light reflected off the polished mahogany of the convoluted staircase which scrolled around and around to a final landing Melrose could not see, and for all he knew, went through the ceiling and up to the heavens in a Boring's meditation on

Brunelleschi's dome, the fly on the lampshade on the desk seemed incapable of movement and would sleep through any swatting.

It was irresistible, this sense of moving through a bed of treacle, and he felt his eyelids go heavy. He shook his head to clear it. For all he was aware of it, he might have been standing here for hours. Boring's ran on its own time, Greenwich Mean not even in the equation. Probably, Melrose thought, Boring's was at the heart of the modern mad science of chaos theory.

When still no one had come to attend to him, he wondered if his feet stuck in this treacle could propel him into the Members' Room and there find both whiskey and assistance. And if he was going to fall asleep, he might as well do it in front of a crackling fire, drink in hand, seated in a comfortable, worn leather chair.

Trueblood had come to collect him at such a grisly gray morning hour, Melrose hadn't even had time to read his newspaper. This was a ritual undertaken only to see if the world was still up, not to see what it was doing. Yet here were issues of all the dailies and Melrose had no desire to look at a single one. He felt rather than heard a person behind him. He turned to see Boring's porter, Young Higgins. Young Higgins was not young, and Melrose declined assistance with his bag. In what was a genuine if somewhat atonal sort of greeting, Young Higgins told Melrose how glad he was to see him at Boring's once again, and asked if he required anything. Melrose said he'd come down later for a drink, thanked Young Higgins and carried his own bag up the wide, softly carpeted stair.

The level of activity in the Members' Room at seven P.M. had increased incrementally with preprandial conversations, the good mood induced both by whiskey and the knowledge that dinner would soon be served. There were a half dozen members sitting here, drinking or snoozing, and Melrose waved to Colonel Neame, who was always in the same chair by the fire, usually with his friend Major Champs.

Richard Jury and Melrose Plant were drinking a very fine malt whiskey, with their own conversation nose-diving into inconsequentiality: both were betting what would be on the menu. Melrose slapped down a five-pound note and said, "Starter: Windsor soup."

Jury frowned. "Five *pounds*? Don't be daft. I'm a public servant; I can't afford to lose fifteen pounds, which is what it'd come to with three courses. Anyway, I was going to say Windsor soup, too." He dug in his pocket for change, his lips moving silently, figuring. "One pound seventy, that's closer."

Melrose groaned and made to tear his hair when a young porter told him there was a call for him and could he take it in reception? Melrose excused himself. As Melrose walked out of the room Jury got up and went across to where Colonel Neame was sitting by the fire.

It was Trueblood on the phone, fixing the time for their drive to Heathrow. "Not that early, for God's sake."

"Well, you know what it's like with security these days."

They argued and settled on a time. "How is Miss Ickley? What does she think of the alleged Masaccio?"

"Hasn't made up her mind yet."

Melrose rang off and returned to the Members' Room where Jury had ordered seconds for them.

Jury said, "Okay, we're still on starters. I'll let you have the soup and I'll take prawn cocktail . . . no, no . . . I'll say avocado stuffed with Stilton."

"Stuffed with Stilton? That's rather elaborate for Boring's."

"Well, avocado like that's all the rage in London at the moment."

"Main course: Dover sole."

Jury said, "I hope it is. I love Dover sole. But I'll say . . . spring lamb. No, it isn't spring yet, so just make it lamb."

Melrose frowned. "A lamb is always a lamb, isn't it? So it's still spring lamb. Anyway, I'm changing mine. I'm saying jugged hare."

"Jugged hare? Do they do that here? That's sort of an acquired taste, isn't it?"

Melrose swept his arm around the room. "What else have we to do here but acquire tastes?"

Jury grunted. "Anyway, you're not supposed to switch from the thing you name first."

"Good God! You're such a stickler for rules. And anyway, when did we ever make up rules?"

"I probably wouldn't like jugged hare. When I see a bunch of animal rights activists I get depressed. I think of Carrie Fleet. Remember?"

"How could I ever forget?"

They drank in silence for a few moments, both remembering Carrie Fleet, both on the edge of a monumental sadness. Melrose jerked around when the young porter (really young, a Dickensian youth with ginger hair) came to announce that dinner was being served and would they care for another whiskey? Both declined, Melrose saying they'd have wine with dinner.

It was a beautiful room—high windows, crown moldings, dark wood polished to such mirror smoothness you could almost see your reflection in it. Ceiling fans turned decorously overhead, a central chandelier tossed beads of light across the tables and chairs.

The sommelier twisted his key and went into a mild ecstasy when Melrose chose a Pinot Noir of clearly exciting (and expensive) vintage. Then he departed and soon Young Higgins settled before each of them the first course: avocado stuffed with Stilton and baked.

Astonished, Melrose asked Jury if this was some new fad.

"I told you, it's very popular at the moment. Remember, I'm one pound seventy into your fiver. We forgot dessert. I'm betting treacle pudding. No, tart."

"Gooseberry . . . no, I'll say some sort of sponge roll."

Said Jury, looking around the room, "I can think of worse places to spend one's twilight years than here at Boring's."

"Your head on a spike at Tower Bridge, perhaps. You wouldn't stand it here, not you. Now, I'm the perfect candidate for retirement."

Jury made a blubbery, dismissive sound with his lips and waved away Plant's candidacy.

"But I *am*. Just look at me, look at my life. I'm retired *now*. I can nip off to Firenze any time I take a fancy to do so. That was Trueblood on the phone." When Jury looked blank, Melrose said, "That phone call I got. Are you engaged in short-term memory loss?"

"Long term, actually." Jury looked off toward the black windowpanes.

"How so?"

The sommelier was there with the wine, which he presented for Melrose's inspection. Melrose approved, and the cork was removed and Melrose declined the tasting of it, telling the sommelier to pour it. He looked slightly shocked, poured and left.

"Why do they do that? You know, show you the label? Would one be suspicious that it was really a bottle of plonk they were foisting off on their guests?"

"Show. Ritual." They ate in silence for a few minutes.

Young Higgins was back, removing their avocado and announcing that the lamb would arrive in just a few moments.

Jury shrugged and raised his hands, smiling, while Melrose sat staring. He calculated. "That's three pounds forty you owe me."

"Let's go to Vegas while your luck is running. Now, what were we talking about?"

"Memory loss. You recall when we were sitting here November a year ago?"

"Certainly, I do."

"We were talking about the war. The Second World War, I mean."

Melrose nodded, hardly shifting his attention at all to the plate of lamb and silver dishes of peas and potatoes Young Higgins now placed before him. "I remember. You said you'd been evacuated, your—cousin, is it?—up in Newcastle told you about it."

Jury nodded. "But she said I wasn't in the Fulham Road house when my mother died. And I was younger, too. Maybe no more than two or three. I'd much rather she died with me there."

"Well, I wouldn't, old chap. Because had you been, probably you wouldn't be sitting here right now. I can understand your feelings, though."

They ate in companionable silence, passing the silver dish of vegetables back and forth, drinking more wine.

Then Melrose said, "How about *her* memory, your cousin's?"

Jury looked up from his plate, which he hadn't touched much. "You mean hers could be faulty?"

"Of course."

"She's years older than I. She'd remember better." Jury smiled. "Her husband, Brendan, thought she was winding me up. She doesn't really like me."

"Is she vicious?"

"Vicious . . . that might be too strong a word."

"Okay, give me a weaker one."

As Young Higgins came to clear their plates away, Jury said, "Resentful, maybe, of me getting so much attention from my uncle. It was my uncle who took me in. My aunt was kind, but not really too keen. And after he died, she didn't feel she could keep me on, not with three of her own. The other two are dead now."

Young Higgins cleared his throat and said, "Your treacle tart will be up in a moment. Would you care to have coffee in the Members' Room?"

Melrose said, yes, they would and stared at Jury as Young Higgins moved off. "You win it all."

Jury smiled and shrugged.

*   *   *

Back in the Members' Room, in the same seats they had occupied, Jury said, "The thing is, she had pictures—snapshots, you know—of me and these other kids. They were kids I remember, too. But that was several years later, in Devon. They were foster children this woman was drawing stipends for—"

"Instead of the kids being the evacuees you thought you'd been among?"

"Yes."

"Pictures may tell part of the truth but not necessarily all of it."

A log split and fell, sparking. The flames sputtered, became no more than live coal and leaped once again into flame. He said, "Lately, that's what I seem to be dealing with—pictures. Memories. Neither being completely reliable as a reconstruction of the past. I have a friend, a DCI in the City police, who showed me some pictures." He told Melrose about Mickey's suspicions.

"Why doesn't he investigate this himself? I know you're awfully good, but it seems odd bringing Scotland Yard into it."

"It does, yes. We're old friends, we go back a long way."

"Still—"

"He's dying."

"Oh. I'm sorry."

"His father was a regular at the Blue Last. He knew the owner, Francis Croft, quite well. Oliver Tynedale and Francis Croft were like brothers. It's impressive that they'd remain that close to each other and stay friends for that long, and also be in business together."

"I can't imagine anything that could sour a friendship quicker than a business relationship. Who was at the helm?"

"Tynedale, I expect. The business seemed to fall roughly between the public relations end and the financial end. I imagine the line between them was pretty much blurred."

"So Francis Croft died and his own fortune got divided among his children?"

"Actually, no. That's another unusual thing. Some of it went to Tynedale's children, as some of Tynedale's will go to Croft's. They really are like one extended family."

"Which sounds as if it complicates things."

"Yes." Jury watched the fire over the edge of his glass of cognac.

"Let's just say that, unlike his father, Simon Croft was crooked. Say he embezzled funds, and a major stockholder found out and—" Melrose mimicked a pistol with his thumb and forefinger. "Except you don't think so, do you?"

"It's more that Mickey doesn't think so."

"He's convinced it's a member of the family."

Jury answered obliquely. "The thing is, Tynedale is very sick; murdering him would be, well, superfluous for an heir of his. His granddaughter, Maisie, will probably get the lion's share. The fortune would then be split— not necessarily equally—among the remaining Tynedale and Croft children—Ian, Simon, Marie-France—oh, and there's Simon's other sister, Emily. She's living in Brighton in one of those assisted-living places."

"Hmm. If the motive's getting a larger share of the inheritance, why would the killer choose Simon Croft over the granddaughter? You've just said she'll undoubtedly get more than the others."

"Depends, I suppose, on how much more," Jury said.

"Isn't it equally likely there's another motive for shooting Simon Croft? What if he knew about this imposture?"

"Which points to the Riordin woman, or, of course, Maisie. She might know, she might not. Anyway, they're the ones who wouldn't want Oliver finding out Maisie isn't Maisie. To wait fifty years for the payoff shows a hell of an emotional investment on the part of Kitty

Riordin. To have that snatched away now—" Jury shrugged.

"Perhaps Simon Croft's killing isn't connected to the identity of Maisie Tynedale. DCI Haggerty could be dead wrong."

A porter came on hushed feet to deposit two more cognacs. Jury insisted on paying for this round and slapped down Melrose's five-pound note.

"Oh, thanks," said Melrose. "You're too generous."

"I know." Jury swirled the cognac, sniffed it and drank. "Another thing that bothers me is this little girl who's Tynedale's ward. Gemma Trimm her name is. She claims someone's tried three times to kill her."

Melrose sat up. "My God. But do you believe her?"

"They found a bullet casing. Southwark police certainly believe there was a shooting; they seemed to put it down to a rash of robberies, that, or some young punk proving how cool he is. As to the choking and poisoning, well, I'm not so sure."

"And what would be the motive in this case?"

"I've no idea. Her presence in that house is mysterious. She seems to be largely ignored except by staff and Oliver Tynedale, who apparently dotes on her."

"Is she a dotable little thing?"

Jury smiled. "Oh, my, yes. Extremely dotable—an earnest child. They say nothing about her. I came upon her quite by accident outside, walking."

"They say nothing about her?"

"I questioned all of them, except for Oliver Tynedale, and no one so much as mentioned Gemma."

"That's damned strange. If the old man is so fond of her you'd think the others would be discounting her all over the place. His ward, you say?"

Jury nodded. "According to her friend Benny."

"God, don't bring anyone else into this tale. I'm back with the cook and the gardener as it is."

"Benny's extremely resourceful. He has four or five shops in the main street he runs errands for. He's the local messenger service. You know, if the bookshop wants a delivery made, he does it. Same for florists, same for butcher and newsagent. What I admire is his ability to fend off questions about home and family. I don't blame him. A lot of people I'd rather not show my ID to, either."

Melrose laughed, sliding down in his chair. "You sound like you're the same age as this boy." He kept laughing, stopped and said, "Maybe that's the secret."

"What secret?"

"You're so good with children. They seem immediately to sense a kindred spirit in you." He sighed. "Whereas with me, it's sensing an unkindred one."

"That's not true—" The doomed lament of the long-case clock gave the half hour. "Christ, ten-thirty already. I've got to go." Jury drank off his cognac and rose.

They were moving toward the door when Colonel Neame called out to Jury, "My dear chap, did you like the avocado and Stilton?"

Jury nodded and waved.

The colonel again called out, "I'd hated to have steered you wrong on that."

At the door, Melrose stopped dead. "I don't *believe* it. That you'd stoop so low . . ."

Jury grinned. "That's why they call us the Filth."

TWENTY-ONE

Mr. Gyp handed the freshly wrapped packets over the counter to Benny, saying, "Here's chops and chine. Just you mind you get that up to the Lodge this morning as Mrs. MacLeish wants to get 'em stuffed and on their way."

Benny really hated meat deliveries and especially Mr. Gyp's as Gyp liked to talk about the cut-up meat as if something about it still lived: "Get 'em on their way." It was as if the poor pig was going off on a trip.

Mr. Gyp was always inviting Benny back to the abattoir and when Benny said no thanks, Gyp told him he hadn't the stomach for life if he couldn't make himself look it in the face.

"All of life ain't an abattoir, Mr. Gyp. Not all of it."

"You'll learn, young Bernard. And your dog." Benny didn't like the way Mr. Gyp said this, sort of sinister like. He was always looking at Sparky, as if taking measurements in his mind. Probably more to make Benny uncomfortable than for any humane reason, Gyp would give him, occasionally, some leftover chops or a bit of mince and often a bone for Sparky. Gyp would slyly hand over a damp, blood-smeared packet of things for Benny to take to his "family." Was it a big one? It must be for all the meat they eat, said Gyp. He was always trying to get Benny to tell him where he lived.

Benny had heard noises coming from the back that would send him flying from the shop, out to the curb where he'd sit with his head on his knees, dizzy. He might have fainted with the horror of it if he hadn't got out. He swore he'd quit, but he didn't. It wasn't because he needed the money. It was because of the way Gyp asked him about his family, asked him why he wasn't in school. Benny told him he was getting homeschooling. Mr. Gyp said he ought to be in a proper school and maybe he, Gyp, should do his duty and "call the Social." Benny didn't know whether he would or not, but he was afraid to take the chance. Funny, but none of the others he worked for ever went on the way Gyp did. Not even Mr. Siptick, who was bad enough. But with the others, there'd only been some friendly questions asked and answered and then forgotten.

Benny didn't have a large family, but what he had—Nancy and the rest of them—were all under Waterloo Bridge.

Before Benny's mother died she'd told him if anything ever happened to her, not to hang around, for if the Social got wind of him, they'd slap him in an orphanage. Never mind about her, she said, just grab up Sparky and run for it. Get to the bridge.

But of course Benny couldn't do it. When his mum died on the pavement outside Selfridges, he'd stood there waiting for her to come back. A crowd gathered and one of them summoned a constable who'd been strolling and enjoying a rare sunny day in June. It was this officer who collected Benny and took him along to the station to see what could be done for him. *Never let the Social get you in its clutches, love.*

But the Social had, in the form of a Miss Magenta who had stood looking at Benny there in the station, measuring him up with her eyes (the way Gyp did later). You could tell she loved her job, even if she didn't love the children who made it possible. For she didn't care about him; he sensed this, but he didn't take it personally. She'd have been this way around any kid, with her cheap shiny smile and her cold pebble eyes.

While the constable was making out some sort of report, Miss Magenta was tidying Benny up. She'd been to the water fountain down the hall and was wiping his face with a damp handkerchief.

Disconsolate, but holding fast to Sparky's thin rope he used for a lead, Benny looked around and saw an elderly lady, rather thin and gray-haired, but still pretty and so richly dressed the effect was stunning. She was sitting on a bench against the wall, waiting for someone or something, and was watching the social worker washing Benny's face with the wet handkerchief. Benny knew what his mum had meant by getting in the "clutches" of someone, for he was definitely in Miss Magenta's. Her small hand on his shoulder felt like an armored mitten.

Her other hand kept washing his face. She said, *"Cleanliness is next to—"*

"Dog turds," Benny interrupted.

She rocked back on her heels, then collected herself and once again applied the damp handkerchief to his chin.

But the old lady, Benny noticed, was laughing, and it made him feel better, as if there were someone else in this chilly room who could share his feelings. He watched her open her purse, take out what looked to be bills and then sit there, seemingly waiting.

When Miss Magenta went once again to the fountain for a good soak of cleanliness, this lady moved with surprising speed to put her back between the fountain and Benny. She stuffed some bills in his cardigan pocket and whispered, "I'll create a diversion; as soon as I've got their attention, run like hell."

"Who is that woman?" asked Miss Magenta in a rather dangerous tone, as if, once the Social got you, you were no longer free to have chance encounters. Nothing from here on in would be left to chance.

The richly dressed lady called to her, "He reminds me of my great-grandson. I'm Irene Albright."

As Miss Magenta was finally putting the damp handkerchief away, there came a loud moan and Irene Albright fell in a heap on the floor. The constable, the desk sergeant, Miss Magenta and two or three others rushed to her aid. Benny was alone with the door only a few steps behind him. He backed up carefully with Sparky, and they were out on the pavement, where they both turned and ran like hell.

When Benny and Sparky got to the Lodge with the packets of chops and chine, Gemma was sitting on the bench with her doll, waiting. Mrs. MacLeish, the cook, had mentioned a delivery that morning and Gemma had come, as always, to wait by the gate. She took the meat and started off to the kitchen, calling over her shoulder she'd come straight back.

Benny climbed up onto the board wedged between the branches of a silver beech and waited. True to her word, Gemma was back before a minute had passed. Breathlessly, she asked, "What's chin? I'm not eating something's chin." She climbed up and sat down across from Benny in the tree seat.

"It ain't—isn't—'chin'; it's 'c-h-i-n-e'; it's some part of the pig, it's between his shoulder blades . . . I think I'll stop eating meat. I can't stand it that pig is slaughtered just so we can have pork chops and chine. And I can't hardly stand Mr. Gyp anymore."

"I hate him. He's covered with blood. I wonder if butchers hate animals. I wonder if that's why they get to be butchers."

Snowball, Katherine Riordin's cat, had come along to annoy Sparky. Snowball hissed.

"Gyp doesn't like Sparky. I can tell that."

Gem shook out her black hair so that it caught a flash of sunlight. "I'm not going to eat meat anymore." She said this as if Benny hadn't said it first. "A policeman was here yesterday."

"He's the same one that came to the bookshop."

"He didn't have a uniform on. It was probably his day off."

"He's a detective. They don't wear uniforms."

"Well, he didn't have a gun either."

"They don't carry guns." Benny wasn't sure this was true, but he said it as if he were. He took this line with most things he said for uncertainty never got you anywhere.

Gem was removing the doll's bonnet and studying its head. "But if there's a fight, they could get killed if they don't have guns."

"Police think carrying a gun only makes things worse, it makes the criminals more likely to shoot." That, he thought, was a really good idea. Maybe he'd read it somewhere.

"If he doesn't have a gun, how can he fight back if someone tries to shoot *me* again?"

Benny looked up through the breeze-shivered leaves of this big tree and thought further: this detective from New Scotland Yard hadn't simply dismissed the danger Gem was in. Benny frowned, concentrating on that. But Gemma—why Gemma? Why would someone want to get rid of her? Was it because old Mr. Tynedale liked her so much? Someone was afraid he would give away most of his money to Gemma?

"Are you thinking?" Gemma climbed down. "I'm going in to get some holy water and a towel. I'll be right back."

Benny grunted, only half hearing. Sparky followed Gem. He seemed to want to protect her.

Could Gemma know something she didn't know was important, and someone had to make sure she never realized it and told? Or maybe she *owned* something important . . . Benny sat up straight, recalling a film he had seen (and he hadn't seen many) and looked at the unnamed doll. His eyes widened; maybe the doll wasn't hollow inside. Maybe someone had opened it up to stash jewels or drugs or something and then sewn it up again. Its torso was of firmly stuffed material, even though its head and limbs were hard plastic. He took the doll up, bareheaded without its bonnet, and prodded and prodded; he put it against his ear and shook it.

"*What are you doing to Richard? Put him down!*" Gem dropped the towel she was carrying and climbed up to the seat and took the doll.

Benny stared from her to the doll. "Richard? *Richard?*"

"I ran across it when I was doing the *R*s." She leaned the doll against her shoulder and patted his back because it had been manhandled so outrageously.

Benny leaned toward her. "The *R*s were things like Ruth, Rachel, Rebecca. *Richard* is a *boy's* name!"

"I *know*. It *is* a boy. I'd never name a girl Richard. We were all wrong, you see." Gem was not about to take the wrongness on her own shoulders.

"She can't be a boy. Not after all this time!" Benny sloughed himself off the tree and paced around. Sparky woofed. It was too infuriating! What a thing for her to pull! He said, "Look how she's dressed, how she's been dressed all this time, in that long female dress!"

Reasonably, Gemma said, "It's christening clothes. It can be either one. Look—" She raised the doll's dress, pointed to the placidly empty space between its legs. "See? Nothing."

Benny blushed furiously. Oh, she looked so *smug*.

TWENTY-TWO

Waterloo Bridge rose out of the fog lying across the Thames, a sleeker, more streamlined and diminished version of what it had been during the war. Benny had never seen the old Waterloo Bridge, but Mags had shown him pictures of it in old magazines. Still, it was quite a sight, rising with the lights of the South Bank behind it, and overhead, crowds of stars and an iridescent moon. He stood looking at the starry bridge until Sparky nudged his shoe, nudging him out of his daydreams so as to set about distributing what was in the packet from Mr. Gyp.

That was the way Benny saw Waterloo Bridge, when, after dark, he came back to his makeshift life on the Embankment. It was always dark now in December when he finished work. Often he stayed to help at the Moonraker, for Miss Penforwarden was often behind-hand with her work: things like sending out notices of new books she'd acquired to customers on her mailing list. There were a lot of books to be posted to people on that list, names kept on cards in one of those round Rolodex files.

It surprised Benny how much work she had to do, and how uncomplaining she was about it. Aside from dithery looks here and there for something she'd set down and *Now where is it? Pencil, Miss Penforwarden? Be-*

hind your ear. Glasses? In your hair. This amused her more than anything else, and Benny thought that this was because she didn't get angry with herself, didn't put herself down like most people (including Benny) were inclined to do. Benny resolved to be like that himself, as he considered it a real virtue.

Miss Penforwarden wanted to pay Benny for the extra time he put in, but Benny absolutely refused, for he was happy to do it. So in place of pay, she invited him and Sparky to have supper with her on those evenings. He gladly accepted. Dinner with Miss Penforwarden came a couple of nights a week and had got to be a regular event.

Miss Penforwarden talked a lot about the past, about her husband, dead now; about her son, dead, too; about her lovely dog Raven, also dead. Benny felt awful about Miss Penforwarden's misfortunes; it seemed more than one person should be asked to bear. But her life was not presented as a tale of woe, and was all the more woeful for not being. It was matter-of-fact, even humorous; it was the way his own mother had been, keeping always at the forefront what was essential. As literally with her last breath she warned Benny about the National Handbag and managed a laugh.

Benny thought Sparky and he were very lucky; still, he reminded himself they gave as good as they got. As far as Benny knew, they were the only ones here camping under the bridge who actually worked for a living. Not that some of the others wouldn't, given half a chance, but a lot of them used drugs and drank themselves to sleep, where he could understand they'd sooner be than awake. Wakefulness for them provided no ease.

The ones who were clear enough in the head, begged. Benny did not look down on this because his own mother had been forced to beg. Before, they had had a nice life, for Benny recalled a solid house with lots of rooms where he had lived with his mother. She had cooked for this wealthy family. Only, one day saw them not so wealthy; the man of the house had gone bankrupt and staff had been let go. *It's through no fault of your own, Mary; we've just got to tighten up.* Bankrupt. A funny word to him as a little boy. Had the bank erupted? He pictured pound notes flying up and outward, falling again like volcanic ash.

Sparky always got first pick from the package and always chose the beef bone, but still he whiffed them all: chops, bones. He took his bone and trotted off to wherever he gnawed it or buried it, saving it, maybe, for a rainy day.

Here under the bridge was the place to be on rainy days, all right. For the most part they were not friendly people, and Benny could hardly blame them. Twice Benny was robbed before he decided to bank his earnings. He had set up a savings account at NatWest and he now had quite a bit of money in it. He would never have been accepted under the bridge, never, if he hadn't stopped here with his mother for the last few months of her life, so they had got used to Benny. When his mother died, several of them had been very kind and offered him food and gin. Mags, wrapped in bunched and knotted shawls, had held him and rocked him, saying, "Poor lad, poor lad." It had been and would always be as far as Benny was concerned the worst day of his life.

And, of course, he was also liked for the occasional packets from the butcher. They could cook the chops over a small fire. The bones did well in a watery soup. There was never enough to go around, of course, but still, it helped.

He had a pallet to sleep on. He had got blankets from the Lodge when he found Mrs. MacLeish was going to donate them to Oxfam. He had explained to her that the RSPCA was always looking for blankets and stuff, and that he put in time there as a volunteer; she was perfectly amenable to having the blankets go there (and also told him what a good child he was to be so concerned about the poor animals).

Benny found the Sergeant reading a book with the aid of his flashlight. He had an old terrier that would sit and bark, but in a friendly manner, at Sparky. Sparky woofed back, also in a friendly manner, and Benny imagined it was by way of having a conversation.

"Ah! Young Bernard. What've we today?"

Benny handed him the paper-wrapped chops. The Sergeant would then distribute them according to "rank," his term, meaning only to whoever was left out last time. Benny preferred not to do the handing out. They knew he brought it, and they certainly appreciated it (and thanked him), but it was better if the Sergeant handed it out himself.

"And is it Mr. Gyp we have to thank for all this?"

It always was, but the Sergeant always said this, making a ritual of handing over the goods.

"The generous Gyp." The Sergeant winked.

For both of them knew that Gyp was not a generous man.

Tonight, Benny watched the Sergeant walk to the enclosure beneath the bridge, and clutched his cap in his hand. In a rusted oil drum they'd got a fire going with newspapers, cardboard boxes, twigs and maybe some skinny branches they'd picked up in Hyde Park or Green Park. Sometimes the air smelled of pine, and he could imagine himself in the freedom of the north woods somewhere, maybe in the Alps or even in the northern United States.

No one here seemed to have the name he was born with, but instead had exchanged it for a name that better suited. "Mags" was not short for Margaret or Megan, but for "magazines," which Mags had collected over time and trundled around in her stolen Safeway shopping cart. About the cart she said, "You'll not see many more of these in future. Now, they lock 'em up. What bloody nonsense. Why, what I got here—" she put her hand on the metal cart "—it's gonna be a collector's item! When I went to Safeway a while back, here they'd fitted the line of carts with this fancy locking thingama-jig where you bung in a pound coin—a whole pound, can you bloody believe it?—and then get your pound back at the end at customer service. Don't think I didn't call the store manager over and gave him what-for. Like what if a person's not got a pound coin on him and was I expected to go wait in line just to get a fiver changed? Had one, too. I keep a fiver by me so's they don't think I'm homeless. Disgraceful! I said. 'I call lockin' up the carts a bloody disgrace! I know there's thieving, but to put your shopper through all this foolery just because a few of these carts gets nicked!' I went on and you bet the women standing there and heard this, they were with me all the way and started in complainin' and get-tin' quite shirty with him. He wanted to throw me out, but with all them women, well, he couldn't very well. So what he did was smile his smarmy smile and plug a pound in the slot and Bob's your uncle, I had me cart. I strolled round the produce with it and then when I didn't see him, I just wheeled it out the door.

"Benny," Mags had gone on, "one thing you always want to do is stay on the offensive. This is the best life lesson you'll learn. For the second you turn *de*fensive, they'll be circling like vultures, for they know you're dead! Act as if you know you're right. Like, if the Bill comes stickin' its nose in when you're jimmying a lock off a lock-up garage, stand your ground, *stand your ground*, and say you lost your key. When they ask you who you bloody are, you hand 'em a card, any card that you carry around—you should always carry some busi-ness cards, don't matter whose. Write a phone number on the back. 'Sorry, officer (you ijit), I recently had the number changed.' That kind of thing throws the Bill. They ain't total ijits and you might not get away with it, but I 'ave more 'n once. It just throws 'em. I could tell you stories, young Ben—"

That was Mags. Benny had no idea what the Sergeant's birth name was. It was the Sergeant who kept watch over the place under the bridge to make sure it got cleared up every morning or the Bill would have something to say. (The Thames police had a station just by Waterloo Bridge, too.) Benny didn't know where the Sergeant stashed the blankets and pallet. But the Sergeant had said that as Benny was working all day and bringing food back for them, the least they could do for him and Sparky was take care of his stuff. Benny could have afforded a bed-sit somewhere nearer his job in Southwark. People were always putting up little cards in Mr. Siptick's window advertising bed-sits and rooms for rent. The problem wasn't money, but age. What landlady would rent to a twelve-year-old boy (and his dog)? What would happen, and he knew it would happen, was the Social. His mum had warned him and so had Mags. For Benny the Social had horns and cloven feet.

Benny loved the Victoria Embankment, Waterloo Bridge and Westminster Bridge beyond it, and up the other way was Blackfriars, and the Thames in the early morning layered in mist. He liked to watch the river and think about the stories the Sergeant was always telling him about the old docks and warehouses, Wapping and Stepney, Whitechapel and Limehouse. All the ships, maybe five hundred of them, coming up the Thames from Gravesend, when the Thames was a real working river. It still was, but now, not much muscle or sinew—too many boats carrying tourists back and forth.

Occasionally, a sunset could be so intense that it looked as if London were burning. Great flares of orange and red that seemed impossible to have ignited over a city so vastly gray, and often dreary, Benny thought, if you didn't look underneath.

There was always underneath. You couldn't take things at face value. He thought of his mother, Mary.

Underneath her head scarf and wool shawl, his mother was never a beggar. She had lost everything in one fell swoop—Benny's father, and his pay, and she having no skills to work going had lost their little house in County Clare. But there had been those fortunate few years when she had worked as cook for the bankrupt family, but that too had gone. It was a terrible thing about coming finally to the streets; it was a long slide that you'd thought you'd stopped once, twice, three times; that you thought you'd got a handle on, and then only to find you'd slid farther down until your bum at last connected with cement.

He could see each of them now with his chop on the end of a stick holding it over the fire, and the Sergeant on his way back. He wore a long, heavy brown coat that had all of its buttons still. He was very proud that it didn't look seedy. It was all he had, the Sergeant had told Benny, from the old life in National Service. "Mucked about in the military police, me, in the war. Be surprised what you learn as an MP. Proper job I had of it, sorting out who done what to who. But it seems I've a mind for that sort of thing."

They had sat down to look out over the river. Benny said, "I met a policeman a couple days ago. A detective from Scotland Yard."

"Scotland Yard? Now that's something, that is. What did he want?"

Benny told him about the murder. "He wanted to know about Gem, too."

"That poor little girl—someone wants her out of the way? Never did hear of such a thing. Terrible."

"The thing is, I always took it that Gem was making it up. You know, so people'd pay attention to her. She hasn't got a proper family, I mean, no mum or dad, sisters, brothers—she hasn't got anyone."

"It's a puzzle, young Ben, it surely is." He was quiet for a few moments. "I wonder . . . now, I had experience as an MP with a young soldier who was, uh, messing around with the captain's wife. I finally twigged it, but what he done, see, was parade a good-looking German tart—ahem, I mean a woman—around just to put us off the scent. With a girl that looked like her, why bother with the wife? What I'm sayin' is, could the business with young Gemma be a distraction?"

Benny frowned. "Distraction? But from what?"

The Sergeant shrugged, wetting cigarette paper with the tip of his tongue. "How about that murder?"

"Yes, but . . . trying to kill Gem, all that happened before the murder."

"Still . . ."

They were silent for a few moments as the Sergeant smoked his cigarette. Benny looked through the dark out over the river to the lights on the far side. "Still, I wish that detective'd come back."

The Sergeant pinched the end of his cigarette before lighting it. "You can bank on that, young Ben. The Bill always comes back."

II

Firenze Farrago

TWENTY-THREE

That part of the Ponte Vecchio that he could see from this upper story of the tiny hotel was drenched in light. Such a distillation, such a concentration of light, Melrose had never seen before. It cast a golden skin across the Arno and beaded the graceful arc of the bridge where the goldsmiths traded, as if even more gold were called for, as if there could never be too much of it, as if the city could dissolve into sheer light and luster.

Florence's abundant charms had laid themselves at his feet last night when, after stowing their things in the high cool rooms of their small hotel, they had gone in search of dinner. Trueblood had picked this hotel, liking its seclusion on a street so narrow it could hardly accommodate more than the two of them walking abreast. The hotel seemed to occupy no more than a floor of a building that seemed otherwise tenantless. Melrose loved it; he loved the lobby-reception room, the antique furnishings of his own small room and everything going about in slippered silence.

Except Trueblood, who now stood in his doorway. "Come on come on come on come on" jabbered Trueblood, with the speed of an auctioneer.

It was, thought Melrose, an unseemly pace for this otherwise slow morning. "Good Lord, allow me to enjoy this vision of Florence."

"We want to go to the Brancacci Chapel. That's first."

Trueblood was carrying the brown-paper-wrapped Masaccio panel, about as convenient as lugging an oar around. There had been a bit of a row with a long-suffering flight attendant over the disposition of this long parcel: Trueblood wanted it sitting in the seat beside him (as if St. Who was not very sturdy on his legs), and the flight attendant had told him no. It must ride somewhere out of people's way. And, no, he could not purchase another ticket for it. Trueblood had given in and put it overhead, but had not been happy. He got a crick in his neck from constantly having to look up.

As Melrose swept coins and credit cards off the nightstand and into his pocket, he said, "Aren't you afraid you'll lose that walking around?"

"No."

They left the room, Melrose sighing and exclaiming he trusted he wasn't to be herded around at this pace the entire time they would be here. Trueblood didn't answer, just went on before him through the little lobby. Melrose loved the cool space of this lobby, with its blush-tinted stone flooring, rich dark moldings and white busts in alcoves. Reception consisted of a Regency desk and the chap behind it. The breakfast room, where Melrose was headed, though Trueblood was not, was large enough for only four tables and gave the impression, since the other three were unoccupied, that it was a dining room of one's own.

Failing to steer Melrose off course, Trueblood resigned himself to sitting down at the table. They were served by the ubiquitous reception-desk-fellow and another young man. The service was swift and pleasant and the food delicious. It would have been an altogether relaxing experience had not Trueblood sat sighing and checking his watch every two minutes. Melrose ignored this and tucked into the hotel's homemade granola. "This is quite good. Have some."

"I did. I ate an hour ago."

"You've already eaten and you'd starve me? No, don't unwrap Masaccio again."

Trueblood was carefully sliding a thumbnail under the tape and folding the brown paper back as tenderly as a baby's bunting. He had acquired a small magnifying glass which he clicked out of its black case and went about moving it all over the exposed part of the panel.

"For God's sake, Marshall, you know every inch of that painting by now. Who is this chap you're dragging me to see?"

"A man named Luzi. Aldo Luzi. An expert, perhaps the most expert in all of Italy on early Renaissance art."

"Really? But what about the Ickley woman? She, you said, was the foremost authority."

"*Then* she was; she was *then*."

"What in hell are you talking about? 'Then'? It was only yesterday. Are entire reputations to be made or broken over this suspect Masaccio?"

Trueblood inspected a small croissant, then took a bite. "She *is* the authority in Britain. I only mean I thought she *was* the foremost authority until she filled me in on this Luzi chap."

"Ah!" Melrose looped a little spoon of plum jam on his toast and said, "Then 'foremost' authority cannot move across borders."

"Don't be a nitwit."

"Okay. Anyway, the Ickley woman couldn't tell if the painting's authentic?"

"It wasn't something she could swear to either way. She could tell the panel, the paint, the varnish, and so forth were right for that period."

"The period being—"

"Early 1400s. You know the Renaissance better than I do."

"But only the British version." Melrose signaled the waiter for more coffee and Trueblood slid down in his chair, eyes closed. "Actually, there was no Renaissance anywhere else; Italy had the whole thing tied up and screaming."

Trueblood sliced him a look as the waiter poured coffee. "Don't prattle on, will you?"

"You sound exactly like Agatha."

Trueblood rewrapped Masaccio, then bounced in his chair a couple of times, displaying the frustration and impatience of a child.

Melrose laughed. "Here's a side of you I've never seen. You're as determined as a four-year-old trying to get his parents to stop eating and get up and go. This, so he can also go and do absolutely nothing."

"Well, I'm not going to do nothing."

Melrose sighed. "All right. I'm ready; bring on the Brancacci."

"Bran-kah-chi, Bran-*kah*-chi." Trueblood separated each syllable as if slovenliness in pronunciation would show a lack of respect that would have all of Florence bolting its doors and turning its back. He rose suddenly and walked toward the door.

"Finished!" said Melrose, throwing up his hands. He carefully folded his big napkin while Trueblood lurked in the doorway.

They descended a marble staircase into the murky depths of the entryway. They walked through the door into white light on pocked gray stone while on the other side of the narrow street purple shadows filled the crouched doorways, watched over by stone sculptures of animals and angels.

They walked, Trueblood in front and occasionally looking back and waving Melrose along.

Finally, they were crossing the Ponte Vecchio, Trueblood giving no quarter for pausing by these windows filled with gold necklaces, bracelets, earrings. The goods, Melrose thought, might have been molded out of the golden surface of the Arno—this morning's dream scene. He was yanked back by Trueblood's iron grip; the only thing he would be allowed to stand and ogle would be inside the Brancacci Chapel.

Melrose insisted on looking in the window of the little glove shop just at the other end of the bridge. Nothing but gloves! They lapped over one another in tiny colored waves of turquoise, lemon yellow, lapis lazuli, cobalt blue, crimson. He got pulled away yet again, and Melrose thought Trueblood must really be smitten if he could ignore such an addition to his wardrobe.

The temptations of the Ponte Vecchio behind them, Trueblood once again got in front; he was pointing at some destination, which in a while composed itself into a piazza and a church. "I forgot this was on the way. It's the Santa Feliceta and there's a fresco in here we want to see, too."

It was a painting of the Annunciation, and Melrose liked the startled *I-can't-believe-what-you-just-said* look on the face of Mary, turning to look at the angel delivering what was supposed to be really good news.

"Marvelous," said Trueblood.

"Have you ever seen an Annunciation painting where Mary looks as if she's saying, 'Hey, cool.' Think about it. I'd probably wear that look if Agatha told me she was moving into Ardry End. Poor Mary." Melrose wished he could tell the Virgin Mary she should be glad that was only the Archangel Gabriel before her and not Marshall Trueblood, who was disappearing up the shadowy nave.

When Melrose found him in the piazza, Trueblood said, "We can skip the Pitti Palace, if you don't mind."

If *he* didn't mind? By no means did he mind. All he wanted was to get back to that glove shop. "Okay. Later."

"Then come on," Trueblood said testily, reclaiming his lead. Over his shoulder, he said, "Next stop, the church of the Carmine. Where the frescoes are. It's on the way to Luzi's."

Nothing was on the way, thought Melrose, lost in a little maze of alleylike streets. They turned off the Via Sant' Agostino to the Via De' Serragli and the church sprang into view—at least into Trueblood's, for he trumpeted, "There it is! You'll be astonished!" He squared his shoulders and secured his picture before him like a shield, as if to defend himself against too much astonishment.

Melrose shrugged and said, "Okay, but listen, when we finish here, I want to go back to that glove shop . . ."

"*Glove* shop? Am I losing my mind?"

Again, Melrose shrugged. "I don't know." He decided he would take dumb rhetorical questions literally from now on. "But I want some gloves even if you don't."

This exchange had taken them into the chapel and down the nave to Trueblood's cherished frescoes, where they now stood. "Melrose, we're standing before perhaps the greatest frescoes ever painted."

"I know, but I'm serious about the glove shop."

Trueblood was carefully undoing the brown paper, which had begun, it appeared, to molt at the creases, light showing through the frayed folds, like a much-read love letter or a whore's stockings. Holding it up, he looked from St. Who upward to St. Peter, nodding and nodding.

"It looks like the same painter," said Melrose, "and looks like the same style, still, you've got to ask yourself—"

"I've asked myself every question in the book." Trueblood's eyes riveted on the fresco. Melrose had to admit all of this was astonishing. He'd seen many representations of Adam and Eve's being drummed out of Paradise, but never with such expressiveness. Eve's expression was especially harrowing: the mouth a rictus of pain, eyelids closed and slanting down as if she'd just been blinded. There were various scenes from the life of St. Peter: the tribute money, healing the sick with his shadow. "The thing is, didn't Masolino paint some of this? Didn't you tell me they worked together?" Melrose looked on the other side of St. Peter's raising someone from the dead, he wasn't sure who, to another rendering of Adam and Eve's expulsion from Paradise. "That's what I mean. Obviously, another painter painted *that* representation; everything about it is different." The two figures seemed completely calm and courtly. "That's a traditional depiction."

Trueblood nodded. "That's the difference between them." He stood and gawked at the frescoes for a good twenty minutes and paced before the frescoes for another ten while Melrose wandered around, stopped at the top of the nave and wondered what would happen if he tossed holy water on his face. Better not. There could be a thunderbolt.

"Time to go!" yelled Trueblood, rewrapping his painting—warmly, as if they were about to be heaved into a Russian winter.

Aldo Luzi lived in the Oltrano in a flaking stone building on a dead-end street running parallel to the river. The flat itself took up all of an upper floor, exquisitely decorated and luxuriously furnished. The materials covering sofas and chairs and footstools ran to damask, velvet, silk and brocade.

Signore Luzi was a scholar; thus, Melrose had expected a small run-down room overflowing with books, more than the bookshelves could accommodate, and stacked in piles and spilling over the worn carpet. Papers, journals in uneven towers. The room should look as crowded as the man's intellect, heaps of quarterlies and journals reflecting heaps of intelligence. Perhaps an owl on a dusty mantel. Something like that.

Nor did Signore Luzi himself fit Melrose's preformed idea of a "foremost expert." One, he was too young (late thirties? early forties?); two, he was too good-looking (where were the bent back, the owlish eyes, the specta-

cles, the unruly gray hair?); three, he was too well
dressed, even for informality. The blue shirt was undoubtedly designer, the scarf Hermès. His mind might
not belong in this sumptuous setting, but his body did.

They were seated in the spacious living room, Melrose
on a dark green damask cloud, Trueblood on its dark
blue twin cloud. They had bypassed the usual small talk,
Melrose was glad to see, to get to the point. The only
concession to the stock formalities was the espresso Luzi
had served. Now, he set down his cup on the sleek coffee
table to take up Trueblood's picture.

Luzi nodded at Trueblood's story of his acquiring this
panel while his eyes stayed on the picture. He had a
black mustache which he liked to tug at, thoughtfully.

For some moments, Luzi said nothing, but let his eyes
rove the room as if trying to decide whether to buy the
place. Melrose looked at his host's painting-covered
walls. They were largely Renaissance, and he was surprised to see among them one of those village-night-
mare works of Stanley Spencer. Higher up was a picture
of a man with a bowed head, stark naked and looking as
if he were being stoned to death. It could be a Lucian
Freud. There was one dreamy pre-Raphaelite painting
that might have been Holman Hunt's as it resembled
his *Ophelia*. It showed a young woman lying by a brook
amid wild flowers that blew like waves gusting back.

Trueblood set his small cup in its saucer and the *clink*
dragged Melrose back from the shores of dreams.

Signore Luzi had been talking: ". . . They were so
much in and out of one another's pockets—Masaccio,
Donatello, Filippo Brunelleschi, Masolino. There were
always the *concori*—the, uh, competitions—and, also,
several different artists might work on one painting or
sculpture at different times and in different years. Masolino and Filippino Lippi worked on Masaccio's *St.
Peter Enthroned*." Luzi took up Trueblood's picture
again. "The Pisa polyptych . . ." He interrupted himself
to inquire whether they'd planned to go there.

"To Pisa?" said Trueblood. "Of course; it's our next stop."

Oh? thought Melrose. No one had bothered to tell him.

"Ah, I am sorry to disappoint you, but that part of the polyptych has been covered or removed temporarily for some small restoration."

Trueblood slid down in his chair, looking forlorn. "Well. Oh, well."

Signore Luzi continued. "Now, several pieces *have* been discovered in churches, true. It's just that in your circumstance, finding this in an antique shop, I would think, no, this cannot be." Still holding the painting, he continued. "Masaccio. It's hard for me to imagine such talent and reputation in a man so young. Does that happen much anymore?"

Trueblood interrupted. "But it is possible. Eleanor Ickley—do you know her?"

"Of course. I was just reading an article by her." He pulled again at the tip of his mustache. "Now," Luzi said, "one real authority on Masaccio is in Siena. A Signore di Bada—"

Melrose sat bolt upright. *Real* as opposed to *foremost?* In Siena? Now that Pisa was dead in a ditch, would they still be making side trips? Oh, surely not!

Oh, surely, yes was Trueblood's response. "Di Bada. Siena, it's not far. It's only—"

"Sixty-five, seventy kilometers." Luzi shrugged. "An hour's drive." Luzi shrugged this distance away.

Trueblood looked at Melrose, not to ask if he acquiesced in the matter of this short journey—it was assumed anyone, even Melrose, would be thrilled to go sleuthing after Masaccio—but to see how soon Melrose wanted to go.

Melrose said nothing.

"We could leave now," said Trueblood.

"We could," said Melrose, "but we won't. I want to go to the glove shop."

Aldo Luzi laughed. "But of course! Such wonderful leathers! And such colors!"

They all took the glove shop as a point of departure, rose and headed for the door. As they shook hands and said their good-byes, Aldo Luzi leaned against the doorjamb and said, "He was only twenty-seven when he died." It was so sad, the way he said it. "Masaccio."

Melrose asked, "What did he die of?"

Luzi thought for a moment. "Want. He died of want."

Melrose colored, thinking that was something none of them, none of their three untalented selves, would die of, and felt diminished.

Outside, with the heavy door and its lion head knocker bolted, Melrose said, trying to keep the annoyance out of his voice, "You can't really mean to go to Siena to yet one more foremost-authority-leading-expert?"

"I certainly do. Should I ditch the whole plan when I'm this close? Come on, Siena's scarcely an hour's drive. We can rent some really fast car."

"*Close?* Marshall, you are not one inch or ounce closer to knowing this—" he tapped the package (once more wrapped and taped and tied) "—is genuine or not."

Trueblood made a show of thinking this over, which Melrose knew he was not. "There're car hire places at the airport."

Melrose took a few steps to the curb and appeared to be throwing himself in front of a Vespa which had materialized out of nowhere, out of the fuel-shocked air of Florence, before dematerializing into the dusk, failing to claim, this time, the life of one more Florentine. Melrose really wanted one of those scooters.

Taking the suicide-attempt hint, Trueblood threw his hands up (one not rising much above chest level, as the package was securely under his arm), "Okay, okay. We can go tomorrow. Let's find a drink."

"But first, but *first* to the glove shop. Thataway." Melrose pointed in the general direction of the Ponte Vecchio.

"I never knew you to be so glove addicted," said Trueblood, as they strolled along. "Maybe there's a twelve-step glove program you could try."

"Come on," Melrose said, taking command.

The knock-you-into-the-Arno scent of leather engulfed him when they entered the little shop. The gloves were in glass cases and also stacked by the hundreds—thousands?—in their own little plastic cases in cubbyholed wooden shelving.

Nine or ten customers preceded them, which was easily enough to fill the tiny shop. Melrose wedged his way in (*"Mi scusi, scusi"*) to look at the gloves in the glass case.

Now it was Trueblood's turn to carp, trying to lever Melrose out and into a trattoria. Melrose stopped listening; he knew it wouldn't be long before Trueblood fell hungrily onto this fashion feast, and it wasn't. After he elbowed an old man so hunched his chin barely cleared the counter, Trueblood was trying different gloves on each hand. This was difficult with his painting pressed under one arm.

To the old man, Melrose bowed and, with a supercilious smile, waved him to his place at the counter.

The old gentleman looked at him with considerable distaste: *"Lasciami in pace!"* he very nearly spit.

Melrose blinked. *"Prego,"* he said, but for some reason he did not really believe he'd been thanked. Back to the gloves, let's see: the black kidskin with the narrow white edging at the wrists would be perfect for Diane; they'd blend with her clothes, her house, her cat. One always had to take back little presents for the ones left behind. This was an excuse to look at (easily) a hundred pairs of gloves. A suede of deep gold, perfect for Vivian.

Noxious apple green for Agatha. Two pairs of lilac for Miss Broadstairs and Miss Vine. (They would probably wear them for gardening gloves.) Several more pairs for others. For himself—he looked down the counter.

Why was Trueblood unwrapping the painting? Why was he now holding it for the saleswoman's close inspection? Why was she raising pince-nez, dangling from a silver chain, up to her eyes? Was Trueblood wanting to fit up St. Who with gloves? If he got testy about it, would the scene resolve itself into *Expulsion from the Glove Shop*?

Melrose went back to his own glove buying, trying to ignore the comments and labored breathing of the people behind him waiting for service. He was taking no more chances in being polite. He picked up a pair of soft leather gloves that poured like double cream onto his hand in a color called Midnight Ashes. They were a gray so dark it just missed being black. He certainly had to have those. This next pair were doeskin in a nice fawn shade. As he was debating buying these also, Trueblood shoved in beside him to show him a pair in a shade something like sea green.

"Nice, eh?"

"Beautiful." Fortunately the painting was rewrapped. "Do you like these—" Melrose held up the nearly black gloves "—or these?" He pointed to the fawn gloves.

"Both. Get them both. See, I bought two." Trueblood held up the bag that contained his purchases.

"Yes, but you needed a pair for St. Who. I'm only gloving myself. And I'd feel rather overly indulgent buying two pairs, I mean, at these prices. Of course I realize they'd cost twice this at home, but that doesn't make them cheaper. No, I think I'll go for the dark gray ones." What Melrose was actually doing was giving Trueblood a chance to do his Christmas shopping. He knew Trueblood loved to purchase things on the sly, once he found that one was particularly taken with a certain article. "I think I'll take one last look at the back, if you don't mind waiting a tic."

"No, no, go on," said Trueblood, "they've some especially nice ones at the back."

When Melrose looked back, Trueblood was in close colloquy with the saleswoman, who was nodding and smiling. *Sì, sì.* Melrose allowed enough time for the transaction at the front. When they left the shop, he smiled, for Trueblood was securing this last flat little parcel beneath the string around his painting.

Melrose felt rather humble about this and determined to stop giving his friend such a hard time over his foremost or leading expert or authority in future.

TWENTY-FOUR

Determined to get to Pietro di Bada in record time, Trueblood told Melrose to turn onto the motorway, a plan quickly scotched by Melrose, who said that if he was going at all he wanted to see the Tuscan countryside, and not from the rush of a motorway.

"You'll want to stop," said Trueblood, churlishly.

"No, I won't."

Of course, he would, which was why he had insisted on driving. And he did, when he spied from a distance the hill town of San Gimignano. Melrose loved the name and kept practicing, trying to get the accent just right (*"San Gim-i'yon-o, San Gim-i'yon-no"*). Its needle-like towers bathed in the sun, some nearly encased in vines and flowers, its feudal walls and narrow windows, its medieval stone—all were irresistible.

Trueblood was reading his guidebook. "There were once something like four hundred towers here. Now it's only around seventy. What happened to the others?"

"Is that the point? I mean, what happened to them just doesn't seem the *point* of this town." Melrose brought the car to a halt in the car park, and, breathing hard, they struggled up the steps onto the cobbled road and still climbed. They found a little trattoria in which to lunch on bruschetta, crostini and wine. Melrose exhausted his Italian when he asked for *la lista dei vini* and *acqua minerale* and as always came up short when the waiter (impressed by their command of the language) made his own contribution: *"Gassata o naturale?"* Melrose shrugged his shoulders in a not-caring gesture. Trueblood was having gin and tonic all over Florence because that was the way it was spelled out: *gin tonic.* Well, they'd never claimed to be linguists, had they? said Trueblood, ordering another *gin tonic.*

The lunch was simple and good—when wasn't it good over here?—and afterward they ambled farther up the hill to come out on a piazza overseen by a charming church. They crossed it and came upon a museum of torture. Here was something to catch Melrose's interest! Once inside with their tickets, they appeared to be the only torture enthusiasts, for they saw no one else in the first room, where they stopped before an exhibit of a kind of iron headpiece, fashioned so as to fit over the head and keep the mouth shut. Women who passed their time in gossip paid heavily for it.

In the next, where the relics really got going, a young lad of perhaps ten or eleven was walking about with a gelato, and Melrose wondered how he'd ever got the dripping cone in here. The boy was standing before the iron maiden, licking the ice cream with fervor.

As Trueblood peeled away and walked pretty much in a trance around the various rooms, Melrose followed the boy. He liked the manner in which the lad could counterfeit the effects of each device. The iron maiden had him pressing his fingers against his chest, distorting his face in pain and emitting low-key shrieks as the spikes penetrated his flesh. Before the neck clamp (another original cure for women with loose lips), the boy turned his hands backward (having finished his ice cream), clutched his neck and stuck out his tongue. A couple of exhibits later in front of what looked like an electric chair, he went rigid, holding out his arms and giving a few quick shivers. Next, to simulate the effect of one's torso being trapped in the metal box while one's limbs were being severed, he bent in half and applied an imaginary saw to his arm, scraping it back and forth. The knives, the clubs, the swords, the chains, the pickaxes all fell to his interpretation.

This kid was in love with pain, thought Melrose. Where were his parents? In the cellar, bound and gagged? The museum was quite entertaining, really, and he wondered the owner didn't charge more. At the entrance was a sign that explained this was a private collection. Children weren't allowed as the displays might be too harrowing for them. Harrowed was what this boy was not. The exhibit finished, Melrose and the boy found themselves at the exit.

Trueblood had ambled out and Melrose saw two adults and a girl, all looking harassed and irritated. The boy's mum and dad and sister, it would appear.

The boy had emerged and the mother was extremely quarrelsome: "Gerald! I told you not to go in there! What were you doing?"

Americans. Did that explain it?

"Nothing. It was boring."

The family turned and walked away. But for one sumptuous moment, the boy looked back over his shoulder at Melrose and winked.

"What we should do," said Trueblood, when they were back on the road, "is divide up Long Pidd into *contrade*." He had purchased a little guide to Siena and was reading from it.

"Suits me, as long as Theo Wrenn Browne and Agatha aren't in mine."

Trueblood slewed a look at him. "Don't you know anything about around here?"

"I know the medieval cure for gossip."

Trueblood grunted. "Well, *contrade* are something like tribes. In Siena there are seventeen. This division of neighborhoods is as old as the Tuscan hills apparently."

"What's so great about that? There are at least that many in London: there's Chelsea, Battersea, Knightsbridge—"

"No, no, *no*. It's not the same at all. Those are just geographic; those are postal zones. These are neighborhoods that are very tight," he said clutching himself, making Melrose think he had a lot in common with the boy back there. "People are very loyal to them, they've got their own flag, their particular emblem—like a goose or an elephant—and they're extremely competitive."

Siena sat on its hill, looking down at them at dusk, full of little lights bathed in mist, a city small, earthy and beautiful.

Dark quickly overtook dusk after they'd left the car again in a car park and climbed up steps and down steps and up again. A soft rain fell, more mist than rain, as they made their way along the Via Di Stalloreggi toward the Duomo. Every once in a while, Trueblood would stop and scrutinize the city map, then nod and continue.

"We're looking for the Via Del Poggio," he said. Trueblood pointed at a plaque. "See?"

Melrose made out what appeared to be a turtle. "So this is the turtle *contrada*?"

"I don't think that's the way they refer to it."

They found the Via Del Poggio. Over one door was a small flag. "That," said Trueblood, "identifies it, too. And there's the plaque, see?" This door opened and as quickly closed. In this flurry of light, Melrose made out another turtle.

"Here's di Bada's house!"

"Good. It's getting cold. But if he's one of your *true* foremost authorities or leading experts, he probably will not be offering drinks."

"What're you talking about?" asked Trueblood, raising the small brass door knocker.

Melrose shrugged. "I don't know."

But he did when the gentleman he supposed to be the one they'd come to see opened the door and peered out over the tops of his glasses (which had ridden down his nose), and squinched his eyes as if blinking in an unaccustomed light and as if the light were out here instead of in there. If Aldo Luzi had been erudition's antithesis, Pietro di Bada was its crowning glory, the very definition of scholar. If symbols could walk! Here was a cherub of a man, quite old and round shouldered, the shoulders covered with a shawl.

Trueblood bowed slightly and said, "Signore di Bada? Professor di Bada? I'm Marshall Trueblood, and this is Mr. Plant—"

"Non capisco, non capisco." The old man waved Trueblood's words away, looking irritated that he had been sucked to the door by some fool who couldn't even speak the language.

Trueblood tried again. Pointing to him, he asked, "Signore Pietro di Bada?"

"Sì, sì."

Ah, they were getting somewhere! "Signore Aldo Luzi was supposed to have called you and explained that we were—"

"Parli lentamente!" Signore di Bada exclaimed, annoyed at being kept in the cold doorway.

Trueblood looked at Melrose, and they both shrugged.

"The phrase book," said Melrose pointing to Trueblood's pocket. "It's some command to speak something. Inuit? Senegalese? Who the hell knows?"

"I found it, I found it! 'Slowly.' We're to speak *slowly.*" Trueblood cleared his throat and with contorted mouth said, "Aldo Luzi. He. Said. You. Were. The. Leading. Au-thor-i-ty on Mas-ac-ci-o."

"For once he's right. Come." His outstretched arm ushered them in.

Melrose said, stupidly (he later realized), *"Parla inglese?"* It was one of his overworked phrases, and he hoped it wasn't Spanish.

"Speak English? It is obvious, is not? Why you two speaking Italian?" Di Bada started laughing fit to kill, as if putting one over on them was what he'd been waiting to do all day. He waved them in, still laughing. It was a gasping sort of laugh, a mildly snorting laugh, somewhere between gasp and hiccup.

This little charade didn't fit the "foremost authority" picture at all. For such a person, humor would be dry, reflective, ironic. Wit, trenchant. However, the milieu reinforced Melrose's picture: books and papers everywhere, light from a green-shaded desk lamp pooling on the scuffed wood of the desk and beaten-up Oriental rug.

Signore di Bada wrestled a couple of straight-backed chairs free of encumbrance, sending a stack of journals and assorted papers spilling to the floor. "Sit, sit." He waved them down, neither of them able to put his feet on anything but papers and journals. Melrose scraped some of the papers together and held them out to di Bada, who said, *"Grazie."*

"Prego," returned Melrose.

Di Bada laughed again. He was, apparently, still jubilant over his little practical joke. *"Mi scusi."* He wiped the tears from his eyes and blew his nose on a handkerchief roughly the size of Northamptonshire, which he then bunched and jammed into his pocket. "So! Luzi said you wanted help about a painting you think is of Masaccio? It isn't, but let's have a look." While Trueblood carefully unwrapped the painting, di Bada asked Melrose, "You been to Siena before? No," he answered himself. "You like Firenze? *Sì, sì,* Firenze, who would not love it? I tell you who. We, the Sienese! I tell you a little story about the Black Death, is very funny."

Melrose was already laughing.

"In fourteenth century, one of our principal fountains was the Fonte Gais. A group of Sienese found and dug up a statue of Venus and set it atop the fountain. Then

came the Black Death, and the preachers and soothsay-
ers said it was having that pagan statue up there that
caused it. So one night, a little group disguised as peas-
ants stole it away, broke it to pieces and then sneaked
across the border to bury the pieces in Florentine land,
so the Black Death would turn from Siena to Firenze."
Here came that hiccupy, snorty laugh that made the old
man shake like a bowl of jelly. He seemed always on the
verge of it. Any old joke or prank, good or bad, was better than no joke at all for Signore di Bada.

"Oh, the panel you brought—" He set it on the floor,
holding it at arm's length. "Hmpf! It looks as if it could
be one panel in a triptych—"

"Polyptych," said Trueblood, eager to move the identification along.

Thick eyebrows floated above black-rimmed glasses
as di Bada peered at Trueblood. "You know so much,
my friend, why do you come to me?"

Trueblood washed his hands around in air, saying,
"No, no, no. Sorry. I only meant it was suggested to me
by this antiques dealer that it might be part of the Pisa
polyptych . . . possibly?"

Di Bada rested the panel against the end of his desk
and crossed his small hands on top of it. He shook his
head slowly back and forth, seemingly at Trueblood's
folly. "Signore Trueblood, you realize how you are an
idiot? Oh, it's true, quite true, that nearly a dozen different parts of that polyptych have turned up, but in
places such as ancient churches—"

"I believe that's where she said she found it. The
church in San Giovanni Valdarno."

Di Bada held up a hand, palm out, as if to push back
this absurdity and said, "That is Masaccio's birthplace.
That a painting so important could be overlooked in
that church? For centuries?" Di Bada flapped his hands
as if wishing them away. "Signore Trueblood, this is ludicrous."

Trueblood objected. "But isn't that the way things

often are found? By some strange confluence of place, time and person? Several pieces of the Pisa polyptych were found in just that way, weren't they?"

Di Bada was waving the words away before Trueblood was half finished. "Perhaps, yes, but I tell you, not by somebody in an art gallery. You go to Pisa? No, it is a shame that the *St. Paul* in the Museo Nationale is taken down. They feared for its safety, I think. You have got in your own country, in London, the center of the altarpiece: *Madonna and Child Enthroned*. Then there is Berlin, where there must be four or five of the panels, and the predella of Saint Julian; one in Naples; another piece in some city in California no one can remember. No, Signore Trueblood, I fear you have been—" he tapped his temple with a finger "—what is the word? 'Duped,' ah yes. Duped."

Melrose, who thought he would never take up Masaccio's cause after all of this trouble he'd been put through, still, even he was irritated by di Bada's attending more to himself than to the panel.

As if he read Melrose's brain waves, di Bada shoved his glasses up on his head, and brought the picture so close to his face his nose was all but touching it. "Masaccio. Hmpf!"

Melrose interpreted the "Hmpf!" not as a sound of dismissal but of curiosity. He watched di Bada rise, move to one of the many bookcases, reach down a dusty-looking volume and riffle its pages. "Masaccio was a man possessed," he said, turning pages. "It's all he cared about—art. He neglected everything else, everyone, including himself. There were long periods when he saw no one. He belonged to this guild—the *Speziali*—who had grocers among its members, and I've always been amused by that. Well, Masaccio got so bad, so afraid others might steal his work, he became—what is the word?" He snapped his fingers several times.

"Paranoid?" Melrose suggested.

"Paranoid, *sì*. So paranoid the only person he would

admit to his lodgings was this grocer. For a time when he
forgot to eat he enlisted the grocer's aid, told him to bring
bread and cheese. The grocer had no more to do with art
than to be a member of the same guild as the painters. He
was trustworthy. He was completely disinterested. Why
not trust the person who can gain nothing, eh? Why not
trust the grocer?" Di Bada returned to his chair behind
the desk and sighed. "You know he died when he was
very young—"

"Twenty-seven," Trueblood put in.

Melrose thought he detected a lump in the throat
here.

"Imagine what he would have accomplished had he
lived even another ten years." The old Italian meditated
on empty air. "The great Brunelleschi; Donatello, perhaps the greatest sculptor since the Greeks; and our
Masaccio, the first great naturalist." He said to Trueblood, "You have been to the Brancacci Chapel? Of
course you have. Then you have seen one of the
strongest uses of perspective in the *St. Peter Healing
with the Fall of His Shadow*. This is said to be the first
Renaissance painting. Your eye plunges down that city
street at the same time St. Peter is walking toward you.
Things *move* in this painting; the shadow of St. Peter
moves. Masaccio developed chiaroscuro; he was the first
to use the cast shadow as a device. You have been of
course to the Santa Maria Novella, no?"

"No. I mean not yet."

Di Bada looked at them as if they were heretics.
"You stay in Firenze and not go to see the *Trinity*?
Well, when you go, look at the *Trinity* from the west
aisle. You will see how the great vaulted ceiling seems
to open from the space in which you stand. It was
Masaccio's purpose to project his subjects into the
earthly sphere to suggest the reality of the supernatu-
ral. See, your eyes meet Mary's eyes. That gaze induces
the belief that she is present. It is revolutionary."

There was a silence suffused (Melrose hoped) with

the proper respect. Trueblood finally broke it, saying, "But I wish you would take another look at the panel, Signore di Bada."

"If it would please you." Di Bada ran his eye over the saintly figure, even got so far as to take out a magnifying glass, a big one with a horn handle. He ran this over the painting, his eye making quick little darts. He returned the magnifying glass to its perch atop a small hill of books. He thought for a little while. "Perhaps you shouldn't rest your case on the opinion of such as I. I am an expert, true. But there is one who knows perhaps even more—"

Melrose tried to keep from slipping down in his chair, but did not wholly succeed. Trueblood was, of course, all ears.

"—this is Tomas Prada who lives in Lucca. It is worth your time to see him. I am sorry I cannot be more helpful. I can only say what I said before, that this is so unlikely to be by Masaccio . . ." Di Bada shrugged.

He went on, with a shake of his head. "Masaccio had nothing. He owed money to others; he possessed nothing; he had pawned his clothes. Yet was he not one of the chosen? I sometimes envy the mental state that simply forgets the material world. Not 'denies' it, for that of course is to acknowledge it before pushing it away. But no, Masaccio forgot that it even existed. He was one of the chosen."

All through dinner—a marvelous fish soup, followed by a *tagliatelle alle noci,* followed by partridge, right into their *dolce,* a warm zabaglione—they argued. Not in a bellicose way, because the restaurant was too fine and the food too good, not even particularly contentiously or continually. They brought it up, let it lie, brought it up again.

Melrose said, "I simply refuse to go to a 'One-who-knows.'"

"It's not that far. Lucca's almost right on the way."

"'Almost' is the operative word here. Now listen: we have already spoken to the foremost authority and leading expert. I refuse to drag myself—"

"'Drag'? It's a Maserati."

"On these drifting hills *nothing* is a Maserati. I refuse to go in search of One-who-knows." Except that Melrose was intrigued by now with this entity he himself had really conjured out of di Bada's phrase. He really wanted to see this inquiry through to its godforsaken end. He did not, however, want to agree to this third leg of their journey without a certain amount of resistance. Anyway, it was fun listening to Trueblood whimper and plead. He picked up his glass of Chianti (which was unlike anything you could get in England) and said, "Oh, all right." He dipped his spoon once again into his Marsala-drowned custard. How could something so simple taste so wonderful?

Trueblood was pleased as punch. Melrose said, "You know, the more we go on with this, the nearer we get to the question, not the answer."

Trueblood looked a little shell-shocked, his eyes like cartoon eyes, *X*s in place of pupils. "What do you mean?"

"I don't know, really. It's just something I felt. Marshall, what are you doing?"

"Huh?"

"Why are you chewing your zabaglione? It's custard."

"I'm not chewing. But I was thinking, shouldn't we go to Pisa; even if we can't see that part of the altarpiece, we could walk around the Carmine to sort of feel the context."

Melrose knew that Trueblood knew *that* entreaty would fall on deaf ears.

He glanced quickly at Melrose and said, "No, I expect not." He had the look of one who had finally discovered his home, only to find the family had been turned out of the house . . .

Melrose took another swallow of the Chianti and asked himself if Trueblood—running all over Tuscany with his questionable painting—if Trueblood weren't, like Masaccio, one of the chosen.

TWENTY-FIVE

The next morning Melrose was awakened at some intransigent hour by Trueblood's banging on his door.

"Sorry," he said when Melrose stumbled to open it. "But just knocking wasn't enough."

"At dawn, it usually isn't."

"Dawn? Good Lord, it's after eight."

"Close enough to dawn for me." Melrose yawned.

The sun had come out yet there was still this ocean of mist at their ankles, and Melrose felt as he had the night before, that he was standing on a ship's prow, looking out over empty water. After coffee and rolls, they stashed their small bags in the trunk and aimed the car toward Lucca.

This time, Melrose didn't have to be argued into taking the *autostrada*. Neither did the Maserati. They flew.

A buxom girl in a dirndl and peasant blouse opened the door, painted an astonishing blue, and said, *"Posso aiutarle?"*

Melrose did not think she'd asked, "What posse of retards are you?" So he assumed it must be something to do with offering help. He asked if she spoke English. "We're English—*inglese*?"

"Ah, *sì, sì!*"

"We'd like to see Signore Prada. I called—"

"*Non capisco . . .*"

She seemed genuinely upset. Melrose put an imaginary phone to his ear and pretended to be dialing. "Mr. Plant? Mr. Trueblood? Called before."

"Ah, *sì! Per favore.*" Her outstretched arm motioned them in to a hallway pleasantly adorned with more photographs than Melrose had ever seen on one wall, a delicate table with a soft-glowing lamp on it, and the scent of a flower he couldn't determine. They followed her down the hall to a door she lightly knocked upon.

"*Avanti!*"

The girl opened the door and let them pass before her. "*Grazie,*" said Trueblood.

"*Prego.*" She nodded and left.

The gentleman who had been standing by the window Melrose assumed to be Tomas Prada. "Signore Prada?" said Melrose. He introduced himself and Trueblood. "We called about the painting."

Tomas Prada, Melrose judged, was somewhere in his late fifties. He had very dark hair and a thick mustache, both of which showed signs of gray. His features were chiseled, his cheekbones and nose sharply defined.

"Ah, yes. The Masaccio. Please, sit." Prada indicated two comfortable-looking armchairs. He himself continued to stand by the window.

He must also have been a painter; Melrose saw the easel and what looked like fresh paint on the canvas, a study of an olive grove, as nearly as he could tell. "You're a painter yourself?"

Prada gave a self-deprecating shrug. "*Sì.* I teach at the Accedemi in Florence. Three days a week only, so I choose to continue to live in Lucca." Prada left the window and came across the room. "Now, let's see this Masaccio you fancy you've found."

Melrose (who for some reason had today put himself at the helm of this little ship) thought his comment rather patronizing and set him straight: "It's not precisely our fancy. Mr. Trueblood has shown this to several people, here and in England, all authorities on Renaissance art, including your friend Pietro di Bada. Neither he nor the others feel they can say definitely that it *isn't* Masaccio's work." Although di Bada had come damned close.

Prada smiled a rather inky smile. His mustache was all over it. "Wall-sitters." He waved away the other authorities, including his friend Pietro.

Melrose frowned. "'Wall-sit . . .'? Oh, you mean *fence*-sitters."

"Those who cannot make their minds up. Let me see." With both hands he took the panel, which he rested upright on the floor against the easel. He gave it a quick once over. Then he took it to the window and made his examination slower. "First, have you run tests on the material?"

"Yes," said Trueblood.

"And the paints, the surface, they are compatible with the fifteenth century?"

Trueblood nodded.

Prada again leaned the panel against the easel, adjusting its position so that it got more light. He looked at it for some time, one arm across his midsection, the other braced there as he indulged the nervous habit of pulling at his mustache. Prada was silent for some moments, staring at St. Who. After a while he said, "These altarpieces were commonly dismantled, the separate parts to be taken by whatever family had commissioned the work in the first place. Sold perhaps, perhaps passing through many hands. None of the Pisa polyptych is in the church of the Carmine anymore, and only one piece is in Pisa itself, in a museum. This is very interesting."

Prada moved to the window again to look at the painting. "You know Donatello had a lock put on his workshop because he feared others would steal or plagiarize his work. Which at least one did. There was so much competition for commissions, for they meant not only money, but more commissions." He said all of this to the painting. Looking up from his examination, Prada sighed. He handed the picture back to Trueblood. "I have a suggestion. You have started at the end of your search. Go back to the beginning."

"Come?"

"The beginning. Instead of the end. Now, how did you come by this picture?"

"In an antique shop. I'm a dealer myself."

"And what about the shop that sold this to you? Is it reliable?"

Trueblood nodded.

"What is the provenance? Where did he find it?"

"She. According to the woman who sold it to me, she found it in San Giovanni Valdarno."

"That is something that tells against it, to claim it was found there. And how could one even entertain the notion that this is part of the Pisa polyptych, and hang it up to sell? No. How much did you pay for it, if I may inquire?"

"Two thousand pounds."

Prada nodded. "In other circumstances, quite a lot of money, but only a fraction of what this would be worth if it was whole and if it was genuine. You said it was tested for its physical properties?"

"Yes," said Trueblood, "as well as could be in a short time."

Prada moved to the easel again. "Would it be St. John the Baptist? He has the weighty form you find in Masaccio's figures. The chiaroscuro—that shadow just there—" he pointed to the side at what Melrose couldn't even make out, it was so subtle "—is Masaccio, yes? And the spatial effects. *Sì* . . . Of course, you know Masaccio was the first to make use of Brunelleschi's architectural perspective? The receding diagonals giving the illusion of reality. The centric point, the vanishing point. You have seen the *Trinity*?"

They both grunted what they hoped would pass for an "Of course."

Tomas Prada smiled beatifically. He could easily have taken the place of one of these panels. "I think not. I think you have not been to the Santa Maria Novella."

What the hell was this, anyway? Did Prada mean to give them a lie-detector test? Wasn't it enough for these Italians they had come *all the way from London*? And driven over half of Tuscany pursuing this dream?

"You must go, obviously. You see, Masaccio made an astonishing leap between the style of the San Giovanni triptych and the *Trinity*. No other painter, not even Leonardo, changed so quickly and with such amazing results. You must see this vaulted ceiling. The perspective, the blurring, the vanishing point. What is interesting is that the doctrine of redemption is also a blurring, a *sfumatura,* of space and time. Christ gives himself once, but then there is the Eucharist, where he gives himself again and again, unendingly, in complete contradiction of time and space. You see? The receding diagonals give the illusion of reality so that one might, in seeing the forms in the painting as real, believe in the subject. Perspective was Masaccio's theology." As he said this he was looking at Trueblood's painting.

"To see what pieces have been recovered of the Carmine polyptych, you would have to go to Vienna, Berlin and, of course, London. The National Gallery houses—" Prada grew thoughtful "—the central panel, I believe. The *Madonna and Child*. The entire predella story is in Berlin. This"—he tapped Trueblood's panel—"would have been one of the wings, the side panels next to the Madonna. St. John or St. Nicholas, probably. I mean if it was authentic."

Melrose shot Trueblood a look to see if Berlin, having got two mentions, was now in the travel plans, but Trueblood was wholly taken up with what Tomas Prada was saying.

Right now, Prada was smiling. "Perhaps I must join my friend di Bada on the wall—"

"Fence?" said Melrose, matching the smile.

"*Sì.* Only, there's one thing that greatly perplexes me, Mr. Trueblood."

"What's that?"

"Well, you see, what we know of the Pisa polyptych in its wholeness, we know only from Vasari's description. We haven't the advantage of seeing these parts in a catalog or as a print, have we? So if this is a fake, a forgery, what was it copied from?"

Trueblood looked befuddled. "A good question, a good question, Signore Prada."

Prada sighed. "A good question, perhaps. But I think a better question might be, 'Can you live without an answer?'"

Trueblood considered. "I could; I'd just rather not."

He was beating his head on the dashboard and loving it.

"Don't be so dramatic," said Melrose, as they drove down the curving road away from the Prada house.

"Why didn't we think of what they were copied from? It's so obvious."

Melrose was enjoying the feel of the car as they rolled through the Tuscan landscape, verdant even in December. They had been here for only three days and it felt like weeks, months, even. Travel had that sort of intensity; sights, events crushed together so that one wound up thinking, *No, it surely must have taken me a week to see that, not merely an hour.*

The fingers of his gloved hand upon the steering wheel (he was wearing his new gloves) tapped out a little tune. He was in good spirits. Trueblood was winched down in the passenger's seat, contemplating nothing except his own thoughts and turning now and then to look at the painting in the back, where it lay, now unwrapped as if it had no more to hide.

*   *   *

That night they dined at the Villa San Michele on an ambrosial fish netted in some heavenly stream. For dessert, there was a soufflé Grand Marnier. When they finished, Trueblood asked the waiter to bring their coffee and cognac out to the terrace. *"Fa caldo, signore."*

"Sì," said Trueblood, not caring whether it was or wasn't. The waiter brought the drinks and withdrew.

"They're so ceremonial," said Melrose, with a laugh. In the dark, they looked down on the city of Florence, its lights spread out across the city like drifts of fallen stars.

Trueblood uttered a giant sigh. "We leave tomorrow."

They sipped their cognac, lighted cigarettes. Standing in the softly scented air, there came what felt to Melrose a mortal silence. Here he was in a place he had not wanted to come to, and which now he did not want to leave. He felt out here an awful longing; he felt like crying, really. Images flickered in and out of consciousness: the vine-wrapped towers of San Gimignano, its laddered, uphill streets; the conspirator's wink of the lad who was hurried away from the Museum of Torture; Siena, the color of warm earth; its purple-shadowed streets; the blue door of the house in Lucca; the echoing stairway of their little hotel.

"Maybe," said Melrose, "Diane was right after all."

"How so?"

"See Florence and die."

III

Moonlight Sonata

TWENTY-SIX

As it happened, it was not Oliver Tynedale who had been prevented by ill health from attending Simon Croft's funeral two days before, but Simon's sister Emily; her heart simply could not accommodate either the travel or the stress. "He looked remarkably chipper," Mickey had said of Oliver Tynedale. "Certainly doesn't look in his nineties." Mickey had told Jury this; Mickey had gone to the funeral, but kept his distance, hanging back beneath the dripping trees.

Jury had hoped to speak to Emily Croft following the funeral, but since he couldn't, that meant a trip to Brighton.

Brighton in December, although still a fairly bustling city, bore little relation to Brighton in June or August. Jury often felt there were few things bleaker than a seaside town in winter. He walked across a beach less sand than shale and broken shells and stood listening to the hollow fall of waves, the hiss and whisper of the foaming tide coming in. He had come here as a child. It was a memory that now receded like the tide. He was no longer sure about memory.

Emily Croft was a thread that had loosened from the tightly knit Croft and Tynedale clans. Not that he expected or even wished that she'd spill all sorts of secrets about the others. It surprised him, though, that she lived here in Brighton in a "facility" such as this that could only be depressing.

Jury thought about this standing in front of a high window that looked over the edge of the bluff to the sea, pewter to dark gray farther out and rather quiet today. He had been shown into this sitting room with its cold and glaring marble fireplace to wait. The furniture was sound but homely, dark blue and brown, the armchairs bulbous with stuffing.

The door opened and Emily Croft walked in. She was wearing yellow, which made him smile. One so seldom saw it in clothes, not a pale, liquid yellow, but a sunny yellow dress and cardigan. She was thin and a little angular, but still, at seventy-three, in possession of skin and cheekbones a model would kill for. She did not look the least bit infirm, nor did she move as if she were ill. He wondered if this iron stamina which both Emily Croft and Oliver Tynedale had in abundance was characteristic of the rest of the families.

"Miss Croft." He held out his hand. He had called from London and arranged to see her. "First, I'm very sorry about your brother."

It was obvious she had been crying, but the Tynedales and Crofts were a resilient sort and he knew there would be little breaking down here.

She smiled. "Superintendent Jury," she said, taking his hand.

"I really like your dress." He rather blurted this out, realizing its inaptness after he'd said it.

She laughed as if the compliment were unexpected. "Thank you. Let's go out here to the sunporch." She extended her arm to indicate a glassed-in sunporch and led the way. "Please sit down."

The furniture was white wicker, the carpet sisal. It was more relaxed out here, and with the sun slanting in, far more cheerful. A better background for a yellow dress.

"You came about Simon's death."

"I'm very sorry about your brother, I truly am."

"So am I, so am I." Her voice wavered and she looked out to the sea, which the sun brightened momentarily. She cleared her throat. "Simon was a stolid person, but a good one. And very, very smart. The idea that anyone would want him dead is so alien to me—" She stopped again and looked out. "I've thought of little else since it happened. I've tried to come up with some reason or other. I can't."

"When did you last see him?"

"About three weeks ago. Simon tried to come every week. Sometimes he didn't make it, but usually he did. Both he and Marie-France, though she doesn't come as often. Ian, too, visits me once in a while, and I know Oliver would if the doctor hadn't offered to chop off his feet." She laughed, but the laugh broke in two. "Let me tell you what happened, since you must be wondering why I'm here and not in London. About five years ago I lived by myself in Knightsbridge. When I developed this heart problem, my doctor advised me to get someone in. People advise you to do that as if it's the easiest thing in the world, when it's really one of the hardest. Living in a two-bedroom flat with a stranger? Please. Oliver asked me to come to the Lodge where there were people around but where there was also privacy. I could have gone to Simon or Marie-France, but there goes the privacy for all of us. The Lodge was ideal; it was perfect. You could walk around for days without running into anyone if you chose." She stopped and reached in the pocket of her dress for cigarettes. She turned the THANK YOU FOR NOT SMOKING sign backward. "That always makes me want to light up."

Jury laughed and took the lighter from her and lit her cigarette. Lighters had such a satisfying little rasp and snap to them.

"You must have been a smoker once, Superintendent, the way you're looking so covetously at this."

"You're right."

"Well, be proud of yourself, though I doubt virtue is much of a reward for you. I've tried several times to give them up and can't."

"And did you choose not to?"

She was puzzled. "Not to what . . . oh! You mean to bump into people at the Lodge?" She laughed again. "If you mean Kitty Riordin, yes. I'm not terribly fond of Maisie either, if it comes to that." She looked at Jury, as if perplexed by his question. "I expect that's why I'm here and not there."

"You didn't get along with Mrs. Riordin."

"I've always thought her a cold fish. I'm rather surprised that Oliver didn't finally get tired of her." She shrugged. "I expect having her there got to be a habit with him. He's a very good judge of character, Oliver. So was my father. He had presence; so does Oliver. But I don't think it comes from wealth and power—and believe me, Oliver has both in abundance. I think, rather, it comes from honesty. Both of them were—are—fueled by honesty. And perhaps we all inherited something of that. I hope so."

"You did."

Emily Croft smoked and rocked. Peacefully, Jury thought. He doubted she would put up with any constant irritation in her life; she would do something about it. "But if it was a choice between you and Kitty Riordin, he wouldn't choose her, would he?"

"No. But I certainly wasn't going to bother him with all of this. He's ninety-six or seven, you know. He's remarkable. As much as I love the Lodge and always have, I decided I'd give this place a try." She looked around, walls and ceiling, as if assessing it for the first time. "You want to know about Simon, I expect."

"I want to know about everybody."

"Yes, of course. You know, I always got along with Simon. Remember, I was years older than Simon and Marie-France; I was eighteen, nearly Alexandra's age. We were fairly close, Alex and I. I expect that's why she confided in me. Did you know she had another child? I don't know if she told anyone else; perhaps she told Kitty, since she was close to Kitty because she took care of Maisie. But I know she told Oliver she'd decided to take a trip to the Continent." Emily laughed. "I wonder how many trips to the Continent could be blamed on illegitimate babies."

"Not Ralph Herrick's?"

"Oh, no. It was just before Ralph came along; they were married that Christmas and Alexandra got pregnant soon after. I've always thought that her sadness at having to give up that first child made her immediately want another."

"She didn't tell you who the father was of that first baby?"

Emily shook her head.

"Tell me about Ralph Herrick."

She threw back her head and laughed. "Ah, Ralph. Yes, I wondered if anyone was going to get around to him. Simon and Ian idolized him, and no wonder. A handsome flier, a hero. Made to order for hero worship. Well, Simon was, what? Ten or eleven? I suppose it's understandable."

"You didn't admire Ralph Herrick as much as the others?"

"Not even with the help of the Victoria Cross, Superintendent. Admittedly, he *was* daring, though 'audacious' might be a better word. Ralph was an opportunist. I've always been a matter-of-fact person, not very imaginative. As I said, I admired Oliver Tynedale and my father because they're fueled by honesty. Ralph was running on empty." She stubbed out her cigarette in a thin, aluminum ashtray and went on. "I really tried to warn Alex, but she wouldn't pay any attention. Neither would I had the situations been reversed." She sighed. "Poor Alexandra. I don't think in the year they were married he turned up more than half a dozen times. If he had been present more, I think she would have discovered he was bad news. He was too plausible. I'm always suspicious of overly credible people. What surprises me is that Oliver and Dad were taken in. They were such cool characters themselves, I'd think they'd be alert to someone who reminds one of those old 1920s Chicago gangsters, one of those smooth racketeers one sees in old American films." She shrugged. "Ralph would've made a wretched father. He hadn't it in him to be anything but."

"What about Maisie?"

"I'm none too fond of her, obviously, since she engineered my leaving. Helped to, I mean. I think she's completely deluded when it comes to Kitty Riordin."

Jury did not want to put words in her mouth. He sat back. "If you'll excuse the curiosity—and there is a reason for it—by the terms of Mr. Croft's will, was anything settled on Kitty Riordin?"

"No. There were no surprises in his will, Superintendent. The bulk of his money and his property come to my sister and me. There were bequests made to Ian and Maisie and—I thought this rather sweet—to Mrs. MacLeish. I understand it was she who found Simon's body, poor woman. You know she came to cook for him, of course. Oh, yes, and Simon left some money in trust for little Gemma Trimm. That was nice of him, I thought, as he had no reason to do it, especially in light of what I expect Gemma will inherit from Oliver. Simon was just a very generous man. Well, so was my father, so is Oliver. But regarding the will, no, as I said, there were no surprises."

Actually, he did know because Mickey had found out. Jury simply wanted to hear what Emily Croft said about the will. He waited. When there was nothing else, he said, "You go up to London occasionally, I understand."

"I do. It's one of the nice things about having money, Mr. Jury. You don't have to constantly disrupt your life. I didn't have to sell my flat in order to live at this place.

Oh—is this by way of asking me if I was in London the day that Simon was shot?" Her smile was sad.

"Were you?"

"Yes, as a matter of fact, I was. I got there in the early afternoon; I wanted to do my Christmas shopping. I stayed overnight, but I didn't get word about Simon's death until the next evening, after I'd returned here. I was simply too exhausted to turn around and go back. My doctor didn't want me going to London in the first place."

Jury nodded. That was no alibi, at least not so far. "What about your brother's house, Miss Croft? You and your sister have inherited it, I expect."

She turned her head to gaze out of the window to the sea, and said, mournfully, "Yes. But I doubt either of us will live there. When you get old, Superintendent, you don't feel much like turning your life over yet once again."

"You'll sell it?"

She gave him a long look, a head-to-feet look. "Are you considering real estate as a night job?"

Jury burst out laughing. He thought it was the first good laugh he'd had since the case started. "Would I make a good one?"

"Oh, probably not. You just seem to worry about the disposal of flats and houses, as if that's a sideline with you." She laughed herself. "No, we won't sell it. I don't want to lose Simon altogether. As I said, it's the nice thing about money. You can keep things as they were."

"Not really, though."

She gave him another long look, this one full of empathy. "Death is always with us, Mr. Jury. Always." She smiled. "'The fellow in the bright nightgown,' is what W. C. Fields called it. I love that image, but I don't agree with it. There is no bright raiment. Death comes along in the same old clothes, nothing new, nothing different from what we're used to seeing. And we do see him, all the time, and know it, and try not to. I find it comforting that death holds no surprises." She looked at him, kindly. "Hold on to that notion, Superintendent. In your line of work, you'd do well to hold on."

Her expression was inscrutable. He felt the need to counter it, he didn't know why.

"'Death is always with us'—that's a bit of a cliché, isn't it?" He smiled.

"No." She smiled, too.

TWENTY-SEVEN

T he Tynedale maid, Rachael, opened the door to admit Jury and a white cat who'd been looking squarely up at him. Jury told the maid he had an appointment to speak to Oliver Tynedale. He was twenty minutes early, he knew. "I'd also like to see Miss Tynedale, if that's possible." Jury looked down. "I can't answer for the cat." Rachael giggled and led him down the hall. The cat followed.

She was writing at a desk in a bow window and rose to greet him. "Superintendent Jury." Her tone was as level as her eyes, neither welcoming; she softened up a little when she saw the cat. "I see you've brought Snowball. She belongs to Mrs. Riordin; she's a strange animal."

The cat resumed its glaring at Jury. "I know all about strange when it comes to cats, believe me. May I sit down?" He detected a hesitation before Maisie held out her arm to indicate the chair he stood by. The cat saw this and walked back to the door.

"Has something else come up?"

"No." He did not elaborate, wanting her to do the talking.

"You upset Kitty Riordin, you know."

"Police have a way of doing that."

"You wanted to talk about the war and about what happened."

"Isn't that what police do? Talk about what happened?"

Maisie seemed to be looking at everything in the room except him. Now, she seemed to be studying whatever document was on her desk blotter. "'What happened,'" she responded to his question, "was Simon being murdered. Not the war, not the Blue Last." She was trying not to show the extent of her anger.

Jury looked at her speculatively. "How do you know that, Miss Tynedale?"

She looked around the desk as if she couldn't lay her hands on what she wanted. "What happened was an air raid, and the Blue Last took a direct hit. This was fifty-five years ago, right after Christmas, December twenty-ninth. East London was devastated. It was the heaviest raid of the war, some seven hundred bombers. My mother's—Alexandra—and Francis Croft's deaths. That's what *happened*."

Half a century ago and she still felt the emotional devastation? Jury didn't think so. "You have all of those details right. They must have been told to you time and again. I was a tiny kid then and I remember nothing; at least, nothing right. And as for your mother's death being so long ago, you know perfectly well one death can affect another, no matter how far apart in time."

"Not in this case. No."

"You're certainly sure about that. Why?"

She merely shook her head.

She wasn't going to answer, so he said, "You didn't mention the Riordin baby."

"Erin, too, of course." Maisie studied her hands. The disjointed fingers seemed still to shame her a little. "I know those bones were discovered."

"Yes."

"I don't see what they tell you. I don't see how you'd know they were my mother and Erin Riordin."

"Many ways. The sex is fairly easy, certainly in the case of the adult. A child that young, well, perhaps not so easy. One has to guess on the basis of other things. The child's skeleton was so near the adult's and there were apparently no other children in the pub . . ." Jury shrugged. "They can go by the composition of the soil, the vegetation—a number of things besides the condition of the bones themselves. Teeth, for instance. Even in infants; the teeth might not have broken through yet but there's maturation below the gum. In the case of your mother and Erin Riordin, there's the bombing itself. Fragments of shells, that sort of thing. Forensic anthropology is quite amazing. You know what can be done with reconstructing a face from the skull, the bone structure."

She studied her hands, then looked, again, around the desk as if searching for something. She was searching, Jury thought, simply for time.

"I'd like to know more about Mrs. Riordin. You're very fond of her."

"Certainly. I hate clichés, but she's been like a mother to me."

Jury wondered why Maisie didn't see the other side, the corollary to that. "How did she come to be employed?"

Maisie reflected. "Well, she had just come over from Dublin—like any number of Irish girls. She was quite young, just a little younger than my mother, Alexandra. My mother went to an agency and found her. Of course, Kitty hadn't told them she had a baby because she knew the agency wouldn't put her on their list. Kitty just hoped whoever interviewed her would be understanding. She was lucky it was Alexandra, who was, from what I've been told, the most understanding person in the world."

"She was with you for how long before that December raid?" He noted the way in which she referred to "my mother" and "Alexandra," and not "mum" or "mummy." Of course, Maisie hadn't really known her mother, but, still . . .

"A little over a year. I guess it was right after I'd been born."

"Your grandfather liked her?"

"Oh, yes. If it hadn't been for Kitty, I'd be dead."

"And she more or less lived with and for the family after that."

"That's so. I've wondered why she didn't marry again. I'm pretty certain she had opportunities."

"Is the family—are the families—so close it might have been, well, consuming?"

She thought about this. "I think not in a bad way. We're very tightly knit, yes."

"The trouble with that is, you pull one strand loose and the piece unravels."

"That metaphor's a bit strained, isn't it? If one of us falls on his face that doesn't mean all of us will."

"It might. Especially since you don't know which one fell."

Maisie ran her hand through her black hair, and it dropped back in place just as neatly as it had been. He imagined this to be like the disturbance of the past, as if the placid surface of a lake had been raked by wind and rain, and then returned to glassy smoothness.

He wondered if this was why she hadn't married, because of her ties to the past and the families who constituted it, or for some other, perhaps more mundane reason. Certainly it couldn't be because she hadn't the opportunity. She was too attractive, too intelligent and too rich. The money alone would be an inducement.

She had risen and was leaning against the desk, her ankles crossed, her face turned down. "My father was in the RAF; he was decorated. The Victoria Cross."

Jury felt himself once again pulled back into something he did not understand. "So was mine. I mean, in the RAF. He was shot down over Dunkirk."

"I'm sorry."

It rather surprised Jury that she seemed to mean it. "It was a long time ago."

She nodded. "I don't like sounding sorry for myself, but I feel really cheated, not only having lost both my mother and father, but having no memories of them either."

"It would be just another version."

"'Version'?"

"Of what really happened. Of reality, I suppose I mean. How well do we remember anything? How well do we remember yesterday?"

She smiled for the first time. "That's sophistry, now. Or you find consolation in thinking that." She had left the desk and now stood by the bow window behind it.

"Oh, I'm unconsoled," he said. Feeling more tired than he knew he should, he rose and went to the window himself. They stood there. The ground was spongy with morning rain and the beech tree, the one with the wood plank between its thick branches, seemed still to bear the weight of the rain.

Jury watched as the gardener, Mr. Murphy, leaned a hoe or rake against the garden wall and bent over a small plot of some delicate-looking white flower. His hand went to the small of his back as he stood upright. Arthritis, rheumatism, probably. He was too old, Jury thought, to take care of this garden all by himself. He wondered where Gemma Trimm was. Had he been more fanciful (but "fancy" he tried to relegate, like whiskey, to his off hours) he might have supposed his encounter with Gemma was imaginary. She seemed so unrelated to this house, so fairy light.

"What are you thinking? You're smiling."

"Tell me about the little girl."

Maisie looked, just for a second, puzzled. Was it possible that Gemma made such tiny inroads on the family consciousness that they really had to stop to think? How could any child living here—much less one as interesting as Gemma Trimm—make so little impression? Further, a child beloved of the patriarch, the man with the money? Did none of them view the child as a threat?

How much *was* Tynedale worth? Perhaps so much that a million here or there scarcely scratched the surface.

"She's Granddad's charge."

An interesting way of putting it. Just as she said it, Gemma appeared at Mr. Murphy's side. It was as if she had physically to appear to remind them all of her existence.

"She has no family? None?" Jury asked. That had a ring of fatalism.

"None I know of. Granddad notified the authorities and tried to find out where she belonged for a good two or three months."

"Even if he had located her relations, I'm sure he could have made some sort of arrangement to keep her."

Her smile was wan. "I'm sure you're right. But don't sound so righteous about it."

"Do I? Sorry, it's just that money makes so many problems go away. Anyone who says it can't buy happiness obviously doesn't have any."

"My goodness, Superintendent, you never struck me as a cynic."

"But I'm not."

Mr. Murphy had wandered beyond their line of vision while Gemma and her doll waited by the flowerbed. He soon returned pushing a wheelbarrow with what looked like a great deal of effort.

"Poor man," said Maisie. "Angus is too old and too rheumatic for all of this work. But we've tried out several gardeners to help him, and none of them seemed very dedicated to the work and only irritated him to death. The last one, Jenny Gessup, just up and left. Now, I expect I'm going to try again. The agencies send such rubbish. But he really needs someone for the hard work."

"Really?"

TWENTY-EIGHT

"I was wondering," said Oliver Tynedale, lying back among the cushions of his very large bed, "when you were ever going to get around to me."

"I'm here in a—what? A semiofficial capacity?"

"Well, hell, if you don't know, be sure I don't. I don't know what semi gets you these days." He reached around to pummel his cushions. "Me, I'm the whole of the Tynedale Brewery."

"I'm doing this because Michael Haggerty asked me to help. If I tax your patience just toss me out."

Oliver Tynedale lay back. "Throw out a Scotland Yard superintendent? That sounds like fun. I don't mind talking to you and I'm not as weak as I look."

"You don't look weak. But they wouldn't let me talk to you when I was here before."

Oliver waved that aside as nonsense. "Bunch of pansies. Who kept you out? Barkins? Not that nurse because I fired her after twenty-four hours. Last, I hope, in a string of them. I'm stuck in bed right now. Worse luck. Wait a minute, I'll show you—"

Jury was rather surprised with the man's alacrity in getting out of his bed. He was very tall, easily as tall as Jury himself, thin (but hardly emaciated) and didn't walk with a stoop or as if he were in pain. He was into his bathroom and out again, pulling his oxygen equipment on a wheeled, stainless-steel trolley. "Don't you wish you had one of these?"

"Lord, yes. Wish I had those pajamas, too." They were printed all over with Mickey, Goofy, and Tweetie Bird.

Oliver had left the trolley behind Jury and come back to sit on the edge of his bed, whereupon he looked down at his pajamas. "Well, you're not getting these, unless I decide at some point I need to bribe you. I know the commissioner, by the way. Word to the wise and so forth." He swung his legs up and under the covers and sat back again among the cushions with a sigh.

No wonder his son Ian was so easy to deal with. He'd inherited his father's pleasant nature and springy genes.

But then Oliver's expression changed and he looked off toward the wide window which showed nothing but a bleak, oyster-colored sky, a few black branches tapping the glass. He had gone lax.

"Mr. Tynedale?"

Oliver looked around at Jury and said, "What happens is, for a moment you forget. You forget what's happened. Maybe that's the merciful side of life. Simon really was like a son. He really was."

Jury leaned toward him and put his hand on the older man's shoulder. It seemed so natural a gesture that he didn't hesitate. "I'm sorry. I'm honestly sorry."

Oliver sighed and pulled the blanket up toward his chin in the way children do. He looked around the room as if something of Simon Croft had materialized there, sitting in that chair, or standing by that window looking down, or pulling a book from those shelves. Jury wondered if the air would grow so thin with desolation they would all need oxygen.

"If you're going to ask me do I know of anyone who could have done this? No."

Jury thought for a moment. "Simon Croft was writing a book, I understand. Did he talk about it?"

Oliver seemed surprised at this turn in the inquiry.

"The book about the war and the pub being bombed? His father, Francis, you see, owned a pub—"

"The Blue Last. Yes, I know. I know it was bombed in December of 1940. Mickey Haggerty told me."

"Yes. His father was one of Francis's very good friends. I knew Haggerty, too, but not so well. I don't really know his son, except for the one time I tried to help him out, but I have it on good authority he's a very good policeman. I think Simon was really enjoying writing this book— though 'enjoy' sounds like the wrong word. What I mean is, he felt he was doing some good for himself and perhaps for the rest of us by delving into it. Like the expiation of a sin, though there was no sin involved. The working out of something. But why do you ask about the book?"

"Because there was no sign of it. No manuscript, no notes, and whoever did this took Croft's laptop, too, and diskettes, assuming there were some and I can't imagine there not being. From what I've heard of him he was a careful man. He'd back up his work."

"I know there *was* a manuscript. He read me a little of it now and then, to see, I think, if he could jog the old memory." Oliver tapped his temple. "He was hoping I'd remember more and more if he could furnish details— you know, setting a scene, putting in details, just as—" he swept his arm over the room "—describing a chair or a sofa might help you see someone out of the past sitting there."

Which Jury had just done.

"They took the damned thing? The manuscript?"

"As far as we can determine. I wasn't questioning its existence, but whether there was something in it that could injure someone—I'm assuming there is, or was. Mr. Tynedale, think."

Oliver nodded and pursed his lips. "You wouldn't have a fag on you?"

Jury laughed. "I wish I did. I stopped."

"Oh, hell. Didn't you find it was easier to think when you had a smoke?"

"No doubt at all."

Oliver leaned back, heavily. There was a silence. "I'm thinking."

Jury smiled and nodded. Behind him he heard a brief hiss and looked around, wondering if something had happened to the oxygen canister. It was Snowball. How had that cat got in here? The door was shut.

"That's the surliest damned animal I've ever come across," said Oliver. "Always in a bad mood. Always turning up where he isn't wanted, which is bloody everywhere. Belongs to Kitty Riordin; she should keep him on a short lead." He scratched his bald pate. "Ralph Herrick—have you come across his name? He was my daughter Alexandra's husband. Not, unfortunately, for very long. He was a fighter pilot, RAF. Very young for a captain, but good enough to shoot down a slew of Messerschmitt 109s. That was the German fighter, the main one. Ralph was pretty dazzling. Just plowed right into them and—" He made a machine gun of his arms and *rat-tat-tatt*ed as if he were ten years old.

Jury grinned. "Yes, I was told that. Had he something to do with this book?"

"Not directly, at least I think not directly. What Simon seemed especially interested in was that Bletchley Park operation. The cryptanalysts, that lot, you know? The Enigma machines. Alan Turing. Anyway, Ralph was involved in that. It was after he was wounded and mustered out that he went to Bletchley Park. He was, apparently, as good at decoding as he was at blasting German planes out of the sky. I don't know what particular skills he had; he'd read philosophy at Oxford. He wasn't a mathematician. But apparently he could read a monalphabetic code just by looking at it. I think he was part of the group in Bedfordshire, an RAF intercept unit. Or Cheadle. A nice boy, a sort of 'glory boy.' Alexandra was besotted with him." Oliver shook his head, sighing.

"No, there's nothing Simon told me about feeling he

was in danger. But then—" he looked at Jury "—I'm not sure he would have, anyway. You're suggesting it might be someone in the family who killed Simon, and I doubt Simon would have told me if he suspected such a person had a grudge against him. Could be he thought he shouldn't spring any bad news on me. Simon would have wanted me to die in peace, with my illusions intact. He'd have been surprised at how few I have." Tynedale smiled at Jury. "He was a good man. I'll miss him."

His voice had grown thin and distant, rain in the wind. Jury changed the subject to one he thought would be a happier one. "I'd like to know more about Gemma Trimm."

Oliver perked up. "Ah! Now *there's* someone to be reckoned with! I take it you've met her?"

"I have indeed. I agree with you about the reckoning. What I've been wondering is, why doesn't anyone speak of her? I had fairly long talks with your son, with Marie-France Muir and with your granddaughter. No one mentioned her. I came upon Gemma by accident."

Oliver gave Jury a whack on the knee. "Just the way *I* did! By accident! It was about three years ago. I'd had lunch with Simon in the City, a place in Cheapside, then wandered around. I like to do that in that area. Things just spring out at you for some reason. Well, one thing that sprang was this little girl standing in the middle of the pavement, in Bread Street. She was completely alone, except for that doll she still carries everywhere. It didn't have any clothes on, just a naked doll. She wasn't crying. She looked serious and abstracted. I asked her if she'd lost someone—her mother, maybe? She shook her head. I told her we should go together to someplace where they could find out where she lived. I took her hand—she didn't resist at all. It was as if she'd been waiting for someone to come along. It was the strangest thing that ever happened to me. Anyway, I walked her to the Snow Hill station, where the police were very kind, but couldn't get anything out of her except her name. 'Gemma Trimm,' she said, just like that. Just hammered it right out, as if she were hammering tin. But she didn't know where she lived. Well, they got a doctor in and he suggested some sort of aphasia or amnesia. A social worker, naturally, got in on it, but I scotched that idea in a hurry. After I'd failed to find any relations or anyone for Gemma—and I looked for a long time—I made her my ward. And to this day, I have never found out one thing about Gemma."

"There's this belief of hers that someone tried to kill her."

He nodded. "That shooting incident. Police didn't know what to make of that, but it did happen. Gemma was out after dark in the greenhouse with a light switched on and someone took a shot at her. Scared the hell out of me, I can tell you." He closed his eyes. "Someone must be damned jealous, that's all I can figure out. Except Ian. I don't think he forgets she's there. Ian's just got his head a little in the clouds, I think. As for the others, I expect they think I'm going to settle a walloping big chunk of the Tynedale Brewery money on Gemma."

"Are you?"

"Of course. In any event, Mr. Jury, everyone in this family is already rich, really. I can't imagine one of them killing for money. I simply can't."

Jury shook his head. "For some people, there can never be enough money. It's an addiction." He rose. "I really appreciate your talking to me, Mr. Tynedale. I think it's been a big help."

"I hope so." Oliver put out his hand. "I hope you come back, too."

"Thank you. I expect I will."

"But since you're going—"

Jury followed his line of vision.

"—take that goddamned cat with you."

TWENTY-NINE

W hen Jury walked into the Members' Room of Boring's, he found Melrose Plant with whiskey in hand, sunk into his leather armchair as if he'd been dropped there by a crane.

"Good Lord," Jury said, "did you walk back?"

"Heh heh, very funny." Melrose sat up a bit, took a drink of whiskey. "I'm exhausted." The fire near his chair sparked once and then went back to doing little but licking hot coal as if in sympathy with Melrose's state of mind and spirit. "Whiskey?" He held up his glass.

Jury took it.

"I didn't mean *mine.*" Melrose retrieved his own drink, then lifted his hand to beckon Young Higgins.

Jury sat down. "Florence is supposed to energize rather than exhaust." He set some books he'd been carrying on the little drum table by his chair.

"Then Florence never met Marshall Trueblood. If one can level a thing by mere looking, the Brancacci Chapel lies in ruins. Take off your coat. We can dine on my memory of *tagliatelle alle noci.*"

"Wow," said Jury. "Chips on the side?"

Young Higgins had come so slowly he might have been doing the Stations of the Cross.

"Two whiskeys, Higgins, please."

"And a hair shirt," said Jury.

Higgins left without questioning either request.

"He'll probably bring one, too. What's it for? Haven't you done your share of suffering today?" said Melrose.

"It's for you. The martyrdom of St. Jerome can't hold a candle."

Melrose slid down in his chair. "My God, don't tell me you're a Masaccio fan."

"Sunderland, actually." Jury heaped his coat across the armchair nearest the fire and sat down again. "You're planning on staying here at Boring's for a while, then?"

"I'm too tired to go home. Anyway, I have to wait for Trueblood."

"You know, you're not really all that well traveled for one of your money and leisure."

"I've been to Baltimore."

"Are you telling me that you didn't enjoy Florence?"

"Oh, I *enjoyed it.* One *enjoys* Florence, after all."

"One hopes one does."

Melrose continued. "And one can't help but have tender feelings toward a place like San Gimignano and those spires. Or Siena, that looks as if some spellbinder put it to sleep and it's only partially awoken. Everything is narrow there—streets, houses—everything echoes." He sighed. "It was just this race Trueblood had me doing, running from one expert in Renaissance art to another—authorities on Masaccio. Imagine devoting your entire life to just one thing."

"Given one or two of my cases, I probably can."

Melrose lit up a cigarette, blew the smoke away from Jury and tilted his head to look at the books. "What are those?"

Jury looked at them. "Couple of books on gardening."

"Well, I'll be jiggered. Are you retiring to till your own pea patch?"

"Not I."

Melrose picked up the larger book and riffled the

pages. *"A Fool and His Garden."* He smiled. "Now there's a fresh approach to gardening."

"It's the acerbic approach. I thought it suited you better than *Sweet Sue's Sweetpeas,* or *Lazy Days with Lobelias.*"

Melrose took the book and opened it. "I like the little drawings." He turned the book, showing Jury an unhappy gardener trampling the petunia patch.

Young Higgins was back with the drinks, setting a glass at each man's elbow, taking up Melrose's old one.

"Bets are off with you," Melrose said to Jury. "Higgins, what have we to dine on tonight?"

Holding his small silver tray to his chest and coughing gently into one fisted hand, Young Higgins said, "We've steak and kidney pudding and roast pork. Both quite delicious."

"No Portobello mushrooms?"

Young Higgins gave him a blank look. "Sir?"

"Never mind. Thanks, Higgins." When the ancient porter had crept off, Melrose sniggered. "See why I come here? What more could one ask of a place that's never heard of Portobello mushrooms?"

"It hasn't heard of much of anything since the Great War, has it?"

"Let's hope they keep it that way." Melrose returned to *A Fool and His Garden.* "Listen to this." He laughed. "'There is something homicidal about he who would prick and prune and plunder thick hedges into the abysmal shape of swan and urn, a man so dangerous he needs stabbing with a sharp-pointed trowel.' Indeed, I like that." He set aside the larger book and picked up the smaller: *Gardening Primer.*

"That one's more or less a grounding in gardening skills."

"Pretty basic, isn't it?" He turned it so that Jury could see the climbing rose. "Maybe I should try my hand at soil tilling. Enter big turnips in the annual Sidbury garden show. Wait a minute: you said these books were 'for you,' meaning me. Why are these books for me?"

Jury shrugged. "Thought they might be helpful." Jury took a drink of whiskey. God, it was good here; they must keep the stuff in a vault. He ignored Melrose's squint. "So, what did you and Trueblood do?"

"What'd we *do?* I just told you. We ran all over looking up experts. Count me the leading expert in Renaissance art in Long Piddleton—no, correction—in the Long Pidd *area*—which takes in Sidbury, Watermeadows and the Blue Parrot. Everything up to Northampton. Perhaps *even* Northampton!"

"What was the result of all of this expert consultation? Did they agree that the painting could be an authentic—what's his name?"

"Masaccio. No, they didn't. Just a bunch of wall-sitters, all of them."

They sat at Melrose's favorite table, a small one in the middle of the room and next to one of the oak pillars. When they'd polished off their artichokes with lemon, Jury asked, "You were saying you were expert. On what?"

"Haven't you been paying attention? Masaccio and Renaissance art. I want another drink—oh, I'll just order a bottle of wine." He gestured to the sommelier, who came to take Melrose's order.

"So, go on." Jury watched with sad longing as two old geezers lit up cigars. He had never smoked cigars, but that made no difference. After all this time without a smoke he would have lit up a cat. He would have dropped a match on Young Higgins, coming now with their steak and kidney pudding, negotiating his way through space and time, unimpeded, but as if he had chosen to cross Piccadilly Circus blindfolded.

Melrose continued, back on Masaccio, "I have quietly extended my knowledge of the twenties—" The sommelier brought the wine for Melrose's inspection, uncorked it and poured.

The scent of steak and kidney pudding wafting around

them, Jury said, "Prohibition in the States, I seem to re-call. Ah, thanks," he added to Higgins.

"Not the *192*0s in New York, the *142*0s in *Florence.*" To Young Higgins, he said, "Looks marvelous." He went on. "I also know something of Masolino, Donatello and Brunelleschi. The perspectival illusion."

"Sounds like a magic act." Jury cut off a big forkful of steak and kidney pudding.

"It was an invention of Giotto, or at least he discovered it. Perspective can't really be invented, can it? Bru-nelleschi and Donatello extended it to architecture. Per-spective in a painting. You know what that is, of course. The art of making an object appear as three dimensional. It's not an easy thing to do, actually, applying mathemat-ics to space. Like the barrel vaulting in the *Trinity.* The ribs diminish in mathematical foreshortening." Melrose held out his arms and brought the tips of his fingers together, *whoosh whoosh.* "The art of the vanishing point. The cen-tric point, the vanishing point, this is the point at which all lines meet in the distance. Where it all comes together, where the pattern's exposed."

"It sounds like the solution to one of my cases. The only thing is, by the time you get to it, the vanishing point, it's gone."

"Yes, I expect it is."

"There's a paradox for you."

Melrose nodded. "Anyway, Trueblood just stopped listening when the subject veered away from Masaccio and his own painting. I could tell; his eyes filmed over. As are yours, right now."

"They are not. I'm extremely interested."

"Don't be ridiculous. Who'd be interested except someone nutty about Italian art?"

Jury smiled. "Actually, I do know such a nut."

Melrose stopped in the act of eating and looked at Jury for a long moment and then resumed. After con-centrating on his glass of wine, he said, "You're fitting me up."

"I don't know what you're talking about."

"Come on. First it's the gardening stuff, then you've had me going on about fifteenth-century Florentine art—"

"How the devil could I do that? I didn't even know Florentine art was *in* the fifteenth century. I didn't even know it was Florentine, for that matter."

"Very funny." Melrose sighed and put down his fork. "Let me tell you something—" He leaned toward Jury as if he meant to grab his tie. "If you've got some notion I can impersonate some leading expert in the field of Italian Renaissance art, forget it. I know next to nothing." Finished, Melrose sat back and took out his cigarettes, having no mercy on Jury at all.

"What are you talking about? You've just held forth for a half hour on the art of Florence."

"Oh, come on. That was a Diane Demorney half hour. The only difference being that Diane takes a half minute to get across her single nugget of knowledge about anything on earth. What you've just heard me say is *it;* it's all I know." He flicked his temperamental old Zippo, lit his cigarette and dropped the lighter in his pocket.

"You know a lot more than you think you know." Jury watched the thin ribbon of smoke stream upward.

"I know a lot *less* than I think I know. Get Trueblood to do it."

"He's too volatile." Jury sipped his wine. "Take that painting along, then. That would be plausible as a reason for paying a visit. You want Ian Tynedale to look at it."

"Ian Tynedale? Is he your authority?"

"Yes. He's Tynedale's son, and Italian Renaissance art's his particular love."

"Richard, I'd never be able to wrench that painting away from Trueblood."

Jury drank his wine and thought for a moment. "Okay, then we'll go to Plan B."

"Yes, Plan A was such a hit, I can hardly wait. So tell me."

Jury told him.

"No," said Melrose. "I'd look stupid."

"Well, yes, but when has that ever bothered you?"

Melrose blew smoke in his face. Jury laughed.

A meal with Plant was one of the few things that could penetrate the ozone layer that Jury sometimes felt masked his ability to think clearly.

He thought about this as he walked along the Victoria Embankment, delaying his homeward journey. He could get the Northern Line at Charing Cross. Or he could keep on walking. It was a good way to order his thoughts. Sometimes he would pretend that he was seeing the problem for the first time, had come upon it suddenly, by accident, and heard the story anew. Rarely did this approach to a case turn up fresh ideas, but it occasionally did work. He liked that paradox of the vanishing point. You find the answer, but the answer dissolves before—what?

In the case of the Tynedales, fresh ideas weren't surfacing now. He did wonder about Kitty Riordin's husband. Had he been more or less expunged from her consciousness? All of her energies were directed toward Maisie Tynedale . . . or Erin Riordin, whichever she was. That smile of Kitty's, that infernal little smile. He couldn't let go of it.

Even this short distance from the Strand, traffic noise dwindled to near nothing and there was a strange stillness. He had passed behind Charing Cross station and Somerset House, and now stopped to look down at the Thames, dark and unmoving, or at least it gave the illusion of being motionless. Yet the middle of this river moved at an incredible speed, he had heard.

Down below he could see the brief spurt of flame, someone lighting a cigarette. A muffled shout, laughter, disembodied. An undercurrent of voices and sounds curling upward like river mist. He knew Waterloo

Bridge was a favorite haunt of the homeless, even with the Thames police at the bridge only a stone's throw away. But they tolerated it, the police, turned a blind eye as long as everything was cleared out by morning. What a life, thought Jury, to have to take down a shelter every morning and run it up again every night.

Jury stopped and leaned against the railing to look at Waterloo Bridge and the South Bank brimming over with lights. It would not have looked that way to Myra before she jumped. It would not have looked that way to Roy either, as he stood in fog thick as fleece and lit a cigarette (Jury was sure of that), and smiled that bittersweet smile, and thought about Myra in her cold Thames grave . . .

He thought of Alexandra Tynedale, that benighted young mother, and Liza Haggerty, another benighted mother. Liza had been a very, very good detective. She could read in a crime scene signs and portents that baffled others as if they were hieroglyphics carved on cave walls. Probably, she had known before Mickey that something was wrong. But, then, he guessed most wives had such instincts about husbands. You didn't need to be a scene of crimes expert to know that.

Really, he should call her, ask her out for a meal or a drink. It might be a sort of relief to her to talk to somebody on the Job. She was bearing up wonderfully, but what must it cost her to know that she'd be left alone with four kids?

He would do that.

THIRTY

Mickey Haggerty leaned against the filing cabinet overflowing with folders and documents. It was the next morning. They were continuing their discussion of Kitty Riordin, begun in the Liberty Bounds.

"I didn't get any sense of loyalty toward the Tynedales, which, really, I thought she'd make an effort to project," said Jury.

"She's obsessive. The only subject she's interested in is Erin Riordin, a.k.a. Maisie Tynedale." He slammed the drawer he'd been searching through shut and went back to his chair, in which he sat down heavily.

Jury said, "How long did your dad know Francis Croft?"

Mickey tilted back in his swivel chair and ran his hands through his hair. "A long time, long as I can remember." He looked off into space. "Croft was a really good man. So is Oliver Tynedale. Both of them would do anything for a friend, no matter how tough. When I was a kid, Mum was in Scotland once, driving from Ballantrae to Stranraer. She meant to catch the ferry across to Belfast. Just as she was taking the car onto the ferry, she passed out. They got her to a hospital and into the CCU. Dad couldn't be reached, he was out on some case. But Oliver Tynedale's name was in her address book, so police got in touch with him. He sent a car for me right away to take me to the Tynedale Brewery airstrip, dragged his pilot out of bed and flew me to Stranraer. If he hadn't done this, I'd never have seen her alive again. He didn't leave either; he stayed with me. Oliver knew how to talk to kids. I always thought he should've been a teacher or something like that. There's this way he has—a manner, a tone of voice—that calms you down straightaway. It's not a quality you see very often. After she died—" Mickey looked down, scraped at his tie. To avoid looking across at Jury. When Mickey finally did, tears stood in his eyes.

"I can understand your not wanting Kitty Riordin getting away with this, if Tynedale is a man like that," said Jury. "What else did you find out about her?"

Mickey pulled the top folder from the pile on his desk, slapped back the cover. "Not much, and not easily. I guess fifty years can do that to a case." He managed a grin. "Katherine—always been known as Kitty—Shea. When she was eighteen she married Aiden Riordin. He had trouble getting work in Ireland—where it was worse than the North—and came here. I get the impression he was to send for her, but then the war happened. Aiden Riordin got caught up—this part's interesting—in the British Union of Fascists."

"The Blackshirts."

"That's right. Pretty hard to take them seriously."

"Hmm. I don't think I'd rush to judgment there. East London got pretty worked up when Mosley was released. But go on."

"There's not a lot about Kitty Riordin to be going on with. She left Ireland, came here, but not, I think, to find her husband. I think she hoped opportunity was more likely to come her way here than in Killarney. It did."

"It did indeed." Jury paused.

Disturbed, Mickey rose, tossed down the pencil he'd been fiddling with. "Croft's murder was an inside job meant to look like an outside job, some unknown intruder. By 'inside' I mean either a family member or someone else with access—staff, acquaintances. I mean that it wasn't some stranger and the motive wasn't robbery." Mickey tented his hands, spoke over the tops. "I told you that: Simon Croft thought someone wanted him dead."

"You did. 'Out to get him' was what you said. Why?"

"He didn't know, did he? He wanted me around as some sort of protection."

"He didn't even hazard a guess?"

"I'm sorry to say I didn't pay a hell of a lot of attention. I honestly couldn't take it seriously. Look: Croft was sixty-three. He had too much money and too much leisure. Apart from this book he was writing, he had little to do."

"Yet he was a broker, a very good one, you told me. He probably still had clients. I would imagine that kept him pretty busy. This book he was writing on the war. He used to read bits of it to Oliver Tynedale."

Mickey beat a short tattoo with two pencils on the edge of his desk. "He talked about it once or twice. British Fascism was some of it. Sir Oswald Mosley—how did he get to be a sir?—and his followers. Did you know that in 1940 police rounded up German nationals—all the men between sixteen and sixty? As if no female and no man over sixty could possibly be a spy?" Mickey laughed.

"She dismissed Aiden as a fool."

"Yeah, well, our Kitty certainly wouldn't've shot Croft to preserve the honor of the Riordin clan. Who would care if Aiden Riordin was goose-stepping all over Hyde Park?" Mickey winced.

"Anything wrong? Do you need something?" Jury was already out of his chair.

Mickey waved a shaky finger in the direction of the water cooler by the door. "Cup o' that." He took a vial of pills out of his desk drawer, shook a couple into his hand.

Jury handed him the paper cup. "I wish they'd fill the damned things with whiskey." He sat down again as Mickey washed down the pills. Jury wanted to ask him about the pain, but thought such a question would be tasteless or morbid, much like the gathering of people around a smashed car. So he kept the question back.

Mickey tossed the pills back in the drawer, slammed it shut, letting off a mild amount of steam in the act. He went back to the subject of the manuscript. "But I agree: if somebody went to the trouble of taking the PC, the diskettes, the hard copy—there's something in it someone doesn't want broadcast."

Mickey had risen again to go to the window. Jury wondered if the getting up and down helped to relieve the pain. The phone rang and he scooped up the receiver. "Haggerty. Yeah . . . Then do it." He hung up. "No, I guess not everybody would say 'publish and be damned.'" Mickey frowned.

"There's someone you haven't paid much attention to."

"Yeah? Who?"

"Ralph Herrick. Alexandra's husband." Jury sat forward. "Simon could have brought something up in his book connected to him, Herrick. I don't mean necessarily about him, just something going on. Oliver Tynedale mentioned Bletchley Park. The decoding that was done there. Very hush-hush stuff."

"Hmm. I remember Herrick was RAF. Decorated, too. Quite the hero. The Victoria Cross."

Jury nodded. "Right. He also was quite brilliant in the reading of codes. He could take one look at a code and see the pattern immediately."

"Christ. Most of the time I can't even look at the alphabet and see a pattern. Now, I do seem to recall that Herrick was one of the Bletchley Park people."

Jury nodded, grew thoughtful. "I wish to hell I could see that manuscript."

Mickey ran his hand down over his face and said,

tiredly, "Maybe this whole case is being looked at wrong. Everything's there, and the answer with it, but our perspective's just wrong."

"Like a painting." Jury smiled. "A friend of mine just got back from Florence. He was talking about fifteenth-century Florentine art. An architect named Brunelleschi. 'Perspective illusion' was the quality that was revolutionary."

"Don't know the chap. I should spend more time at the Tate."

Jury looked at Mickey for a moment and then looked away. "Ian Tynedale is passionate about the art of the Renaissance."

"Yeah, I know." Mickey squeaked back in his swivel chair. "It's one reason I know the motive for this murder wasn't robbery. What thief would have left the paintings on the walls? Especially the one near the desk? According to Tynedale, who got it for him, it's worth a cool quarter of a million."

Jury smiled and got up. "Maybe whoever did it wasn't much of a critic."

THIRTY-ONE

Angus Murphy looked up, suspicious. "Ya got t' much education fer this job, is wha' I think." The gardener wiped his face with a bleached blue handkerchief that made his blue eyes look even more faded. "Why, there I'd go breakin' ya in and off ya'd go the minute ya saw somthin' ya'd be more ac-clim-ated to."

Angus Murphy was short, wiry, ageless and (Melrose thought) loved impressive words. He had been dropping them in whenever he could with no real care for aptness. His slate blue eyes seemed to be permanently narrowed, as if the eyelids had been loosely stitched.

"—an' ya'd be off like a bird, off like greased lightning, off like—" He paused.

"—a bat out of hell?" Melrose prompted. Angus Murphy was a man who liked his metaphor, no matter how worn. "But actually, Mr. Murphy, it would be very unlikely that would happen, as I've reached some *détente*—" (Melrose spoke this carefully) "—between my brain's needs and my body's. I don't deny I'm well educated. But I've reached this point, you see, where the only thing that will satisfy me is getting down on my knees and grubbing around in the soil."

The eyes narrowed even more. "What was that ya said? 'Day-somethin'?"

"Détente?" Melrose was pleased he'd been right about the impressive words.

"That's it. What's that mean, then?"

"It means things at war with one another have reached some point of relaxation."

"Ah!" said Murphy, nodding sagely, and then working it around in his mouth for a moment.

They were standing by an ornamental pond in the rear garden of Tynedale Lodge, following Melrose's interview with the butler, Mr. Barkins. Melrose found it hard to keep from dropping the "mister" and calling him "Barkins." He had had the foresight to bring a flat cap so that he could turn it around in his hands, occasionally squashing it, to make himself appear humble. He thought it was pretty rum that this oaf of a Barkins should have the privilege of hiring and firing staff. But Barkins clearly loved it, loved exerting what small measure of power he had in the household. As far as the new gardener, Ambrose Plant, was concerned, Barkins only thought he had the power. Oliver Tynedale was the one who had it after Jury had called him to explain what he wanted.

In the big, slightly chilly kitchen, Melrose had finally been invited to sit down and have a cup of coffee—elevenses, a brief respite from toil Melrose knew about only through the incessant visits of Agatha to Ardry End. Otherwise, he couldn't tell a respite of toil from a tenner, nor, really, could his "staff," a generalization he hesitated to use since, except for Martha, his cook, the only others were his butler, Ruthven, and his grounds-keeper, Mr. Momaday. Ruthven did indeed work, but he didn't toil. He carried out his duties as smoothly as an Olympic skater. On the other hand, Momaday was completely hopeless, walking all over the land with a shotgun broken over his arm, looking for something to shoot.

Melrose had thought about all of this in preparation for his morning interview with Ian Tynedale, which he thought was far more congenial than the one with

Barkins. He'd be the first to admit he was lazy, but he didn't care. Right now he was having his coffee at the long table where he supposed meals were taken by staff and he'd be one of them.

Sitting at the bottom of the table as Barkins was grilling the candidate for undergardener was a beautiful child with midnight black hair and skin so translucent one could almost see through it. She was eating a piece of bread and butter and keeping a close watch on Melrose. He wondered if this was the little girl named Gemma Trimm. No one had bothered telling him.

Barkins wondered how it was that if Mr. Plant had had as much experience as he'd said, he'd never been head gardener. Because, Mr. Plant had responded, he didn't like administrative work. Barkins thought that an odd answer, but went to the phone and called the numbers given him, the recommendations Melrose had supplied. After a few minutes he was back, saying both of the previous employers had been most satisfied with his work. They were, of course, Marshall Trueblood and Diane Demorney.

"They were indeed effusive, Mr. Plant."

Then Barkins asked him the usual boring questions as to why Mr. Plant had left these two satisfied employers. Mr. Plant had wanted to move to London, et cetera, et cetera.

The little girl had finished sizing him up (reaching her conclusions far faster than the butler) and had gathered up her strange doll and gone outside.

Barkins thought he would do with having a trial run for a week or two. Melrose had reacted with proper humility.

Which is why he was standing by the pond, at either end of which he had pointed out the gardener's still-thriving hakonechloa and Rubrum grasses, the Rubrum's sprays of delicate flowers still going strong in

December. Then there was that New Zealand grass with its drooping flowerheads at the far end, over there. Melrose made much of these grasses, they being about the only thing he knew. "Hakonechloa" he had learned—as he had a few other gardening nuggets of wisdom—from Diane Demorney.

"Point out," Diane had told him in the Jack and Hammer, "that hakonechloa is a must-have for every snob around who knows nothing at all about gardening—I certainly don't, nor do I want to—point out that the name is simply on everybody's lips."

"But . . . what is it?"

"Some sort of grassy thing."

"Well, but what does it look like?"

"Melrose, don't be simple. How should I know? If it's a grass, I expect it's green. Tallish." Her hand measured off air. "Look: when you don't know a damned thing about a subject, you rattle off one or two esoteric bits that hardly anyone knows—"

"Well, hakonechloa won't do, then. You said it was on everybody's lips."

"But people don't *know* it's on everybody's lips, do they? One or two bits and then learn the Latin—I think it's Latin—names for this or that and toss them in occasionally."

"You mean even if I've got the names wrong?"

Diane looked over her shoulder to the bar where Dick Scroggs stood reading the paper. She gave him the queen's wave, meaning two more drinks. To Melrose she said, "I expect it *will* be wrong, but who cares, as long as it's Latin."

"But a gardener might know."

Diane sighed deeply. "Even if he does, you just finesse whatever you're looking at for something that doesn't grow around there—a palm tree or something."

"Diane, how could I mistake a plant or a flower for a palm tree?"

"Then say something that grows around a palm

tree—at the base of it. He won't know what you're talking about."

"That'll make two of us." But Melrose had to admit he was enamored of the Demorney grasp of one-up-manship. "Okay—" He read from one of the three-by-five cards on which he was taking notes.

("*Notes!* Lord," Diane had said with a shiver.)

At first, Melrose had done what he thought to be the sensible thing, and gone to the little library, where he'd pulled down a book, slogged through it for a while and realized facts without color, without conversation, without nuance, were boring and hard to absorb. He had only two days before he returned to London, and knew what he needed was a crash course. He needed the gestalt of gardening—watching someone do it, hearing someone speak of it. To this end he had gone in search of Alice Broadstairs, who, along with Lavinia Vine, competed at the annual Sidbury Flower Show. The trouble with this approach, Melrose should have known, was that Miss Broadstairs was *such* a gardening enthusiast, she rattled on and on about her roses and orchids, covering entirely too much ground (literal and metaphoric), so that Melrose was bombarded by facts he couldn't assimilate, and, more important, that would probably do him no good. He took notes, though, for among all of this fall of blossom was the odd bit that would help: a rose called Midsummer Beauty that was still brilliant in December; the Mahonia japonica, that he could remember because it rhymed; and Diane's hakonechloa. He came, in other words, to realize that knowledge was style: it's not what you know, it's how you know it. Diane was the person for this, and she would be having lunch (the two olives) at the Jack and Hammer.

She had said, "Do something with mistletoe. Christmas is just around the corner, unfortunately." Diane could only make it through the holiday season with a breakfast of eggnog.

"'Do something'? I'm not *decorating* the garden."

"I mean, look up one or two kinds of mistletoe and trot them out if you're looking at a bush."

"Doesn't mistletoe grow on trees?"

Diane tapped her stirrer with its marinated olive gently on the rim of her glass. "I have no idea. Find out what kind, then."

Melrose made a note on his card. "What if this house doesn't have the kind mistletoe grows on?"

Diane rolled her eyes and ate her olive, after which she said, "Then you ask him *why* this kind of tree isn't in the garden." Languidly, she fixed a cigarette into her black holder. "You're usually inventive. One must be able to turn things to one's advantage. How was Florence?"

"Magnificent, absolutely magnificent." Somehow, this galloping trip that had irritated him to death (except, of course, at the end) had turned in his mind to something gorgeous and fragile. "My favorite place was San Gimignano." Not only did Melrose pronounce this correctly, but he managed to sound like a native when he blended that second "i" with the "y." He had practiced a lot.

"Say that again."

"San *Gim-i'yan-o.*"

"How fascinating. I love Italian names. 'San Gimignano.' Hmm."

It annoyed Melrose that she pronounced it exactly right without any practice at all. For some reason, Diane was good at things like that.

"San Gimignano (he liked saying it) is about twenty miles outside of Florence. It's like suddenly finding yourself back in the Middle Ages. The town's famous for its towers. Once there were hundreds of them, so many you could walk across town on the rooftops."

"I can hardly walk across town on the pavements."

"I imagine this 'tower' business was a kind of ego thing. Oh, the towers permitted fortification—you know, pouring boiling oil down on your enemy—but I bet the whole idea got out of hand and everyone tried building a tower taller than his neighbor's, so they just kept building taller towers."

Diane tapped her cigarette free of ash. "Sounds like Las Vegas. Now, tossing things like that name into conversation, well, it would stop everyone but the mayor of San Gimignano dead in his tracks."

"Meaning?"

"Meaning people don't give much of a damn what you say. It's the way you say it. Knowledge is presentation."

Exactly. Melrose smiled.

Angus Murphy's voice drew him back from the Jack and Hammer, saying, "Ya do seem t' know y'r grasses, ah'll say that. Come wi' me."

Melrose followed him to a bed of largish, flat-headed white perennials. "Achillea, this lot is. Hardy flower." He looked even more narrowly at Melrose. "But you must know that, ah expect."

He could not believe his luck! He was first out of the gate on this one. He knew only this species because he liked its common name. "This white one has always interested me: *ptarmica,* sneezewort, I believe it's called."

"That's it, aye. Surprised you'd know that one—"

(So was Melrose.)

"—not got much to recommend it."

"Now I'm rather partial to the *A. millefolium Heidi* (only because it was described as 'fading beautifully'), but I don't seem to see any in your garden . . ."

Murphy grunted. "Can't get everything in, can ah? What'd ya do about fertilizing this lot?" They had moved to another bed of purple flowers Melrose couldn't identify for the life of him. "Ya can see they've got pretty straggly."

Melrose sighed and shook his head. "Yes, it's quite sad when an entire bed falls into a state of desuetude."

Murphy blinked. "State o' wha'?"

"Desuetude. But, look, you can't be everywhere, Mr. Murphy!" Melrose rang out cheerfully while flinging his arm out toward the sneezewort.

"Now, how d' ya spell that?"

"Spell what?"

"That word begins with 'des.'"

"Oh. 'Desuetude'?"

Murphy was handing him a pencil stub and an empty seed packet. "Write it down there."

Melrose managed to crowd the word onto the border. Then, for good measure, wrote *détente* on the other narrow border. The picture on the packet displayed a bright grouping of Michaelmas daisies. He handed the packet and pencil back with a smile. "You know, with Christmas coming in just a few days, I wonder you don't have some mistletoe about."

Murphy was practicing *desuetude* and not attending. Finally, he put away the seed packet and led Melrose into the greenhouse. "Got a rose ah'm foolin' with ah want ya t' see."

The world of roses had managed to bar its doors against Melrose. He had not attempted to learn the hundreds of different kinds; he felt it could take a lifetime for any serious researcher to master the subject. Roses. Between Alice Broadstairs and Lavinia Vine, he had heard all he ever wanted to, as they were always cross-breeding, inbreeding, mutating to come up with a new species and beat each other out of the first prize at the Sidbury Flower Show. Roses ignited them.

"This here 'un. What d'ya think o' this?"

The rose in question was an exquisite golden, peachy color. "Breathtaking," said Melrose. It was, too. He just didn't know its name.

"Nearly took the blue ribbon at the Chelsea Flower Show, this did."

"What I'd like to see is the rose that beat it."

Murphy chortled. "Tha's a good'un. Now, what won,

d' ya guess? Come on, now," he added when he saw Melrose hesitate.

Melrose simpered a bit as he said, "Probably one of those revisionist roses that Gertrude Jekyll and that lot were always coming up with. The Sissinghurst syndrome. You remember that, don't you?"

It was clear Murphy not only didn't remember, far more important, he didn't know how to say it. His eyelids were stitched even closer as his fingers went to his pocket to draw out his stub of pencil and the seed packet. Thinking even harder, he drew out two. Melrose took them as Murphy said, "Both o' them words."

"'Revisionist'? 'Syndrome'?"

Murphy flicked his finger at the packets, a nod that told Melrose to get on with it.

Then, being thoroughly satisfied that Melrose had the collective wisdom of ten gardeners, Murphy went in to his lunch, Melrose declining the invitation in favor of a walk around the garden where he might pick up clues from the furrowed rows and seed packets that would give him future ammunition if he was grilled again.

THIRTY-TWO

Hunkered down over a flowerbed, where a seed packet picturing a bouquet of bluebells was stuck to a marker, Melrose heard a voice:

"Those aren't bluebells in there."

Quickly, he turned. It was the little girl who'd been sitting at the kitchen table. Here she was sitting on a board that had been squeezed between the sturdy branches of a beech tree. "No? This seed packet says bluebell."

"I changed the seed packet with those ones." She pointed toward another flowerbed.

"Why did you do that?"

Moving her doll (dressed in an impossibly long frock) to her other side, she said, "Because I'd rather have bluebells in there than the other stuff. Benny switched the packets for me."

"Oh. I thought bluebells were wildflowers, anyway."

She considered that. "Not around here, they aren't."

This all seemed perfectly logical. "And who is this garden marauder, Benny?"

"My friend. He makes deliveries for Mr. Gyp, who's really nasty. I'm not eating meat anymore. Benny brings books, too, from the Moonraker. Mr. Tynedale likes me to read books to him. I mean I read *parts* of books. Little bits. Right now we're reading a book about a man named Gatsby. I really like the big eye. Do you want to sit down? I'll move Richard."

Melrose had always considered he had a quick mind, but he was having trouble processing all of this information. Yet she appeared to think it was all in a day's talk. "Thank you, I think I probably need to sit down." When he'd hoisted himself up beside her—there was just barely room if she held the doll on her lap—he decided to take her information from the top. "If you can read *The Great Gatsby*, you must be an excellent reader."

The eyes she turned on him were killingly honest. "Parts, I said. Little bits."

"Well, the little bit about the eye. I don't remember that."

"It was on a sign of a doctor who makes eyeglasses. Mr. Tynedale says it's like the eye of God. But I don't think so." She leaned backward into empty air, so that her black hair nearly touched the tree roots. She went on, from her almost-upside-down position: "It's probably Cyclops."

Melrose was even more surprised. "Are you referring to *The Odyssey*?"

"It's by Homer. I don't know his last name. It's a really good story."

"It is indeed. Did you read it in translation or just stick to the original Greek?"

When she did not bother answering, Melrose said, "Mr. Tynedale must be an excellent man if he has you doing all this reading of books that even adults don't often tackle."

"He is. He's very excellent. You can help baptize him."

Melrose had a startled moment before he realized she was now speaking of her doll and not the excellent Mr. Tynedale. Then, of course, he still had to stumble over the "him." "Him?" He regarded the doll. "I assumed your doll was a 'her.'"

"No, he's not. See?" She pulled back the long gown and pointed toward the torso, the joined legs and undisclosed sex. "It's smooth, see. Nothing's there."

"You don't happen to know the Crippses, do you?"

"No."

He was surprised at her rather sophisticated acceptance of this sexual ambiguity. "Well, but it could be a girl, couldn't it? On the evidence we've got?"

"It *could* be a girl, but I don't want him to be. His name's Richard. When I thought he was a girl I was going to name her Rhonda. I was on the *R*s. I was waiting for Benny to come, but you'd do just as good."

So attendance at the baptism was not an honor conferred but a need for assistance. "Were you going to do it now?"

"We might as well since we're not doing anything else."

"Excuse me, *you* might not be, but I have that load of dirt—" he pointed to a wheelbarrow full and waiting "—to take around to the bedding area out front. I'm your new undergardener."

She scratched her ear and looked at him, not entirely unlike the way Angus Murphy had looked at him. It was that sizing him up, waiting to catch him out look. He gave in. "Okay."

"Come on!" She shoved herself off the board, and so did he, glad to leave it. Off she ran between the hedge and the sneezewort to the pond where Melrose and Angus Murphy had stood and considered grasses. She turned and ran backward with a shout to him to hurry.

Before the pond with its sinister goldfish, she jumped from one foot to another as if she had to pee. When he arrived by her side, she thrust the doll (in its too-much-handled frock) toward Melrose.

"Me? Just a moment, why are you giving this job to me?"

"You look more like a vicar than me and I don't want to get wet."

"What are you talking about? Why should anyone get wet?" He held the doll away from him.

"Because you have to be in there to dunk him." She nodded toward the pond.

"I'm not going in that water!" He did not add, with those goldfish!

"But someone has to!"

"All you need to do is dip your fingers in the pond and make a cross on his forehead. I've been to a lot of baptisms (he had been to none) and that's how it's done."

"No it isn't. I mean, it isn't always. Benny told me, and so did the vicar, there were people who went into the water up to their chins. The vicar would shove their heads all the way in. I guess they had to hold their breath. Benny says it doesn't take unless you're all the way in."

Melrose snorted. "Well, if this Benny is such an authority I'd think you'd rather wait for him. Besides he knows Richard—" *Richard?* "—a lot better than I do."

He knew that hands-on-hips posture. Every child he'd ever had any dealings with resorted to it. Resolute. Determined. Implacable. A swell recommendation if you were running for a seat in Commons, but dire when it came to someone's being baptized.

"I've been mistaken for a lot of things in my life, but never for a vicar" was his weak rejoinder to the hands-on-hips.

"You're only wasting time arguing."

Melrose raised the gown up and inspected the back. Its head and jointed limbs were hard plastic, its torso firmly stuffed and covered with a smooth, flesh-colored fabric, seamed down the back. A few threads were loosening, and a bit of stuffing was about to work its way out. Smugly, he said, "You know what will happen to this doll if you dunk him all the way into the pond?"

Her hands came away from her hips and she looked unsure. "Nothing will. He'll just be wet."

"Not only wet but *waterlogged*," he said, cunningly. "You see this little seam here? Water will get in and Richard will squish for the rest of his life." He shook the doll. "Or maybe even come apart."

Truly uncertain now, she shook her head. "No, he won't."

Melrose gave a great sigh and a shrug and said, "Okay, if you're so sure—" He removed one shoe and started on the other preparatory (it looked like) to his dive into the pond.

"No, wait!" She grabbed the doll back and chewed her lip. "I'll have to think about it."

"And I have to take that load of dirt to the bedding-out area."

"I'll go with you."

She seemed relieved not to have to debate the baptism any longer.

"All right." Melrose could not recall if he had ever had a wheelbarrow in his hands. He took hold of the handles and shoved it along while she trod by his side, looking up into his face to see whatever it was she wanted to see. He didn't know. Trundling the barrow between the white columns and the line of cedars, he said, "What does he want all of this dirt for?"

"It's fertilizer, not dirt."

Was he to be saddled with a child who would contest his every word? (Didn't they all?) "'It's fertilizer, not dirt,'" he mimed in a high, squeaky voice. "What's the difference, then?"

"It says on the bag: 'fertilizer.'"

"Well, you don't expect them to put 'dirt' on it, do you?"

For a moment she was skeptical. On both sides of the large bedding area in front were white stone benches. She lay down on one as if the stone were a bed. She set Richard on her chest and moved his arms back and forth. "He could be a detective."

Melrose had stopped the barrow by the edge of the

bed and was reaching for the shovel. "Detective? Who are you talking about?"

"Richard. I'm only saying he *could* be. We're not sure."

Melrose dug in with the shovel. "Well, let me know when you are."

As he shoveled and she watched, a silence descended. He doubted it had anything to do with their mutual respect for work. Around the far corner of the house, a white cat ran and after it a small dog, a terrier of some sort, with a white coat that looked springy, like lamb's wool.

"Sparky!" Gemma called, and the dog left off chasing the cat and came to sit beside the flowerbed.

Melrose raised himself up, feeling the small of his back. Arthritis was no doubt setting in. He looked down at the dog who slapped his tail on the ground. "'What fresh hell is this'?"

"It's Benny's dog, Sparky." The dog bounded over to her and did some more tail pumping. She ruffed up his neck and made some of those irritating childish sounds one makes over babies.

"And where's Benny, then? I mean to enlist him for the baptism immediately."

"Sometimes Sparky comes by himself. He's really smart. Benny says he goes out at night and walks all around till dawn. He remembers everything."

"If he's that smart, let *him* do the baptizing."

Sparky trotted off; the cat had disappeared down the drive to a little cottage. Gemma said, "See down there?" She was pointing to that cottage inside the gates. "That's where Mrs. Riordin lives. She's lived there for years. I can get into it. She always goes into the shops on Wednesdays. Then I go in. You can, too, if you want to look."

Had Jury deputized this child? "Why on earth would I want to do that?" When she shrugged, he went on. "And what are you doing it for? They'll have you up on a B and E one of these days."

"What's a B and E?"

"The only police jargon I know. It means 'breaking and entering.' In case you didn't know, it's illegal." *Plop* went another shovelful of fertilizer onto the bed. He hoped he was doing it right.

"If I take anything I only keep it a little while and then I always put it back," Gemma informed him, from her prone position, the B&E jungle holding no terrors for her.

Melrose stabbed the tip of the shovel into the soft earth. "You shouldn't be *taking* it in the first place." He saw her draw something out of the pocket of her plaid skirt.

"Here's an earring." She held it out for him to see.

It was a nondescript gold earring, certainly not worth stealing. "Did you just take one?"

She nodded. "I don't want to wear it. I just like holding something in my hand that belongs to somebody else. I always put things back in case you think I'm a robber." This was pointed out in a fairly indignant tone. "You can go inside if you want. We can get inside; there's a window round back that doesn't shut properly."

"Don't pretend you're going to rope me into your life of crime." He stopped his work to look down toward the cottage. "Which window?"

THIRTY-THREE

Having made a note of the window but taken a raincheck on the B&E, Melrose pushed the roots of another shrub in the ground as if he were burying a time capsule. He'd been on his knees for forty-five minutes now, probably more than he had during his entire childhood of churchgoing. If the Buddha had spent a half hour planting shrubs, he might not have been all that enamored of the full lotus position. God, the back! The recalcitrant back! He was tamping down earth when he was treated to the sight of a pair of paws and some shaggy breathing.

Melrose sighed. He really wasn't in the mood for that boulevardier Sparky and his wanderings, but here he was, probably eager to debate planting in December. "I agree," said Melrose, taking out his cigarettes and old Zippo. "But if Murphy says do it, I do it." The Zippo rasped but did not fire. "You wouldn't happen to have a light on you, would you?"

Sparky was standing there flinging his stubby tail from side to side. Did he want Melrose to go someplace? He was making those small, backing up movements that, had he been a puma, would have been worrying.

Melrose deposited his unlit cigarette behind his ear and sat back on the cold ground. "That does it for now.

Where's your companion boy?" He heard a hiss, looked behind him and saw the thug-cat Snowball, its face looking as if it were mashed up against a pane of glass. He was glooming away, sitting between Sparky and Snowball and wondering what his attraction was to these animals when he heard his name called.

"Mr. Plant!"

When he couldn't immediately make out the direction from which it had come, the voice called "Ambrose!" as if being staff, he could only recognize his given name. He turned and saw Ian Tynedale standing in the open doorway that led to the patio. He motioned Melrose toward him. "I've something I want to show you."

"Certainly, sir." Melrose would have tugged at his forelock, except he couldn't find it.

He followed Tynedale into the library, the same place where Ian had interviewed him. The interview had quickly veered off into art and Melrose had disclosed he was a great fan of the Italian Renaissance. Melrose had balked at doing this, but Jury had thought it a good idea, even if a little out of character for a gardener.

"Just tell him your mum was Italian. An Italian countess or something."

"You sound like Diane Demorney."

How was it, Melrose wondered, the Tynedales managed to hold on to their looks? Genes, most likely. Old age sank into most people over sixty like Dracula's teeth. He only hoped that when he got to the geriatric stage he'd look half as good as Ian Tynedale. And as far as he could see, the Tynedales had all sorts of bad habits—drinking, smoking, eating rich food (an impression formed seeing the *crème brûleé* the cook had prepared)—that made no inroad on them. How refreshing. Tynedale drew a cigar out of a black humidor and sat back in his leather swivel chair. Melrose wondered: Did Ian Tynedale suspect he wasn't who he said he was? No, Melrose doubted he suspected anything. All he wanted was to have someone as an audience for his acquisitions. It was the art enthusiast in him; he'd have had Snowball and Sparky in here if they'd shown the least inclination toward Italian Renaissance art.

That was what Ian was now talking about and Melrose said, "Isn't that redundant, sir?"

Ian raised his eyebrows. "How so?"

"Italian Renaissance art. The Italians *owned* the Renaissance, didn't they?" Melrose thought maybe all of this was a bit thick, coming from an undergardener, even an overeducated one. He decided he was a show-off and told himself to stop it. "What I mean is, I, uh, read that somewhere."

Ian seemed pleased that here was a person who read. "Good point! Of course, you're right. Sit down, sit down, man." He waved Melrose into the chair opposite.

Melrose sat. Why wasn't Tynedale suspicious? Probably because he wanted only to have someone to talk to about Florentine art and Florence. *I'm your man!* thought Melrose.

Ian pulled a heavy paper out from between two thin boards and held it up for Melrose to look at. "What do you think?" Ian tapped the paper.

It wasn't a painting; it was a sketch. Melrose chewed his lip. It looked like a study of perspective, two flat surfaces, one probably a mirror, held opposite one another, lines intersecting. Melrose cast his mind back to di Bada talking about Brunelleschi. It could have been done by a number of artists but Melrose thought Brunelleschi a safe bet since the drawing wasn't an original, anyway. "Well . . . I'd say Brunelleschi. Uh . . . maybe."

"I think this is Giotto. He rediscovered perspective, didn't he? The Greeks would have known about it. Indeed, Plato called perspective 'deceit.'"

"Plato called everything deceit."

Ian laughed. "It's plain to see you haven't always been a gardener."

"Undergardener," Melrose corrected him. "But this sketch, you're not saying it's an original."

"Oh, don't I *wish*!" Ian laughed again and pulled out another sketch, this one of the Duomo. "I don't remember how I came by this one. The dome of Santa Maria Novella. I have no idea who the artist is. But it's quite beautiful."

"Well, if that sketch was by Brunelleschi, it'd be worth the contents of the London silver vaults."

His eyes still on the paper, Ian rubbed the back of his neck. "Of course, it isn't about money."

A sentiment generally favored by the rich, Melrose had found. While Ian brooded over this picture, Melrose took the opportunity of looking around the walls on which were hung priceless paintings. The collection reminded him of what Jury had said about Simon Croft's collection. He wished he could steer the conversation around to that.

He didn't have to.

Leaning back in his chair and holding the drawing up at arm's length, Ian said, "A very good friend of mine died a week ago. He'd have appreciated this." He sighed and placed the paper back between the protective boards. "He was murdered."

"How awful. How did it happen?"

"Someone broke into the house—a place on the Thames—"

Melrose interrupted. "But that was in all the papers. His name was—" Melrose paused, in an effort of remembrance.

"Simon Croft. Our families were very close." Ian picked up the other drawing, the one of the Duomo. "A marvel of engineering. I wish I'd been there."

"Up on the scaffolding drinking watered wine?"

Ian laughed. "No. Down on the piazza, drinking Tynedale beer." He picked up the neglected cigar. "Imagine the company we'd have: Brunelleschi, Leonardo, Masaccio . . ." He shook his head slowly in wonder.

"You know, I read somewhere that Masaccio was so worried someone might steal his work, he wouldn't let anyone in his rooms except his grocer."

Ian laughed. "Sounds like Simon."

"Does it?"

Ian seemed contrite at having mentioned Simon's name in this facetious context. He changed the subject. "How are you getting on with Murphy?"

"Fine."

Ian smiled. "He's an irascible fellow. The last person quit without notice. Just stopped coming. Well, she was young. One makes allowances. Maybe she was scared off by the shooting incident. I expect Murphy told you."

"Told me what?"

"Back in October, someone fired into the greenhouse. At first the Southwark police put it down to another in a rash of attempted robberies around Southwark and Greenwich. Lewisham, too, I seem to recall."

"Was anything stolen here?"

"No, thank God." Ian glanced around the walls.

Melrose tried not to seem any more inquisitive than any curious person would have been. "You said, 'at first.' What did the police finally put it down to?"

"Kids running around with a gun. Will Southwark soon be Miami?"

"Would we really mind, considering the weather? Tell me something: this house is surrounded by a high wall. If you were a kid bent on shooting things up for no particular purpose, would you go to the bother of trying to scale the wall just for a target that meant nothing to you?"

"No, now you mention it. You think the police were wrong?"

"Don't you?"

Ian thought for a moment. "Oliver—Dad—doesn't exactly have the chief constable in his pocket, but he does have clout. The commissioner's a good friend. I don't think they'd blow off an investigation. Gemma—the little girl—is sure the shooter was shooting at her because she was in the greenhouse. Gemma's imagination works overtime."

"But you say she was in the greenhouse when this happened."

Ian shook his head. "Police didn't think she had anything to do with it—I mean, that she was the target."

"Generally speaking, a person standing in the path of a bullet usually *is* the target."

"I see what you mean, only—well, why would anyone want to hurt Gemma? She's only nine years old. It doesn't make sense."

"It makes as much sense as some boy with a gun climbing over your wall."

He had left the Lodge after his "tea" (which he made sure to keep to the drink itself) and had gone to the main street where he could hail a taxi on some unobtrusive corner and return to Boring's. That was when he saw the butcher's shop open, the one Gemma had mentioned.

GYP THE BUTCHER was scrolled in shiny black letters over the doorway of a half-timbered shop behind whose big glass window sat meat displays surrounded by parsley, looking more like precious stones than chops and rashers. He peered through the glass and saw the tall thin proprietor. Melrose could hear him talking. He stood by the door and lit up a cigarette.

". . . mind you. Yes, I know it's your time to go home, but these here orders only just now come in and they're wanted tonight. Business ain't always at your convenience."

"But it's my friend's birthday, Mr. Gyp, like I told you. If it wasn't for that, I'd be glad—"

"Oh, that's as may be, but I'm sure the Lodge don't mean to wait on any birthdays, so you best hop it . . ."

The voice trailed off, but not, Melrose imagined, from lack of malice. Melrose knew a tormentor when he heard one. Children were especially desirable as objects for such people because they were relatively helpless and (it was assumed) weak. But they weren't weak, at least not the ones who had been left to rely on themselves.

The voice droned on: "You best look elsewhere if you can't take the odd late hour. It ain't as though there's no one else'd like the job."

All the while Gyp was delivering himself of his stored-up acrimony, the boy, who looked anything but stupid (which also went for the dog, Sparky), kept trying to wedge a word in, but found no chink in the wall of talk. The little dog, however, growled softly, its dog patience stretched to the limit.

Gyp recoiled and said, "We'll have none o' that dog o' yours, young Bernard. You control that animal or—"

"It's only Sparky! You know he never bit anybody—"

"Always a first time. That animal ought to be on a lead—"

"He never has and don't call him 'that animal.' His name's Sparky, as you well know."

Melrose liked the boy already. He wouldn't defend himself, but he leaped to the defense of his dog.

Gyp droned on. "Now, here's the chops for the Lodge. The beef silverside and rashers, they go to the Roots. Rashers is a bit fat, but if he complains you just tell him that's good bacon, that is."

Melrose decided this was as good a time as any to go in, so he pitched his cap a little forward and stuck his fingers in the small pockets of his jeans and entered.

"Evenin'," he said, bringing two fingers to the bill of his cap in a deferential salute. "This the butcher wot supplies the Lodge up there?" He jerked his thumb over his shoulder. "And you be Mr. Gyp?" Barely waiting for the butcher to accede to this, Melrose went on. "I just come from there and as I'm goin' back, I can take the parcel for you and save the lad a trip. Couldn't 'elp over'earin' what you said."

Before Gyp could object (as he was certainly about to), Melrose hurried on. "'Not a butcher in all London can touch 'im' is what that Mr. Barkins said. 'Ain't one of 'em can do a crown roast'"—Melrose's eyes flicked to the board where lay pork chops fanned out in perfect symmetry like a chorus line—"'or cut chops the artful way does Mr. Gyp. Almost too pretty to eat, them chops. No, that Mr. Gyp's a marvel, and an upright, honest man with it. I've never 'ad a doubt Gyp gives honest weight. We're lucky to have our Mr. Gyp.' That last was said by cook and it's somethin' to get *her* praise." Melrose halted, not for lack of other fanciful compliments, but because he felt like a vicar delivering a good-bye over the body of the lately dead. Gyp, he saw, had grown increasingly pleased as all of these compliments showered down on him. The boy and his dog stared at Melrose with eyes like full moons, disbelieving that anyone would find Gyp praiseworthy. Only an idiot (Melrose was sure Benny was thinking) could have listened to this lot spoken in as poor a North London accent as this toff was doing: a dropped *h,* an eclipsed *t* was about all Melrose could manage. (Just because he was undergardener didn't mean he could talk like one. Jury never seemed to learn that.)

Melrose leaned down to give Sparky a pat and the dog pumped his tail.

In a silky tone and a wipe of his hands on his blood-streaked apron, Gyp asked, "An' who might you be, sir?"

Melrose stuck out his hand to shake Gyp's (which he found cold as death) and said, "New gardener up to the Lodge. Ambrose Plant's the name. A pleasure to step into such a well-kept shop as this one."

Gyp clearly thought in Melrose he'd found a mate and would probably be wanting to nip along to the Scurvy Ferret for a pint. "Well, ain't it nice to have a new face to look at, and one that doesn't mind working outside his set hours. I was just trying to advise young Bernard here on the importance of bein' flexible."

"Ah, you're right there, Mr. Gyp, indeed you are."

Benny squinted up at Melrose in utter disbelief. Even Sparky managed a disbelieving cock of the head. Here was a boy and his dog story worth hearing.

"And o'course," continued Melrose, "I'd be 'appy to deliver that other l'il package too on my way."

"Now, that's most kind of you, Mr. Plant, on'y the Elys, they're a bit peculiar about strangers comin' to their door—"

Benny objected: "No, they're not—"

Gyp stamped on whatever Benny was going to say. "The old lady, she's the suspicious type."

Benny looked from the one to the other of these men as if they were both mad. Had they been dogs, Sparky would have done the same.

"Ely? Did you say Ely, Mr. Gyp? Could that be . . . what was his name . . . ?"

"Brian Ely. Lives with his old mum over in Mickel-white Street."

Melrose clapped his head. "Brian, of course! And the old lady! Well, ain't that a turnup for the books! It's been ten years since Brian and yours truly lifted a pint at the Scurvy Ferret." Since Melrose knew the only reason Gyp didn't want him making the Ely delivery was to force Benny here to do it and thus delay the boy's departure, he said, "This lad can show me the way."

Gyp thoroughly approved this scheme and stood washing his hands and grinning a sort of death's head grin.

But poor Benny, who'd seen deliverance only a moment ago, now saw his hopes dashed once again, or at least partly dashed. Melrose collected the packets and with false bonhomie told Gyp that he'd see him again soon. Then man and boy and dog departed.

Outside, Melrose gave Benny's shoulder a little shake. "Look, I'm not really who that Gyp thinks I am."

"Yeah? You're not who I think you are, neither."

"Oh? Oh? And who do *you* think I am?"

"You ain't someone what lives within the sound of Bow Bells, if you take my meaning. More some toff puttin' on an accent. It's really bad, I guess you know."

"This is the thanks I get for helping you with deliveries?"

"No, mister. That's really swell of you. Only now, I'll still never get to my friend's birthday in time with the cake." He held up the white box he'd been hanging on to.

Melrose looked up and down the dark street for a cab. He saw two, but they already carried passengers. "All we need do is take a cab, first to the Lodge and then the Elys."

As if cabs were as far beyond his reach as stars, Benny halted beside Melrose. "A taxicab?"

"Of course. Here comes one now."

"That's a mini-cab, that is."

Melrose sighed as he sliced his arm up and down. "So it's a mini-cab. So the driver talks to us in Portuguese. It has wheels, so hop it."

The white car lurched to a stop and the driver stuck his head out and called something incomprehensible. Melrose and Benny ducked into the back and Benny gave the address. The car lurched off as it had lurched in.

The driver pulled to a stop at the Lodge, where Benny directed him. He then disappeared through a garden gate while Sparky waited in the car, anxiously flapping his tail. The boy was back inside of two minutes. He told the driver the Elys' address and after much incomprehensible talk from the driver, the cab swerved around and shot down the road.

The Elys' house was in a stingy little street behind one of many churches attributed to Wren. Here Benny told the driver to keep the engine running, he'd be back in a tic, as if the cab were a getaway car. In syllables that still baffled Melrose, the driver went on about something—the gold standard? The Palestinian crisis? Standing on hind legs, paws against the window, Sparky watched Benny go.

Mr. Ely, if that's who it was, appeared in silhouette against the backdrop of a lighted hallway and, after a moment of hello and good-bye, closed the door. Benny rushed back, clambered in and told the driver to go to Waterloo Bridge, the other side, the Embankment side.

"And then where?" asked Melrose.

"Nowhere. I'll just get out there." Benny held the cake on his lap and watched the night slip by.

Melrose frowned. "But your birthday party—?"

"It's around there."

With Sparky up on the seat beside him now, Melrose pondered. It was pretty clear Benny didn't wish to discuss the matter and Melrose would never force it. "How long have you been working for this Gyp person?"

"Over a year. But it ain't—it's not—just him. I make deliveries for Delphinium and Mr. Siptick, too. He's the newsagent. And the Moonraker. Miss Penforwarden is really nice." He started humming.

"How about school, though?" Melrose then congratulated himself for asking the most detestable question man ever put to child: *How about school?*

But Benny didn't mind. "Oh, my mum takes care of that. I mean, she teaches me at home. See, I'm chesty—" Here he released several labored coughs for Melrose's edification. It was the first time Melrose had heard the boy cough. Apparently feeling called upon to demonstrate his reason for skipping school, Benny kept hacking away.

"Okay, you can stop that now. It's none of my business, anyway."

"You're the first person ever said that."

Crossing Waterloo Bridge, Melrose looked up and down the river, to Blackfriars, to London Bridge, to Tower Bridge, to this whole panoply of bridges lighted all along their length. He thought the scene was gorgeous. He supposed this was how a New Yorker must feel crossing over a bridge to Manhattan. He remembered seeing the backdrop of Manhattan when he'd been watching a news presentation. The skyscrapers' tops had been lit with colored lights, pink and yellow and green, surreal colors that seemed to float behind the news presenter.

When the mini-cab stopped and set Benny down near the Embankment, Melrose felt a pang. He told the boy to wait a minute as he wrote down Boring's number on the back of one of his old calling cards.

"Just ring me if you need another ride. Or anything."

"This here says you're an earl." Speculatively, Benny looked from the card to Melrose.

"Not I. A friend of mine." Melrose carried the card for emergencies.

Benny nodded and put it in his pocket and did not move. He was waiting for the car to leave, Melrose guessed, so as not to give away his own movement.

Melrose told the driver, "Mayfair. Boring's."

THIRTY-FOUR

Jury was in the St. James pub leaning against a post when Liza walked in. She was carrying an Oxford Street shopping bag that bristled with ribbon-wrapped boxes. She was wearing an unfashionable black coat and a scarf over her hair, but she still turned heads. Up and down the bar, men swiveled around to get another look. Liza would be married again within a year, he bet, four kids or not. Probably she would have to remarry, no matter how much she still loved Mickey. On her own, merely providing for four kids would be a huge problem; keeping them happy and out of harm's way with no one to help would be even worse.

"Hello, Richard." She kissed his cheek; he could have done with more.

"Hello. Let's go upstairs. There's nowhere to sit down here. Better yet, you go upstairs while I get you a drink. Lager? Gin and tonic?"

"What I'd really like is a brandy. I'm beat."

"It's yours."

Jury collected the drinks at the bar and made his way upstairs. At the top of the staircase, looking over at her, he thought how much she reminded him of a small girl inside a coat too big for her. She had deposited the shopping bag on one of the chairs. He set down their drinks, a double brandy for her, a pint for himself.

"Thanks. And thanks for asking me here. It was really nice of you."

He smiled. "Hardly a sacrifice on my part. All I had to do was cross the street." He gestured behind him in the direction of New Scotland Yard.

"You know what I mean. You see, there are very few people I can talk to—or Mickey himself when it comes to that—because very few know about his cancer. He must really need your help for him to tell you about it."

"I suppose so. I'm helping as much as I can, Liza."

"I know." She had not removed the coat. It was as if every transaction now were so fleeting, it would be useless to settle in to any encounter. She put her hand on the shopping bag. "Buying presents. It's difficult trying to celebrate. It's damned difficult looking at all those carefree faces."

"But they're not, not really. Look at the suicide rate around Christmas."

"Then why do we waste all of this energy pretending it's such a happy time?"

"Is it wasted? I guess I'm of the old 'assume-a-virtue-if-you-have-it-not' school."

She smiled. "Who said that? Shakespeare?"

"Hamlet, I imagine."

"Why not? He said everything else." She laughed and sipped her brandy. "I feel better. I expect this is what I needed."

Jury was quiet, waiting for her to go on. That she needed to talk was painfully obvious. It must be like a punishment, the tragedy you couldn't talk about.

Liza leaned closer and said, "I'm worried about him, Richard. That must sound ridiculous—of course I'd be worried—but I mean the toll this is taking on him emotionally."

"But, of course—"

She raised her hand, palm out, as if to push away some easy comfort. "I know what you're going to say: it's natural he'd be having emotional swings, but he's become so involved with this case—it wasn't even a case when it started, just identifying old bones. And then the murder of this Croft and now it *is* a case." Her hand went up to her mouth, to cover it, to try to keep from crying. She took a deep breath and went on. "The thing is, Mickey can't seem to focus on anything else. What is it about this damned case, Richard? Now, of course, it's in the City, and the City means Mickey. It's devastating to find him mentally elsewhere all of the time, all of the time elsewhere, knowing that in a little while he won't be anywhere. When I think of a world without Mickey in it—" She stopped. Her fisted hand was over her mouth, denial shaking her head from side to side, sending the tears flying instead of falling.

"Liza, listen. I think I can answer your question. This case, he needs it; he needs to be engulfed by it; he needs something larger than life. It isn't just this case. It could have been any case. When I talked to him in his office he needed a case that would make him think because he didn't want to think about himself."

"He's taking the case so personally, though."

"His father was a good friend of Francis Croft. In that way, it is personal."

"God, what the hell difference does it make if this woman is or isn't who she says she is? He's probably wrong anyway."

"I don't think so."

Liza looked surprised. "You mean you think the woman isn't this man's daughter?"

"Granddaughter. I don't think she is, no."

She sat back, drank the brandy. "It's just so consuming . . ." Her voice trailed off.

"So is the disease. Maybe he needs something outside of himself to match it." It was what he'd said before, different words. He wasn't convincing Liza, that was plain. He wasn't convincing himself.

THIRTY-FIVE

To the frustration of the mini-cab driver, Boring's, in its narrow Mayfair street, was identifiable only by its number and an old street lamp at the bottom of the steps. Its members apparently felt that if you didn't know where Boring's was, you probably shouldn't be going to it.

Melrose paid the driver a monstrous sum for carting them all over the West End searching for the club and added a monstrous tip because he, Melrose, did not speak Senegalese; he had been quite obliging, at least, from what Melrose could make out.

It was by now a little after seven o'clock. He had his room on the first floor and took the stairs two at a time, feeling quite youthfully athletic after his afternoon in the open air. While he was slamming drawers around looking for his silver cufflinks, he reminded himself the afternoon hadn't been entirely given over to exercise. There were the intervals around the pond and the beech tree.

In the Members' Room, several elderly men sat in various stages of predinner expectancy, with their predinner whiskeys or gins. Melrose spotted Colonel Neame in his usual chair by the fire. The feet jutting out from the other wing chair undoubtedly belonged to Major Champs, Colonel Neame's lifelong friend. He had met both of them last year at about this time; it had been in November. They were fixtures. But then all of the members were pretty much fixtures. A thin blade of fear creased Melrose's heart as he wondered if he too would become one.

The old men were gazing dreamily into the blazing fire when Melrose walked up and said, "Colonel Neame," and smiled down at the white-haired man with the rubicund face. "Major Champs," he said to the other.

Both of them started and began their slow acceleration into speech: "Um . . . uh . . . wha . . . well . . . um . . . um. My boy!"

Colonel Neame, his monocle falling from his eye and suspended by its black cord, was the first to utter actual words: "I say—will you look who's here, Champs! Delighted, delighted!"

Both of them rose to insist Melrose join them. Melrose, on his part, insisted on buying the drinks. This was met with happy-sounding *umphs, ums, lovely.* Melrose beckoned the young porter over, young by Boring's standards, all of whose staff were fairly over the hill. His name was Barney and he had bright ginger hair.

Melrose took the club chair on the other side of Major Champs as Barney went off to fetch the drinks. While they waited, they settled down to talk about something or nothing as to health and well-being; it mattered little just as long as drinks were on their way and pipes and cigars were to hand and lighted. Then the drinks came and approval rose from the chairs like smoke signals. Thought need not play much of a role in all of this, but Melrose was about to do it when a familiar voice sounded at his back.

"Good evening, Colonel Neame, Major Champs, Lord Ardry."

"Ah! Superintendent Jury!" Neame rose and Champs almost did, stopped in midrise by a laborious wheeze.

Neame went on. "We're relieved it's only dinner that brings you here tonight and not police business."

"My presence reminds you of Mr. Pitt, I expect. I'm sorry."

"Ah, don't apologize, Superintendent. Everything reminds me."

"Must you go through that 'Lord Ardry' business?"

Jury drank the wine Plant had ordered, a bottle of Puligny-Montrachet which was open and breathing on their table when they walked in. "That's how those two know you. You're the one introduced yourself as Lord Ardry. You don't want to disillusion them, do you?"

Young Higgins tacked their way with a tray of soup.

"Oxblood."

"No surprise."

And they didn't discuss the case until their bowls were empty, Jury ladling up his in less than a minute.

"I'm starving," he said, then looked at Melrose, who was rummaging in his pockets. "You're not going to smoke, are you?" His tone was vexed as a teacher's on having discovered graffiti on her blackboard.

"No-o," Melrose said, acerbically. "One doesn't smoke between courses. It's bad manners. But you always said somebody else smoking didn't bother you."

Jury frowned. "Well, it does. For some reason." He was quite gloomy tonight.

"It's your friend."

"What?"

"Your friend, in the City police, this DCI Haggerty. You're thinking about his smoking and his cancer, even if it is isn't specifically lung cancer."

Jury was silent, looking at Melrose. "You're right. Why didn't I work that out?"

"Because he's your friend." They both took a swallow of wine. "Boring's wine cellar is up to snuff, I'll say that."

Young Higgins was back with their dinners, which he set before them. Roast chicken, peas, potatoes, cauliflower, the vegetables in a silver serving dish. They thanked him appreciatively.

Jury said, "I just had a drink with Liza—that's his wife. She's in a bad way."

"Because of him."

"Because of him, yes. Not just the cancer itself, but his emotional balance. She says it's changed."

"I expect mine would change too if I knew I was going to die in a few months."

"That's what I told her." Jury swallowed the rest of his wine and set the glass down. "I don't think it's even going to be a 'few' months. I don't think it'll be that long."

Melrose looked at him. "That's—I'm sorry."

Jury took a deep breath. "How did you get on at the Lodge?"

"Lovely. Spent a lot of my time with Gemma Trimm. She's clearly taken with you. As usual." Melrose sighed.

Jury laughed. "What the hell does that mean? 'As usual'?"

"Nothing. Listen, little Gemma told me how she could get into the cottage—you know, Kitty Riordin's—whenever our Kitty comes to Oxford Street for a spot of shopping. She offered to get me in there."

"I hope you took her up on it."

Melrose made a face. "No, not right then, at least."

"You're a poor candidate for a B and E."

Smugly, Melrose said, "That's just what I told her."

"I see you started out on the right foot with a child. As usual."

"What's that mean? 'As usual'?"

Jury smiled. "Nothing."

Melrose speared a new potato. "Do you think it's remotely possible that she could be related? I'm thinking of—"

"Great-granddaughter?" Jury sat back. "The thing is, Oliver Tynedale's not the sort of man who'd hide the fact this little girl is his great-granddaughter. Whatever the reason for her abandonment—that she was illegitimate, or whatever—it wouldn't bother him; he'd tell the world."

"He couldn't tell the world if he didn't know it himself."

"You mean someone maneuvered Gemma into the household?"

"To surprise him in the end; to make him so grateful for this belated piece of knowledge he'd change his will. Remember Kitty Riordin."

"And now another little child comes along, Gemma Trimm, and the scenario's basically the same? I just think it unlikely there would be two cases of hidden identity in that house. And in the case of Gemma, Tynedale wouldn't have to be kept in the dark in order for the interested party to rake in a lot of money. He'd leave it to her in any event."

"But *if* there's truth in this, what if Simon Croft knew it? Wouldn't that be a reason to get him out of the way?"

"Could be, yes."

"Speaking of children, did you meet Benny?"

Jury laughed. "I did, yes."

"And did you speak with his nemesis, the butcher, Gyp? Horrible person." Melrose told him the story of the birthday cake. "He enjoys making young Benny's life a misery."

"Real sadist, it sounds like. I must remember to pay him a visit."

Melrose surveyed the table. "You've eaten everything, even the butter."

"I was hungry. Maybe I'll have some more." Jury craned his neck, looking for Young Higgins.

"Are you putting on weight?"

Jury shrugged. "How would I know? I can't see myself."

"There *are* mirrors."

"I don't look in them. Anyway, if I'm getting fat, you-know-who would let me know *tout de suite.*"

"I don't know you-know-who."

"Take my word for it. What's for dessert?"

THIRTY-SIX

When Jury returned to his flat, you-know-who was cooking a fry-up in his kitchen. The mingled scents of sausage, fried bread and Samsura made the air on the first floor landing positively seductive.

Carole-anne was frying away and humming a tune Jury thought he had heard. He tossed his keys in the large glass ashtray that had served him well and was now starved for ashes. He looked at the Christmas tree over in the corner, also starved, but for decorations, and assumed these metaphors were inspired by the action in his kitchen.

"Hey, Super! I'm out here!" called Carole-anne, as if the kitchen hovered somewhere between Islington and the moon. "My cooker quit working again."

This happened periodically. The landlord, Mr. Moshegiian, had promised her a new cooker, but it hadn't materialized. Jury assumed there was an honest difficulty here, as Mr. Mosh did not make empty promises to Carole-anne. Few did.

The kitchen swam in the mingled scents of sausage and perfume. He leaned against the doorjamb and said, "It's nearly eleven; isn't that kind of late for one of your fry-ups?"

"I was hungry. I've been dancing." She went on humming.

"At the Nine-One-Nine? Stan Keeler doesn't play dance music."

"He does sometimes." She sang a few bars of what she'd been humming. "'My baby don't care for furs and laces—'"

A little hip action here.

"'My baby don't care for *high*-toned plaaa-ces!'"

Some more hip action.

"That might be danceable coming from U-2, but not from Stan Keeler." Dancing to Stan's music would be like trying to glide over shards of glass. He wished she'd sing another couple of lines, though, with a little more hip action.

Carole-anne sighed. "You shouldn't always be talking about things you don't know about."

Always? "And just what else do I not know about besides 'My baby don't care for sausage fry-ups'?"

Ignoring him, her humming became a sort of whispered singing as she flipped eggs—four, Jury noticed—"'My baby don't care for rings . . . da da de da da da daaaah.'"

The fry-up, he had to admit, was beautiful—sausages succulent, fried bread crisp and golden, eggs smooth as silk. It was sort of the taste equivalent of Carole-anne's looks. Tonight she wore a turquoise blue tank top the color of her eyes and a sequined peachy miniskirt close to the color of her hair. This outfit on another woman would have clashed; on Carole-anne it merely melted like a Caribbean sunset.

She was dividing the contents of the skillet onto two plates.

"I ate dinner. I don't want any of that artery-clogging meal." Actually, he did; he was hungry again. It was hard for Carole-anne to look woebegone, given her dramatic coloring, but if she tried really hard, she could. On the spatula lay a beautifully fried egg. "Well, maybe just a little," he said.

She smiled and slid the egg onto his plate, removing one of the two sausages from his plate to hers.

"No, no. Put that sausage back. I can manage two. Just." He adored sausages.

Plates loaded, they went into his living room and sat down, Carole-anne at the end of the sofa near the starved tree. "That tree wants trimming, Super. You got some little blue and white lights somewhere, don't you? Mrs. W has hers all done up with snow and tinsel over the lights and a silver star on top. It's lovely." When he just went on eating a sausage, she shrugged. "I guess I'll have to do it as you're not in a very Christmasy mood, are you?"

"I was the one who went and got the trees, remember?" He'd bought a large one for Mrs. Wassermann, a small one for himself, a smaller one yet for Carole-anne, since she had a studio on the top floor and little room.

Still, she looked sad at its unencumbered state. It was a bit shabby, Jury thought, a secondhand tree. He had waited too long and the shapely ones were gone.

"It needs lights, it needs color."

"Go stand by it."

She frowned over a wedge of fried bread. "Is that a compliment? I can never tell."

Jury sniggered over his bread.

"Anyway, there's a surprise present Mrs. W wants. Oh, and me, I want one, too. I said I'd tell you what it was."

"If you tell me, then where's the surprise?"

"Right now, before I tell you. What we want is that you take us to see *The Mousetrap.*"

He just looked at her.

"You know. That Agatha Christie play that's been here for years and years."

Dashing her hopes, Jury said, "I've seen it." He did not add that it was so long ago he couldn't remember it.

Carole-anne was the only woman he'd ever seen make a significant gesture out of hands-on-hips sitting down. "You *could* see it again."

"I didn't know you liked mysteries. You're even reading an Agatha Christie." He nodded toward the book on the coffee table. Books were not Carole-anne's raison d'être.

She picked up the book, tossed it down. "That's just to study up on before we see the play."

Study up on Agatha Christie before one sees her? Well, one might read Dante before going to Florence or T. S. Eliot before visiting Burnt Norton. "I don't like mysteries, love; there's already too much mystery in my own life."

"*Life?* Mysteries don't have anything to do with life! They're completely unlife; they're nonlife. There's no relation to reality at all."

Jury felt as if he should defend this sorry genre. "Some of them do, don't they?"

"No. So if that's why you don't like them, well, you can stop now."

How was it her argument was so inherently refutable, yet he could think of no refutation?

"I called and they had tickets for the week between Christmas and New Year's?" It was put as a question; her look implored.

Jury was surprised she'd resisted buying them.

"You will, won't you, Super?"

Of course, he'd take them. To tell the truth, he sometimes thought they were all in the same boat, whatever that might be. "I'll think about it." Her expression implored, but he refused to capitulate to that deep turquoise look, at least not immediately.

Carole-anne speared a sausage bite and continued. "We decided we'd have Christmas dinner at Mrs. W's instead of here."

By "here" she meant Jury's own flat. Looking around his small living room and the round table covered with a runner that would seat one comfortably, he said, "Can't imagine why. But why not go out to someplace where the furniture is actually geared to people sitting down and eating?"

She looked blank.

"A restaurant."

Nearly tilting a rasher of bacon and fried bread from her plate when she sat up, shocked, she said, "On Christmas Day? You must be daft."

"Well, there must be a whole host of the daft out there because a lot of people eat out. Saves cooking, washing up, talking to people you have nothing to say to, et cetera, et cetera."

"I should certainly hope you don't mean our Mrs. W."

That he might mean Carole-anne was beyond all reason. He smiled. "Of course not. I love talking to both of you."

She resumed her eating.

He spiked a bite of sausage with his fork. "I'd better stop eating so much. I'm getting fat." He glanced at her to see how she'd take this.

"You? *Fat.* Oh, don't be daft. If you were getting fat I'd be the first one to tell you."

He smiled. "Wasn't there one more sausage?"

The next morning, Jury stopped by Mrs. Wassermann's garden flat. It was "garden" only by virtue of its being lower ground floor and its promise of opening out onto great vistas in the rear of the house. But that remained only a promise, much like the one for the new cooker. The flat could have been as easily (and more honestly) called "basement."

Mrs. Wassermann opened the door—or rather "undid" it—as there was much unbolting and sliding of locks and chains before it opened.

"Mr. Jury!" She clasped the collar of her chenille robe together. Her hair was still rolled and under wraps—didn't that bonnet she was wearing used to be called a mob cloth? She said, "Pardon me for looking so—*deshabillé.* Is that the word?"

It was, but Mrs. Wassermann wasn't it. Carole-anne was it, a lot of the time. Jury smiled. "You look exactly like you should a little after eight A.M." He regarded the flowered cap.

She followed his glance and explained. "Carole-anne thought my hair would look nicer with just a bit of color. She thought it would give me more of the *demimonde* look."

Where was Carole-anne picking up these words? Hanging around Tony and Guy's salon in her off hours? The thing that amused him was that they were archaic.

"As far as I'm concerned, you don't need a new look. I like the old one, especially your hair." She had lovely hair—not gray, not white. Platinum. "But then I expect we all get bored with the way we look."

"Come in, come in, Mr. Jury. I'm leaving you standing in the cold." With a strong gesturing of her arm, as if she would encompass all of him, she waved him into the flat. "I wanted you to see my tree, anyway. I just put the kettle on; I hope you'll have a cup of tea."

"Thanks, I'd like that." He watched her go off to the kitchen and turned to look at the tree. Mrs. Wassermann had always been as much Christian as Jew; he remembered years ago her discomfort at this, as if she were doing something neither Christian nor Jew would ever countenance. Jury had the impression that her mother had not been a Jew, but this had not saved either of them from the concentration camps.

The tree was as beautiful as Carole-anne had said. White lights winked behind shimmering tinsel, patches of cotton looked amazingly real and a big silver star glittered in the reflected light. Beneath the tree were several presents, wrapped in a paper he wasn't used to seeing anymore, figures of skaters on ponds, of families joining hands around the Christmas tree, of people singing carols. The colors were dull reds, browns and greens. Nothing glittered, nothing shone. In among the faded packages sat a small crèche, and he crouched down to get a closer look. The little wooden figures he could almost hold in the palm of his hand, including the

three Wise Men and the camel. The lamb, the goat and
the dog stood as he supposed they always would.

He was suddenly drawn back to that pub near
Durham called Jerusalem Inn, and the little girl—
Chrissie? Was that her name? Her doll had been enlisted to play the role of the Christ child. Chrissie had
not liked that, and had kept taking the doll away. Scenes
came to him in a rush—that Christmas at Old Hall,
Helen Minton and that long expanse of sea and beach
in Sunderland. He was flooded with memories; he could
barely breathe for the sudden sharp pain. It was ridiculous, absurd. He tried to laugh but had no breath for it
and the effort only made the pain get worse. *This is not
the way it's supposed to happen.* Wondering if the
weight of memory was killing him, he took shallow
breaths. Breath that barely touched the diaphragm.
God, but he felt woozy: was he going to faint? He didn't
move. The pain stopped just as suddenly as it had
started.

He forced his eyes open and looked at the crèche and
waited for his head to come round, his thoughts to clear.
The pain, he thought, was too sudden and swift to be serious. He was still crouched down, looking at the crèche.
Chrissie made him think of Gemma, Gemma out in the
greenhouse in the dark, the greenhouse itself lighted,
the light pooling below the windows, shadows looming
like closet monsters.

"Here's tea, Mr. Jury. I used my Fortnum and Mason
Christmas tea." When he didn't answer, she asked, "But
are you all right, Mr. Jury?" She put a delicate hand on
his shoulder as he crouched there.

He rose tentatively to his feet. "I'm fine, Mrs. Wassermann; I was just admiring your crèche." He accepted the
cup of tea she held out to him.

"You know, I've had it forever, since I was a girl. Yes,
I know it sounds impossible I could have kept it through
all that happened. How I kept it in the camp was to hide
the pieces on me—down my front, Mary under my scarf,

the Wise Men in my socks and shoes. It's a miracle they never found them. I only lost one camel."

Jury smiled. "One camel. I guess I could live with that."

Looking at him, she said with all the mildness in the world, "But you never had to, Mr. Jury."

He knew it was not a reproach; she would never reproach him. It was a simple statement of fact, but he felt it nonetheless, what separated them, an unbridgeable gulf.

He raised his teacup. "Land of hope and glory, Mrs. Wassermann."

"Happy Christmas, Mr. Jury."

THIRTY-SEVEN

"Get your skates on, Wiggins, we're going to Southwark. I need your fine-tuning."

Wiggins had just set down the telephone receiver and picked up a glass of gummy-looking pink liquid. "Fine-tuning, sir?"

Jury was at his desk now, sorting through a sheaf of papers from Fraud and routed through Chief Superintendent Racer to Jury. Thinking aloud, Jury said, "What the hell's he trying to fit up Danny Wu for now?" Danny, he bet, was running something on the side, but it wasn't arms, opium or hookers.

Wiggins tried again. "Fine-tuning you said?"

"Huh?" Jury skimmed several papers off the top of the pile and shoved the others in a file drawer. "That's right, Wiggins. Have they still got you shackled to that Greenwich case?"

Wiggins smiled. "Still shackled, sir, but nothing's stirring at the moment."

"Good. Southwark is where we're going as soon as Racer disses me for whatever's on the menu today. What I need is your well-nuanced, closely calibrated method of interviewing."

"Well, thank you, but when it comes to questioning witnesses, there's nobody better than you, and I mean that."

"Wrong, Wiggins. You are." Jury flashed him a smile and left the office.

"Two more murders in Limehouse." Racer seethed. "Obviously gang related and you're resting on the laurels of that Brixton shoot-out. Since when did you start carrying a gun, Jury?"

"Since the assistant commissioner's last decree."

"You carrying now?"

"Of course not."

"Too bad. You could've put a bullet in that cat. He's in here, somewhere. I can smell him." Then Racer went on about Brixton and Limehouse while Jury's eyes scanned the room.

A new piece of furniture had been delivered and occupied a space near the library shelves, behind whose bottom doors Racer kept his supply of whiskey. It was locked up as tight as a crowd of Millwall supporters at a match. This had not been done to keep out people, but to keep out the cat Cyril.

Jury would have been delighted to give Cyril a home—so would Fiona, so would Wiggins—but removing him from these offices would so seriously curtail Cyril's activities, it would be cruel. Racer had tried every way imaginable of getting rid of Cyril—poisoning, trapping, electrocuting. The bowl of milk on the floor with the live wires running into it hadn't worked either, surprise, surprise.

The doors of the secretary were open, revealing a lineup of little cubbyholes, much like the ones behind a hotel desk into which mail and keys are slotted. Behind the cubbyholes was empty space. Jury knew this well, remembering a similar piece of furniture in Trueblood's antiques; that one had housed a dead body. The cubbyholes were no doubt intended to house little writerly items such as quills, wax, ink or cat's eye. This is what Jury saw peering from behind a cubbyhole. The eye looked at him and then moved on to another hole. Jury smiled.

(Not for long.) "Jury!"

Jury flinched. "Sir!"

"I can do without your damned sarcasm today. You've been working on that murder in the City that's none of our business—"

"Begging your pardon, sir, but it is our business now as the City police asked us for help." *Well, me, at least.*

"They don't need our help. They've got their own little fiefdom there."

Jury scratched down a number, tore it from his notebook and handed it across the desk. "Call DCI Michael Haggerty and he'll tell you."

"Then why in hell didn't this go through me?"

"An oversight, I expect."

"You're doing nothing about this Dan Wu business. Except eating for free at his restaurant."

"His restaurant is where he is nearly all the time."

"Yeah, but that doesn't mean you've got to stuff yourself with spring rolls and Jeweled Duck just to talk to him."

"You've been there yourself, I see."

Racer flapped a dismissive hand. "I want you working more closely with Limehouse police on this."

"To coin a phrase, they don't need our help."

"Oh, yes they do." Racer was getting up and into his black vicuña coat. "Get over there. See if there's anything new—I'm late!" He looked at his watch and stormed toward the door.

"Christmas shopping, sir?"

Racer was through the outer office and slamming the door behind him.

Jury moved over to the *secretaire,* knocked twice on the loose top and said, "All clear."

He was talking to Fiona Clingmore, who was busy with an overhaul of her face—green eyeshadow, blush, mascara—when Cyril ambled in, looking as if he headed a royal procession, looking as if his brilliant copper fur were a robe of state.

Fiona said to the cat, "You've been in that desk again, haven't you? Don't look for sympathy here if he catches you." She clicked her compact shut.

Cyril yawned. He sat with his tail lapped about his legs and gave Jury and Fiona slow blinks. He was sitting in a patch of sunlight and when the sun wavered, he sparked. Why would he bother with live wires, being one himself?

"Have you ever had a heart attack, Wiggins?"

They were driving across Southwark Bridge, Jury looking out over the gray and wind-troubled Thames.

"Me? Heart attack? My God, no. Why?"

"I thought I might be having one this morning. I mean even *before* I went to Racer's office."

"What kind of pain? A squeezing one?"

"No. Sharp. Just very sharp. It hurt to breathe. It didn't last longer than a minute, probably not even that."

"That sounds like heartburn, indigestion. Or a panic attack."

"Why would I be having a panic attack?"

"Don't know. Too much on your plate, maybe."

"No, I don't think so."

They were silent for a moment, then Wiggins gave a little bark of laughter. "If I was having a heart attack, believe me, you'd have heard about it."

Jury smiled. And heard. And heard.

THIRTY-EIGHT

arkins opened the door, clearly displeased to see policemen again. Jury told him he wished to see Maisie Tynedale. The butler sighed. "Any time, night or day, you people call. Scotland Yard simply doesn't care. You run rough shod over everyone. Nothing," said Barkins, in his most disapproving tone, "must stand in the way of a police investigation."

"Good of you to recognize that. Most people aren't so obliging," said Wiggins, unwinding his endless black wool scarf.

Barkins looked as if he'd choke, and Jury wondered if Wiggins was making a rare foray into irony. "Thanks," he said, "I'll keep it." Jury was referring to his coat, which Barkins had made no move to take.

"If you'll just wait, sir, I shall see if she's available." Barkins swanned off toward the double door to their right, knocked and entered. He was back in a tic, telling them Miss Tynedale would see them.

"Just me," said Jury. "Sergeant Wiggins will go with you to the kitchen, where he'll have questions for the staff."

Barkins stiffened even more and informed them that Mrs. MacLeish was extremely busy with all of the Christmas preparations.

Wiggins drew out his notebook and flapped it a couple of times in front of Barkins.

Heaving a great sigh, Barkins said, "Oh, very well." To Jury he said. "I'll just show you in—"

"Never mind; I can find my own way."

"Superintendent Jury."

"Miss Tynedale. How are you?"

"I'm all right." Her hand gestured to a chair, which Jury took. She sat behind the desk in the window embrasure, as she had before. Through the window Jury could see the brittle winter garden—sacking covering the more delicate plants, flowerbeds mulched down, roses and rhododendron cut back, hanging matting over the climbing vines on the garden wall. It should have looked bleak, but it didn't, not to Jury. The colonnade, the white arbor, the weak sunlight to him looked romantic.

"You said you weren't surprised that Mrs. Riordin didn't marry again." Jury wondered if her eyes grew wary, or if it was simply his imagination. She flicked a lighter before he came up with the folder of matches he carried about for old time's sake.

Maisie frowned. "Her husband walked out on her."

Jury thought that rather an oblique answer. "Are you suggesting that because of the way her husband treated her, she couldn't trust any man?"

"It's possible." With a degree of impatience, she pushed her chair back. "I don't see what Kitty's marrying or not has to do with Simon's murder."

"I don't either. But I think it does have to do with Mrs. Riordin's devotion to the Tynedale family. You'd hardly disagree that she *is* devoted to all of you."

"I'd say it was an exceptionally nice position. I told you before: Grandfather was so grateful I was alive, he'd have given her almost anything. Look, you have no idea what the loss of my mother meant to him."

"I think I do." Jury paused. "I want to talk some more about Gemma Trimm. What about these alleged attempts on her life?"

Maisie laughed. "Gemma has an overactive imagination."

"She'd better, since she's all by herself. A bullet shattering the glass of the greenhouse isn't really explained by imagination, now is it?"

She hesitated. "Police thought it might just be a stray bullet—"

"Someone hunting the queen's deer in Southwark, you mean?"

Maisie gave Jury a look and a strained smile. "The police said it was probably 'some kid got hold of his dad's gun.' Those were his words. But then there was that night when she swore somebody was trying to smother her and then somebody was trying to poison her. Why would *anyone* try to kill that child?"

Jury didn't answer.

"And why do you need to know all of this in relation to Simon's murder, though?"

"It's family history. Family history might be helpful. You've employed a new gardener, have you?" Jury nodded toward the window. Melrose Plant was passing by carrying a bucket in each hand.

"What?" She turned. "Oh, him. Yes. Ian just hired him. I don't know how he'd heard I wanted one; he simply came here and applied. Our main gardener thinks he's quite good, if a little overeducated." Her short laugh was edgy. "You certainly do switch the conversation around."

"It isn't conversation." Jury drew a notebook from his inside pocket. "He replaced another gardener—a Jenny Gessup?" He flipped the notebook shut. "I'd like to talk to Miss Gessup."

Maisie sat down again. "Why?"

"Did she give notice? Or did you sack her?"

She flinched. "Neither. She just didn't turn up for work one day."

"When was this?"

"Back in October."

"How long did she work here?"

"Six months, perhaps. You can ask Angus Murphy, he'd be more exact as to times. He'd remember where she lived, too. She wasn't much good, you know."

"Meaning?"

"She wasn't really interested. She was careless and somewhat lazy, although she did stay sometimes until after dark. The thing is, she'd sometimes be out in the greenhouse late, just as an excuse to stay after dark and I believe she'd come into the house and, well, go through things, papers, that sort of thing, not that she ever took anything; at least I never missed anything. She was a bit of a flirt, too."

"With whom?"

"Ian, for one. I know, I know he's far too old for the likes of Jenny Gessup to be flirting with. But he looks much younger than he is, and with some women, age makes no difference."

"It would make a lot if she could interest him. He's a wealthy man."

"That's just ridiculous. For a man like Ian—" She made a dismissive gesture. "And she kept flirting with Archie, kept him from his work. Archie Milbank, he's employed to do a little of everything. Maintenance things."

She turned and Jury saw her profile outlined in pale gold light. Her dark hair was webbed with it. She looked much younger than she was, too; they all did. With some people, the older they grew, the more elusive time became. To a young person, fifty would seem antique. If only the young knew how quickly they'd come to it.

Jury said, "Simon Croft's sister Emily. She lived here, with you, at least for a while." When all he got was a nod of the head, he went on. "She's living in an assisted-living facility in Brighton?" Jury loved the euphemism.

"Emily. Yes, she is."

"Why? You could afford in-house care, if that's what was needed."

Her arms folded, she turned to him. "I can't explain that very easily. Of course, we could afford home care. Emily has a steadily worsening heart condition, but it doesn't require constant monitoring, at least not yet. Her doctor wanted someone around, though, in case of emergency. She refused to have anyone in her flat, so we asked her to come here. Occasionally, she returns to the flat, but not for long."

"You're right, that doesn't explain it."

Maisie sighed, played with the curtain's tassel. "Emily and Kitty just didn't get along."

Jury waited, assuming there must be more. When there wasn't he said, "Mrs. Riordin is staff. Instead of turning out a member of the staff, you'd turn out a woman who is, for all intents and purposes, family?"

She flushed. By way of defense, she went on about the "facility." "The place is quite lovely. She has her own rooms, so she's really independent."

Jury hated this sort of rationalizing. "I don't see how, if her living has to be assisted."

"Yes. Well. St. Andrew's Hall, it's called."

"I know. I've been there."

Maisie was astonished. "Been there? Then you've already talked to Emily. I'm sure she told you about her condition. Why are you asking me these questions?"

"Police do that sort of thing." His smile was chilly.

"Granddad wouldn't hear of Kitty's leaving. I've told you how attached he was to her."

This didn't sound like the Oliver Tynedale Jury had met. He would never have allowed one of the Crofts to leave because Kitty Riordin didn't like her. "Did he know?"

"I beg your pardon?"

"Did your grandfather know the reason for Emily Croft's leaving?"

"No."

There was a silence while, Jury imagined, she examined this cold-blooded removal of a woman who was probably surrogate aunt to her. More than that he wondered at the influence over the family Kitty Riordin had achieved.

"It's really quite a nice place, St. Andrew's Hall. It overlooks the sea. I've always thought the sea a sort of balm to the soul."

Jury rose. "So did Virginia Woolf. For a while."

Small deposits of the recent snow had been driven between the colonnade's white pillars and clung to the cypresses that lined the path across the way. From one of the closely packed branches an icicle dropped silently to the leaf-packed ground.

Gemma was sitting on the same bench she and Jury had shared two days ago, the one closed in on two sides by lattice. This bench and the seat in the beech tree seemed to be her favorite places. She sat with her doll, dressed up this time in trousers and shirt much too big and a scrap of red material as a neckerchief.

"Hello, Gemma. Remember me?"

"Yes. You're the policeman."

"That's right. Richard Jury."

With some gravity she said, lifting up the doll, "His name's Richard, too. You can sit down if you want."

"Thanks." Jury sat down and picked up the doll from where she had lain it. He looked at it for some time.

"Does he look okay?" said Gemma. "I know his pants are way too big."

She sounded anxious about the doll's transformation from supposed female to supposed male. "Oh, yes, he's fine. I was just thinking—"

Gemma's eyes, wide and dark, seemed to implore him not to think about the doll, or at least not too much.

"—thinking how nice it must be to be a doll."

Her expression changed to simple curiosity. "Why?"

"Well, you can be pretty much anything you want to be."

Curiosity changed to doubt. "No, he can't. Not if I don't want him to be."

Jury made no comment. This apparently made her more anxious still and she edged closer to him. He said, "That's true, in a way, but remember: you don't know everything about him. Only some things."

This giving the doll a life of its own didn't sit well with her. Her frown was deep as she lay her hand on the doll's chest, very near Jury's fingers.

"Remember how you thought this doll was a girl?"

Gemma rushed in to say, "He can be *either.*"

"Yes, but you didn't really know that then."

Her mouth worked with possible answers to this charge, but she came up with nothing.

"All I'm saying is, you might want Richard here to have some sort of identification." Jury took out his and showed her. "Like this."

The thought seemed to fill her with wonder. "You mean Richard's a *policeman*?"

"Could be, but I'm only guessing. Plain clothes, of course. A detective, more likely."

Full of this idea, especially since she'd already thought of it, Gemma studied Jury's ID. "How can he get one?"

"I expect I could fit him up with one from Scotland Yard."

Gemma looked thoroughly bowled over by this. She took the doll Richard back and looked him over carefully to see if there might be any flaws in his detective persona.

"Of course," Jury went on, "he might want to ask you questions."

"Like what?" She looked sharply at Jury.

"I don't know." He shrugged.

There was a period of silence while Gemma looked off in the distance, thinking. "I bet he wants to know about when I was in the greenhouse and somebody shot at me. They missed."

"Yes, I remember you told me that. It must have been frightening."

"It was. I'm still scared about it because that's not all!"

There was a silence. Gemma studied the doll. Finally she whispered to Jury, "Isn't he going to ask me what else?"

"I think he did. You just didn't hear him."

"Oh. Well, the rest is someone came in my bedroom and tried to smother me!"

There was another silence.

She said, "He's not a very good detective."

"He hasn't been at it very long."

"Well, he should ask me if I was asleep when it happened."

Jury held the doll to his ear and nodded. "That's what he's asking." Then Jury made a point of looking around at the lattice work, at the beech tree and at Melrose Plant, down at the other end with Angus Murphy, both of them dumping buckets of something onto the ground. "Richard has to keep his voice low because you don't know who might hear. Look down there." Jury nodded in the direction of the two gardeners.

"That's only Ambrose. He's okay. He's the new gardener," said Gemma, her voice low. "He's pretty nice but he argues a lot. His eyes are really green."

Ambrose? "Hmm. You're sure they're not just green contact lenses? He could be in disguise."

Gemma's mouth crimped up like an old lady's at a particularly juicy piece of gossip. "I thought there was something funny about him when he wouldn't baptize Richard."

Jury made a sound meant to dismiss the gardener's expertise. Then he said, "But about your being asleep—"

"It woke me up! Would it wake you up if somebody was choking you?"

"Fast."

She dropped Richard (whom Jury moved quickly enough to catch) and turned her hands so that she could encircle her neck. She stuck her tongue out and made choking noises.

"Terrible!" said Jury. "I wonder you could get the hands off you."

Gemma missed a beat or two and said, "Oh, they just went away."

"But then how about being smothered?"

Suddenly recalling this important detail, she said, "That's right, the hands came back and picked up a pillow and smothered me. I only just managed to bump the pillow off."

"Thank God. You must be strong."

Uninterested in her strength and the subject of smothering, she gave a shrug and said, "I guess."

There came another silence which she broke finally by saying in a fluting voice, "Well? Well? Isn't Richard going to ask?"

Jury scratched his ear and looked at Richard (who looked supremely indifferent). He was thoughtful while Gemma started jumping as if she could hardly wait to tell the rest of her story. "You mean, what happened next?"

"Yes!" She took Richard from Jury's hands and looked at him gravely. "I was almost poisoned."

"I remember that. And the cook very nearly quit."

"Benny told me about the way this family in Italy used to poison each other. The Medicines. They'd keep poison in all sorts of places, like in a ring. And when the victim was about to drink, they'd click open the ring and dump the poison in. That's what happened."

"To you?" When she nodded, Jury said, "The poison was in a ring someone was wearing?"

Emphatically, Gemma nodded.

"But you don't know who?"

This time she shook her head, just as emphatically, sending her hair swinging like leaves in the wind. She had finished and was now rearranging Richard's neckerchief.

"That's really some story." Jury brought out his small

notebook and the stub of a pencil he kept telling himself to throw away. "Here."

She frowned. "What's that for?"

"For your statement. That's what it's called, a statement. What you do now is write down whatever happened. Didn't Richard tell you about this?"

Her mouth gaped. "*No!*"

"Then he's very lax. Witnesses always have to write their stories down, make their statements."

"But I've already *stated*!"

"Yes, to me. But it has to be written down, if that's what actually happened."

Gemma looked horrified. "It'll take *days* to write it. Months! I don't write very good."

"Oh, don't worry about that. Scotland Yard sees all sorts of writing."

Gemma gave Richard a sharp rap against the lattice. "Nobody ever told me, not those police who came, they never told me."

Jury sighed. "That's too bad; they should've taken your statement."

She was clearly angry with Richard and gave him back to Jury. She stood there, arms folded, looking at the notebook Jury held, and the pencil. "You said, 'whatever happened.'"

"That's right. We'd hardly need a statement of what *didn't* happen."

Gemma scratched her elbows. "Well, maybe some of it didn't. Some of it could've been—you know—like a bad dream. Like the choking part. It *did* wake me up, I mean I thought it did, but maybe I was dreaming it all and got mixed up."

"Hmm." Jury grew thoughtful again. "That's certainly possible."

"And the smothering part, too. It was as if it'd happened. It felt real."

"If it was a dream, well, of course, you wouldn't need to put it in a statement."

With her hands on his knees for support, she jigged on one leg, then the other, kicking her feet back.

"What about the poison, then? Could you have dreamed that, too?"

She shook her head. Dark leaves swirled as she bounced from one foot to another. "I was . . . just . . . thinking about what Benny told me . . . so much . . . I must've . . . thought it . . . happened."

"Well, yes, I can see that."

She stopped, a sober look on her face. "But the shooting really did happen."

"Yes, there's proof of that. You said you went to the greenhouse. Tell me, did Jenny Gessup ever go out there?"

"Sometimes she did, but she's gone." Hence, scarcely worth the breath to talk about.

"Was Richard with you in the greenhouse?" Jury gave the doll a pat.

"Yes, except he wasn't Richard yet. He was—Ruth or Rebecca or Rachael or Rose or Rhonda . . ." She shrugged.

Richard's tenure on earth as a girl still gave Gemma trouble. Jury was glad the litany of names ended.

She said, "If it'd been Richard, then he could have caught whoever did it."

"That's right. You turned the light on when you went in?"

Clasping Richard to her chest, she said, "I had to *see,* didn't I? I only turned one on, anyway."

"What happened then?"

"I heard a kind of crack, then the window broke and glass scattered everywhere. Then it was like a mosquito *whrr'd* past me. I got down."

"That was smart."

The corners of her mouth stretched down, indicating exasperation at being questioned yet again. "I guess I have to write a statement about being shot at."

Jury was looking off across the garden, where Melrose was dumping another bucket into the flowerbed.

Mulch, maybe. "You know what? If you tell this to—what's your new gardener's name?"

"Ambrose." Looking in the same direction, she squinted.

"Tell Ambrose and he can write it down. As soon as he's finished his garden chores, of course."

Although this arrangement was preferable to writing herself, there were still reservations. "He'll just argue about every little thing."

"He can't. He wasn't here, after all. He didn't witness it."

"He'll still say I saw it the wrong way round."

Jury didn't know what to make of this little conundrum. "I'll tell him just to write down what you say and not argue about it."

Gemma murmured, "He won't pay any attention."

"If you think I'm going to carry buckets until you sort all this, well—"

They were standing near the greenhouse. "You're doing the job so well I'd say you were a natural—*ow!*"

Melrose had just dropped a bucket of fertilizer on Jury's foot. "Oh, sorry about that."

Jury rubbed at his ankle. "Sure. Now, what did Angus Murphy have to say about this Jenny Gessup?"

"Unreliable, useless, uninterested, or, as he put it, in a state of desuetude."

"Funny word to be using."

"Isn't it? He says she didn't have the strength for some of the jobs, such as carrying buckets for hours on end. This—" Melrose said of the bucket on the ground "—must be the dozenth today."

"What's in it?"

"Who cares? Fertilizer, I expect."

"Listen: I want you to write down the account of the shooting Gemma's going to tell you."

"What? *What?* That would be one of the labors of

Hercules, I suppose you know. And if she's told you already, why—"

"Because sometimes details turn up with repetition. You know that. She might mention something left out of what she told me."

Melrose frowned. "What about the poisoning and the choking?"

"That didn't happen. I suspected that. The shooting clearly did. Being shot at gave her bad dreams, and the choking, smothering business was only that. A dream. The poisoning didn't happen either; it was the result of someone's talking about poisoning in general."

"But that still leaves the question, why shoot her?"

"No, it doesn't, not if that was the only attempt made."

"Sorry, I don't follow."

"Gemma might not have been the target. People assumed she was because of these other two fictionalized attempts. If they hadn't occurred, police would have brought up the other possibility: it wasn't Gemma."

"Then . . . who and why?"

"One of two things might have happened: it could have been a prearranged meeting in the greenhouse between the shooter and his or her target—just to get the person out of the house probably. Or the shooter saw someone in the greenhouse, thought the person was the target, took the opportunity and got a gun. An impulse. As I said, those are just possibilities. But it wasn't necessarily Gemma the shooter was after."

"Good Lord, you're not suggesting it was old Angus Murphy?"

"No. He's still around after several months. Had it been Murphy he'd most likely be dead by now. My guess is Jenny Gessup, who I'm going to see as soon as I can gather up Wiggins."

Melrose bent, cursing, to pick up the bucket. "The antiques appraiser was chicken feed to this."

"With that attitude, you'll never make first base at the

Chelsea Flower Show." Jury turned to leave. "And don't forget to take down that statement."

Melrose called to Jury's swift departure, "All she'll do is argue."

Jury smiled. *Full circle.*

In the kitchen, a tea party appeared to be in progress, with Sergeant Wiggins at the center of things. Around the table also sat an elderly but robust-looking woman who must be the cook, two young ones who were probably maids and a thin, acne-scarred lad who would have been a groom, if there'd been horses. Leaving that occupation, Jury imagined he was Archie Milbank, who did odd jobs under the gimlet eye of Barkins, who was not present at the table.

The kitchen was wonderfully massive and cozy at the same time, partly owing to an inglenook fireplace blazing away as if initiating the Great Fire of London. It was flanked by a large industrial-size Aga and a modern column which housed a microwave oven and what looked like a rotisserie. The cook was not hurting for modern conveniences.

When Jury walked in, Wiggins rose and the others looked at Jury with simple delight, as if he were one of the Wise Men come with a bucket of frankincense. (Jury had trouble getting that image of Melrose Plant out of his mind.)

Jury's smile only increased the general air of beneficence as Wiggins introduced him around the table. Here was Mrs. MacLeish, cook; Rachael Brown, maid; Clara Mount, cook's helper; Archie Milbank, "maintenance."

Jury thanked Mrs. MacLeish for the mug of tea she was pressing into his hand and asked if he could have a word with her. Of course, of course. They went to Barkins's little sitting room.

"First," said Jury, "I'm awfully sorry about Mr. Croft. You knew him from childhood, didn't you?"

Her eyes grew glassy with tears, against which she drew a handkerchief from her apron. "I did that, yes. Mr. Simon was a lovely man, just lovely. Like the rest of the family, scarcely ever a cross word."

"It's been suggested he was afraid of someone or something. Did you get that impression?"

She frowned. "He did seem not to want to see people, or at least some people. I thought it was because of that book he was writing. Spending all his time on that, he was. Of course, I never did see him much as I went to the house only twice a week to do the cooking. Mr. Simon wasn't big on cooking for himself. Sometimes he got Partridge's to cater. I do know he got that policeman—a friend of the family, he was—to stop in every once in a while. So I expect he could've been afraid, couldn't he? Maybe it was for some of those valuable paintings and things?"

"Possibly, yes."

Jury thanked her and rose.

They were in the car with Wiggins thumbing through his notes. As always, they were copious. "According to Mrs. MacLeish, who went to Simon Croft's house to prepare meals for him, the only people who got inside the house were the grocer and your DCI Michael Haggerty. Maisie Tynedale called. But Croft did not want her inside and told Mrs. MacLeish to say he was busy with work that couldn't be interrupted. He had taken to doing this several weeks before."

"This is the paranoia we've been hearing about?"

"Yes. She says the policeman—meaning DCI Haggerty—had a cup of tea with her in the kitchen when he came round, and so did the grocer, a Mr. Smith. Anyway, they had tea—"

"Occupational hazard."

"What?"

"Nothing. Go on."

"—had their tea and a good chat."

"About what?"

"Oh, the new millennium dome. I was telling you—"

"Yes, yes." The last thing Jury wanted was for Wiggins to get stuck on that. He wondered if he'd last until the millennium.

"What it looks like is Simon Croft could have been suspicious of any of them, anyone in the family."

"Good thinking on his part. So am I. You know, I don't get this: here's Croft with money enough to be catered for by Partridge's or Fortnum and Mason. Why would he be using Mrs. MacLeish to cook his meals?"

Wiggins gave a smart little nod and said, with authority, "I can answer that, sir, I believe. Mrs. MacLeish has cooked for the Tynedales and the Crofts for decades, ever since the older men were young ones. Simon Croft has always depended on her and wouldn't give it up, not for love nor money. He was spoiled. They're all spoiled, if I'm any judge. They get used to how things were done a long time ago and they're not about to change that."

"It sounds almost incestuous. That's the trouble with closely knit families; they don't know when the hell to stop."

THIRTY-NINE

Dulwich always surprised Jury. It was a real village within the Greater London area, home of Dulwich College and one of the best picture galleries in the country.

The house Jenny Gessup lived in was a small, attractive, yellow painted-brick one, with front garden given over to winter despoilment: hedges straggly, earth stone hard, flowers gone, probably some time ago.

Jury raised the brass dolphin-shaped door knocker several times. Finally, a young woman opened the door. She was short, with a trim build and delicate cheekbones. She did not appear to be one to handle wheelbarrows and buckets, but apparently had, as Angus Murphy hadn't complained about her lack of ability, only her laziness. Her hair was a hybrid grayish-brown the color of tree trunks. She did not appear best pleased to find two strangers on her doorstep.

"Miss Gessup?"

"It's with a hard *G* like 'guess,' not like 'Jesus.'"

Jury could tell she was delighted at being able immediately to take them to task. He smiled. "I'm Richard Jury with a *J*. Exactly like 'Jesus.'" He showed her his identification.

Jenny Gessup's face was red. "You're public servants; you ought not to get smart with those who pay your salary." She flung the door wide and marched herself into her sitting room, leaving the two of them to find their way by following their noses. They did.

Jury made himself comfortable on a small sofa slipcovered in lavender linen. The color on walls and woodwork was a pastel, a faded peach; chairs were covered in stronger garden colors: delphinium blue, daffodil yellow. It was as if summer had retreated here, having lost its brief campaign with the winter outside, and here was its last ditch stand.

"Miss Gessup, you worked at Tynedale Lodge." She pulled back and, Jury thought, became wary.

"You could say."

Jury smiled. "I do say. But you weren't there long, were you?"

Defensively, her voice raised a notch or two. "I only took the job as a lark, anyway."

"According to Miss Tynedale, you stopped coming."

Jenny gave a dismissive wave of her hand. "Oh, *her*. She acts like the lady of the manor."

"She is. Why don't you like her?" Jury could almost see a door close in her mind. All she did was shrug and study her bitten fingernails. "Why did you quit, then?"

"I told you. I wasn't serious about that job."

"Then why did you take it on in the first place?"

"Extra money, of course. I'm saving up to buy a car."

"Are you working now?"

She shook her head.

"Have you since you left the Lodge?"

"Can't find anything that suits."

The illogic of that answer, given she signed on as a gardener, which didn't suit either, Jury did not explore. She had quickly reached that point where her answers would be static or lies.

"You remember Gemma Trimm?"

"Gemma?" Jenny brightened a bit. "Yes, of course. We were kind of friends. I liked Gemma, but no one else paid much attention to her. Sad." Her voice was wistful. "There was that shooting up at the Lodge. The Southwark police said it was robbers first off and then said it was some boys acting up. Well, Gemma thought it was someone trying to kill her. That's daft."

"What if the shooting wasn't random? What if the shooter was after someone else?"

Her fine brown eyebrows drew together in puzzlement.

"I mean, is it possible the killer thought it was you in the greenhouse?"

Her eyes widened. "Oh, that's ridiculous." Not meeting his eyes, she picked at a bit of skin around her fingernail.

Jury left the idea on the table. He said nothing.

"Anyway," she went on, "if they were trying to shoot somebody besides Gemma, why not Angus Murphy? He was in the greenhouse a lot more than me."

"Too big. No one would have mistaken him for you."

"If you know something that might make you a danger to someone else," said Wiggins, "you'd better say."

Just then a woman appeared, holding branches of greenery of the sort one collects to make wreaths. Holly, perhaps. She stood in the doorway to a courtyard, smiling.

Jury and Wiggins both rose. Jenny stayed put on the sofa. "It's my aunt Mary."

The aunt put the holly on a table by the door and held out her hand, saying, "Mary Gessup." She pronounced it with a *J* sound.

Jury returned the smile and introduced himself and Wiggins. He brought out his ID again.

"Good Lord." She looked from them to her niece. "What's going on?"

Jenny said, "They're just asking about what happened at the Lodge. You know, about that shooting."

"But that was over two months ago."

"We're looking into the death of Simon Croft. He had a close association to the Tynedale family."

"Croft. Yes, I read about that. He had something to do with finance in the City."

"There may be a connection. We're simply trying to sort the details."

"Do please sit down. Would you like some tea?" Before Jury could say no, they'd just had some, she went on: "Jenny, do go and make some, will you?"

Truculently, Jenny rose and walked out. Her aunt watched her go, then said, "I thought you might want to talk without Jenny around. There must be more to this than Jenny's working at the Lodge."

"There is. We told your niece that whoever fired on the greenhouse might have actually had in mind to shoot your niece."

Mary Gessup stared at him. "Jenny? But *why*—?"

"That's what we want to find out. Mind you, I could be dead wrong."

"I know. She was scared, she said, which was understandable. But wasn't that a robbery attempt?"

Jury did not answer directly. "Has she been in trouble before?"

Mary Gessup hesitated. "Yes, but not seriously."

"What was 'not serious,' then?"

"Well . . . she was working for an old woman in the village and was discovered going through her things. I don't know what it is in Jenny that causes her to do that. She didn't take anything. The woman didn't press charges."

"Is it compulsive?"

Mary looked a question.

"Compulsive behavior?"

Mary was standing by the fireplace. "It could be, yes."

"Because that could be serious; that could be deadly. Even if she didn't take anything. I get the impression she isn't steady."

"'Steady'?"

"You know—dependable."

Mary nodded. "She's scattered; she can't keep her mind on a thing for very long. More so than most girls."

"She could have stumbled onto something at the Lodge and not known it."

Mary Gessup looked beleaguered. She shook her head, not in denial, but as if to clear it. "Of course, that's possible, Superintendent—"

"I'm only saying that *if* she found out something she shouldn't have, it would be in her best interests to tell us. That's all."

Jenny was back with the tea tray and seeming in better temper. Restoring, the prospect of tea was, thought Jury. No one knew that better than Wiggins, for whom this would make the fourth or fifth cup. Jury himself declined.

Jury said to Jenny, "You didn't much care for Miss Tynedale; what about her grandfather, Oliver?"

Immediately, her face brightened. She was holding the teapot in air as she said, "Oh, yes. Do you know what he said when I first met him?"

They did not.

"It was a poem. 'Jenny kissed me when we met,/Jumping from the chair she sat in . . .' I don't remember the rest. But wasn't that lovely?"

Wiggins put down his cup, and said,

> *"Say I'm weary, say I'm sad*
> *Say that health and wealth have missed me.*
> *Say I'm growing old, but add*
> *Jenny kissed me."*

They all gazed at Wiggins, astonished, none more than Jury. He had never known his sergeant to quote poetry. "That's beautiful." Then to Jenny, he said, "No wonder you liked him."

"He was Gemma's and my favorite."

And it occurred to Jury, and saddened him, that Jenny seemed to be putting herself in a category with Gemma Trimm. They were friends, Jenny had said, as if they were of an age together. Maybe that's what characterized Jenny Gessup: she seemed like a little girl.

When the others had drunk their tea, largely in silence, Jury thanked them and rose. "You've been very helpful. I hope we can clear things up."

"Where to, sir?" Wiggins had started the car.

"The village. I'd like a few words with the trustworthy grocer and the florists." After a few moments of driving, Jury said, "Rather remarkable you knowing that poem. Written by—" Jury snapped his fingers "—one of those poets with three names."

"Sir? Walter Savage Landor."

"Ah. Anyway, it's not the best known poem. How do you come to know it?"

"Jenny was my sister's name."

Again, he surprised Jury. "But I didn't know you had two sisters. I've heard you speak of only one, the one in Manchester."

"I don't have the other anymore. She died."

Never had an announcement of death been uttered with such restraint. "I'm sorry, Wiggins, really." He felt the inadequacy of such a statement. "A while back, was this?"

"Twenty-two years. This Christmas."

Jury felt doubly inadequate. "She died on Christmas Day?"

"Yes, sir. We were all in the parlor, around the tree, opening our presents, when Jenny said she felt sick and went upstairs to lie down. Mum went up with her and then Mum came down, saying she had a high temperature. You can imagine how eager a doctor would be to come out on Christmas Day. One did, though. It was meningitis and she died at midnight."

"My God, Wiggins. How awful. Was she younger than you?"

Wiggins nodded. He said nothing else.

FORTY

"That's the shop, right up there."

When they pulled up, Mr. Smith was weighing potatoes for a customer, a tall woman with shrapnel eyes which she kept trained on the scales. Jury wondered if any shopkeeper had ever got away with giving her bad weight. The grocer spun the brown sack around to close it and exchanged the potatoes for coin. The woman took herself off, casting suspicious glances at Jury and Wiggins.

"Mr. Smith?" Jury took out his identification.

"Oh, my! Scotland Yard. My, my." He wasn't displeased. "This must be about Mr. Croft. I had the City police with me just yesterday. My. Well, just who owns this case, anyway, you might ask."

"Technically, the City police. That's where the victim lived—and died. But there was a lot of spillover—" Jury left the explanation hanging. "Could we have a word with you, Mr. Smith?"

"Of course, of course. I'll just have my girl down to keep an eye on the place. Come along."

The three of them went inside where the grocer opened a door at the bottom of some steps and yelled upward for "Pru" to come on down. "Make it snappy now, girl!"

Pru, a stout, sullen girl in carpet slippers, could no

more make it snappy than fly to the moon. *Slap slap* the
slippers sounded on the stair. When Pru finally emerged
from the staircase and saw Jury, she lightened up a bit.
One hand went to her hair and the other to the bottom
of her rust-colored jumper, arranging both more satis-
factorily.

"'Lo" was all she said, tongue wetting her lips, but it
was clear she wanted to speak volumes of clever repar-
tee. Her eyes slid off Wiggins like water over stone and
wended their way back to Jury.

Her father told her, "You take care of customers here
while I talk to these detectives."

Pru's skin pinked up beneath a plump face full of
freckles. "Wha's it about, then? You done somethin' you
oughtn't, Dad?" Even her smile was pudgy.

"Never you mind."

Like a manservant escorting his visitors to an audience with royalty, Mr. Smith extended his arm and
briefly bowed. "This way, gentlemen, back to my office."

The office consisted of a desk and four chairs, old
black leatherette with aluminum arms and legs. There
was a strong smell of cabbage and damp wood.

Mr. Smith pulled two chairs around. Not until he himself was seated behind his desk did he ask, "Now, gentlemen, what can I do for you?"

"I don't want to waste your time (*meaning mine,* Jury
thought), so I'll tell you what I understand. You continued to deliver groceries to Simon Croft even after he
took up residence across the river. That's quite a lot of
trouble to go to for a pound of potatoes."

Even as Jury spoke, Mr. Smith was shutting his eyes
against the thickheadedness of Scotland Yard. With a
superior little smile playing about his lips, he said,
"That's how much you know, Superintendent, as to the
ways of Mr. Croft—or any of the clans, the Crofts and
the Tynedales."

"Well, then, enlighten me."

Mr. Smith was glad to do so. He sat forward. "Mr.

Simon Croft was one of the people who hate changing anything at all. Even where he gets his groceries. Why, he even laughed about it. 'You'd think I'd grow up, wouldn't you, Mr. Smith?' See, he even had the Tynedale Lodge cook come twice a week and do for him. Mrs. MacLeish, she is. She'd cook up several days' dinners at once. He was that attached to the Lodge."

"Then why did he move?" asked Wiggins, who had his notebook out and was frowning to beat the band. "Why did he leave Tynedale Lodge?"

"He wanted to be nearer the City. That's what he told Mrs. MacLeish. It's where he worked."

Not satisfied with this reason, Wiggins wrote it down, nonetheless.

Jury asked, "How often did you make these deliveries, Mr. Smith?"

"Once a week, dependable as clockwork. And other times if he needed more for dinner guests or drink parties, though I'm sure there weren't many of those. And he'd get Partridges to cater for him, too."

"Mrs. MacLeish must have talked about him to you."

"Mrs. Mac's never been one to gossip about her employers, and I admire that."

"So do I," said Jury, smiling wryly, "but it's not much help to us now. Both of you must have remarked on Mr. Croft's life—as they say—'style.'" He did not want to put ideas in the grocer's mind, nor words in his mouth.

Mr. Smith's chin was resting in his hand, his elbow on the desk. Narrowly, he regarded Jury, as if gauging his trustworthiness. "I recall being there in the kitchen with Mrs. Mac when she had to go to the front door and tell that Maisie Tynedale that Mr. Croft couldn't see her as he wasn't feeling well, but it wasn't so, for he was in his library working away."

Mr. Smith set about recalling. "It must've been back the end of October—no, hold on a minute, beginning of November, that's it, for I recall talking about Guy Fawkes and fireworks and wondering if we'd see them along the river there. Around the time that somebody was shootin' away up at the Lodge. Well, it was all over the manor, wasn't it? Nasty, these kids are today, some of 'em. Everyone was talkin' about it, the Daffs was all over it."

"Daffs?"

"The toy boys, the daffodils, the two that own that flower shop across the street. You talked with them?"

"Briefly, yes."

"Well, Mr. Croft got his flowers from them to the day he died—pardon that, it's just the expression. Very particular he was about his flowers."

"Mr. Peake and Mr. Rice?"

"Aye, that's them. Now they might be able to tell you somethin' I don't know." From his expression it was fairly clear Mr. Smith didn't think this even remotely possible. Then he stretched back in his chair and ran his hands over his bald pate in quick succession. "As I recall now the Daffs made a delivery just before the man was murdered." He smiled and waited for the next question.

"You've been most helpful, Mr. Smith." Jury rose and Wiggins stowed his notebook in his inside coat pocket and rose also.

Mr. Smith, however, remained seated, apparently prepared to stop there and answer questions through eternity.

"Mr. Smith?" Jury gently brought him back to his greengrocer business.

"Huh? Oh, sorry. Yes, I'll just see you out."

Pru seemed as reluctant to see them go as did her father.

Outside, Wiggins said, "A person might be suspicious of someone being that willing to answer questions."

"Why so cynical?" asked Jury, intent on jaywalking and looking for an opening between a removal van barreling down the road and two Volvos coming from different directions. "There are still a few people who find this an opportunity for a good gossip and couldn't care less if you're police or the Queen Mother. Come on—" They made a dive toward the opposite pavement.

The shop DELPHINIUM was as colorful outside as in. The sign that stretched along one side of the building was decorated with flowers, mushrooms and little green people Jury took for wood sprites or aliens.

Inside, the smell was simply heavenly, the mingled scents of lavender, jasmine and roses. Odysseus could not have fared better among the lotus eaters. Jugs and tall aluminum flower holders sat on the floor and they had to negotiate down an aisle lined with camellia plants to reach the back of the shop. Tommy Peake and Basil Rice were well-dressed men who could have been nearly any age at all. They were arranging roses and oriental lilies in what looked like a cut-glass crystal vase and another of plain crystal, clear but for a ribbon of amethyst that wound vinelike around it.

"Mr. Peake, Mr. Rice, you may remember I stopped in a couple of days ago?" Jury introduced Sergeant Wiggins. One florist tucked a pale strand of hair behind his ear and the other tried to find seating for the two detectives. Both were rather thrilled. Jury told them not to bother, that they wouldn't mind standing at all, that they would probably swoon anyway from the delicious scents in here.

"I wanted to talk to you about Simon Croft."

Basil slapped his hand to his forehead.

Jury pegged him as the more histrionic of the two. "You made fairly regular deliveries to Mr. Croft in the City."

"We can guess," said Peake, "who told you *that*. That old gossip, Smith—" He nodded toward the greengrocer's shop.

Basil showed more sympathy for the victim. "That poor, poor man. What a dreadful thing to have happen."

Tommy Peake said, astutely, "But you're from New Scotland Yard. Why would you be investigating this?"

"The City police have jurisdiction, of course. My part in this is a bit complicated."

Basil asked if he might be allowed to continue arranging flowers as "Miss Bosley wants this *tout de suite,* and you know what she's like!"

Jury smiled and said he didn't, really. It occurred to him that Basil lived in a world where everybody knew everybody else. Basil flipped his hand and waved away police ignorance as if the Bosleys had often roamed the corridors of Scotland Yard and meeting up with Miss Bosley was merely a matter of time.

"What's interesting is Mr. Croft continued to use your services even though there are plenty of florists on the other side of the river. He lived not far from Covent Garden."

"We *are* quite good at this business," said Basil.

Tommy shook his head. "Oh, we're good, but that isn't the reason. Simon was one of those people who hate change."

Sententiously, Wiggins said, "But we all have to resign ourselves to it, don't we?"

Tommy looked at Wiggins. "You're talking about age and infirmity. Death. Yes, but there are things you can control. Such as where you get your bloody bouquets." His smile, Jury thought, shimmered.

"Did Simon Croft have a standing order with you?"

Tommy nodded. "There were also times he wanted something particular. Otherwise, his instruction was to make up whatever we thought looked good and just take it along. But there were times he just hankered for a particular flower, you know?"

Jury could not remember the last time he'd even seen a bouquet, much less hankered for one. "When was the last time you made a delivery?"

Tommy pursed his lips and remembered. "That was just the week before he was shot." He shivered slightly. "Got as far as the front door with 'em. That cook—the one who works at the Lodge and, I guess, went to Simon's house, too—she's the one took the flowers in."

He seemed disgruntled; they both did. "Ordinarily he had you in?"

"Well, of course!" said Basil. "Usually made a real *fuss* over them. Right, Tommy?"

Wiggins said, "So you knew Simon Croft quite well?"

Basil backpedaled. "Not all that well, no."

"You were on a first-name basis with him?"

"Oh, we're on a first-name basis with *everybody*."

"Not with us, you aren't," said Wiggins. "Sir?"

Jury hid a smile. "I think that'll be all, for now."

As they started toward the door, Jury said, "You're on a roll, Wiggins." He stopped and turned. "Do you deliver to Islington, Mr. Peake?"

"We can do."

Retracing his steps, Jury walked back to the counter. He looked at the cut glass, at the crystal with its ribbon of amethyst. "I'm afraid my policeman's moiety doesn't run to this." He tapped the crystal vase.

"These—? Oh, good Lord, Superintendent, don't think we furnish vases like these. No, they belong to customers who bring them in each time for an arrangement. Particular, they are. What we usually do is furnish a glass vase and we can also do a very nice arrangement tied with twine. Or a box, of course. What sort of flowers have you in mind?"

Jury scratched his neck and looked at the cold behind the glass doors. "One is an elderly woman—"

"Lavender," said Tommy and looked at Basil.

"And heather. And perhaps two of those roses—" He pointed to roses of an exquisite shade of lavender. "That'll do for her, trust me. Perfect."

"Okay. The other's a young lady—"

Both assumed their thinking positions, leaning over the counter.

"Hmm." Basil said, "What's her coloring?"

"Hers? Oh. Hair kind of fiery, eyes this color—" He touched the ribbon of glass winding around the vase.

"Ah!" Basil stood up and plucked a colored pencil from a cup of them and drew it across the pad. Then he did the same with another. "What colors does she like?"

"Emerald green, hot pink, lapis lazuli—"

"God," said Tommy, with a wink, "she's lucky to have someone who notices and remembers. Can't ask a husband those questions; he wouldn't have a clue."

Jury watched Basil with yet another colored pencil. He turned the notebook around so Jury could see it, and said, "This might look an odd combination, but believe me, she'll go for it."

Jury was astonished that with so few strokes in so little time, Basil had drawn a complete arrangement of flowers.

"We've got the bells of Shannon, and we can get iris—can we, Tommy?"

"Absolutely."

"And these coppery roses, they'd be perfect."

Jury slowly shook his head. "No wonder Simon Croft didn't want to give you up."

"I don't get it, Wiggins. Why the grocer but not the florists? Why would Croft admit Smith and not those two?"

They were waiting for two lorries and a Morris to pass in front of them.

"You're assuming who he saw and who he didn't is significant. Maybe he just didn't feel like diving into the pool with those two on that day."

Jury laughed. "Of course, that could easily be it."

"Or maybe Simon found them a shade too you-know?"

They were crossing the street now. "Wiggins, they've been 'you-know' for as long as he knew them." Jury looked up the street. "There's the butcher's; I want a word with him. Come on."

Gyp was just pulling down the grill in front of his window, preparatory to closing. Jury found him to be wiry and angular, his chin sharp, his nose pointed, his shoulder blades as thin and spiny as sharks' fins. He could tell that Gyp was cutting-edge mean. The bloody apron he wore did nothing to soften the portrait. Even his voice was reedy and ragged and without resonance.

"Sorry, gentlemen, but it's closing time. All work and no play makes Gyp a dull boy." His laugh was more of a giggle.

"Prepare to bore us then, Mr. Gyp." Jury flashed his identification. "And lead the way inside."

Gyp was one of those people whose reaction to a policeman on the pavement was to run. All the little meannesses, the little tricks and swindles he had contrived to work on his fellows would leak from the corners of his mind and lubricate memory. Jury could see it in his black and oily eyes. And this was not to mention the fate of the benighted animals that fell under his cleaver. There was one in the window right now, a suckling pig scored with slices of orange and studded with cloves. If Gyp kept a cat it would only be to kill mice. Admittedly, Jury disliked butchers. He had seen their plump and smiling faces looking out from the pages of magazines, rosy and self-satisfied, as if they were choking on rubies.

"It's my closing time. Like I said. It's half-five—"

"That's good; we won't be disturbed. Come on."

Muttering, Gyp led the way.

Several chairs lined the aisle between counter and wall and Gyp sat but Jury and Wiggins remained standing. More intimidating.

Gyp said, anxiety clotting his voice, "It's about that lad, ain't it? Benny? I knew I should've reported him not goin' to school."

Jury said nothing. Let the man babble. He went on about Benny, school and "that mutt o' his" and the "thieving" that went on in the shop. "It ain't only school; it's where that boy lives, and with who. Headed for Borstal, he is, probably been there already."

"Scotland Yard," said Wiggins, "isn't here to track down truants."

Jury said, "We're looking into the death of Simon Croft."

"Croft?" Gyp's tallow-colored skin drew up in furrows. "That one from the Lodge? He moved to the City. Why'd you be asking *me* about Simon Croft?"

"You did know him."

"So did everybody. But you think he'd come in and ask for a pound o' mince? Well, he didn't. People at the Lodge don't deal with the likes o' Gyp." He hooked his thumb toward his chest. "Too high 'n' mighty for that."

"How long did you know Mr. Croft?"

"Didn't I just say I hardly did?"

"Then how long did you hardly know him?" Jury itched to hit this man.

"Long as I had me shop here. That'd be, oh, twenty years about." With long fingers he stroked a sunken cheek.

"He didn't like you, right?" Jury supposed this was a safe bet.

"I'm too busy to care who likes me and who don't."

"Well, I'm not too busy, Mr. Gyp." Jury moved to the chair, reached down and twisted the neck of the collarless shirt tightly enough it raised the butcher from the seat; he did this slowly, which made it even more threatening. "Now you listen to me, Gyp. If anything happens to Benny Keegan or his dog—*or* his dog—"

"You're choking me! I'm choking!" he declared in a strangled voice.

"—I'll be back, so you better work hard at keeping them healthy and out of traffic." Jury suddenly released his hand and Gyp fell back against the wall. Jury nodded to Wiggins and they started toward the door.

Behind them, Gyp called out, "I'm reportin' this, don't think I won't!"

Jury took out his small cache of cards and flipped one in Gyp's direction. "Just in case you forget my name."

Jury liked the musty air of the Moonraker Bookshop, the slightly acidic smell of ink, the thought of brittle old paper crumbling like memory. Dust, poor light and nostalgia, these were his notions of places like the Moonraker. Or perhaps this was just his romantic notion; God only knew Waterstone's didn't fit the image. He liked the wooden sign above the steps that led down to "garden" level, too. MOONRAKER BOOKSHOP, S. PENFORWARDEN, PROP.

"He was very interested in the war," said Sybil Penforwarden, speaking of Simon Croft. "Prodigiously interested. I must've ordered a dozen books for him. The last ones were—" She stopped and considered. "*Fourteen Days,* that was one, and *Solemn December*—an unfortunate try at assonance, don't you think? At any rate, Simon had a high regard for both. The *December* one, of course, is the one set in 1940. We talked about the war, we talked about it quite a lot. We'd both been children then, seven or eight, I believe I was. He'd have been a bit older, and we both had memories which we tried to pin down." She took a sip of tea. She had kindly invited Jury and Wiggins to join her for tea. "I always have my tea around five o'clock and I've just baked a seed cake."

Which Jury was tucking into with his second slice, as was Wiggins. A longcase clock ticked somewhere at the end of an aisle of shelves; except for that the room was deathly quiet. Had some customer been reading back there in the shelves, one would have heard the pages turn.

Jury eased down a little farther in his slipcovered chair, careful not to lean his head against it for fear of dozing off, and feeling for the first time that day completely comfortable, and hungry and thirsty, too. He slid his cup toward the pot and Miss Penforwarden poured out tea, adding a measure of milk.

"Croft's interest wasn't just historical, then. It was personal."

"Oh, yes. Very." She held the pot aloft, signaling Sergeant Wiggins, who, of course, wanted a refill. "You see, his father, Francis Croft, owned a pub named the Blue Last. It was in the City. It was demolished during the London blitz. That would have been—" She closed her eyes and calculated.

Jury did it for her: "December 29, 1940."

Miss Penforwarden was astonished. "You're certainly a student of history."

Jury smiled. "Not really. I was told about the Blue Last."

"Of course. There was that item in the paper about its being the last London bomb site. Some developer had bought it up and in the course of digging they unearthed bones. Well, they could have been anybody, couldn't they?"

Jury ignored this. "This book Mr. Croft was writing. His interest was personal, you agree; did he ever discuss the particulars?"

Sybil Penforwarden sat back with her cup that trembled ever so slightly in its saucer. She thought. "Now, that's a very perspicacious question, Superintendent—"

(Jury would've enjoyed hearing her talk to Angus Murphy.)

"—very. 'A family thing,' I recall he said. It's coming back to me in bits and pieces. I'll just toss them out as I recall, shall I?"

"Absolutely."

Wiggins retrieved his notebook from the little end table where he'd deposited it when the tea and cake had arrived.

She went on. "Now, I recall that he talked about Oswald Mosley—you know, the dreadful Fascist? Simon was interested in him because he'd discovered that Mrs. Riordin's husband—she lives at the Lodge, you know—was one of Mosley's followers. He said to me that many people took Mosley to be a cartoon character, a laughingstock, but, he said, 'the man was dangerous, extremely dangerous. People have forgotten that.' Simon wondered why Riordin would desert his wife just to join up with that 'rascal'—which is what he called Mosley. Simon could be old-fashioned in his choice of words." Miss Penforwarden smiled.

Jury wondered how well she knew Simon Croft. "But he didn't ask Katherine Riordin herself?"

"That I don't know."

"Could he have been upset or incensed by things that we come to take almost for granted anymore? Abortion, divorce, unmarried couples, homosexuality. Things that—whether rightly or wrongly—the public finds more acceptable now?"

"Yes, he was old-fashioned in that respect. But not sanctimonious or sermonizing, if you know what I mean. It's just that he believed so fervently in—attachments."

"Loyalty, for instance?"

"Absolutely. Yes."

"To king and country?" Jury smiled.

"You might laugh, but—"

"I'm not laughing, Miss Penforwarden."

"He was very fond of Alexandra's husband, Ralph Herrick. Ralph was in the RAF. Simon himself was quite young and Ralph was his hero. Ralph Herrick really was a hero, too. He was awarded the Victoria Cross for valor. I don't remember precisely what he did; Simon said he was a daredevil pilot."

Jury thought for a moment, absently regarding Wiggins, who was faithfully taking notes. There was loyalty for you: sitting there with his third cup of tea (having poured himself another) and his notebook on his knee. Jury smiled. He knew how he'd feel if Wiggins was shot and killed. He'd get the bastard who did it. One could not, however, get the entire Luftwaffe.

"Simon talked about impostors," said Miss Penforwarden.

"What?"

"You know, the enemy posing as someone else, the ridiculous notion that the Germans would pop up everywhere in England disguised. Such as the idea circulated about German parachutists—that they'd fall to earth disguised as nuns. That and the fifth column idea. Traitors out in their gardens signaling to the German planes with electric torches. Silly stuff. But once such an idea takes hold, he said, it's very hard to disabuse one's mind of it."

"Yes. He would not like the idea of betrayal."

Wiggins put in, "Would you, sir? Would any of us?"

Miss Penforwarden pursed her lips and returned her cup to its saucer. The tea was cold, anyway. "You know, I sometimes felt there was something other than the war that urged him on to do this research."

"But he didn't say what it was."

"Outright? No."

"You say you saw him two weeks ago. Did you notice a difference in his behavior?"

She looked puzzled. "No. He was the same as always. He'd talk about the forties, the devastation. Hitler would send over five hundred planes a *night*. Simon had a journal, or notebook he kept, and he'd tell me facts such as that. I wondered how he remembered them and he held up the journal that he always carried. 'Never be without this,' he said."

"Some people seem to think he'd grown a little paranoid during the last weeks of his life. To the extent that he wouldn't let family members come into his house. And the owners of the flower shop weren't admitted when they brought flowers he'd ordered."

"But how did they know, these people who were turned away?"

"How did they know?"

"That he'd changed; that he'd grown a little paranoid."

"Perhaps because he wouldn't see them. He appeared to be afraid."

She was obviously doubtful. "I can only say he seemed the same to me."

"Well, perhaps that's because he felt far more comfortable around you than he did around others."

She waved a self-deprecating hand. "I can't imagine that's so."

"I can." Jury rose and gathered up his coat. "I think we'll be going. You've been extremely helpful, Miss Penforwarden. You ready, Wiggins?"

"Sir," said Wiggins snappily.

A moment ago he'd looked rather dozy. Jury said as they ducked under the low lintel, "That's what three cups of tea and three pieces of cake do to a person, Sergeant."

"But it was worth it, wasn't it?" They walked toward the car. "We got a different picture of Simon Croft."

"So eating all that cake was a kind of martyrdom that paid off?"

"You could say that. I'm pretty full. Now where to?"

Jury shoved himself into the cramped seat, thinking he'd be just as comfortable riding in the trunk. "Drop me off at the Croft house."

"What would you expect to find? The crime scene people did a thorough check—"

"Yes. But sometimes it helps to look at things on your own."

FORTY-ONE

Private residences on the Thames were rare, especially in the City, which had always been the financial and trading heart (if trade can have a heart) of London: the Bank of England, Mincing Lane, Lloyd's. Now, such conversions were seeping into the City as had been going on for years in Docklands, and continued throughout the areas of Whitechapel, Limehouse and Wapham. These were the old buildings that sentimentalists would still have preferred to be left standing, memorials to London's past, the docks, the stews. But what had been lost in the way of romance had been made up for in eye-catching livable space. The developers and builders were right for a change. The improvement really was an improvement, except to those sentimental souls who believed the past was inviolate and did not want change.

Jury knew he was one of those souls. So had Simon Croft been. This useless romance that Jury was caught up in did not profit his work, though for the most part he could set it aside. But then came a case that demanded one take a long look back.

Simon Croft's house was not the result of a conversion. It was Georgian, not terribly interesting architecturally, but its gray stone bulk was imposing, partly because of its age. It was flat fronted, with long windows on the ground and first floors, smaller sash windows on the two upper floors. In front was a small forecourt large enough for five or six cars. The only one presently here was Croft's own Mercedes.

When he had been here the night of Croft's death, he had noticed the house was full of stunning antiques, a fortune in furniture. He was standing now in a large, nearly empty drawing room or reception room. Against one wall stood a credenza, probably seventeenth century, on whose door and sides were painted fading flowers in pink and green. The only other furniture sat near the center of the room: a fainting couch, covered in deep blue velvet, and a Chippendale elbow chair with a silvery green damask seat.

The same feeling of emptiness Jury had courted outside came back to him now. It was the sort of emptiness one associates with houses whose occupants have suddenly packed and fled. It reminded him of his first visit to Watermeadows, that beautiful Italianate house and gardens which had Ardry End as its neighbor, despite their grounds extending over a quarter mile before meeting. He shut his eyes and thought of Hannah Lean. *Don't go there,* he told himself. But, of course, by the time you think of that, you're already there. That room in Watermeadows had been even larger than this one, emptier, with scarcely any furniture—a sofa, a chair—giving rise to that same baffled feeling that the owners had made a quick departure, and, as in war, as in an enemy occupation, had taken whatever transportable belongings they could and vanished. He left the room.

He walked down the black and white marbled hall, bisected by a wide mahogany staircase, to the library where Mrs. MacLeish had discovered Simon Croft and called the City police. It was quite a different room, crowded with chairs and tables and books. Jury switched on the desk lamp, an elaborate one with a brass elephant as its base. He looked over what the police hadn't taken away in evidence bags. There was a chased silver inkpot, several Mont Blanc pens, a blotter and a stack of printer paper held down with a heavy glass weight, the printer itself on a small table in the window embrasure. There was a handsome rosewood piece that looked like a bureau but was really a filing cabinet. Chairs were the roomy sort, deeply cushioned and covered with linen or leather. Jury could almost feel the room embracing him.

Books were shelved floor to ceiling around three walls, two of them separated by narrow leaded windows. It was interesting to him that the killer had removed all trace of the book Simon Croft had been working on— manuscript, hard drive, diskettes—yet had forgotten intellectual content, or, given he or she had no time for inspecting the books, simply hoped that no one would think of searching Croft's bookshelves.

It had to have been here somewhere, the reason for Simon Croft's murder, and perhaps it still was. There was no sign even of the notes he must have made. No sign either of the pocket-size journal Miss Penforwarden had alluded to (*"He always carried it. 'Never be without this,' he said."*) And no sign of this year's diary, which he must have kept too, as there were diaries from the last fifteen years placed side by side on one of the shelves in such an orderly fashion the gap told of the absence of at least one, this year's.

Jury imagined that the books Croft had consulted most would be together rather than parceled out according to subject, author or alphabet. He took out his notebook and read again the titles Miss Penforwarden had given him, then looked for those two books. They were, as he had supposed, together on a section of shelf nearest the leather chair. It was a chair that would have suited Boring's. It was well worn, and Jury assumed it was Simon's favorite. He sat down to look at the books purchased from the Moonraker. He leafed through them and saw numerous markings and marginalia.

Solemn December, although fairly recently acquired,

was much read. There were scraps of paper and yellow Post-It notes on a number of pages. The subtitle of the book was *Britain, 1940*. As Miss Penforwarden had suggested, the book was unquestionably on his subject. A good third of it was composed of photographs, and the text itself dealt with the hardships and courage of the British people—the wardens, the volunteers, the shopkeepers and ordinary citizens. It was nostalgic, a hope and glory book. As such, Jury somehow imagined it was of limited textual value to Croft, not dense enough. The picture he had built up of Simon Croft was of a complex man. He was someone who could (and did) set great store by family and the past, but who would not, at the same time, be hoodwinked. "Hoodwinked" by what exactly Jury couldn't say. Certainly the identity of Maisie Tynedale was in the running.

Again he wondered: if the purpose of taking Croft's computer, journal, diary, notes and hard copy was to eradicate whatever knowledge Croft had stumbled on, why hadn't these books been removed, too? This next one, titled *Fourteen Days*, was very heavily marked up. Notes, marginalia. A much-used book which appeared to be, unlike the other one, sinewy, full of material.

Jury had to begin with what he knew about motive in this murder, and the only one he had yet sorted was the alleged motive of Kitty Riordin and her daughter, Erin. That Croft had unearthed this imposture (*"Simon talked about impostors"*) and confronted Riordin with it would have been motive enough for her to kill him.

Another point was the supposed attempt to shoot the person in the greenhouse. But were these two shootings connected? Perhaps not, but Jury hated coincidence.

A cigarette box inlaid with mother-of-pearl (*"I'm beautiful, Jury; have one."*) sat on the table beside his armchair. He got up and walked around the room trying to think his way into Simon Croft's mind. Though he was loath to mix it into this brew because it widened the field so much, Jury knew he had to consider the likelihood that Croft's murder was related to his work as a broker rather than his family or his past, as Plant had suggested. Perhaps he had caused a loss to one of his clients; perhaps there was fraud. Perhaps. Jury doubted it. Croft just didn't sound the type. More than that, Croft's behavior during his last visit with Miss Penforwarden did not sound like that of a desperate man who'd been caught with his hands in the till. No. But then Miss Penforwarden's assessment of Croft's state of mind had been different from Mrs. MacLeish's, or Haggerty's, or the grocer Smith's or the Delphinium boys'. That was interesting.

Jury had made two circuits of the room, standing here and there, and now stopped before the rosewood filing cabinet. Bless the man for his orderliness. He removed a folder labeled "correspondence." He guessed the order of the letters would be by date, the ones in front being the most recent, given Croft's meticulous disposal of papers. Jury went through them and found the whole lot disappointing. There were letters of appreciation from satisfied clients, acknowledging the good job Simon had done with their brokerage accounts; a letter inviting him to a weekend in Invernessshire; a few letters from his solicitors regarding "minor" changes in the wording of his will. That would hardly constitute changing beneficiaries, thought Jury. That was about all. Letters might, of course, have been removed.

He went back to his chair, sat down and picked up *Fourteen Days,* which sounded almost like the title of a thriller. He read about the hammering East London and part of the City had taken on the nights of December 19 and 20. He was surprised to read that Hitler had for some time before the blitzkrieg been convinced that Britain would come to its senses and simply capitulate. And given the German successes, it was a wonder Britain didn't. It was a blessing that his country had been totally unaware of the disasters suffered by the British Expeditionary Forces. France had been a disaster. Also, Germany had taken Holland, Brussels and, worst, had advanced to the English Channel.

There were a number of marginal notations, which was not surprising, considering how conscientious a note taker Croft was. In one margin was penned in RALPH (?). Not familiar with Herrick's wartime maneuvers Jury couldn't, of course, see the relationship between Ralph Herrick and the account in the book of the GAF daytime raids on aircraft fields in the southeast of England. The bombers were turned back or brought down by RAF fighter pilots. Then again, two pages later in the margin, RALPH (???). Here, again, several pages were devoted to accounts of Göring's near success in wiping out the RAF airfields, which would have meant wiping out the RAF. In other words, winning the war in the air. Winning, period.

For some reason, those three question marks disturbed Jury. The single question mark on the page before might simply have indicated curiosity. But here the marks suggested a real need to know. Know what? This entry was also cross-referenced: (CF. P. 208, F.H.).

"F.H." A title, perhaps? An author? He went back to the bookshelf and ran his finger along the spines of the books Croft seemed to have used most for research and found the title *Finest Hours* (a borrowing of one of Churchill's titles). He thumbed up page 208 and read an account of German bombers over the Isle of Wight. In the margin was written "R"? What was Simon asking? Whether Ralph had participated in this particular battle? Or that Ralph had talked about it? What could Simon otherwise be alluding to? Jury went to the three other pages indicated in the margin, but the details of the combat meant little to him.

Except, of course, in his own private world, where they meant a great deal. Jury had not known his father except as the face in his mother's photographs, and

whatever he himself had contrived to imagine about his
father, a litany to repeat again and again before he fell
asleep. Definitely handsome, undoubtedly brave.

He thought of photographs. Croft would probably
have an album; anyone this precise, this organized,
this dedicated to preserving memories would have
pictures, snapshots and so forth. The book itself,
wouldn't it contain photographs as studies of this kind
so often did? He made a cursory examination of the
shelves on which were kept the journals and diaries,
but saw nothing.

Frustrated he went back to his chair and picked up
Finest Hours again. What was Croft thinking about?
Jury riffled the pages and stopped at more marginalia,
this time a column of dates:

> 5.24.41   [BISMRCK]
> 8 & 9-'40   [ATTACKS, AIRFIELDS]
> 10.40   COV.

Jury skimmed the page in whose margin these dates
appeared, in a neat row. There were no corresponding
dates in the text of this page or the ones before or
after. He went to every page where Simon had made
marginal notes. No such dates appeared in the text, so
there were obviously other sources he was using. But
he could not find reference to them. How could he
match up dates to events? How could he find the common denominator? Was there one and was it Ralph?
No one had talked very much about him, but, then,
he'd been around so little that the family hadn't really
known him well. Simon and Ian had idolized Ralph;
that did not constitute knowledge. The marriage to
Alexandra was brief and wartime. What all knew and
mentioned was that the young flier had been awarded
the Victoria Cross.

On the last page of the book at the very bottom,
Simon had written,

COVENTRY
ULTRA
CHICK. BED.
HATSTON
ENIGMA B.P.
—GOD I DON'T BELIEVE THIS.

"Enigma." Jury frowned.

He sat thinking in the chair for some time. Then he crossed to the telephone and took out his small notebook. He rang Marie-France Muir.

After that, he rang Boring's.

FORTY-TWO

Marie-France Muir lived in Chapel Street. The house was not commodious, but knowing the value of square footage in Belgravia it didn't have to be to mark the owner as well off. The furnishings would also have told the story. Against one wall sat a walnut kneehole desk flanked by an ornate pier glass and an exceptionally beautiful painting of woods, sheep and drifted snow that seemed to be lit from within. In an embrasure near the fireplace sat a walnut chest on chest of rich patination. The fireplace itself was an ornate green marble, guarded by an elaborate fire screen, decorated with birds and butterflies. A glass and rosewood paneled display piece holding fine china that Jury would have lumped under *étagère* was undoubtedly something else, something rarer. It was over six feet tall, nearly as tall as he was. Through the door into what must have been the dining room he glimpsed carved walnut chairs and the end of a dark dining-room table.

Yet what dominated the living room was not the furniture but the art, paintings largely of the French Impressionists and post-Impressionists. They hung one above the other in rococo gilt frames. It looked like a gallery. He wondered how many of them were originals; he wondered if *all* were originals.

The sofa and chairs were of humbler origins and

more comfortable ones, slipcovered in a restful gray linen. "This is really a nice room," Jury said, sitting back in the deep chair with the coffee Marie-France had had the foresight to make. He was almost hesitant to lift the paper-thin cup, which looked as if it would break if he blew on it.

"Thank you." She looked around as if assessing everything anew, in light of his comment. "Much of the art was acquired by Ian. It's his field, painting. A few pieces came from Simon's house—" The fragile cup trembled in the saucer and she set it on the table beside her chair. She was silent for a while and so was Jury. He did not intrude upon such silences, the ones caused by grief. He did not intrude unless the other person made it clear there was something he could offer.

"It's just made such a difference," she said. "Simon and I didn't see each other all that much, but you don't have to, do you? To know the other person is there. The thing is, we were quite self-sufficient, and though we might give the impression of living in one another's pockets, we really don't, and didn't. I mean all of us, including the Tynedales. I think his self-sufficiency might be the reason Ian never married, or, at least, one of the reasons." She smiled. "Lord knows, he could have had his pick. It's too bad in a way, none of us having children. I certainly wanted them and so did my husband." She shrugged, almost by way of apology.

"Then you wouldn't have—" Jury rephrased it. "How often had you seen your brother in the past two months?"

Marie-France considered. "Once at his house, once here. The last time was, oh, back in early November."

"Did he seem in some way different?"

She frowned slightly. "No. All of us are always pretty much the same. Boring, but true."

"A few people I've talked to got the impression he was afraid of something or someone. To the point, really, of paranoia."

The smile she gave Jury could have charmed the gold butterflies right off the fire screen. "Mr. Jury, that's the most ridiculous thing I've ever heard."

His smile matched hers. "Perhaps. But remember, you'd seen him only twice and the last time was over a month ago."

"I'm not basing my opinion on seeing him; I'm basing it on knowing Simon. He was the easiest person I've ever known, the most composed. Simon and paranoia just don't go together. Who's said he was afraid and why?"

"He asked DCI Haggerty to come by the house when he could; your brother appeared to be afraid of someone. He wouldn't admit tradespeople to the house or family members. Maisie Tynedale, for instance."

"But he didn't say what he was afraid of?"

Jury shook his head.

She sighed. "As for the tradespeople, I don't particularly put out the red carpet for the butcher and baker, either. And as for Maisie—" She looked away and waved her hand in a dismissive gesture. "Simon never liked her."

"Why not?"

"He thought she was pushy on the one hand and somewhat of a sycophant on the other. Probably a few other things in between." She picked up the silver pot and poured Jury more coffee. No question, coffee tasted better coming from a silver pot and delicate china.

"How about you? Do you agree?"

"About Maisie? Yes. I find her very cold."

"And her grandfather? How does he feel about her?"

"When it comes to Oliver, I can't really say. Maisie's not only Alexandra's daughter, but the *only* grandchild. Those are two reasons for him to adore her." She frowned. "But he doesn't seem to. Adore her, I mean. Certainly, not in the way he does that little girl, Gemma. But of course she's only eight or nine. Perhaps when Maisie was nine, Oliver felt the same way..." She shrugged. "The one person who seems to get on with

Maisie is that Riordin woman. I don't like her at all. There's something almost, ah, creepy about her. When she was still a young woman she tied herself down to living at the Lodge. I find that odd."

"She must think there's something in it for her. I imagine she expects to come into at least part of Mr. Tynedale's estate. Don't you?"

"Yes, but, well, certainly there'll be a bequest, but I shouldn't think enough to warrant giving over one's life to it." She sighed and sipped her coffee.

Jury leaned forward. "Have you ever thought there might be more to it than that?"

"What do you mean?" She looked off toward the window as if a fresh aspect were to be found there. "My Lord, are you suggesting they were lovers?"

Jury laughed. "That never entered my mind. Perhaps it should have."

With an oblique look at Jury, she said, "No, it shouldn't. I'm surprised it entered mine. Oliver is simply not—I don't know how to say it. Anyway, he's not, take my word for it. Then what did you mean?"

Given that Ian Tynedale and Marie-France disliked Maisie and Kitty Riordin, and also were such obviously intelligent people, he was surprised neither of them wondered about Maisie's parentage. But they were also ingenuous; maybe they couldn't comprehend something so monstrous as an imposture lasting more than half a century. "I don't know. I'm fishing, I expect."

"Well, you need some better bait, Superintendent." This was accompanied by her immensely charming smile. "The rest of us manage to rub along with Kitty, but not Emily. Emily never did get along with her; Emily thinks she's a fraud."

"In what way?"

"Kitty took credit—no, that's not exactly right—she was being credited with something she didn't do: she didn't save Maisie's life. It was chance, pure chance. But Kitty began to believe she saved the baby's life."

Jury nodded. "There's something I wonder, though: why would she have taken either child out during the blitz? That was savage bombing the Luftwaffe was doing."

"Savage, but erratic. Simon talked about it often. He was moved to write this book, not surprisingly, because our father, Francis, had died in the blitz. Simon thought what a lot of people mistook as strategic bombing was simply systematic bombing. Göring's last-ditch stand. He'd already lost in his attempt to destroy our air force by bombing the airfields.

"For us young ones, the whole thing was exciting— look at those ruins, that rubble we could investigate for treasure. It was rather like a film. Well, I'm trying to answer your questions. That sort of illusion wasn't restricted to children. Grown-ups felt it too."

Marie-France went on. "What I'm saying is that there were times we thought of it as a fairy tale. That sounds outrageous, I know, but that was the climate of opinion sometimes. Add to that that Kitty Riordin was a headstrong girl, and if she thought a baby needed some fresh air, I suppose she wasn't going to hide in the Blue Last waiting for the war to blow over."

"And Alexandra?"

"Alex was more sensible, more realistic."

"Why would she allow *her* baby to be taken out, then?"

"It's a good question. I can't answer that. But you know we're sitting here second-guessing what happened fifty-five years ago."

Jury smiled. "I spend most of my life doing that."

"I can see you'd have to."

Jury put down his cup. "This book your brother was writing. Ralph Herrick apparently figured in it."

This surprised her. "Ralph?" Bemused, she repeated the name as if it were some magical incantation. "Ralph. I don't recall Simon mentioning him with regard to his book, though when we were children, I know Ralph seemed to us ever so glamorous. He was a hero; he was handsome; he was married to Alexandra. Simon and Ian both idolized him. They thought it wizard that he flew a Spitfire."

"Do you remember Herrick as anything other than an icon?"

Marie-France thought for a moment, sipping her coffee. "You know, that's well put, Superintendent. I think that's just how we saw him. He represented something in the war that was noble and good. But as for knowing him, Ralph wasn't really around much. He was rarely at home, even after he married Alex, and they were married only a little over a year when she was killed. And then . . . ?" She paused, trying to remember. "I'm not sure what happened to him."

"Herrick joined the people at Bletchley Park. You remember, the mathematicians like Turing who were working on Hitler's Enigma machines."

She looked at Jury with raised eyebrows. "Really? No, I don't think I ever did know that. I would think Simon must've, though." She was looking out of the window to where a shaft of sunlight was turning a vase of roses a deeper shade of pink. The small gilt clock on the mantel chimed seven.

"I've got to go. I really appreciate you talking to me." Jury rose.

"You're very welcome, Superintendent." As she rose to see him out, she laughed. "I really can't get over someone's saying Simon was paranoid. If there was ever a person I can't picture having enemies, it was Simon."

Jury looked at her. "Then I'm afraid you'd be wrong."

FORTY-THREE

"I have my coat on and money," said Gemma. From the coat pocket she drew a small, shiny-blue change purse with a zipper and decorated with a bright pink plastic flower. She was sitting with Benny on the wooden plank in the beech tree.

"I can't take you to Piccadilly," he said, feeling guilty. "I'm too—busy." He was too young, he meant. Not for himself—he could go to Piccadilly and back ten times over. He was too young to take the responsibility of Gemma is what he meant. He'd never get permission. That made him laugh. He was too young to be doing most of the things he *was* doing. The thing was, Benny wanted to see the windows at Fortnum and Mason, too. "They're really the best Christmas windows around, is what I've heard." But it did worry him something might happen to her.

"I know. Don't you want to see them?"

He shrugged. "I wouldn't mind."

"Then let's."

He sighed. "Gemma, they'd never let you go with me, even if we did take a cab there and back." He'd seen she had a lot of money in that little purse. Enough for cabs, he bet.

"Then don't ask."

Benny sighed again. He'd been watching Sparky

make his way over the ground, stopping at stalks and hedges, sniffing as if he'd never been in this garden before. Now he was going into the greenhouse. He never dug up around flowerbeds; he was very good that way, but sometimes you had to watch him. Mr. Murphy didn't like dogs much, anyway.

"Christmas is in only three days."

She was picking at a stitch on Richard's blue trousers. She had cut off some of the excess material and sewn up the sides, which now fanned out and were still too big. Her needlework was not very good. "I sewed this. Do you like it?" She turned Richard slowly around so that his outfit could be viewed front to back.

"It's a lot better than that old nightgown. But couldn't you have used blue thread instead of white?"

Gemma looked doubtful. "Maybe." She added, "But I couldn't find any." She hadn't looked.

"It's nice."

"He needs new clothes for Christmas. He needs a mac."

"Uh-huh."

Gem went on picking at the thread. "Do you think about your mother?" Her voice seemed to shrink.

Benny was surprised. "Sometimes."

She raised her eyes from the trousers and looked right at him.

It's awful to have somebody know you're lying, Benny thought. "Okay, like a lot of the time." Now his own voice sounded strange; it sounded hollow.

"I would too if I could remember mine. I don't know even what she looked like."

Benny thought a moment. "Like you. Think of you, only older. You know who you look like? Like Maisie's mother. Remember? You showed me her picture once."

Gemma frowned. "That makes me look like *Maisie.* I don't want to."

Benny didn't either. He shook his head. "No, no. Her *mother.* Mr. Tynedale's daughter is who you look like.

Maisie doesn't really look like her even if she's got that dark hair and stuff. Like her face isn't the same shape. Maisie's mother's is heart shaped. So is yours. It's like a little heart."

Gemma put Richard down and felt her face all around. "I don't think so."

"Gem, you can't *feel* heart shaped. Just look in a mirror."

"Okay," she said. She looked into Richard's face for a moment and then said, "I don't believe in Father Christmas anymore. Of course, I used to."

This irritated Benny. "Well, how long ago was 'used to'? I mean, it couldn't be very, could it? You're only nine."

"I'm nearly ten. I'm as good as ten right now."

"How long ago was it, then? When you believed in Father Christmas?"

"A long time. When I used to be five."

This really irked Benny no end. He didn't believe in him anymore but he was so much older than she. He'd been looking forward to talking to her about Father Christmas—the kinds of things he got up to and the dwarfs and all. Actually, he'd been looking forward to feeling superior. That was one of the nice things about little kids being around, the way you could feel superior to them. "That's not much time for believing. I mean, you wouldn't even have thought much about Father Christmas until you were four, say. So if you stopped at age five—well, it was hardly worth it, believing. You might as well just have gone ahead and disbelieved." Benny did not know what this fuddled need for accuracy was. Was it because the subject of his mum had arisen and talking about her made him cold and anxious? Yet the need to talk about her was as strong as the fear of talking.

The way she had lived and died was to him courageous, but to another would be contemptible, which is how the ones under Waterloo Bridge were thought of by other people. Benny had gone out with his mother most days. When one day they had collected scarcely enough for Sparky's dog food, Benny leaned against his mother and cried. *"We got nothing, nothing, nothing."* And she had answered, *"Neither does God."* And he had said, "But He doesn't have a dog." His mum laughed.

But that's the way she always was, not hopeful that things would change, for she knew they wouldn't, yet not seeming to care that much. He remembered a Selfridges bag walking past them (for they were sitting on the pavement) with three white boxes Benny could see over its rim. His mother said, *"She's just bought three new pairs of shoes. Those boxes are shoe boxes. Now you know what'll happen to them? They'll spend their lives in her closet. She'll wear them a few times and then they'll sit amongst the other shoes and she'll buy more."*

She actually didn't seem to mind having to beg. It made him furious to think of this, for she had deserved so much better, and in Dublin they'd *had* so much better.

"What's wrong?" asked Gem in a worried way. "You look mad."

"I'm not." But he was. He turned to her and asked, "Do you mind not having anything?"

She frowned. "What do you mean?"

Benny swept his arm out to encircle the house and the grounds. "I mean all this of the Tynedales. Does it bother you none of this is yours? Not even a little bit is yours?"

Gem's face, to his horror, began to crumple.

"I'm sorry, Gem. I didn't mean it the way it sounded."

Gem wailed and clamped Richard to her chest.

Benny put his arm around her, genuinely remorseful that because he didn't have anything, he didn't want her to, either, nor did he understand any of this. "I'm really sorry."

She went on wailing.

"Stop that."

She stopped; she stopped as though she'd never started and went back to inspecting Richard's trousers.

Now Benny was really irritated. "How'd you do that?" For her wailing had certainly been a convincing example of brokenheartedness.

"Do what?" She was humming now and wiping at Richard's shirt from where she'd cried on it.

"You were just crying and yelling to beat the band."

"I *know* I was. I was sad."

"Well, obviously, but—" Exasperated, Benny thought, *What's the use?*

Melrose considered the shrub.

Why Murphy couldn't just leave it alone he didn't know. The shrub looked okay to him, boxed as it was inside its yew hedge. There was a whole line of shrubs within hedges, a box parterre he believed it was called. So it was a trifle scraggly and needed a bit of shaping—like one of Polly Praed's mysteries—still, the shrub presented itself to the world as fairly in line with the others.

"*That shrub there,*" Murphy had said, "*that shrub's got desuetude written all over it.*" Melrose was glad that Murphy had gone for the day.

He heard a car rev up and looked behind him to see Kitty Riordin in her little VW making a turn in the gravel drive. She rolled down the window and called to him. "Ambrose! When you've finished here, would you just give my bit of garden a weeding? Thank you!" She threw up her arm in a wave good-bye and rolled off. It was her day for shopping in Oxford Street and Piccadilly.

Kitty Riordin was a person who ran to schedules, all of her appointments, rendezvous and pleasure hunting neatly written in on her calendar, boxed like the shrubs inside squares he was examining now for a cosmetic fix.

Melrose studied the ball of shrub and decided to have a cigarette as he looked off at the cottage.

FORTY-FOUR

Keeper's Cottage sat about a hundred yards from the Lodge and had been, presumably, a caretaker's lodge. It was sheltered from view by several large tulip trees and a magnificent larch. In front of the little cottage was a remnant of garden, one clearly not tended by Angus Murphy, nor would it be by Melrose. Now, in winter, it was a haven for cold stalks, brittle-looking stems and sodden leaves.

He went around to the back and tried the window Gemma had told him about. He raised it easily and dropped down into the kitchen. Nothing interesting here, so he went through to the living room. It was warm and with the signature English cottage ambiance of cretonne, exposed timbers, cuteness and cat. Snowball sat and stared at Melrose. He wondered why he had this effect on animals; they found him as entrancing as a box parterre. They stared; they washed.

He looked at the pictures on a round table by the window (cutely curtained in a print of flowers and butterflies). There were a number of framed photographs, mostly of the snapshot-by-the-sea variety, showing a younger Kitty Riordin with a younger Maisie Tynedale. At least the child looked like Maisie, here probably ten or twelve. There was also one of (presumably) Maisie as a baby. On the corner of the silver frame dangled a silver bracelet with an engraved heart: *M*. The bracelet adorned her tiny wrist in the photograph and, looking closely at the hand which lay against Kitty's breast, he could make out the flaw in the tiny fingers, which would have been, he guessed, prior to the accident during the bombings. He was surprised, though, that the Tynedale fortune hadn't been able to secure a surgeon to put the flawed little hand to rights.

He walked up *très* cute narrow stairs into a bedroom the same size as the room beneath it. Bathroom over the kitchen. Definitely a house for one person, but that said, it seemed comfortable and with the fringe benefit of meals taken at the Lodge.

Snowball had followed him into the room and regarded him with an expression usually reserved for bus conductors. Melrose told the cat to go away, an order which would have gone down equally well with a bus conductor.

Melrose wondered if Kitty Riordin would bother hiding incriminating evidence. Or was she confident that so much time had passed, no one would be searching her premises? There was a desk with pigeonholes and writing implements against the front wall between the two windows. The top held shelves for books behind two glass doors. He stood and looked, believing this to be better police procedure than immediately knocking about the room and busying his fingers with poking things about. Having looked without success, he busied his fingers poking through the cubbyholes and little drawers. Nothing. He looked through her bureau drawers. Very neat, nothing there either.

The cat, who had been creeping about and sniffing as if he had never been in the room before, made a bound to the bed where Melrose was now sitting and another bound to the night table, knocking over a picture. Finding nothing further to maul and hit, Snowball gave up trying to find anything remotely interesting and padded downstairs. *Good riddance.*

Melrose picked up the picture of Kitty and another baby and the little bracelet that had dangled (as had the one downstairs) on one corner of the frame. On this one the heart was engraved with the letter *E*. Melrose sat with this little bracelet and looked to the window where a narrow branch of the tulip tree tapped in the wind. There was nothing surprising in Kitty Riordin's keeping this memento of babyhood, certainly not the bracelet worn by her own baby, Erin, and not Maisie's either, although she could have handed it over to Maisie herself or even Oliver. But that was splitting hairs. Only . . .

. . . assuming the child brought back from the walk that night was actually Maisie, how had Kitty come by Erin's bracelet? Could she have found it in the course of frantically sifting through the rubble of the Blue Last? Surely not. He held it up, swinging it on his finger. It struck him as bloody unlikely but he would have to allow it was possible. The question then was, why? Why would she search for it? Other than as a memento, what purpose would it serve? The bracelet downstairs with the *M* would *indicate* the baby was Maisie—not *prove* it, since anyone can switch a bracelet from one little wrist to another.

He went back to looking at the photograph. The baby had both of its hands on Kitty's forearm. He could see the fingers separately and clearly. In some way the picture made Melrose think of Masaccio's *Madonna and Child* in the Uffizi. He recalled that the hands of the baby Jesus curled on his mother's arm, just as Erin's did here. The plump little hands were perfect and unmarked. This was taken before that awful night, the final night of the Blue Last, when little Maisie's arm and hand were hit by flying rubble.

Or was it Erin's?

Melrose kept looking from the photograph to the bracelet to the tapping branch of the tulip tree outside. It was almost enough to make him believe that Kitty Riordin knew the pub would be bombed. But not even Kitty Riordin could control the skies.

He hoped.

FORTY-FIVE

loomy thoughts. But it wouldn't be the first time
a mother had done something like that.
  And it had been, after all, for Erin's own good.
Melrose was in his room at Boring's trying to decide
what to change into for dinner. For God's sake, he told
himself (snippily), you have only six articles to choose
from—two jackets, a black cashmere and a greenish
wool-silk; two pairs of trousers, one of those being the
new black jeans he had bought at the Army-Navy Store
for gardening and the other a black wool; two shirts, one
white, one a black turtleneck. Still he felt all the indeci-
sion of a teenager trying to decide what to wear to the
dance.

He looked his wardrobe over. Black. Now *that* was an
interesting idea. What, he wondered, would be the effect
if he pulled on the black jeans—

(He did.)

Pulled down the black turtleneck.

(He did.)

Then yanking it from its hanger, pulled on the black
cashmere jacket.

He did this too, then stepped back from the long mirror, whipped out a comb and snapped it through his
gold-licked hair, cool as John Travolta. He caught the

whole effect and smiled. He made a gun of his thumb and index finger, *pow.*

Back at you.

In the Members' Room, Melrose waved hello to Major Champs and Colonel Neame, but sat down on the other side of the room, after procuring for himself a newspaper from the rack near the desk, one of the twenty or so different papers Boring's supplied. Melrose could understand keeping *Le Monde* on the rack, but did anyone in here speak Arabic? Swahili? Cigarette in his mouth, he flicked his Zippo and lowered his face to bathe in shadows and fire. Unfortunately, there was no way to see just what the effect was, but he thought it fitted his black-clothed persona.

"Cool."

Quickly, he turned, nearly dropping the lighter. "Polly!"

Polly Praed smiled as Melrose jumped up, mouth unhinged. He'd caught the cigarette as it fell.

Polly ran her eyes from his head to his toes and then back up again. "*Way* cool." She stood by a leather chair, companion to his own. She said, "I may have to revise my opinion."

"What the devil are you doing here in *Boring's*?"

"Oh, don't be such a stick, Melrose. These places let anybody in nowadays. Light?"

He lit the cigarette she was waggling in her mouth. She hadn't changed a jot in these last couple of years. She still had the only amethyst eyes in the world, excepting Elizabeth Taylor's.

"But how did you know I'd be here? Sit down, sit down."

Polly sat in the wide leather chair opposite him and placed a brown paper parcel she'd been carrying between herself and the arm.

"Did you come here to see me or what?"

"To see my editor."

Melrose looked around the room. "He's here?"

"No-o. I mean I came to London to see him."

"How did you know *I'd* be here?"

"It was really hard, like tracking down the Jackal. I called your house." She blew smoke in his direction. "Ardry End," she added, as if he might have forgotten.

"We haven't seen each other in over two years. Last time was when I came to Littlebourne—"

"Looking for Jenny Kennington."

More smoke. "I wasn't looking for her for *myself.*" Was she jealous?

"Who, then, were you looking for her for?"

"J—" He caught himself before he said *Jury* and just in time to substitute "Jenny was wanted by the Shakespeare police."

"The what?"

"Stratford-upon-Avon police."

"Why did they want Jenny Kennington?"

"She was chief suspect in a murder—didn't you read it in the paper?"

"Was she convicted?" She sat eagerly forward.

What shameful hope he saw in her amethyst eyes! "No. She didn't do it."

"Oh." Hope sinking, she fell back in her chair.

"Polly!"

They both looked around to see Richard Jury. Polly's expression changed immediately from the sardonic to the devotional. Oh, she could treat *him,* Melrose, all any-old-how, but when it came to Richard Jury, whom she ranked with a total eclipse of the sun or a lunar meltdown (sun and moon coming in second and third)—well, that was quite another matter. Her eyes widened, her black curls shivered around as if they were being launched into space.

Melrose said, "I didn't know you were coming. Did you leave a message here?"

"Nope. Didn't come to see you, actually." He turned and sketched a salute to Neame and Champs. "I came to have a chat with Colonel Neame, over there."

Melrose frowned. "Really?"

Jury nodded and returned his attention to Polly, who gave every indication of not wanting it, looking here, there, everywhere except at Jury, who now sat down on the arm of her chair. "How'd you storm this bastion of male enterprise, Polly?"

Rubbing her thumb across her wrinkled forehead, she mumbled, "Oh, you know . . ."

"She's in London for the day to see her editor." Melrose helped her out. "She cleverly found out my whereabouts. Good detective, Polly."

Polly once more sat back and rolled her eyes. "Oh, for heaven's sake! Why do people think just because you write mysteries you're Sam Spade?"

"No one would take you for Sam Spade, Polly," said Jury. His proximity, there on the chair arm, would probably bring on a seizure at any minute. "Have you got a new book in the works?"

"Uh-huh."

"Did you bring a manuscript along here for your friend to read?" He cocked his head at Melrose.

"Uh-huh."

Melrose sat forward. Was that an "*uh*-huh" or a "*nu*-huh"? He hoped it was a *nu-huh* for he really was in no temper for Polly's prose. Yet there was that brown paper-wrapped package squashed between her and the chair arm. Maybe if no one mentioned it, it would ooze down farther and under the seat . . . *Ooze,* Melrose prayed.

"This it?" Jury whisked it out.

Stupidly, she nodded. "Uh-huh."

Jury smiled and excused himself. He saw Colonel Neame; he would be back. Dinner, perhaps?

"Uh-huh," said Melrose.

*　　*　　*

"Bletchley Park, 1939. Yes, it was after I'd finished at Oxford and before I joined up. RAF, I think I told you. Some days those were! Bletchley. Crazy," said Colonel Neame.

"What took you there, Colonel?"

"Oh, call me Joss, please do. What took me there was recruitment. You see, they needed many more people . . . Thank you, Higgins."

Jury had ordered whiskey all around and Major Champs, upon receiving his, rose. "You two have business; I'll just sit over there and read my paper."

Jury invited him to stay, but he walked off, making little backward waves with his downturned hand and re-settled himself on a sofa.

Neame sipped his whiskey. "Anyway, cracking a code as complex as the Enigma needed an odd combination of the artistic and the bookkeeping mind. Hard to find. They weren't, you see, just after mathematicians. It took a different sort of mind altogether. You can imagine how much plodding had to be done in working through the range of possible matches—"

"How did it work? The Enigma code?"

"Codes, Superintendent. Different codes and different machines. To explain how the damned thing worked would take more time than I daresay you have. The Poles broke it in the thirties. Didn't help them much, poor devils. At that point the Germans were using a monalphabetic code—you know, the simpler kind. But they used a dozen *different* monos, so it was hardly simple. Now, when we graduated to the polyalphabetic ciphers, it became even harder.

"The machine was made up of rotors—wheels—so you had your wheels, your ring settings, your steckers. That was a plugboard on the machine that scrambled the identity of letters. Now all of that was difficult enough, but the Germans changed the settings every day to make matters worse. It would have been impossible to break the code by pure plodding; at some point, intuition, the ability to actually think *irrationally* was needed. Genius was needed, like Turing's and a few others'. They could see the ghost behind the scrambled letters, if you understand what I mean. It's impossible to obliterate language completely. There's always a ghost of the original meaning, and if you're good at it, you can see the ghost; you can see the pattern. I'm not doing the whole thing justice, the way I'm explaining it. It was infernally complicated, that Enigma stuff. Devilishly." He tossed back the remainder of his whiskey. "You know the type of person who makes a good cryptanalyst? A paranoid."

Jury was startled. "Why do you say that? I don't see that thinking people are out to get you would do much by way of making you good at decoding."

"No, no." Impatiently, Colonel Neame shook his head. "You're using only one definition of the word. I mean 'paranoid' in the sense of being able to think irrationally. Being able to see something that no one else can see. *That* is 'paranoid.' You see something no one else does. In the way you used the word, which is the way most people use it, you mean you alone see danger and must therefore be imagining it. But that's a dilution of the meaning of 'paranoid.'"

"Did you ever know a young fellow named Ralph Herrick? RAF, also. And what's more, awarded the Victoria Cross. As I believe you were?"

"My stint came later, but Ralph Herrick?" He gave the name the other pronunciation: *Rafe.* "Absolutely! Don't forget, I was young once too, though a bit younger than Herrick. Ralph was at Oxford, also, though I hadn't known him there. My goodness, yes, I remember him. He was in the Crib room, if memory serves me correctly. That's what he had this incredible knack for. He was brilliant when it came to cribs—you know, the 'educated guess' sort of thing. You guess at some words and then see if those letters could be decoded into others. Ralph had an uncanny ability to do this. They sent him to Chicksands; that was the RAF intercept. Myself, I was in hut three. I was working on the Red key—the Luftwaffe."

"Red key?"

"Yes. The keys were colors, a different color assigned to each branch of the service. Red, was the Luftwaffe. Green, army."

Jury had pulled Simon Croft's book from his pocket, and now opened it to one of the notations. "What about these dates in September of 1940?"

"Hmm. Well, I do remember in August and September of that year the Luftwaffe very nearly crippled the RAF with attacks on our airfields. If Göring had stuck to it, bombing the Isle of Wight—that was the Ventron station—radar, you know—I have no doubt they would have won the war in the air. But it was a strange thing about both of those men, Göring and Hitler; they had no patience; they expected to win quickly. I wonder if it's the earmark of a megalomaniac that he thinks what he wants will happen quickly and painlessly. That it *should* happen that way and if it doesn't, and he doesn't get immediate results, he pulls out. I can tell you one thing, though: it's a mistake Churchill never made. That man was tenacious; he believed in hanging on like a pit bull."

Jury turned the book around so that Neame could read Simon Croft's notations.

Which he did, after adjusting the monocle in his eye.

"Is that the place you mentioned, Chicksands? It's abbreviated here."

"Indeed. Yes. It's in Bedfordshire." Neame's eye fell on the other abbreviated words in the list. "*Cov.* Coventry. Ah, yes. You know about Coventry. No, you wouldn't have been born then."

"I was born, believe me. But I have only a foggy notion."

"Of Coventry. Terrible destruction. Bloody awful. We got word there was to be an attack, but not that Coventry was the target. London, Manchester, maybe Reading. Industrial cities. Never Coventry. Remember, one thing about breaking a code is, you obviously have to go to some pains not to let it be known you've broken it. Because of that, Churchill came in for a horrendous attack, being accused of having known ahead of time that Coventry was the mark and not doing anything about it because he didn't want the Germans to know we'd broken the code. That's rubbish. It's vile. Churchill might have had his dirty little secrets, but Coventry wasn't one of them. We didn't get the right decrypt, that's all. The Chicksands unit didn't have as much experience, and all you have to do—"

"The decrypt came from Chicksands?"

"Far as I know, yes."

"You said Ralph Herrick was assigned there."

Furrowing his brow, Neame took another drink of whiskey. "Yes, but you know, I think Ralph had clearance for just about everywhere. He was able to go between the huts at Bletchley Park, one of the few who had that kind of clearance." Still holding the book, Neame looked back down at the rest of Croft's list. "What is this, then? Whose is it?"

Jury told him about Croft's relationship to Herrick and about the account of the war Croft was writing.

Colonel Neame handed the book back to Jury; the monocle fell from his eye. "Hmm." Neame studied his nearly empty glass. "What you need is someone who was in GC and CS—"

"Is that 'Code and Cypher'?"

"Government Code and Cypher School, right. I'm trying to think who's left who still—Ah! There's Maples. At least he was alive a couple of years ago. His picture was in the paper. Got an OBE and also the George Cross for the work he did at Bletchley. Sir Oswald Maples. I expect he'd be easy enough to find."

Jury smiled. "You were certainly a much-decorated bunch." He rose and when Colonel Neame started up,

Jury waved him back down. "Please don't get up. You've been an enormous help, Colonel."

"Seem to have left you with questions instead of answers."

Jury smiled. "That might be what's helpful."

"What happened to Polly?" asked Jury, returning to Melrose's chair. "Isn't she having dinner?"

"Gone. We're having breakfast tomorrow. She's staying in Bloomsbury. I think she hopes the literary swank will rub off on her." Melrose polished off his whiskey. "How about you? Ready for some more oxblood soup?"

"Any time."

Having brought the wine, Young Higgins floated off like milkweed. The wine was a Bâtard-Montrachet, "the finest white wine," Melrose had said, "in the world." They raised their glasses and drank.

"What on earth were you into with Colonel Neame?"

"Bletchley Park. The Enigma code. Codes." Jury smiled. "Neame isn't just taking up space in Boring's."

"Did I say he was? He's a nice old codger."

"I expect that's it; we tend to condescend to old guys like that."

"What about Bletchley Park?"

Jury pulled Croft's book from his pocket. "The book Croft was writing about the war. Since there was no manuscript, no laptop, no notes I could find, I had a look at a few of his books, presumably ones he used to research his subject. He wrote stuff in the margins—" Jury turned to the list on the last page, held it up for Melrose to see.

Melrose frowned.

"This is what I was talking to Colonel Neame about." He told Melrose what Neame had said.

Melrose stared. "What are you making of this?"

"I'm not sure." Jury picked up his wineglass, swirled the contents. "This might just be the best in the world."

"It is."

"How about Kitty Riordin, then?"

Melrose told him what he'd found in Keeper's Cottage. "I think he's right, your friend Haggerty."

"I take your point about the bracelet. It's unlikely she'd find it in the rubble."

"She could have had another one engraved afterward. The only difference is the initial in the little heart. Links has them. I checked."

"Links wasn't around in 1940."

"No. I simply mean such silver jewelry for babies is not hard to come by. She could easily have had the *M* engraved on the bracelet you saw, making it appear that's what little Maisie had worn. I mean, she could've simply purchased a new bracelet. She didn't have to dig it out of the rubble."

"She didn't really have to have it at all."

"Well, its *absence* wouldn't prove anything; its *presence*, though, suggests the baby really was Maisie."

Jury nodded. "I see Mickey Haggerty's point. All Kitty had to do was smash Erin's hand. She thinks very quickly on her feet. I'd say she immediately sussed out the situation and in the noise and fright and confusion took little Erin somewhere and *wham!*—" Jury's fist smashed down on the table, making the dishes and the remaining diners jump. His mind went back to that smile on Kitty Riordin's face. "She's cold-blooded enough."

"There's no way of proving any of this, though, short of finding the jeweler who engraved the bracelet and hope he's still alive and has an elephantine memory. Pretty impossible."

In silence, they finished off their dinners, bet on the dessert. Melrose said trifle, Jury said pudding. Young Higgins eventually produced Queen of Puddings, and Jury collected his fiver from Melrose.

"You always win."

"I deserve it."

They were silent, eating, until Jury looked up and said, "Why was she there?"

Melrose frowned. "Who? The Riordin woman?"

"No, Alexandra. Why was she at the Blue Last?"

Melrose shrugged. "Didn't you tell me she and the baby visited there often?"

Jury folded his hands and rested his chin on his thumbs. Only his eyes were visible above the fingers. "Look, though: why would she leave Tynedale Lodge to go sleep over in a pub, and haul the baby with her to boot? The blitz wasn't a stroll through Green Park."

"Those two families are addicted to each other. At least they were then."

"I know. Which means Alexandra Tynedale Herrick and Francis Croft, they were too."

Melrose set down his wineglass, dropped his spoon on his plate. "Are you suggesting—"

Jury nodded.

"Wait. You're not saying little *Maisie* was *Croft's*?"

"No, I'm not. Alexandra had an illegitimate child when she was—nineteen, I think. She took herself off somewhere. It was hushed up, not surprisingly; that sort of thing wasn't all the fashion in the forties."

"Money is, though. Money is always in fashion and Oliver Tynedale has enough to make anything go away. He could have taken care of a scandal in a dozen different ways."

"Oliver didn't know," said Jury.

"How in hell do you know *that*?"

"Because the baby was given up for adoption. His grandchild? Not in a million years. Tynedale wouldn't give a damn for convention anyway. He's the publish-and-be-damned type. Easier to be that way if you have money and, as you say, it's always in fashion. My guess is Alexandra didn't tell him because she was afraid Oliver would discover who the father was."

"Thrash him within an inch of his life, you mean?"

"Wake up." Jury snapped his fingers. "That Château-whatever is putting you under."

Melrose looked at him. "Are you saying—"

"That Alexandra couldn't have her father finding out Francis Croft was the father."

Melrose sat back. "That's pure speculation."

"At least it's pure." Jury smiled. "Tynedale is a man who I think is very forgiving. But not in this case. In this case he'd have to be a fucking saint to forgive Croft. His best friend. His life*long* friend. A betrayal that would have ruined everything. God*damn*! It's infuriating all of this had to happen a half century ago. But I'll still have Wiggins go to Somerset House and do a record search."

"And I still say it's much too tenuous."

"Tenuous is all I've got."

They were back in the Members' Room, Young Higgins having poured and deposited the French press pot on the table and Jury's coat on the arm of the chair. Jury had asked him to bring it.

"My knowledge of the Second World War is shamefully small."

"So's mine. Except I do remember Dunkirk, the BEF being evacuated. I remember it mostly because it's where my father's plane went down."

Melrose did not know whether to delve into this or not. "What was he flying?"

"A Hurricane. They were good planes. Except their engines weren't fuel injected; they were carburetor driven. If they were forced into a dive, the engine quit. That's what happened." Jury looked away toward the part of Boring's Christmas tree he could see, the tips of branches on one side. From one of them, a silvery angel hung precariously. "The RAF whacked the Luftwaffe over Dunkirk."

They were silent for a while. Colonel Neame and

Major Champs had gone upstairs. There was no one left in the Members' Room save for them.

Melrose said, "Listen, tomorrow is Christmas Eve. Come to Ardry End for Christmas."

"That would be nice. But I really have to spend Christmas in Islington. You know."

"Yes. Well, then come for dinner tomorrow night. Christmas Eve. You can spend the night and drive back to London the next morning. It's not a long drive. Well, you know; you've done it often enough."

Jury nodded. "Sounds good to me." Then, "I like your new look."

"What look?"

"The black clothes."

Melrose looked down, seemingly surprised that he was he. "Oh." He shrugged. "I just tossed on what was there. Didn't have much to choose from."

Jury shook his head. "Come on. That look's assembled."

Melrose was irritated at being found out about his clothes. Was his mind never to have any privacy? Did everybody know what went on in it? "Polly thought it was cool. '*Way* cool' I believe is how she put it."

"Oh, it's way cool all right. A lot different from your usual get-ups."

Get-ups? "What do you mean? That sounds like posturing?"

"No, no. Merely conservative. Expensive, of course— Michel Axel, Coveri, Ferre, Zegna, Cerruti—but conservative nonetheless."

"Who are those people? Designers? If so, how do you happen to be acquainted with them?"

Jury laughed. "I'm not a total nincompoop when it comes to clothes. Although I expect you might not be able to tell from looking at me."

"People look at you and they don't even see your clothes. They see six-two and a smile. And of course your identity card. But you're probably right; I guess I do look like I'm making a statement."

"'Fear wearing black.'"

"What?" Melrose laughed, briefly.

"It's the definition of 'cool.' 'Fear wearing black.' Makes sense if you remember what 'cool' really meant before it got debased into meaning anything anyone approves of. 'Keeping your cool'—the idea is that you don't *show* any anxiety or fear. So there you are, as calm a dude as can be. And what's icier than black?"

"'Fear wearing black.' I like that."

"Thought you would."

FORTY-SIX

"I suppose you know Christmas is the day after tomorrow," said Polly Praed.

She made it sound as though its propinquity were Melrose's fault. They were having breakfast in a restaurant across the street from Polly's Bloomsbury hotel. That the hotel was in Bloomsbury did not make it fashionable. It was called Rummage's, not the happiest choice of names. Although he wouldn't go so far as to call it a dump, it was far from being a hotel haunted by the *cognoscenti*.

Breakfast was included in the price of the room—not the breakfast they presently shared, but the Rummage breakfast, which they announced in their brochure (Melrose had read it waiting for Polly) as a "cooked breakfast." Melrose guessed that the cooking was not done to order, but everything was cooked before the first frail traveler descended into the bowels of the "garden level" dining room. In other words, the basement.

To Polly's statement that the hotel will cook your eggs any way you want, Melrose said they cook them one way only: "eggs overnight."

Polly scoffed and said he was always criticizing, and Melrose answered, yes, he would always criticize Rummage's, and would kick it if he ever saw it again, and that they could have breakfast at that nice little café across the street, *faux* Left Bank, which is where they now sat.

Or had been sitting. Melrose said he needed to get going soon because he had to get his Christmas shopping done before returning to Long Piddleton, but that they had time for another cappuccino if she liked.

"Do you really do it, Melrose?"

Melrose was making little waves in his cappuccino foam. "What? Do what?"

"Your own Christmas shopping."

It seemed to be a genuine question. Had Polly landed that recently from the planet Uranus? "What are you talking about? Of course I do it."

"Don't get shirty. I just thought maybe you paid someone to do it for you. Or maybe your man Ruthven does it. Or someone."

"Ye gods, Polly. What sort of life do you think I lead?"

She appeared to be thinking. "Well, the life of the idle rich, certainly. I just can't picture you in Harrods mulling over the socks."

"I can't either, but that's because I refuse to go into Harrods. It'd suck me right down. To go into Harrods means you must be prepared for quicksand at every turning. Have you seen the number of *people* in Harrods?"

"Yes. But, of course, it's for people. That's why it's there."

"Wretchedly there. No, I prefer Fortnum's. It's crowded on the food floor but quite bracing on the floors above. Oxygen and plenty of it. No, Fortnum's is the place. I can get everything I want in a minute."

"It's too late for hampers now; you'll be disappointed."

Melrose signaled the waiter for another round of cappuccino. "Polly, do you know you sound like my aunt Agatha sometimes, the way she's always telling me how I'll feel?"

Polly was not offended. This was because she liked taking her own line, and not paying that much attention to

Melrose's. Right now she put down the spoon with which she'd been eating Weetabix (Melrose had never known anyone to actually *order* Weetabix in a restaurant) and asked, "What are you and Richard Jury working on?"

"How do you know we are?"

"I know. You're obvious."

"Can't discuss it. Sorry."

Polly made little jumps in her chair, "Oh, come on, Melrose; you can tell me a little, can't you?"

"Okay." He told her about the murder of Simon Croft. "It was in the papers; maybe you read about it."

She shook her head. "What else?"

"Nothing else." Melrose had imbibed too much of Divisional Commander Macalvie's philosophy: don't.

Yet he felt moved to tell her about Gemma and the shooting.

"My God, Melrose! Whoever would murder a nine-year-old child?"

"Because it happens, doesn't it? A child abducted, beaten, maimed, raped, held hostage. Murdered. I know someone to whom it's happened."

"Who?"

Melrose shrugged, sorry he'd brought it up. He was thinking of Brian Macalvie again. "You wouldn't know him."

"But in these circumstances? Her home, her family?"

The waiter set two fresh cups before them with a waiterly flourish and Melrose asked for the bill.

"In any event, Jury thinks it's possible someone else was the target. A girl employed as undergardener who often went into the greenhouse."

"Did she tell him that?"

"No."

"Then how does he know?"

Melrose stopped his spoonful of foam on the way to his mouth. "What do you mean?"

"What makes you think this undergardener and not the nine-year-old was the target?"

"It seemed more—plausible. The girl often worked in the greenhouse after dark. Also, she quit right after the shooting."

"So would I. Yet she *wasn't* in the greenhouse and the little girl *was.* Unless the shooter was blind."

"The undergardener is quite small. The greenhouse is shadowy, murky. The killer expected the girl to be there. Add that up and it's possible."

"It's possible, but is it probable? You're going to quite a bit of trouble twisting the facts to suit what you want to believe." She sighed. "Mysteries, mysteries, mysteries, mysteries." Her head wagged from side to side as if she were shaking water out of her ears or auditioning for the role in the next *Exorcist* film. "I'm getting to loathe mysteries, including my own. Maybe *mostly* my own."

Melrose was relieved to get away from the Gemma affair. Was Polly smarter than they? "Good heavens, Polly, that's terrible. But you do write other books."

"I could have written *À la recherche* et cetera and they'd still have me swimming the genre gutter."

"But I like your Inspector Guermantes. Of the Sûreté." He'd like him better if Polly weren't fishing names out of Proust.

"So do I, but that doesn't mean I have to dance every dance with him. Only, if I don't I'll probably have to go back to being a wallflower."

"That you will never be." Melrose pushed back from the table and signed for the waiter, lurking back there in the shadows with two others. "I've got to go, Polly."

Polly regarded her empty Weetabix bowl. "Yes, I guess I should, too."

"Polly, when are you ever going to come visit me? I've asked you several times."

"I'd like to." She gathered her coat around her. It was one of Polly's unflattering colors, a rust shade that really looked rusty. "But I'd undoubtedly be overwhelmed. By your house and your ritzy friends."

"You're no competition for Mrs. Withersby, that's

sure." Tired of waiting for his bill, Melrose dumped money on the table, including a hefty tip.

"Who's she?"

"One of my ritzy friends."

Melrose's first stop was in Regent Street, where he went into Hamley's. Given that this was only two days before Christmas, he had not been mistaken about the crowd. The place was jammed, understandably, with children.

Ill-advisedly stopping to inspect this year's toy rage—some sort of lunar space station manned by robotic personnel—he found himself surrounded by kiddies, one of whom got her sticky fingers on his black jeans and looked at him as if he were a ladder she was about to climb for a front-row seat. Her little look was so baleful, he sighed and picked her up and set her on his shoulders. Now she got her fingers into his hair, and he listened to the chattering, gasping children who coveted this toy. The place thronged and thrummed with pre-Christmas anticipation.

The parents of these children were all mucking about with apparently no care that their little darlings might be in the arms of the Regent Street Ripper. Tired of his hair being shredded, Melrose set the little girl down where she promptly began wailing to be taken up again, her little arms reaching pitifully upward. He patted her head and strong-armed his way through a crowd as thick as treacle. A haggard sales assistant pointed him in the right direction.

He searched the tables and walls but found nothing he wanted. He turned away when his eye lit on one article that just might do as it was very stretchy. He plucked it from the long hook on the wall and plowed through the field of wildflower children to the cash register.

Outside, he stopped on the pavement to think. People swam around him as if he were no more than an irritating rock in the middle of a stream. Then he walked the short distance to Liberty's and into its stationery department. There he purchased a pad of paper and ventured down to the coffee shop where he got himself an espresso. He sat down with the pad and carefully drew a picture.

Following this he found a pay phone still working in Oxford Street and called Mr. Beaton. Melrose told him what he wanted and apologized for such dreadfully short notice.

After this, he took a cab to the Old Brompton Road.

Mr. Beaton, whose premises were above a sweet shop, was delighted to see him again after—what was it—three years?

"My lord," said Mr. Beaton with but a marginal bow.

Melrose had never had the heart to tell Mr. Beaton that he'd given up his titles years before. Mr. Beaton would put it down to carelessness at best, slovenliness at worst. Mr. Beaton never changed: always the morning coat, always the tape measure. If Melrose had his way he would hang the George Cross on the ends of that tape measure.

Mr. Beaton's apprentice—this one, tall and angular with a shock of ginger hair—copied the fractional bow.

"Now, if you brought your drawing, I'll see what I can do."

Melrose produced the picture he'd drawn in Liberty's coffee shop. "I'm pretty certain it's to size, Mr. Beaton. I've a good memory for things like this." Had he?

Mr. Beaton instructed his apprentice to bring out certain bolts of cloth. The young man slipped into a room at the rear and was back in a few seconds, carrying the bolts of material.

"Just feel this, now, Lord Ardry." Tenderly, the tailor held out several inches of material from one of the bolts.

Melrose always felt humbled in the presence of Mr. Beaton, for the old man's attitude toward cloth was as reverent as a priest's toward the chalice. Just then, providentially, sunlight filtered through the small panes, fretting the cloth. Melrose fingered the wool and sighed. Woven air, spun sunlight, Melrose had never felt anything as soft and weightless.

"It's a silk worsted, quite fine. Would it do?"

"It'll do wonderfully, Mr. Beaton."

Pulling at his earlobe, the tailor studied Melrose's sketch. "Quite a pleasant little challenge this will be. I've never done anything like it. Now: when would you be wanting this, Lord Ardry?"

Melrose blushed. "Well, I hate to ask it of you—I mean, given it's Christmas and all—but, you see, I'll be going back to Northamptonshire tonight—this is something I'd really like to deliver before I go—if it's possible?"

"In other words, right away."

"Could you possibly?"

Mr. Beaton removed his pocket watch from an honest-to-God pocket and said, "It's getting on for three . . . Shall we say six? Or you can call me at five and see how I'm doing here."

"Admirable. I can come back then. And, of course, don't worry, it doesn't have to be perfect."

Mr. Beaton raised his eyebrows. "I beg your pardon?"

The apprentice blinked once, hard. For even he had caught this graceless remark.

So Melrose slunk down the narrow stairs, feeling gauche and crude, and with an eye unalive to anything aesthetically pleasing.

When Mr. Beaton plied his scissors and thread, there was no such thing as "less than perfect."

Melrose taxied back to Boring's, where he fidgeted, packed and bit his nails, a childish habit he had never been able to shake; he seemed to bite them only when he was deep into something—really deep, and that seldom happened, only when he was reading Henry James or Proust or working on one of Jury's cases. (Would Jury be complimented? Proust, after all, was no slouch.) He was certainly deep into this case. He lay on the bed thinking deeply. There was something neither of them had seen, and he thought it was something obvious. He could feel it as obvious. He gave up and stumbled downstairs with his single bag.

It was after five o'clock, and Melrose decided not to call, but simply to go back to Mr. Beaton's. He had a whiskey as he waited for the boy who dealt with keys and cars, who drove them off to some mysterious parking arrangement (garage? rooftop?) only the boy knew about; then he drove them back to appear magically outside of Boring's door.

Melrose tipped him handsomely, remarking to the lad that he probably had the most important job in London; people would probably die to have someone else park their cars. Then he got in, turned his face skyward in the deepening dark and thanked God for money.

When he got to the Old Brompton Road, he parked illegally (as there was no other option) and took the steps two at a time to Mr. Beaton's rooms.

"Absolutely perfect, Mr. Beaton. You're a wonder." Melrose held up the garments, marveling. "I don't suppose you'd have a box—"

The apprentice immediately went into the back again and returned with a small box, perfect for the clothes. "Is it a gift, sir? I rather thought it might be and found this silvery paper if you need it—? I could wrap it up."

Melrose thanked him profusely. "That's very kind and it would be a big help." He turned to Mr. Beaton. "Mr. Beaton, I would be happy to pay you now, if—"

Eyes closed, Mr. Beaton shook his head. "Not at all, not at all. I'll put it on your account, my lord. Happy to do it."

After securing his package, Melrose thanked them again and raced down to his car.

*　　*　　*

Sir Oswald Maples lived alone in a cream-painted mews house off Cadogan Square. He lived by himself despite the fact that he needed two canes in order to get to the door in the wake of Jury's ring.

He said, holding up one of the canes as if to shake Jury's hand, "It's not as bad as it looks. I don't always need these, just when the knees start going underneath me. Come on in." He used a cane to wave Jury into the living room.

Jury thanked him and removed his coat, which Sir Oswald told him to toss over the banister. Then—again with the cane—he pointed to an overstuffed armchair across from a sofa where he'd been sitting himself. He must be over eighty, yet brandished the canes in the high good humor of a boy. Watching him whip them around to lean against the arm of the sofa, Jury wondered if he thought they were playthings. Had there been a servant and a buzzer to call him hence, Jury was sure he would have used the tip of the cane to press the button.

"It's rheumatoid arthritis, but the discomfort comes and goes. Would you like a drink, Superintendent?" He pointed to a tumbler beside him containing a finger of whiskey. "Or is it a bit early in the day for you?"

It wasn't yet noon, but Jury felt a sadness descend on him whose source he couldn't name—or perhaps he could. He felt as if he needed a drink, after all. Sure. *Needing a drink* was the first step. Or maybe it was the last. But he hated to see Maples drink alone . . . No. *That* was the last. "No thanks. I just drank a bucketful of coffee."

Maples nodded and leaned back against the green love seat. "You wanted some information, you said on the telephone, about Ralph Herrick."

"Yes. As I told you, it was Colonel Joss Neame who mentioned you as possibly remembering Herrick. You knew him."

The older man nodded. "I did, yes."

"You were with the code and cypher branch of intelligence?"

"Ah, yes. GC and CS."

"I'm involved in a homicide investigation. A man named Simon Croft was shot. You might have read about it."

"Oh, yes. I've seen that house on the Thames. Often wondered who lived there."

"Simon Croft did. Alone. He was writing a book about certain years of the Second World War. Croft knew Ralph Herrick. Croft was only a boy, but he rather idolized the man. A fighter pilot, a hero. Not surprising, I suppose."

"Indeed not. No, there was no question about Herrick's heroism. His courage was almost—wanton."

Jury smiled. "A strange way of putting it."

"I know. But it was almost seductive, that courage, and he did throw it around. I don't mean he bragged; that was the last thing he'd do. I mean—it was as if courage were an afterthought. God knows he had it, though. He took out, nearly single-handedly, four Junkers over Driffield, in Yorkshire. The bombers didn't have a fighter escort; they realized finally they couldn't send bombers without escort by Messerschmitts, but the 109s didn't have the range to fly all the way from Norway." He grew thoughtful. "Herrick commanded a squadron of Spitfires that intercepted the German bombers which were hammering one of the Chain Home radar stations. Absolutely critical. Herrick's squadron downed all but one. No, there was no question about his courage, Superintendent."

Jury thought for a moment. "His family—rather, the one he married into—talk about him as though he were, well, an idol. He was idolized by more than one member. But one person took exception to this picture. She said she found him much too 'plausible . . . one of those smooth racketeers one sees in old American films.' That was her description."

Maples threw back his head in a soundless laugh. "That's very good, that is. Let me tell you something about Herrick: a great deal of that courage he displayed was of the daredevil kind. I think it came from his not giving a bloody damn about much of anything. In some way I think he felt the whole war was a card game and he had an ace in the hole."

Jury smiled. "Did he play it?"

Maples reached for the decanter he had placed on a table beside him, poured himself another drink and raised the decanter in question to Jury, who again declined. "Oh, I'm quite certain he played it. But the important thing was the game itself."

Jury handed him the book, opened to the page on which Simon had listed the dates. "This book belonged to Simon Croft, Sir Oswald. Joss Neame helped identify some of this marginalia. He thought you'd be able to help."

Maples took the book, took up his rimless spectacles and bent over it.

"And the last page, that list of words, I marked."

Turning to the page, Maples read off the list. "'Enigma' . . . God, I don't believe this." Sir Oswald nodded. "Pretty obviously worried about it, wouldn't you say? Ralph Herrick's work with the Enigma codes is what I wondered about. It could be what this Croft fellow wondered about, too." Maples put down his glasses, tented his hands and regarded Jury over the tips of his fingers. "We learned from certain decrypts—and also a POW—about an operation that was going down in the middle of November on the night of a full moon—thirteenth, fourteenth, fifteenth. It was to be a three-stage operation: code name 'Moonlight Sonata'— a sonata, you see, being a three-part piece. So the note there—" he pointed to Jury's book "—refers to that plan of attack."

"This was the attack on Coventry? There was no advance warning?"

Maples seemed to be studying the pattern in the wallpaper behind Jury. "Not precisely true, although a lot of people think it is. We knew Coventry and Birmingham were possible targets, but an enciphered map showed the locations to be London and the Home Counties. I'm simplifying the code business here, but the map misled us; the decrypt was wrong. That wasn't the only time I wondered," Maples said, musingly. "Rather I didn't wonder at the time or I'd have done something. I wondered when it did no particular good."

Jury frowned. "You had reason to believe Herrick had something to do with the mistaken decrypt?"

"Oh, I'm fairly certain he did; it was through his hands the map passed. I mean, he did the final decrypt."

"An honest mistake?"

"Could have been, yes. But the 'honest mistakes' were building. There was the *Bismarck* business." Maples motioned with two fingers toward Jury's notes. "That date you have there. May 24, 1941. That was the day of the attack on the *Bismarck*. We had one hell of a time with the naval Enigma. It was some time before we finally broke it." Reflectively, Maples scratched the neck beneath his collar. "The biggest problem was not being able to read the code far enough in advance to take action."

"But could someone have been working on both keys? The RAF and the Admiralty?"

"Good question. Ordinarily, no. But Ralph had clearance to go from one place to another. At Bletchley, the keys worked on were in different huts. Security was hard to maintain. It was too easy for things to slip out. And there were so many people involved. I expect it wasn't until after Herrick had gone to the Orkneys that I seriously started wondering. Hatston, that's where our Fleet Air arm base was. Also we had one of our satellite interception sections based there."

"Herrick died there, I understand."

"Hmm. You haven't, I suppose, talked to anyone in military intelligence? MI5, MI6?"

Jury shook his head.

"I mention that because I think they were on to Herrick and posted him there, as a temporary measure. Or, indeed, intelligence outfits being the bastards we always were, sent him on a permanent basis. You see, he was murdered a few months later. Of course, it was made to look like an accident, a drowning. Very convenient, I think." Sir Oswald puffed out his cheeks and sat forward fixing Jury with steely gray eyes. "Then there was 'Julia.'"

"Julia? Who was she?"

Maples smiled. "She turned up in the GAF—German Air Force—traffic. We had been having great success with that particular traffic until 'Julia' appeared. This was a word that kept turning up in decrypts that we could never pin down. I'll tell you it messed things up for quite a while. You see, it's the main reason I know that Herrick was one of theirs. Indeed, I wouldn't be surprised to discover he'd been a double agent. It would have suited his love of game playing. Anyway, just before the end, which I think he could see coming, he wrote me a note." Maples pointed with one of the canes at the bookshelves behind Jury's chair. "Would you just get me the large volume on the end of that bottom shelf?"

Jury rose and pulled out a thick and much-used book. He took it to the sofa.

Maples adjusted his glasses and opened the book to a page with a note for a marker. "This is quite famous. Listen:

> *Whenas in silks my Julia goes,*
> *Then, then (methinks) how sweetly flows*
> *That liquefaction of her clothes.*

There are at least a dozen poems, all written for Julia, not just that one. That one, though, is the best known.

It's that wonderful word 'liquefaction' that makes us remember it, I suppose."

Sir Oswald paused and Jury prompted him: "And—?"

"Well, it's the poet, isn't it, Superintendent? Robert Herrick."

There was a lengthy silence in which they regarded one another. Then Jury said, "It really was a game for Herrick, wasn't it?"

Sir Oswald nodded. "It was, yes." He removed the paper and unfolded it. Adjusting his glasses, he read: "'I'm surprised at you, Ozzie, for never having worked out Julia. You, such a lover of seventeenth-century poetry.' It's signed, simply, '*Ralph.*'"

"What a bastard."

Maples nodded again. "Exactly. Especially"—here he shut the book with a snap—"for calling me Ozzie."

IV

Fear Wearing Black

FORTY-SEVEN

Snow fell, carelessly, languidly, large flakes drifting by the window of the drawing room at Ardry End where Melrose sat, musing. It was Christmas Eve, or rather Christmas Eve late morning. He was waiting for Jury to arrive.

He imagined some weary sojourner stopping to look in from outside, finding the scene so agreeable he might be transported back to his childhood in a cozy house, sitting before a fireplace with a dog like Sparky and a cat like Cyril. Melrose could almost see a pale face at the window, begging, *Letmein letmein letmein.*

Misguided soul.

"Did you finish your shopping, Melrose, or did you just waste your time in London?" Agatha set about dolloping jam on her scone.

How many scones was that? Eleven? "You mean after Marshall and I wasted our time all over Florence?"

"Now *that* would be the place to do one's Christmas shopping!"

"It was and one did." Melrose checked his wristwatch. Ten-thirty. Jack and Hammer not open yet.

Agatha was so surprised by this answer she nearly forgot to put double cream on top of the jam. "Really?" She simpered, spooning on the cream. "Well, I've always said you can be quite thoughtful when you want to be."

"Isn't it a shame how seldom I want to be?"

"It's too bad you had Trueblood along. With his ridiculous picture."

"It's the reason we went to Italy in the first place, Agatha. If the ridiculous picture is really a Masaccio, it's worth a fortune." Which was not the point, certainly, but money was one of the few things Agatha could understand as a motive for doing anything.

"I seriously doubt it was." She polished off the scone. "I saw one just like it in Swinton Barrow." She looked at the cobalt blue plate. "Are there no more scones?"

Melrose stared at her. "What?"

"More scones."

"No, I mean what painting?"

"A painting just like Trueblood's in a Swinton Barrow shop. Well, not *exactly* like it, but the same sort of subject."

"Where in Swinton Barrow?"

"One of those antique shops; you know Swinton Barrow has so many of them. Trueblood thinks he's so lucky in that painting. Wait until he finds out!"

"The shop wasn't Jasperson's, was it?"

"I don't recall the name. It faced the green . . . yes, and directly opposite a pub. The Owl, I think it's called. I'm sure you could find the pub." Simper, simper. "I told Theo about it. He was so amused. Both of us were."

To think the painting's fate—meaning Trueblood's fate—lay in the hands of Agatha and that snake, Theo Wrenn Browne, was not to be borne. Melrose sat with his unlit cigarette, his fingers turning the lighter over and over, his mind in time with it—over and over: *buy her silence, scare her witless, kill her where she sits.* He rather favored the last of these (as it was the only sure-fire way of stopping her). The trouble was that Agatha never kept her word so he couldn't really buy it; she would be holding the blackmail bag and could hit him for money whenever she felt like it. The only way he would have half a chance to shut her up was to convince her that this new painting she'd seen made no difference to anyone. "Oh, yes, I've just remembered. *That* painting. You needn't bother telling Trueblood; he's already seen it. He isn't interested."

She looked crestfallen, having been deprived of her bad news. "He isn't?"

"He went over to Swinetown—"

"Swinton."

"He went there yesterday afternoon. He doesn't want it, anyway."

Agatha was truly miffed. It was Marshall Trueblood who had made fools of both her and Theo Wrenn Browne at the trial, the one now known as the Chamberpot Caper. Melrose smiled just thinking about that. What a moment!

"Not only that," continued Melrose, "a triptych did go missing from a chapel—where? I can't recall—in 14-something, and for all we know that might have been it. Or one of them, I mean one of the panels, and wouldn't that be a find!" Melrose then loaded on every scrap of information he had about "clumsy Tom" (which was what Masaccio was called by his friends), and was pleased with himself that he remembered so much. "*St. Peter Healing the Sick with His Shadow* is one of the marvelous frescoes in the Brancacci Chapel; you really should see it, Agatha, it's quite magnificent." Then he described, in lavish detail, the *Tribute Money*, "restored after that terrible fire in the 1770s and you can imagine what a job that must have been!" For even Agatha's weasel imagination could operate on this level.

But wouldn't, since her eyelids were fluttering and she was swaying on the sofa, eyes now shut against Masolino's and Masaccio's friendship and their painting together many of those frescoes. Melrose went on until he heard a hiccupy snore.

He went to the sofa and shouted "Agatha!" Scaring her awake was always so much fun.

Her eyes snapped open. "I have to be going. Good heavens, Melrose, how long have you kept me here with your nattering?" She gathered up purse and carry-all (which she had not had a chance to fill with his cook Martha's confections), got up and tugged at her girdle.

"Going?" Thank the Lord.

"I'm off!"

Bloody hell! he thought, as soon as she'd left. "Find my car keys, Ruthven!"

Swinton Barrow was twenty-five miles to the southwest of Long Piddleton and was a little like it, but on a larger scale. Swinton just had more of everything—larger village green, antique shops, bookstores.

At this moment Melrose was sizing up the antique shops on the other side of the green. He had slanted the car in between others outside of the sign of the Owl. He was looking across the green, which was a flat expanse of box hedges and benches, still with snow clinging to them, trapped in the hedges' wiry surface. Frills of snow lined the backs of the benches. It was a pleasant, wintry scene. Jasperson's was directly across from the pub, as Agatha had said (in one of her rare moments of accurate reportage).

A bell jangled as he opened the door on a large room that smelled of wood polish and money. Trueblood could spend a week here. C. Jasperson knew his stuff. In the middle of the room was a center table with a green marble top on a gilded pediment adorned with *putti*. To someone else, the piece would have been quite gorgeous, but Melrose couldn't stand cherub adornments; he had a hard time to keep from kicking them. To his right was a Queen Anne mirrored bookcase he wouldn't have minded having for Ardry End. Near it was an inlaid walnut writing table on which sat an ormolu tea caddy. Melrose loved to find things inside other things and was delighted to see three little tea caddies nesting inside the big one. He smiled and put the cover back on. Near these pieces was a work table, a porcelain plaque inlaid on its top, the interior mirrored. Vivian would like this. He appeared to be doing his Christmas shopping all over again. As he moved from piece to piece, his eyes traveled over the walls, looking for the painting—or plaque—Agatha had claimed to be like Trueblood's. He didn't see it until he'd stepped closer to a little alcove on his left, and there it was. For once Agatha was right. The painting was either of a saint or a monk and could have been a companion piece to Trueblood's. That this painting too might be a section of Masaccio's altarpiece was ludicrous.

"Hello."

The soft voice made him jump. He turned and found himself face-to-face with the Platonic Idea of Grandmother. It was this pink-complexioned, sky-blue-eyed, rousingly coral-lipsticked mouth that everyone wanted for a grandmother and nobody ever got. She smiled and looked, well, merry. "Could I help you?"

Melrose made a slight bow. "I'm interested in this. You know, a friend of mine told me he'd found one in Swinton very much like this. Are you Miss Eccleston?"

"Yes, I am. Amy Eccleston. Why, he was here very recently, about two weeks ago it must have been. He was quite taken by that panel. I believe both *could* be the side panels of a triptych or polyptych. Excuse me for a minute." The telephone was ringing and she whisked herself away into another room. He spent the odd few minutes studying the so-called Masaccio (as she hadn't yet called it) and trying to remember what di Bada had told them about Vasari's description of the Pisa polyptych in that church in Pisa. St. Jerome? St. Julian? St. Nicholas?

She was back. "I'm sorry. It's been busy today."

"Mr. Trueblood is under the impression his is an original Masaccio. Is that what you told him?"

"Oh, my goodness, *no*." Her laugh was breathy. "But there's a *possibility* it might be. Mr. Jasperson's been trying to authenticate them. You're familiar with

Masaccio? A fifteenth-century painter of the Italian Renaissance—"

"And is Mr. Jasperson having some success in doing this? What's the provenance?"

She shook her head. "We don't know. I found them in a little old church in Tuscany. Of course, I didn't guess at their value then, but when I brought them into the shop, well, Mr. Jasperson was more than a little astonished."

"Because they were so valuable?"

"Because they were so *divine.*"

Turning to the panel, they breathed in a little divinity.

She said, "I'll tell you what might be possible. Possibly, your friend mentioned that his might be a *copy* of a panel by Masaccio. On the other hand, they could be panels of the polyptych originally in a church in Pisa. The Santa Maria del Carmine. An altarpiece, most of which was recovered. Part, you see, is still missing."

That little morsel wafted down as gently as the morning's snow, as quietly and unobtrusively as a snowflake.

"Then this," Melrose said innocently, "might be original?"

"I tremble to think." Her blue eyes widened.

Melrose laughed. "I'm sure you do. Though if you believed it, the panel wouldn't be selling for—" Melrose fingered the white tag "—two thousand pounds." He dropped the tag and looked at her.

"No, of course it wouldn't."

"At auction how much might it fetch?"

"Oh, heavens, it would be priceless."

In his mind's eye, Melrose saw Trueblood clutching his picture, carrying it all over Tuscany. He smiled. "Priceless, I agree."

In silence, they regarded the panel.

Melrose said, "Now, Miss Eccleston, here's the thing: that friend of mine believes he possesses something utterly unique. He's been to Florence to try to authenticate the work. It doesn't surprise me your proprietor here has had no luck. No one could swear either way.

The thing is, though, with this—" Melrose nodded toward the second St. Who "—that if other pieces keep turning up, Mr. Trueblood will be terrifically disappointed, for I'm sure you agree any more panels would seem to dilute the notion of originality, wouldn't they? To find even one under the circumstances you've related appears nearly impossible. And more than that . . . well . . ." He shrugged.

She nodded and nodded.

"What I propose is that *I* purchase this, which would prevent his seeing it and, *and,* Miss Eccleston, should Mr. Jasperson—or you—come across any *other* such, you will be so good as to let me know right away. Agreed?"

Oh, she was happy! "Why, yes, of course. Yes."

Melrose took out his checkbook, slapped it open on the writing table, pushed over the tea caddy and said, "I want this too."

"Oh," she said, as if he'd pinched her. "Certainly. That's three hundred, that is."

Melrose wrote out a check for twenty-three hundred pounds and ripped it out. "There you are. Now, I'd like you to keep the panel here until I can come and collect it. The thing is, I'm meeting Mr. Trueblood and wouldn't want him to start asking what's in the parcel."

"Delighted, delighted to hold it for you. I'll just put it in back."

"I'll take the tea caddy. You needn't wrap it."

She ferried the panel away.

On the way to the door, Melrose hauled off and kicked the *putti.*

Then he drove back to Long Piddleton; he had shut up Agatha and now he would have to shut up Theo Wrenn Browne.

The bell over the door of the Wrenn's Nest Bookshop jangled unpleasantly, like a pinched nerve, as if anything coming under the purview of the store's owner reflected the owner's temperament.

Melrose waited, tapping his fingers on the counter, looking out of the shop's bay window at the Jack and Hammer directly across the street. His friends were gathered there, apparently having a merry time. Trueblood, in particular. Theo Wrenn Browne would be waltzing right over there when he saw them in that window seat, eager to impart any unwanted information he had to share about Trueblood's painting.

"Why, Mr. Plant. What a pleasant surprise!"

Liar.

"Whatever brings *you* here?"

"Books, oddly enough. Where are your art history books?"

"Art? History?" A finely wrought eyebrow was raised.

"Now, put those two words together, Mr. Browne, and you'll be very close to what I came in for." He should, he supposed, be milder, but Browne was such a goddamned fool.

Theo Wrenn Browne tilted his head in the direction of some shelves. "Over here."

Melrose followed him. The pickings were slim, which didn't bother Melrose at all, since he didn't intend to pick anything. What he wanted was to know exactly what Browne knew about the other panel in Jasperson's shop. Certainly, Browne would be delighted at any opportunity to burst Trueblood's little balloon.

"Now, here's a nice one." Browne tried to foist Andy Warhol on him.

"No." Melrose pulled down some lackluster study on Flemish art, then reshelved it. Only one book bore at all on the subject—that is, to get the subject going: *Early Renaissance Art.* He started thumbing through the thick slick pages. "Ah. Brunelleschi . . . Donatello . . . Masolino . . ." he read in a whisper.

"What are you looking for, Mr. Plant?"

"Italian Renaissance paintings." And he continued in that reverent way: "Giotto . . . Masaccio . . ."

"Oh!" said Theo, happy to recognize a name, happier to have bad news to impart. "Mr. Trueblood's so-called painting."

"'So-called'?" Melrose managed to look confused. "I don't know why you say that. We've just got back from Florence." He turned back to the book and muttered, "The Church of San Giovenale a Carcia—"

"And—?" Theo prompted him.

"And what?"

"You said you just got back from Florence."

"That's right." Melrose continued his whispered communion with the book. "San Gimignano . . . Monteriggioni . . ." The pages fluttered. Melrose hadn't the vaguest notion what he was doing. But he had some dim idea that it would come to him.

Frustrated, Theo insisted. "You said you just got back from *Florence.*"

"Uh-huh."

"But you said it as if that *explained* something."

"Florence—" Melrose paused. "Florence explains *every*thing!" He clapped an arm about Browne's shoulders, a gesture that completely stumped Theo. He tried to step back, but Melrose had him in a lock.

"The Brancacci Chapel!" Here Melrose threw out his other arm and drew, between thumb and forefinger, a banner in air and, as if reading the print thereon, exclaimed, "The Brancacci Chapel! You've seen it, of course?"

"I? Uh, no, no. Now if you'd just let me get back to—"

Melrose's arm tightened and he began to walk both of them to the store's big bay window. "Imagine!" he exclaimed. Across the street were his friends seated at their favorite table—Trueblood, Diane Demorney, Joanna the Mad, Vivian Rivington. "Imagine we are within this glorious chapel, face-to-face with the frescoes. Just close your eyes—"

Theo didn't want to.

"And imagine seeing Adam and Eve and the expulsion from Paradise." Trueblood had his head in his hands much like the figure of Adam, and Joanna, her head thrown back in a rictus of laughter that bore a stunning resemblance to Eve's howl. Melrose was rather enjoying this reenactment. "Then we have *Tribute Money*—" Dick Scroggs had entered the perimeter of the window. "Next, we have *St. Peter Healing the Sick with His Shadow*." Melrose made a wiping motion with his hand, as if scenes were appearing and disappearing, as if they were watching a dumb show. Mrs. Withersby hove into view, the veritable model for the poor wretch begging for St. Peter's help. In the case of Withersby, it was bumming cigarettes and whatever else life had on offer.

"Uh, Mr. Plant, I think, yes, I think that's my phone ringing!"

Melrose hugged him closer. "Let it ring, let it ring. Let me tell you about San Gimignano—" And Melrose did so, told him about San Gimignano and Siena, in mind-withering detail, all the while enclosing the bookseller in an iron grip. Finally, he released him and said, "I must be on my way. Coming to the pub, are you?"

"Uh, no. No, I think not. Not this evening." He took several steps backward.

"Pity. Good evening, then." Melrose whistled himself out the door.

"Good Lord, Melrose! Where have you been? We're all dining at Ardry End tonight. It's Christmas Eve." Diane Demorney made these announcements as if they had just then come to mind unbidden by outside exigency. "Are we exchanging presents tonight, then?"

Marshall Trueblood lit a cigarette. "You mean for what you actually want?"

"Very funny. But were we to get something for

everyone? That would make—" She counted the people around the table by actually pointing her finger. "If Agatha's coming, that's, let's see, *six*. If everyone is to give everyone else a gift, that's—" Running out of fingers, she squeezed her eyes and put her hand to her forehead.

Joanna said, "Count me out, Diane. I've got to be on my way to Devon this afternoon. Promised I'd turn up for Christmas dinner tomorrow."

"Where in Devon?" Diane asked, not happy with a further refinement on a problem she hadn't yet solved.

"Exmoor."

Diane's martini actually stopped on its way to her mouth. *"Exmoor? But people don't live there, do they? It's a moor."*

"You've never been righter, Diane."

People waited patiently, for Diane's present count. Finally, Vivian said, "Diane, if there are six people and all six are giving each of the others a gift, then—" Vivian made an encouraging noise.

"Easy for you to say, Vivian, you've already *done* yours."

"That's beside the point; the point is the number."

Melrose wished he was back in the Brancacci Chapel. "Actually, there will be seven, not six."

Diane looked as if he had thrown the final spanner in the works. "Who else?"

"I've invited Mr. Steptoe."

They all looked blank.

"Our new greengrocer."

They still looked blank. Finally, Vivian said, "That's sweet of you Melrose. He can get to know people."

"Yes, I thought so."

From the bar, where he was reading the Sidbury paper, Dick Scroggs called over, "Don't see your horoscope column today, Miss Demorney."

"The stars are on holiday, Dick."

"No presents," said Melrose. "You have to do that on your own, go house to house, or whatever."

Diane heaved a sigh of relief, tapped a red fingernail against her empty martini glass and gave Dick Scroggs a little wave. "Did you set a time, Melrose? I mean will we be having drinkies beforehand?"

"We're having drinkies beforehand right now." He smiled. "But, yes, more drinkies will be on offer this evening. Come at seven."

FORTY-EIGHT

Richard Jury reached over to the ice bucket Ruthven had left, at Jury's request, plucked up a cube and dropped it in his whiskey. He had inclined lately toward as bitter a cold as he could get—cold walks, cold drinks, cold rooms, bitter and anesthetizing cold. He did not know why other than wanting to arm himself against the specter of Christmas past, present and probably future. He did not like Christmas; he felt depleted by it.

"That's a thirty-year-old single malt you're watering down," said Melrose Plant. They were seated in comfortable chairs next to the fire.

"It'll be gone before the ice melts. Now, back to St. Jerome."

"I think it's John, St. John."

"You didn't see whatever's left of this polyptych in the church in Pisa?"

"It's no longer there. That's part of the point. Parts have found their way into various churches and museums in Europe. And some of the panels are still missing."

Jury nodded and drank his whiskey. "What's this dealer's name?"

"Jasperson. The woman who's selling them is named Amy Eccleston."

Jury leaned over and set his empty glass on the table.

"I'd like a word with Jasperson. Do you have his number?"

"Here." Melrose handed over a card from his jacket pocket.

"Where's the phone?" Jury rose.

Melrose waved him down. "No, sit down. Ruthven can bring it." Melrose pressed the enamel button beneath the table beside his chair.

Ruthven appeared, was duly dispatched and returned with the phone. Jury thanked him.

"I could easily have gone to the phone rather than the phone coming to me."

"Hell, no. I want to hear what you say."

Jury dialed as Melrose refilled their glasses and plopped another ice cube in Jury's. Jury leaned back and waited and said to Melrose, "I'd be surprised to get anybody on Christmas Eve—hello. Mr. Jasperson, please. This is—? Mr. Jasperson, I'm Superintendent Richard Jury of Scotland Yard . . . No, nothing's wrong . . ." Jury asked him about the two paintings and whether he'd had them authenticated and where they'd come from. "The thing is, Mr. Jasperson, what I've been led to believe is that what you've got there might be a panel from an altarpiece by Masaccio—"

On his end, Jasperson's response must have been forceful—cried or cursed or laughed—for Jury moved the receiver away from his ear, regarded Plant with a shrug, then put the receiver back as Jasperson said something else, making Jury laugh. "I suppose not. Would anyone else connected with your shop possibly know . . . ? No . . . Miss Eccleston, I see. Well, I might just pop round there for five minutes and see what is . . . Yes. Oh, no, you needn't go there. Bad enough to be bothered at all on Christmas . . . Yes. Thanks. Wait. Tell me, if one of these panels did turn out to be by Masaccio, how much would it fetch at auction? . . . You don't say. Thank you."

Jury hung up. "Never saw them."

Melrose sat forward, eyes wide.

"I think we should have a little talk with Amy Eccleston, don't you?"

Melrose was up like a shot. "Let's go."

With their coats on and going out the door, Melrose asked, "How much did he say a Masaccio would get?"

"Around twenty-five, thirty million pounds."

"My God! But why would she be selling it for a measly two thousand, then?"

"Maybe she doesn't know anyone with thirty million."

There were two other customers when Jury walked into C. Jasperson's, American from the sound of them, middle-aged women in jumpers and slacks browsing and apparently giving sod all about the holiday. He liked that attitude.

Amy Eccleston, who had been conferring with them, excused herself and threaded her way through tables and chairs and objets d'art to join Jury near the front of the room. Her smile diminished fractionally when she saw his identification. "Oh." Then the telephone rang and she was off to answer it, no doubt grateful for the pause it gave her.

Jury studied the table in the middle of the room, frowning at the gilt and fat cherubs embracing the table legs. Why would anyone need such a piece, much less at this shocking price? He let the tag dangle.

The middle-aged Americans smiled at him on their way out and he returned the smile. So they smiled again, perhaps thinking they had shortchanged this man in the smile department. The bell jittered as they left.

Melrose, who had spent a few minutes outside contemplating the green, passed them in the doorway. He and Jury had decided it would be better if they entered separately so as not to arouse Amy Eccleston's suspicions, at least not immediately.

Returning from the telephone call, Miss Eccleston

saw Melrose and made a delighted sound. She said she'd fetch his painting in just a moment. To Jury she said, "Now, what did you want, Inspector?"

"Superintendent, actually. I understand you've sold two paintings lately attributed to the Italian painter Masaccio?"

With a self-righteous air, she corrected him. "No, indeed *not*! I didn't say they were by Masaccio. I merely said there's the *possibility*."

"You came across them yourself, did you?"

"Yes. In Italy. I found them in a little church in San Giovanni Valdarno. I thought they were unusual and very striking. Of course, that they might have been painted by Masaccio didn't occur to me at the time."

"Even though," put in Melrose, coming up on the two, "San Giovanni Valdarno was his place of birth?"

She looked from the one to the other, clearly disturbed that they appeared now to be together. "I wasn't thinking of that. Superintendent, what's wrong here? You seem to be accusing me of something."

Jury had been making notes in his small notebook. "What makes all of this suspect is that Mr. Jasperson knows absolutely nothing about these two paintings. Yet they're hanging here—or were—in his shop."

"Mr. *Jasperson*?" Her face looked chalky.

Jury just looked at her.

"I've been with Mr. Jasperson for three years now. He's always—"

"Too bad you won't be with him for three more, Miss Eccleston. The way I see it is this: you've been doing this for some time. You're here by yourself every Friday and on the occasional holiday. On those Fridays you hang your latest acquisition. You might have a buyer, you might not. If not, you merely wait until the next Friday. Certainly this elegant and pricy shop is a wonderful venue for expensive paintings. You pocket one hundred percent of the sale. Not bad. This week's takings are four thousand pounds, no VAT. That's a good return on an investment. It's also extremely daring. What if one of your buyers happened to bring back whatever you'd sold when Mr. Jasperson was here?"

"This is ridiculous. I don't need to—" She started to turn away.

Jury turned her back. "Oh, yes, you do need to. What you'll need to do is leave this place. Leave the village. You won't say anything—not *anything*—about these two paintings. Under no circumstances try to contact Mr. Trueblood. You'll write Mr. Plant here a letter relinquishing all interest in the paintings. Then you have forty-eight hours to get out of town."

"But what about Mr. Jasperson? I can't just leave."

"What you tell Mr. Jasperson is your own business. I'm sure you can think of something plausible." He paused. "You're getting off very lightly, Miss Eccleston. Thank your lucky stars that for some people, art really means more than money."

She looked absolutely white.

Jury smiled. "Gather up your painting, Mr. Plant."

Melrose didn't bother with the wrapping paper.

"Merry Christmas," said Jury.

"Good Lord," said Melrose, as they backed the car out of the parking place. "What could you do to her?"

"Nothing. But she doesn't know that. Of course, Jasperson could have her up on any number of charges."

Melrose was carrying his painting with him in the front seat. He leaned it back and looked at it. "The thing is, we still don't know."

"Whether it's genuine?"

"I don't see how it could be. How could something like this have been missed for all of these years by experts in the field. I mean, how could it have just sat there in some little church—and no Italian Renaissance nut twigged it?" Melrose paused. "But as Tomas Prada— one of the experts—pointed out, what could these panels have been copied from, given the original paintings are missing?"

"Hmm. That's a point, certainly. Can't you live with it this way?"

"Not knowing?"

"Yes."

"That's what Prada asked Trueblood."

"And what did Trueblood answer?"

Melrose smiled. "He said, 'I could; I'd just rather not.'"

Jury laughed. "Sounds like him."

FORTY-NINE

"**Y**our broccoli, now," began Mr. Steptoe, who might have been Irish or might have been English. "Your broccoli, now, the best of your broccoli's dark, so dark it's purple. That has all the nutrients in it twice over the lighter green sort. And any that's yellow, just you pass it up. Yellow means it's finished, no nutrients at all." He ate the stub of broccoli on which he had just passed judgment.

Mr. Steptoe, the new greengrocer in Long Piddleton, sat between Agatha and Diane. They were one woman short, so that meant two men would be cracking elbows. Melrose had seated Agatha between himself and Mr. Steptoe; this had immediately resulted in a whispered exchange, Agatha insisting that she preferred not to sit next to a grocer who would have no conversation at all. *"But I'll be on your left hand, dear aunt, and you know I'll have all sorts of conversation."* This irritated her even more, as Melrose knew it would.

But as it turned out, Mr. Steptoe had endless conversation, though it was all about vegetables. Mr. Steptoe had done beetroot, asparagus, parsnips and potatoes, had gone right around the dishes brought in by Ruthven and the slightly emaciated young lad Ruthven had dug up to help serve. Mr. Steptoe had pronounced each of these vegetables of excellent quality, which prompted Melrose to remark that they should be, for weren't they purchased at Steptoe's? Mr. Steptoe had thought that marvelously funny, and had excused himself from bragging by saying he honestly hadn't had that in mind at all.

"It's just that the right kind of vegetable, properly cooked, does indeed make the difference between a poor meal and a good one."

"Remember," said Trueblood, turning to Melrose, "the excellent flageolet beans at the Villa San Michele?"

Mr. Steptoe made a little noise. "Ah, flageolet! The best are in France, of course."

Melrose thought his guests might as well be at Le Manoir aux Quatre Saisons, listening to Raymond Blanc.

Mr. Steptoe continued: "Yes, I had a very tasty dish of flageolet cooked with apricots in Paris."

"The staple food of the Hunzas," said Diane.

All eyes turned to Diane upon hearing this runic remark.

"Apricots," she said. "Their staple food."

"Diane," said Melrose, "who in hell are the Hunzas?"

Diane waved the question away with ruby-painted nails. "Some Indian or other. Have we finished our dinner? Am I sitting in the smoking section? I'm way down at the end here, absolutely ostracized."

"You've got me, Diane," said Jury, taking her lighter to light her cigarette.

"Oh, don't I *wish*."

"Funny," said Melrose, "I certainly remember clearly the Villa San Michele—the magnificent vaulted ceilings, the faded frescoes on the walls of the lobby, the subdued service in the dining room and that knock-out view of Florence from the balcony. But I don't seem to recall the flageolet."

"Trust Melrose," said Agatha, "to sap all of the senti-

ment from any experience." She went back to prodding
a flower of broccoli around her plate.

"Not *any* experience, Agatha. Not the Masaccio experience, certainly. It had got to where I felt I knew him.
Right, Marshall? You, me and Masaccio: we three, we
happy three, we band of brothers."

Thoughtfully, Diane exhaled a plume of smoke. "That
has a familiar ring. And I agree with Melrose." Having
not been on the trip, Diane could take any side she
wanted. "You know, some writer said Florence was absolutely *overflowing*. It was Henry . . . Henry . . . Oh,
you know that writer who was so enamored of Italy."

"Henry James?" said Vivian.

"That's the one, yes." Diane exhaled another artistic-
looking stream of smoke. "You know, Superintendent,
you'd enjoy Florence. They've all sorts of crime, I mean
interesting crimes, society murders, that sort of thing.
Who was that count? The Conti di Rabilant, I think, was
murdered there. And you'd look marvelous in the uniform of the *carabinieri*. Quite smart." Diane smiled at
him in her sultry way. "What are you working on at the
moment?"

"A shooting."

Diane was interested. "Tell us about it, this shooting.
We might be able to help; we might come up with one or
two good ideas. Why you've seen—" Diane spread her
black velvet-garbed arm "—how we are!"

"Indeed he has," said Melrose.

Trueblood made a sound between a hiccup and a
laugh. "Dream on, Diane."

"But you never know how the details will strike
someone unfamiliar with a case. Don't you agree, Superintendent? Looking at something too long makes
it all so familiar you can think it's always been that
way."

"What are you talking about?" asked Trueblood.

"I thought it rather well put," said Jury. "Only, look,
it's Christmas. Can't we take a holiday from crime?"

Ruthven and his young helper had cleared away the dinner plates, and Ruthven reappeared with the Christmas pudding, which he placed before Melrose. "Shall I do it, sir?"

"No. This is the most fun I have all year. Give me the lighter."

Ruthven handed over the sort of lighter one uses for cigars. The butler then wrapped a napkin around a bottle of Champagne and circled the table, pouring.

Melrose flicked the lighter and held it to the base of the pudding. Flames shot up amidst murmurs of pleasure. Everyone clapped. Melrose stood up and waited for Ruthven to fill the glasses, then he raised his. "A toast! To 'we few, we happy few, we band of brothers.'" He looked around the table. "And sisters."

As everyone touched glasses, Diane said, "There it is again. I *know* I've heard that somewhere."

"King Henry the Fourth," said Melrose.

"Of *course*. The one who beheaded all of those wives."

"Whoever," said Melrose.

In dreams that night, Melrose found himself in the Brancacci Chapel watching the progress of several painters, one of whom was Trueblood. Only here, Melrose didn't seem to know him any better than the others. He had been watching an infernally long time—days, weeks, months? How was he to know? He was starving hungry. Looking around he saw that each worker had a lunch box, but he had nothing. Seeing one of the lunch boxes lying open and also seeing it contained an apple, he took it and started munching while one of the painters up there delicately lined Eve's face.

"Come on, come on!" Melrose yelled to him. "I've booked a table at the Villa San Michele, remember?"

Lithely, the youngest of the painters jumped down from the scaffolding and did a double somersault.

"Show-off," said Melrose.

The show-off plucked the rest of the apple from Melrose's hand and took a bite. "Nice dish o' flageolet and I'm a happy man," said Masaccio.

FIFTY

They must be really angry.

Gemma had raised her hand to knock on the door of Keeper's Cottage when she heard their raised voices and this made her drop her hand and take a step back. She had come to deliver a message from Mrs. MacLeish about Christmas dinner. But their voices made her back away.

It was Kitty Riordin and Maisie arguing. She could make out a few words: earring. The fight had to do with an earring. Gemma wondered if Kitty had discovered the gold one was missing. Did she think Maisie had taken it?

The voices were furious, frightening. Gemma gripped Richard as if she were afraid too much anger might knock him out of her hands. He was wearing the new clothes that Ambrose had given him for Christmas. The outfit was black: black jacket, trousers and a sweater. The suit was so soft, she liked to rub Richard on her cheek to feel it. *"Black is cool,"* Ambrose had said in his note. Gemma marveled at all of this. Richard looked wonderful in his new clothes. He looked smart and dangerous, virtues he had always had, but hidden under the old long dress.

Earring? No, that wasn't it. It had something to do with an errand. Gemma thought she made out, "You've got to do this errand."

The window was open just a little. The old mullioned panes prevented her seeing people clearly in there; they showed only as forms, wavering, distended, as if she were seeing them at the bottom of a pool.

The arguing stopped, suddenly. Silence. The door flew open before Gemma could get away. "Gemma! What are you doing here? How long have you been there?"

Gemma's throat felt thick with sounds she couldn't say. Maisie Tynedale turned and called to Kitty Riordin to come.

When she saw Gemma on the doorsill, Kitty sucked in her breath and asked the question again: "How long have you been there?"

Gemma swallowed and shook her head. Her feet seemed stuck. Then she managed to lift one but before she could move, Maisie Tynedale gripped her arm and pulled her into the cottage. Then she slammed the door shut.

Kitty was in her bathrobe and her hair was down from its smooth coiled bun. She looked much older with no makeup on. She was probably a hundred.

"Gemma," she said, "come on in, dear."

Fear sluiced through Gemma's body as she clutched Richard closer. It was the "dear" that did it. Kitty never called her anything like that. She made a dash for the door, but Maisie was right there, her fingers like pincers on Gemma's arm.

"For heaven's sake, child, I thought you'd like some cocoa," Kitty said. "Come back to the kitchen; I have it heating."

Gemma's eyes were riveted on her. Kitty Riordin, for all that Gemma avoided her, had never seemed so dangerous as right now, when she was trying to appear to be nice.

The kitchen was ordinary—cooker, fridge, a table against the biscuit-colored wall with three straight chairs, a clock on the wall decorated with a red rooster. The rooster was the only color there was.

Gemma unzipped her down coat and put Richard inside in case someone decided to grab at him. She zipped it up again.

They had sat her down on one of the hard chairs, and now Kitty placed a mug of cocoa in front of her, telling her it would warm her up. There were two other mugs sitting on the counter but she didn't fill those. Instead, she watched to see that Gemma drank hers. Maisie had gone into the front room and come back with a bottle of whiskey, which she had poured into a couple of small glasses.

Gemma did not want to drink this cocoa, although it looked very good and rich. She didn't want to, but she knew something worse might happen if she didn't. With Kitty standing over her and Maisie watching, she drank it. No one spoke. They seemed to be waiting. Gemma rested her head against the wall and tried to think of something nice, for thinking about how to get away from this cottage was useless and she just gave up.

She thought about what a strange Christmas this was. How it lacked the usual excitement and suspense (though that had certainly changed in the last half hour!). She had not *felt* it to be Christmas Eve until she had wandered out after her evening meal and found—to her mystification and surprise—a package lying on her seat in the beech tree. It was wrapped with silver paper and white ribbon, and the note said, *"Merry Christmas, Richard."* This had simply floored her: that someone would buy Richard a present! It had turned out to be Richard's new black clothes. It was from Ambrose.

Earlier, Benny and Sparky had come with their Christmas presents for her. Sparky carried a bouquet of bluebells in his teeth which he set down at her feet and sneezed and stepped back, waiting for congratulations. Gemma thanked him and gave him the bone she had got for him. Her present for Benny (which she had wrapped with a lot of paper to disguise its book shape) was the *David Copperfield* Miss Penforwarden had told her Benny was always reading. She had asked Miss Penforwarden had she any ideas for a present, and this was it.

Benny had asked her not to open his present until Christmas morning and made her promise. She opened it, of course, the minute he was gone. It had made her jump with joy: a bottle of Bluebell perfume from Penhaligon's. She straight away uncapped it and dabbed some on.

This had all gone on, this soft afternoon and evening, in a sort of dream.

Now, she supposed, here was the nightmare to finish things off. She felt herself slipping away as if she were turning liquid. The last thing her ears could pick out from their talking was something about "bread and water." So she guessed she was going to prison and slept.

Bread and water. They were the first things she saw when she woke. Her head ached and she felt like going back to sleep, but she didn't. Immediately, she felt her jacket to see if Richard was there and he was. She unzipped her coat and took him out.

With the bread and water there was also a wedge of cheese, all sitting atop a small counter on which there were plates, a couple of pans and a microwave oven. The room was cramped and shadowy, no light except for a wall sconce above one of the two narrow beds. It was small, but still it was rather nice. Cozy and warm. Above the beds were little windows; beside this one was a table with a drawer she yanked out. It was full of junk, but also rolls of coins and keys. She wondered what the keys were to.

To see out of the window, she would have to stand on the bed. Just as she did so, there came a frightening roar and then the room rocked and she was knocked back down. The contents of the drawer fell out, the coins rolling away under the bed. When things quieted down and straightened out, she got up on the bed again and looked out of the window.

"Richard! This is a *boat*! We're on a boat on the *river*!"

FIFTY-ONE

Sparky could always find his way to and back even in dead dark, but there was plenty of light along this bank and across on the other bank thousands of bulbs of light. Massive black heaps—lighted too—spanned the two sides of the river and seemed to have no purpose other than for cars to flow over and back, and, of course, to give shelter to the boy and his friends. This was the most important function of the nearest black heap.

Sometimes Sparky looked up at the people he passed, who walked like robots, staring straight ahead, listening only to what was in their heads and their ears. He wanted to shout! *Down look down, look down, come down and get your noses to the ground and Sniff!* There's a whole sniffing life down here you're passing up. The closest anyone came, and those were few, was reaching down to pet him, but they never stopped long.

Sniffing along the narrow concrete walk, he would spend hours nosing through trash and rags. He was only glad he no longer had to look through this stuff for food. It had been bad when he was little until the boy had found him and fed him and gone on feeding him. Yes, he loved the boy as much as a good sniff around a place.

He could stay up all hours, travel around, sleep all day

if he wanted (well, except, of course, for deliveries). And he'd been given a name—Barky? Sparky? Perky?—it made no difference. The name was for the boy's sake. Bernie? Benny? Bunny? Well.

Sparky was patrolling the bank all along the river and through the confluence of narrow dark streets which had once held nothing but warehouses, but were now where people lived and fancy cars sizzled through the rain.

Here was a bundle of rags. The smells shocked his senses so much that he came near to retreating even before the voice shouted, "Piss off, ya fuckin' mutt!"

Sparky trotted on, feeling stupid, as it wasn't the first time this had happened, and by now he should have learned when a bundle of rags wasn't a bundle of rags. The man was looking for something to throw when Sparky ran. He should be more careful about these wretches. Once, as he was sniffing one over, the wretch grabbed him, tossed a rope over his neck and took him up to the Strand for the day's begging. It always helped to have a dog with you, Sparky knew that. He also knew he could get away. These people couldn't keep their minds on things. When two pound coins were dropped in his old hat, the wretch got so excited and eager to pocket the coins that he let go of the rope and Sparky took off at a gallop, tore from the Strand to the Embankment and in a hop-skip-jump was back with the boy. The boy was overjoyed to see him. Poor Barney (Bernie?) was clearly worried to death, and Sparky wished he could convey to him how spectacular his talent for homing was, how infallible his nose. At times he thought he should have been a wine taster instead of a delivery dog. Or a florist, like the ones in the place of blue flowers.

There have been stories, he recalled, about the incredible homing feats of dogs like himself, such as the one who'd traveled all the way from Bognor Regis to Bath, searching for his owner who'd moved. Oh, sure, thought Sparky, don't we *wish*?

Now, where was he? Stink Street. He called it that for it was home to more smells than any other single place he knew, except for marketplaces. Stink Street came close to knocking him out; it was in amongst all these old warehouses that were home to a lot of youngish snobs with good jobs and money. What he smelled was the rich odor of furs; the scent of the animals they had been ripped from still clung. New tires, cars, leather, sweetish smell of weed. Perfume. The mingling of perfumed scents strong enough to lift you off your legs.

Stink Street was a heady experience. He had to be careful of places like that; they could come to be necessary; they would not let you go. Sparky moved on out toward the river.

The door at the top of the ladderlike steps, which reminded her of an attic door, was not locked and this surprised her. Gemma pushed up one side and suddenly saw the night sky of stars and the white moon riding behind a gauzy cloud. With Richard again tucked inside her coat, she climbed out on the deck of the boat and looked around. She unzipped her coat and took Richard out so that he could see, too. The boat was fairly big; she'd never seen it before and could not imagine why she'd been put here.

"So you couldn't get away," she heard Richard say.

"Well, what am I supposed to do, then?"

"Get away, of course."

There were times he just irritated her to death with his solutions to her problems. Ever since he'd got his new black clothes, he was impossibly bossy.

"It's not impos—"

Gemma shoved him back inside her coat to shut him up. Then she got her bearings: the boat was closer to the one bank than the other. It was much closer to the Big Ben side than it was to the Southwark Cathedral side. There was one bridge fairly close; she did not know its name. Benny had shown her pictures of the next one down, and she knew it was Waterloo Bridge. Around the curve of the river was Big Ben. So she knew where she was, pretty much.

Glad the boat was still, or the river was, she walked all around the deck, which didn't take long. There were benches with plastic cushions built in on both sides; the place where you drove the boat was toward the front. That's where the wheel was, with glass all around like a windshield that the captain could look through to see where he was going. She would never be able to figure out how to drive it. Anyway, the boat was anchored. Over there she saw what looked like a dock. And beyond the dock, a big squarish house. So the boat probably belonged to that house and the dock was for the boat. Maybe it was too big to pull up there, so it anchored here.

Richard was getting ready to tell her to swim for it, she bet, so before he could, she said, "I can't swim!"

"Don't mope or you'll never—" came the muffled words from inside.

"I don't mope!" Gemma closed her eyes, hoping if she didn't give her mind any new sights to see it would be better able to concentrate on her problem. Wait a minute! Her eyes snapped open. There had to be a way to get from the bank—the dock—to the boat. It was somebody's boat and if that person could get to it, then there had to be a way.

"Good good good good!" Richard cried.

But if that was the only boat . . . ? Gemma walked around the deck again slowly, peering over the side. A smaller boat, a rowboat it looked like, was tied to the side of the big boat. She wondered if it was okay, if it had any leaks in it, but if it had, it would already have sunk, wouldn't it?

She shrank back. But I can't get down there—

"You can too; it's hardly any distance at all. Find a rope; there are always ropes on boats. Don't just stand there."

"I'm only nine. How can I—?"

"Oh, for God's sake! Get me out of here and I'll find a rope!"

Gemma took Richard out from under her coat and held him in front of her. While she walked, she turned him different ways so that he could inspect the deck. Slowly around the deck they walked.

"Right there!"

Not only was there a coil of rope, but it appeared to be tied, sturdily tied, to a short pole. She stuffed Richard back inside her coat (while he was still barking orders), picked up the rope and dragged it back to the part of the deck just above the rowboat. It was plenty long. She let the end down, played the rope out to the rowboat. Then she put all her weight into it and yanked hard to see if back there the rope held to the pole. Yes! Only, how was she to move the oars. She could never handle two, one on each side.

"Sure, you can."

"Shut up, Richard! You don't know *every*thing!"

"Pretty much. Find something you can use for oars."

At that moment, something in Gemma switched off and something else switched on. It was no longer a question of would she drown in the Thames, but whether she was smarter than the two women who had stuck her out here. She ran to the flat door and stumbled down the staircase. She yanked out drawers in the little kitchen and tossed stuff out—useless silverware, scissors, plastic things—things in the drawers were all anyhow—knives, bottle caps, string. She finally came to a large spatula and it made her think of the way Mrs. MacLeish made omelettes. She would draw the cooked egg back with the spatula and the uncooked would run around it. Like water around an oar. Well, it was better than nothing. Among the rest of the utensils she found a big ladle. That would have to do.

She stopped, sat down on one of the beds and chewed the inside of her cheek, thinking. Then she remembered the rolls of coins that had rolled under the bed and got down and tried to fish them out, but couldn't reach. With her other hand she groped on top of the bed and found the ladle. With it, she got the two rolls out. Then she looked at the utensils that had landed on the floor and picked up a paring knife.

She sat up and took Richard out. "I hate to do this . . ."

"What? What? No knives!"

"It won't hurt. Much. Be quiet." She removed his clothes, turned him over and with the knife, carefully pried the stitches out along the back seam. Oh! There were protests! Then she removed half of the stuffing and replaced it with the two rolls of coins. She didn't have anything to sew him up again, so she bound him tightly together with the string. She went over the seam again and made sure the string would hold. She shoved his clothes into one coat pocket and the stuffing into the other. Then she collected the spatula and ladle and hurried up the steps.

Sparky sneezed. It was explosive and set him down on his rump. He sneezed again and shook his head as if to render it sneeze free. He trotted over to the place in the courtyard where, in the spring, tulips grew. Whatever had been there was stone cold dead. Then he inspected a planter usually filled with primroses. It wasn't now. He looked around but saw nothing else.

Sparky enjoyed coming to this house; he liked the forecourt. It was pleasant to sniff around in. In the distance, Big Ben sounded whatever hour it was. Sparky could count up to four. Why he could do this was a mystery to him, but for some reason the boy had taught him this trick, which had to do with the street and filling the hat with coins. You'd think he could remember the name of the boy who'd saved him from a dustbin life, but what did names matter? If you could tell you were being summoned by look and gesture, why was the name important? He wasn't even sure what his own name was. Big Benny. Sparky loved that.

He could remember the woman, even by name. This was rare for him to do, but then she had been rare. Where had she gone? He drooped; it made him sad.

Then he sneezed.

The rope had held and Gemma was in the boat, rocking. The boat felt less substantial than it had appeared when she'd been looking down on it. She patted her coat just to make sure Richard was still there, although she knew he was from the extra weight. Slowly and carefully, Gemma turned around in the boat. She faced the land she was heading for and put the spatula in the water. Then she tried to put the ladle in and realized she couldn't do both because her arms weren't long enough. It didn't work, anyway, for they were too small to push back enough water for the boat to move. "How stupid I am!" she said aloud.

"I wouldn't disag—"

"Be quiet!"

She wrenched the oar from its lock, shoved the end against the boat and pushed the rowboat away. One oar could be managed if she used both hands; she'd never have been able to row with two of them. She tried this and found the boat wouldn't go straight with just one, so she moved it from side to side. The boat moved forward, and though she couldn't go fast, she could see the house over there and the dock inch closer.

If her hands had been free, Gemma would have clapped. As it was, she settled for telling Richard, "You're not the only one that's smart."

His answer was muffled, but not complimentary.

Bluebells.

That was what he smelled; that was what made him

sneeze. It got stronger as he sniffed his way around the side of the house. He was baffled; that smell shouldn't be here, but back there where the girl lived with the bluebells he'd brought her. (Jimmy? Janie? Jemima?) Was she here? Had she been here?

He sniffed along the dock. He hated being this close to water. His head came up for he sensed something. Right at the end of the dock, he looked out over the river and saw a little rowboat moving his way. He paced back and forth, back and forth.

Then he saw her and barked.

Gemma could hardly believe it when she heard a dog. Why would a dog be running back and forth on the dock, pulsing with barks—?

"Sparky!"

The boat bumped against the dock and turned around. Sparky looked over the edge. The dock was too high for the girl (Jimmy? Jeanna?) to reach. In a minute, a rope tied to something landed on the dock. Was it that damned doll? It was tied to the end of the rope. He got his teeth around the doll; there was a lot of slack, but he clamped down and pulled the rope up on the dock.

Gemma thought, how would he know what to do with the rope? He was only a dog, for heaven's sake. Yes, but a very smart one. She wanted him to wrap the rope around something, anything that would take it. One of the pilings would do it. She only needed a little purchase so she could climb up. The distance wasn't much. As she looked at the pilings, she saw a second rowboat drifting in and out from under the dock, only this one had a motor attached to it. It wasn't very securely tied.

Gemma imagined Maisie Tynedale must have been in a big hurry to leave.

When all of the slack was taken up, Sparky still held the doll (which was pretty heavy) in his mouth and looked around. He dragged the doll and the rope over to a piling and had just enough room to maneuver the rope around and around again. After she tugged at it and it held, she started climbing.

Sparky bounced about, completely giddy when Jimmy managed to heave herself up, hand over hand, onto the dock.

"Sparky!" Gemma grabbed him and squeezed him to her chest until he could only *just* breathe. He could do without this part of it.

She untied Richard. Remarkably, he was still the same; he hadn't even gotten wet. She was checking to see if the string still held, when she heard the car.

Both of them heard the car.

The car pulled into the forecourt, slammed its door, left its engine running and its headlights on. Gemma knew it was them, or one of them, either Kitty or Maisie. One of them had brought her here. She had expected it, but she was still afraid. Even if she could have jumped down into the boat, there was no time to do it.

The woman came toward them bathed in the glare of the headlights. But when she got to the dock, she stopped, stunned. It was Maisie. Her eyes, looking at Gemma, were immense. "My God! How on earth—?"

Gemma got down to Sparky's level. "Go, Sparky!"

Sparky jumped. He had never really *gone* before, and now he saw his chance. He plummeted toward Maisie, grabbed her ankle and let himself be shaken and shaken, yelled at to get off, get off. Cursed. Good.

Clutching Richard, Gemma watched. "Get her down, Sparky, get her head down!" Gemma moved nearer to them.

Sparky let go of the ankle and sprang up to Maisie's forearm. To dislodge the dog, she had to bend down, get her head down—

Gemma rushed at her just as Sparky had, pulled her own arm back and with every single ounce of strength left to her, brought Richard down on Maisie's head. Giving a small exhalation of breath, Maisie slumped on the boards with a dull thud.

"Let me hit her again! Hit her again!"

That was Richard. Gemma thought he'd earned the right, so she hauled off and brought the doll down on Maisie's head again. Then for good measure, hit her once more. Gemma would have liked to kill her, to roll her off the dock and let her drown.

But she didn't; they left her lying there.

FIFTY-TWO

Sparky led; Gemma followed. All she knew was this was along the Thames, but she had no idea where Swan Lane was, a name they'd just passed. He seemed to know exactly where he was going and stopped every so often to make sure she was right there behind him.

At one point a car stopped, just pulled up to the curb and the driver leaned across as far as he could and said, "Want a lift, love. I'm just on my way to—"

Gemma never found out where because Sparky hurled himself against the car door, mere inches from the nose of this person making his offer.

"Bloody hell!" the man yelled, jerking away from the window, then stalling the engine out when he tried to accelerate, and Sparky, all the while like a pole vaulter, snarling and launching himself at the car. It made Gemma laugh. The man finally got out like the devils in hell were at his heels.

Gemma skipped along as if this were a walk in Kensington Gardens. She hadn't felt like skipping in a long time, but now she did. She wished she could throw herself, as Sparky had done, up against things and scare them and make them run away. But then she'd have to have Sparky's bark and Sparky's bite to do that.

By now they were coming up on the Victoria Embankment, and Waterloo Bridge, vast and black, was a short distance before them. She loved the lights across the Thames, oceans of them as if the whole of London were layered in little lights. Sparky was descending some steps, his nails clicking on the cold concrete. Gemma wondered where they were going, but didn't mind all of this walking as she was still in a little daze over having escaped from whatever horrible plan the two women had made for her. She wondered if she *had* killed Maisie and allowed herself the consolation of thinking she could blame it on Richard, anyway.

"Hey, hey!"

"Oh, be quiet, Richard." She shook him a little. He was dressed again in his black outfit. Sparky had waited patiently while she had sat on the step of a building back there and got the clothes on him and the stuffing back inside. She would sew him back up later when she had a needle and thread.

They had crossed the wide street, garnering a few curious glances from people in cars—why all this traffic?—but not curious enough to stop. They were right by Waterloo Bridge and, after descending a few more steps, right under it. Gemma was astonished to see all of these sleeping forms. People under the bridge. She thought she must be in the middle of a fairy tale. Then she wondered if these were the "homeless" she'd heard spoken of. About them she had always had a kind of shifting image of men and women wandering around dazed, looking for their houses, the places they had nearly forgotten, or been forgotten by.

The thing was, Gemma had scarcely been out in the wide world after she had first walked into Tynedale Lodge. The only person who'd have taken her out to parks and stores and films was too sick now to do it. The others most of the time didn't seem to know she was around. But the staff did; Mr. Barkins didn't like her, but Rachael the maid took her out to do Christmas shopping, which Gemma loved. That was how she'd found *David Copperfield* to give to Benny. Miss Penforwarden was just as nice as Benny said she was. She sat Gemma and Rachael down and gave them tea and some little cakes. She talked to Rachael while Gemma walked around the store, dazzled by all of the books. Mr. Tynedale had a library, it was true, but not all of these shelves with books front and back.

Christmas! It must be after midnight by now, so that meant today was Christmas Day! Sparky was rooting around one of the sleepers and when this person finally sat up Gemma was astonished to see Benny. She nearly dropped Richard. Was there no end to the astonishments of this night? Was it to be one thing right after another, horrible and wonderful in their turn?

"Benny!"

His voice was sleepy. "Gemma?" He shook his head, then looked from Sparky to Gemma and back again.

Now, faced at last with an actual person who could help her, Gemma felt a floodgate open and a squall of tears took hold of her. "Someone tried to *kill me*!"

Forgetting the very strange occurrence of Gemma's appearing in the middle of the night under Waterloo Bridge, all Benny could say was, "Not again!" before he fell right back on his pallet.

FIFTY-THREE

The knock on the door wrenched Jury from a sleep as deep and as soft as the down comforter that covered him and the Italian sheets he lay between. The knock was followed by Ruthven's entrance, in robe and slippers, to tell the superintendent he had a phone call and to place a telephone by his bed.

Last night, Ruthven had brought him a nightcap on a silver tray and asked him if he required anything else. Looking around, Jury had said, "Only to stay in this room in my declining years."

Ruthven had tittered and remarked that the superintendent offered no visible signs of any decline.

The room, Jury thought, as he'd looked around it, was an antidote to a life of lumpy mattresses, threadbare carpets, sprung sofas. One wall was filled with shelves of books and, at intervals along those shelves, small brass lamps were bolted, to cast light on whatever section one might want to explore. In front of the bookshelves sat a leather armchair of a red so deep it was black in the shadows, and a table to hold one's teacup or one's whiskey glass. It was an arrangement that all but begged the room's occupant to pluck out a book and sit down. The wall opposite this was full of windows and velvet curtains. Jury had looked down at a white and crumbling statue in the rear garden by a small pool overhung with willows. All in all, this was the most romantic room Jury had ever seen, the most complete, the most becalmed. He thought, climbing into the sensuous bed the night before, that he could sleep for a year.

Instead, this telephone appeared at 3:30 A.M. with a call from the City police. It was Mickey, who told Jury what had happened—or as much as he knew—and to whom. "But she won't tell anybody the details, except you or Ambrose. Who's Ambrose?" asked Mickey.

"A friend. How can she be so cool about it? My God, she's only nine."

"Don't forget the dog; he can't be more than two or three."

Jury was already standing by this time. He said, "I'll be right there."

"At Croft's house. The kids are here. You apparently know these kids; they certainly know you. I'd like to get more than monosyllables out of the girl."

"Ask the dog."

"Very funny.

"Miss Tynedale, a.k.a. Riordin, has been taken to hospital. Couple of bumps on the head, but nothing serious. She's awake but not talking. The one I want to go after is her mother. What about the kids?"

"Right now I think they should go home, have some Horlick's, go to bed. That poor little girl must be in a state."

Mickey turned away from the phone; Jury could hear Gemma's voice quite clearly, and clearly objecting. "She hates Horlick's, wants a cup of black coffee. And they want to stay here until you come."

"Okay, but tell them they've got to lie down somewhere in the house and get some sleep."

Mickey laughed. "It's obvious you don't have kids, Richard."

Jury felt oddly stung by that comment. But he didn't answer, *Yet it's me they want to talk to, Mickey.* All he said was good-bye.

Melrose Plant was not only awake, but dressed and with a pot of coffee when Jury got downstairs. "Ruthven told me it was the police."

"Haggerty. Thanks." Jury drank down the coffee in one go. "Gemma Trimm was abducted—"

Melrose started up from his chair.

"—but she's perfectly okay now. She wants to see you and me."

Melrose collected his car keys and his coat. "Let's go, then." He stuck his arms into the sleeves of his black cashmere overcoat.

Jury said, "You've got your black clothes on again."

"Ah! But these are different black clothes."

"Cool. Let's go, dude."

They headed out into the frosty predawn morning.

The house flooded the river with light and a strong police presence in the form of a dozen or more men and women, uniformed and plain clothes, stood near the house and down on the dock.

"Where's DCI Haggerty?"asked Jury.

"Gone to Tynedale Lodge to collect the Riordin woman," said a detective sergeant whose name was Knobbs and who didn't like Jury. Or, at least, didn't like New Scotland Yard's presence.

Jury wondered—but not aloud—if picking up Kitty Riordin was premature.

"The kids are in the library. Here, I'll show you—"

"No need, Detective. I've been here before. Thanks."

Knobbs was giving Melrose Plant a careful scrutiny. Jury didn't bother with introductions. "He's mine."

"Your what?" asked Melrose, as they moved off toward the library.

When they walked in, Gemma and Benny bounced up. Gemma was flinging black looks at Jury, sweet ones at Melrose.

Benny started in: "I never heard nothing like it, Mr. Jury. How Gemma here got off that boat—"

Jury knelt down and put his hands on her arms. "What happened, love?"

Looking mad as a hornet, Gemma said, "They were going to kill me is all. They made me their prisoner and gave me bread and water."

"And cheese, you said," said Benny.

"*Benny*, I'm telling it. It was only a *little* cheese. I was on that boat out there—" she pointed "—and I'd probably have died except for Richard."

Jury smiled. "I'm glad I was some kind of help, though I can't see—"

"*You?* You didn't do *nothing*! You'd have just let me be killed. I mean Richard *here*. She stuck the doll in Jury's face, and then, thinking better of it she started slugging Jury, giving him some whacks in the chest, then yelling, "You knew something bad could happen to me and you just left, *you just left!*" She was flailing, kicking Jury's legs, pummeling his chest. Crying, tears flying everywhere. "You're not any good. Ambrose helped me more than you did. Even Sparky helped save me!"

Hearing his name (what he recalled of it) Sparky rushed over and barked at Jury.

Jury pulled Gemma to him, arms around her, patting her back, saying she was right to be mad and he was sorry. He was terribly, terribly sorry he hadn't been here, and yes, he should have been looking out for her. Finally, she quieted down, and he gave her his fresh handkerchief.

Melrose said, "I wasn't here either, Gemma. How did I help?"

She shoved the doll Richard out again as testament to either success or folly. "You got him new clothes."

"Black," said Jury.

"And that helped?"

"Well, of course. Before he only had that awful old

gown to wear. But his new black clothes make him *think*."

"Cool," said Jury, smiling.

"*Way* cool," said Melrose.

And then they all sat down (including Sparky) and Jury and Melrose heard a whale of a good yarn.

FIFTY-FOUR

ickey had taken her to the Snow Hill station. When Jury got there, the two of them were seated in a room furnished with a table and two chairs of tubular steel. The room was painted white, walls and ceiling. The effect was slightly disorienting: a bright, white, scarcely furnished world, absent of warmth, color, kith, kin. A vacancy.

Jury stood against the wall, arms crossed. Kitty Riordin looked up at him with an unreadable expression.

Mickey shoved his pack of Silk Cut toward her, at the same time telling the tape recorder that Jury had just entered. Then he asked, "When did you tell her? How long ago?"

"I didn't; she found out, she suspected something—call it intuition shored up by old photos and maybe more important, the suspicion that Oliver Tynedale didn't much like her. For him not to like his own grandchild would be simply impossible. No matter what he or she did. He was like that."

She spoke not with the lilting grace of an Irish girl, but with the assurance of one long bred to wealth and privilege. It had rubbed off on her, the authority granted by money and power. Ironic that Oliver Tynedale didn't see money and power in that light at all.

"He didn't like Erin?"

"He didn't like her *much*. Not the way he dotes on that child Gemma, who just walked in off the street."

"That's why you took a shot at her? You were afraid she would supplant Maisie—Erin, that is—as a major inheritor of your *employer's* money?"

Jury smiled. *Nice shot, Mickey.* But he didn't think it was the inheritance altogether; Kitty's wanting to get rid of Gemma was prompted as much by Gemma's supplanting Maisie in Oliver's heart as it was by the Tynedale fortune. Imagine all of that effort—the initial danger of this impersonation, the ongoing anxiety that she might be discovered, the grooming of her daughter, Erin, turning her into Maisie Tynedale and breaking into the Tynedale dynasty. The effort of proving that Kitty Riordin wasn't "pig-track Irish." *Where do we get these notions of who we are?* Jury wondered.

"Yes," Kitty said in answer to Mickey's question. "All Oliver Tynedale wanted was a granddaughter."

"So Gemma Trimm comes from nowhere—"

Wryly, Kitty smiled. "What difference does that make? Gemma, you should be able to see, is more of a Tynedale than my Erin would ever have been. Gemma's tough. I mean really tough. It would take a force of nature, a tidal wave, a tornado, to bring that child down."

"That's why you tried again tonight to get her out of the way?"

"She heard me talking to Erin. She heard the name. I had to see Gemma didn't tell anyone, didn't I? Erin's too soft. She really hated leaving the child on that boat. She should have made sure the rowboat was unhitched and let it drift away. That's what she should have done; instead, she rationalizes it, says there was no way that Gemma could have used it."

Mickey was silent, looking at her. The silence lengthened; Mickey could be unnerving that way.

"And Simon Croft," he finally asked.

"What about him?"

Jury's antennae went up. He shoved away from the wall.

Mickey said, "He found out, right?"

"Not that I know of."

"Then why—?"

"Why what?"

"Why did you shoot him?"

"I didn't."

Mickey was half out of his chair, galvanized.

Kitty seemed actually to be amused. "I'm sorry to disappoint you. Simon might have found out something, but that wasn't it." Coolly, she dusted a bit of ash from her sleeve. "You'll just have to start all over again sorting it, so."

Mickey and Jury looked at one another.

"You said Simon Croft might have found something—?"

"Possibly. Something about Alexandra's husband."

"Ralph Herrick. You knew him."

"Slightly. He was hardly ever at home."

She stopped and Jury said, "Would you elaborate?" He was surprised that Kitty hadn't asked for a solicitor during all of this.

"I can't. I overheard Simon talking to Oliver one day, something to do with Ralph and this book Simon was writing."

"So it could've been anything?" Mickey said this and got up to rove the room.

"Did Alexandra ever mention her other child to you?" asked Jury.

Mickey stopped pacing. He looked at Jury, surprised.

Kitty seemed surprised, too. "Yes. The baby was adopted."

"What else did she say?"

"She said the experience was a calamity. The worst thing that had ever happened to her."

"Did she say why?"

Mickey put in, "Maybe because an illegitimate baby would've been a hell of a lot less acceptable than it is now."

"Yes," said Jury. "But 'worst thing'? 'Calamity'? That's pretty strong for someone in Alexandra's position. Her father could have fixed anything. And unless I'm wrong about him, Tynedale would have wanted a grandchild."

"All I know is she said she left for several months, told Oliver she wanted to go around France with a friend. The baby was born on Guy Fawkes night; she liked to pretend all the fireworks were for her. I got the feeling it was very hard on her, giving the baby up."

They were silent for a while until Mickey said, "You never told Tynedale about this baby. Why not?"

"Why would I have? It would hardly be in my interests, or Erin's."

Jury supposed that was how she took the measure of everything.

"Now, haven't I helped you enough?" She looked from Mickey to Jury. "Especially considering why I'm here."

Mickey walked over to the door, looked out.

Jury said, "Just one more question. Did anyone else know about this? Did Francis Croft, for instance?" Emily Croft knew, but he didn't mention that.

"I don't know. I doubt it."

Jury was still asking questions when a police constable, a woman, came into the room to take Kitty away. "How was this adoption handled?"

She didn't answer that; she was led away by the WPC.

It had grown light as they'd been talking to Kitty Riordin. Jury said, "No one has mentioned the father of that illegitimate child. Has it ever occurred to you it just might be Francis Croft?"

Surprise pulled Mickey away from the door Kitty Riordin had walked through. "*What?* Oh, come on, Rich!"

"It makes sense, doesn't it? What would be the reason for keeping that pregnancy a secret? The only one I can think of is that the father would come as such a shock, be so totally unacceptable to Oliver Tynedale, that Alexandra couldn't tell him."

Mickey washed his hands down over his face. He looked exhausted. "It makes some kind of sense, I guess." Mickey smiled wanly. "Look, it's Christmas and we've both been up most of the night." He sighed. "Looks like we're back to bloody square one with Simon Croft. Unless we don't believe her."

"No, I do believe her. We're not back to square one. And you haven't talked to Erin Riordin yet." Jury looked at Mickey, concerned. "You've found out what you wanted to know. You were right."

"I found out *more* than I bloody wanted to know." Mickey chuckled.

"As you said, it's Christmas. Look, go home to Liza and the kids. Go. I can work on this."

"I think I will. What are you going to do?"

"Track down wherever that wee babe was taken. Somehow I don't think it would have been a regular orphanage. Alexandra had money; she would have sought out something better."

"Money, yes. But the presence of mind to sort through that kind of information? I mean, with no one helping her—?"

"Oh, I think she had help. She had Francis Croft."

The City police wouldn't hold the children any longer than absolutely necessary, so Gemma would no doubt be back at Tynedale Lodge. Where Benny would be, he couldn't be sure. Jury knew he could have commandeered a car and driver, but he wanted to think. The element of thought right now was not a car. So he took the tube to Charing Cross station. His fellow passengers looked even more disenfranchised than he himself: an unshaven man who could have been old, who could have been young, impossible to say, talking to himself; a woman wearing a hat with a bird perched and bobbing on its brim; a teenager slipped so far down in his seat, his spine was nearly on the floor. Jury thought about Erin Riordin. Since she was not the daughter of Ralph Herrick, would she (or Kitty) be scandalized by the appearance of Simon Croft's book? Maisie would be, certainly; she'd be the daughter of a traitor to her country. Yes, it was still a strong motive for murder because Erin intended to go on being Maisie Tynedale.

He left Charing Cross station and walked down Villiers Street to the Embankment. When he was near Waterloo Bridge, he stopped and thought: how arrogant of him to think this boy who had been making his way for years with his friends under the bridge would need him, Jury, to take his interest to heart. Jury had come here probably more for his own sake than for Benny's. He crossed the rain-slick road, walked along the pavement, then down the few stairs to the area beneath the bridge. There were only two people there now, an older woman swathed in a blanket and a hat not unlike the one he had just seen on the underground and a man in a greatcoat. They were talking but stopped when he walked up to them.

"I'm looking for a lad named Benny Keegan. Would you know him?"

"An' who be you?"

Jury wasn't going to get anything out of these two; they knew he was a cop. "Just a friend."

The man in the greatcoat sputtered his disbelief. "Ah, sure, and I'm on the short list for the bloody Booker Prize." He drew a slim book from his pocket and waved it at Jury. "We don't know no Benny. Never 'eard o' 'im. Right, Mags?"

"Right," said Mags.

"Right," said Jury and walked away.

He should have realized Benny wouldn't be there this night; he wouldn't have led police to their spot beneath the bridge. Probably, he went to the Lodge with

Gemma; if not, there was always the Moonraker. Miss Penforwarden would always be glad to see Benny.

He climbed the steps to Waterloo Bridge and walked a little way, and stopped. He looked off toward the South Bank and thought again about that last scene in the movie, Robert Taylor—Roy—and his artful little smile. Jury sighed. He thought about Alexandra Tynedale and Erin Riordin, about Gemma Trimm who looked like Alexandra: black hair, heart-shaped face—

Oh, for God's sake, man, so will the next dark-haired woman you pass. You're obsessing. Stop this bloody romanticizing everything.

It had been so early when he had started this Christmas Day that he could hardly believe it wasn't yet noon. The sun floated dully in the sky, throwing off a scarf of light and mist about the Houses of Parliament. London. London did not have the allure of Paris or the burning energy of New York, but it was still a knock-out city, London.

FIFTY-FIVE

"If a Tynedale wants the birth of a child kept secret—?" Wiggins's shrug was his silent assessment of Jury's and his mission. Useless. And he was to go to Manchester in an hour to have Christmas dinner with his sister and her "brood," as he called them.

"We've got it pinned down to a few hours, Wiggins. Can't be that many babies born on Guy Fawkes night in 1939." Jury had found an almanac to tell him at what time on that day in November it had turned dark.

Wiggins looked at the last document he had put in his pile and removed it. He removed the one underneath, too. Too early. Night had fallen around five P.M.

They were looking at documents in the registry office at Somerset House. There were tons of them it looked like, judging from box after box on shelf after shelf. The clerk they'd found and dragged down here to open the place hadn't been happy. *It's Christmas, after all.*

"Yes, sir," said Wiggins. "But I could use some hot—" He raised his paper cup of cooling tea.

Jury nodded. "Go ahead." Wiggins left Somerset House for the kiosk out on the pavement, its owner keeping the canteen full even on Christmas morning. "Some people," he had said when Wiggins expressed surprise at this diligence, "still gotta push the envelope, well, look at you lot."

"Push the envelope? Been too many American CEOs hanging about his tea canteen," said Jury, as he added another certificate to the stack before him. There must have been three dozen here. He winnowed out several as having been born too early in the day for the fireworks. It was amazing how many children seemed to be born all of the time. He was looking only at babies born after five P.M. Staggering, really.

"Here's something, sir. Baby girl, Olivia—" Wiggins paused in surprise.

"What?"

"The baby's name here is given as Olivia Croft."

Jury snatched the paper out of Wiggins's hands. "That's a turnup, that is. Croft." He continued reading. "Born eight P.M., November 5, 1939. At a place called Chewley Hill. It's near Princes Risborough in the Chilterns. Call the place, will you? Tell them I'm on my way. Tell them who it's about. And when they say, 'But it's *Christmas*!' just pretend you didn't know."

"But, it *is* Christmas, sir!"

Jury was shoving his arms into his coat. "Could've fooled me. Do that, Wiggins, then get the hell out of town and on your way to Manchester." Out the door, Jury came back. "And thanks, Wiggins. Happy Christmas."

"And to you, sir."

Chewley Hill, both house and hill, sat at the edge of the Chilterns in a winter light that lent the surroundings a dreamy quality. The ambient light informed the surrounding fields and the bell tower of the church in the town below as if nothing too bright, too harsh should disturb the house's serenity—hard won, Jury would say.

He stood in a galleried hall, looking up the gracefully

arcing staircase on both sides and thought that any young woman with the means to come here should feel lucky—though, of course, she wouldn't. Two very pregnant young ladies (girls, really) standing near the stairwell with their heads together and giggling looked his way. He smiled. Surely, they'd had enough of flirting for the time being, hadn't they?

That the woman who had headed up this tastefully appointed house in 1939 was still heading it up struck Jury as little more than miraculous. Miss Judy Heron did too, and she enjoyed the miracle. "Fifty-five years, Superintendent. I was twenty-four back then and I'm seventy-nine now. I'm very fortunate and so, I think, is Chewley, having that kind of continuity. No, you could say there's little turnover in help here." She smiled.

So did Jury. "I can see why, Miss Heron." He felt the name suited her, for she struck Jury as some tall, thin, graceful wading bird, slow moving and delicate. The unhurried movement was not a sign of her advanced years, but more one of temperament. He could see her even at twenty-four moving in this same, underwater way. She was a calm and calming presence. And so was this room, with its mingling of easy chairs and antique settee, its wall of books, its pale gray walls and warming fire. Even time passed effortlessly, softly ticked away by the longcase clock near the window.

"Sometimes I regret that these girls do not come back to visit. But it's not an experience one cares to be reminded of, I expect. An unwanted pregnancy is a very sad thing. It was then, and it is now. In spite of all the new freedom that women enjoy, there are some heartbreaks that never change, never."

"That's what you find it to be?"

"Of course."

"I don't know, Miss Heron. The two women I saw out there looked pretty much to be taking pregnancy in their stride."

"I'm glad. It won't last long. That will end when their babies are born and they have to give them up. It's emotionally devastating. Frankly, I favor abortion."

Jury tried to mask his shock, but didn't manage it. "You? But—"

She smiled. "You'd think just the opposite, because I run this house? That's rather sanctimonious of you, Superintendent. Abortion as an issue is beyond the means of common morality to penetrate, I think. Oh, common morality is necessary of course. But it's an abstraction. If you saw, time after time, the effect giving up her child has on a young woman, you might agree with me." She looked sadly around her office, more a drawing room with a desk. She sat behind it, surrounded by neat stacks of paper and a folder positioned on the blotter beneath her hands. "I'm sorry for going on. How can I help you? You said—or, rather, your sergeant did—that you were on a case that had to do with the Tynedale family. Alexandra's family."

"That's right. It's a homicide. A man named Simon Croft." He waited for her to react to the name.

"Croft." She looked at him. "I thought she'd just chosen the name out of the clear blue. I see not. Olivia was the baby's first name. The couple who adopted the baby probably changed her first name as well as her last. They often do that; I expect it makes them feel a bit more like her real parents."

Jury waited.

She was silent; then she said, "Superintendent, you can understand that I wouldn't want to break faith with these young women—"

"Something broke faith long ago, Miss Heron. The war did. Alexandra was killed in the London blitz."

"I know, yes, I know."

Jury supposed she had a battery of lawyers beamed in her direction, but they probably wouldn't get far when the confidentiality angle was obstructing the investigation of a homicide. He thought she probably was considering this.

He sat regarding her for a moment and then nodded toward the folder her arms were crossed over. "Is that Alexandra's file?"

"Yes."

They looked at each other while the clock ticked softly. It occurred to Jury that her eyes were as intelligent as any he had ever seen and he thought then of Emily Croft. They were much alike. Jury cocked his head. "You've spoken to the parents already, haven't you?"

"Olivia's adoptive parents are dead. But there is an aunt. I felt I should alert her to the possibility of your going there. I do hope that's not stealing New Scotland Yard's thunder?"

Jury laughed. "Thunder is in short supply, believe me."

She smiled and handed him the folder. "The parents' name, and also the aunt's, is Woburn, Elizabeth Woburn. She lives in Chipping Camden. The Woburns, Alice and Samuel, lived there also. There is really little else I can tell you." She handed him the file. "But I expect Elizabeth Woburn can tell you a great deal more. She's expecting your call."

"Thank you." Jury opened the file and looked at the one page.

Judy Heron nodded. "You may keep that, Superintendent. After your sergeant called, I made you a copy."

He grinned. "God, you certainly do anticipate, Miss Heron."

"I know. It's a faculty I've developed over the years. I deal largely with overwrought people. You can infer that these young women are hardly jubilant when they come here. It's such a pity to be a mother and not be able to feel good about it." She looked at Jury. "Couldn't you get by without knowing the ending, Superintendent?"

It recalled to him the question put to Trueblood by

the Italian art experts. *Can't you live without the answer, Mr. Jury?*

"No. I can't."

He thanked Judy Heron, and rose and left.

V

Vanishing Point

FIFTY-SIX

Awakened by a sharp tug on consciousness, Melrose sat straight up in bed and looked wildly around.

"The grocer!" he said to himself. "My God, the *grocer!*"

He reached for the phone, realized he hadn't the number, started to buzz Ruthven, changed his mind and, fueled by like amounts of fury and fright, ran downstairs to the library to the phone and his small phone book. He found the number and yanked up the receiver. Although Jury probably wouldn't be there, he dialed and heard the phone ring in the Islington flat. He listened to the repeated *brr-brr* and then an answering machine switched on. Thank God, at least there was a chance of getting a message to him. After Jury announced himself and told the caller to leave a message after the tone, Melrose waited. There was a series of clicks and then the tone, which went on and on. Who in hell was calling Jury? The cast of the Royal Shakespeare Company? The Bolshoi Ballet? The "tone" was not a tone; it was a total eclipse of all other sound bites. Melrose slammed down the receiver to call—where? New Scotland Yard? Jury wouldn't be there, surely. Hadn't Jury said he was going to have Christmas dinner with Carole-anne . . . last name? *last name?* and Mrs., Mrs., Mrs.—hell! How could he get their numbers if he didn't know their last names. Zimmermann, Zinnemann, Waltersonn . . . Hell!

I'll have to get going. He was glad he'd fallen asleep fully dressed.

When he turned to the library door, Ruthven was there. "Can I do something for you, m'lord?"

"Absolutely. Get me some tea and the car keys. I'm going back to London."

Ruthven frowned. "You're going *back*, m'lord? But you only just returned two hours ago."

Melrose had passed by him and was already taking the stairs two at a time. "That's right."

"Which car?" Ruthven called up the stairs.

"Batmobile."

The three of them sat about, relaxed and drinking whiskey, beer and sherry, talking about old times they'd shared—pints at the Angel pub, that rock concert at the Hammersmith Odeon, all of those prospective tenants for the flat upstairs that Carole-anne had turned away . . . Until Stan Keeler came along, and *voilà*!

Primly, Carole-anne said, "It's because he was most suitable, that's all. I could tell Stan was a responsible, dependable person."

"Oh, sure," said Jury.

"Old times, old times," said Mrs. Wassermann, still caught up in that cloud of nostalgia we all keep our heads in from time to time. And why not?

"Only the times can't be that old, Mrs. Wassermann," said Jury. "Carole-anne's only fifteen."

Carole-anne, the soberest of the three, picked a copy of *The Lady* from the coffee table and gave Jury a couple of thwacks with it. She was wearing a dress of some sort of glimmering material that shifted, in different lights, from violet to turquoise. Jury warded off the blows with his forearm.

Carole-anne stopped the magazine in midthwack and

looked up at the ceiling. "That your phone, Super?" They fell deathly quiet in that way people do when trying to make out sound that vanishes just as one listens for it. Carole-anne shrugged and said, "If it is, your answering machine'll pick it up. Aren't you glad I got you one?"

"No. It never works right." Jury yawned, completely full of the best turkey and stuffing he could ever recall eating, a dinner, on the whole, as good as the dinner at Ardry End, though in a different way.

"Yes, it does. It does for me, anyway. You're one of those people machines don't like is what I think. I'm surprised your watch runs right with you setting off negative vibes the way you do. Next, you need a cell phone. Like that call right then—" she looked up at the ceiling "—you wouldn't've missed that call if you'd had your cell phone."

"I'm glad I didn't, then. You want a cell phone ringing during Christmas dinner? The world is a damned call box these days."

"Never mind. I think it's scandalous the department doesn't issue cell phones. Scandalous!"

"You're probably right, but I'd send out the same vibes over it, too."

"It's a disgrace, Mr. Jury," said Mrs. Wassermann. "With the life you have to lead. Yes, Carole-anne is right." She made her way out to the kitchen to start the next round of fat-fueling food. Dessert was to be Christmas pudding *and* trifle. She was weaving ever so slightly and turned to wag her finger at Carole-anne. "But don't call him negative, Carole-anne. You should be ashamed, with all he's done for you!" She went on to the kitchen, calling for Carole-anne to come and help her with the dessert.

Carole-anne followed, carrying her beer, and saying, "All I done for *him*, I'd say!"

Jury smiled up at the ceiling, wondering if that *had* been his telephone, and if he should check out the answering machine to see if it was working for once.

He had called Elizabeth Woburn, probably interrupted her Christmas dinner, but she had been quite civil nonetheless, and said he would be welcome, though not on Christmas Day, of course; if he could come Boxing Day or the day after? He really had to let Mickey know what had happened at Chewley Hill.

He called to Mrs. Wassermann that he was just going up to his flat for a few minutes and would be right back. Of course, she couldn't hear him because Carole-anne was in there with her, talking a mile a minute.

Upstairs, Jury checked the answering machine, found nothing on it but that damned clicking sound and wondered into what answering machine graveyard the call had gone, assuming that it had been his telephone that rang. He dialed Haggerty's number.

"Mickey," said Jury, "I've got something that may be helpful, maybe not, but—"

"Hold it while whoever's choking on a turkey bone coughs it up—*quiet!* for God's sake."

There was the briefest lull while Mickey turned back to pick up the conversation and then the background noise erupted at even greater pitch, amplified by a host of giggles. Christmas was certainly giggling season. He was relieved that Mickey and his family were having what sounded like a genuinely good time. It might be the last good time.

"Sorry, Richie, you were saying—?"

"I found the people who adopted Alexandra Tynedale's baby. It was a girl; she named it Olivia Croft."

"*What?* Why would she do that, for God's sake? She wants to keep the birth a secret and then names the baby *Croft.* Why?"

"An acknowledgment is my guess. According to the woman who runs the place, giving up a child is the most painful thing a woman has to do. Alexandra said to Kitty that it was the worst thing that ever happened to her. Oh, of course, the adoptive parents would change the name, but at least the child would be a Croft to

Alexandra until that happened. The couple themselves, named Woburn, are both dead now but an aunt is still alive and living in Chipping Camden. Her name's Elizabeth Woburn. I'm seeing her tomorrow, noonish. Little Olivia was an only child and Elizabeth Woburn sounded extremely fond of her."

"I'll be damned. Well, good work, but my money's still on Kitty or Erin."

"Maybe." Jury sat with one shoe off, an ankle across the other knee, trying to work a pebble or whatever it was out of his sock. Maybe, but Jury didn't think so; he didn't think Kitty Riordin had shot Simon Croft. Erin? Perhaps. Admittedly, this would come under the heading of "hunch." "What about Maisie? Or, rather, Erin? What did she say?"

"Zilch, zero—nothing until her lawyer shows up. What? No, I told you"—Mickey had turned away from the phone—"come on, don't 'But, Dad' me. Go ask your mother." Mickey laughed, returned to Jury. "That's discipline, right? 'Ask your mother'?" Voices rose again in the background. "Listen: I stopped by the Croft house earlier and—" He was cut off again by a child's screaming demands. "Rich, this place is an effing madhouse. I want to talk to you; I want to show you something at the Croft house. Whenever you're done with whatever monster celebration you've got going, do you think you could meet me there?"

"It's pretty much wound down, except for dessert, which I don't think I could eat anyway. I could meet you there, sure. I could do it now, if you like."

"Say, a half hour or forty-five minutes?"

"Right." Jury hung up, checked the answering machine again and would happily have thrown it out of the window, except he'd never hear the end of it from Carole-anne.

Melrose sat in one of Boring's soft leather armchairs as if he'd been painted there. His hand was not so much holding a glass of whiskey as it was wedded to it. He had hoped the drink would unstick his mind, but it didn't seem to be helping.

Snow Hill! That was it; that was the name of DCI Haggerty's station. The Snow Hill station. The telephone was sitting on a table at his elbow and he put in a call. He asked if Superintendent Jury happened to be there or if they knew where he was. Jury hadn't been seen since that morning, the sergeant said and, no, DCI Haggerty was at home. It was Christmas, after all. Melrose wished people would stop saying that. He asked for Haggerty's home phone and was refused it. Melrose inveighed against this refusal, insisting it was an emergency and the sergeant said, yes, sir, it always is.

Damn! He decided to try Jury again. What he got was the same sandblast tone that went on and on and—stopped! He was permitted now to leave a message at least. He got through the first bit of what he wanted to say and then *click click click click*. The damned machine cut him off. He dialed the number again and heard the endless tone.

Melrose slammed down the receiver. Even if Jury hadn't the foggiest notion as to what the truncated message meant, he would at least know that Melrose was trying to get in touch with him and that it was important. Maybe he'd call Ardry End. Yes, he probably would. Ruthven could tell him—wait! Ruthven didn't know he was at Boring's. Melrose dialed again and when Ruthven answered (thank the Lord a *person* on the other end), Melrose told him he was at Boring's and that if Superintendent Jury called to tell him not to speak to anybody until Melrose had had a chance to talk to him.

There. Not much, but something was better than nothing. Catching Young Higgins's eye, Melrose made a circle over the rim of his glass, signaling for a refill. Then he continued to think. Who else, who, who, *who* did he and Jury know in common? The Crippses. Not bloody likely Jury would be checking in there. Melrose ran the cold glass across his forehead, glad of the ice cube, even though it diluted (slightly) the effect of the whiskey, and slid down in his chair. He felt he should be actively *finding* Jury—

Keeler! Was he in town? Was it possible that club was open on Christmas Day? Melrose motioned Higgins to come over, which the old porter did, if slowly. "Higgins, would you please get a number for a club called the Nine-One-Nine, ring it and see if it's open and ask if a Mr. Keeler is doing his gig there? Thanks."

Young Higgins frowned. "Gig, sir?"

"Ah . . . never mind, Higgins, just ask if the club is open tonight."

The old porter shuffled off, leaving Melrose to drum his fingers on the arm of his chair. Young Higgins was back in record time telling Melrose that yes, the club was open.

"Get me a cab, *now!*"

The Nine-One-Nine was a place he'd never have found unless he'd known exactly where it was, a half dozen steps down and bearing no identification except for its street number. He had been here years before, after that rock concert and just before seeing Vivian off on the *Orient Express*.

There was an air of smoke and languor about the club that put Melrose in mind of those 1930s prewar Berlin clubs that exist only in films and imagination. He stood at the bar and ordered another whiskey (his fourth tonight? fifth?). As he glanced at the other patrons, he thought he detected a few approving glances from the women and put this down to his black clothes. He was still wearing them.

When the group (what was its name?) broke, Melrose immediately pushed his way up to the small stage area and cut in front of the two girls hanging on Stan's leather jacket and every word. "Mr. Keeler? You don't remember me, but—"

"Hey! Your earlship, sure I remember. What's up?"

"I've got to find Richard Jury and don't even know his address and as you live in the same house—"

"Haven't seen him today, but I know he was having Christmas dinner with Carole-anne and Mrs. Wassermann."

(Wassermann, of course!)

"What's going on? Is something wrong? . . . *Later*," he said to a girl with a helmet of slick black hair who was trying to engage his attention.

"I can't get him on the phone."

"That's probably from Carole-anne messing with that answering machine. You got a car? I'd drive you, man, except I'm locked in here for another couple hours." Stan was writing the address on a paper napkin. "Here."

"Thanks."

"Listen, come back and let me know if anything's wrong. Please." Stan looked worried.

For an icon, thought Melrose, he was *way* cool. Melrose sketched a salute and left.

Outside, Jury had stopped on his way to his car to thank Mrs. Wassermann again for the dinner, when he heard the phone ring, thought it was his again, but knew it would stop before he could get up there to answer. Let the answering machine do what it's paid for, for once.

"I'll come back for that in a while," he said to Mrs. Wassermann, with a nod at the dessert.

She was holding a green glass plate on which was a portion of pudding. "I'll keep it for you and when you come back—" Suddenly, she stopped, as if the words had stuck in her throat.

"Mrs. Wassermann?" Jury put his hands on her shoulders. "Mrs. *Wassermann*?" He tilted his head, trying to see her face. It was bent over the plate of pudding. Then she raised her face and her look was so sorrowful, Jury was alarmed. "What is it?"

"Nothing, nothing. It was just for a moment I had this—"

"Yes?" Jury's tone was encouraging. When she didn't go on, he said, "You look so awfully worried."

"It was—" She shook her head. "Where are you going?"

Jury was so surprised by her questioning him he took a step back. Mrs. Wassermann never asked questions that might be construed as prying. So scrupulous was she and with so strong a sense of privacy that a question like this one would be considered an invasion of it.

He said, "Just to meet someone. The case we're working on."

She kept looking at him, hard, when upstairs a window flew up and Carole-anne leaned out of it. It was Jury's window, not Carole-anne's. "Super! There's a message on your machine!" She seemed proud that the machine was functioning.

"Who?" The light in the flat behind her flooded her hair and made her dress glisten. What a sight.

"Well, I don't know, do I? He never said his name. What I think was he got cut off in the middle of talking. It was a peculiar message anyway."

Jury was looking up, waiting. Carole-anne seemed to be thinking, if one could judge thought from down here on the pavement. "What did he say?"

"It was something like, you could only trust your greengrocer. No, *don't* trust your greengrocer. Something like that."

Knowing Carole-anne's penchant for messing up messages, Jury bet it was "something like that." For a weird moment all he could think of was Mr. Steptoe. Jury told Mrs. Wassermann he was going back to his flat and for her not to worry. "It's too cold for being out here without a coat. Go back inside and I'll see you later." He knew he sounded impossibly condescending, which he hated.

Shimmering, silver-dust fingernails on shimmering turquoise hip, Carole-anne punched the replay button. Melrose Plant's voice, sounding surprisingly untaped, said, "*Don't* trust your grocer, like Masaccio, and don't—" End of message.

"He got cut off," said Carole-anne, reproachfully. "It's something wrong with the machine."

Jury found the number for Ardry End and dialed. Carole-anne was looking so troubled, he winked at her, then said, "Ruthven, this is Richard Jury. Is Mr. Plant there?"

"No, sir. But he wanted me to give you a message—" (Jury hoped it wasn't the one about the grocer.)

"—that he'd be at his club and for you to ring him there. And you weren't to talk to anyone until you'd talked to him. He was most emphatic on that point, sir."

Jury frowned. "But—what's he doing at Boring's? I thought he drove back to Northamptonshire this morning."

"He did, sir. But this afternoon he turned right around and returned to London. I should say that he did so in an enormous hurry and in a highly agitated state."

Jury smiled fractionally. He wondered if he'd ever seen Melrose Plant in a "highly agitated state." He rang off and saw that Carole-anne was herself looking agitated and put his arm around her shoulders. Then he thumbed his small telephone index and came up with Boring's number. Carole-anne seemed to be settling in, head against his chest. Everyone was acting queerly tonight, including, he supposed, himself. When the porter answered (not Young Higgins, but the ginger-haired lad) Jury asked for Mr. Plant. After some asking around had been done, the young porter returned and said that Mr. Plant had just left.

"Not more'n five minutes ago, sir. Is there a message?"

The night seemed made of nothing but messages. "Just tell him Superintendent Jury called, will you?"

His arm still around Carole-anne, he frowned, wondering what was going on. Obviously, Plant knew something, or had come up with something, but ... Masaccio's grocer? What the hell was that supposed to mean?

"Super?"

"Huh?"

"What's going on? And where are you off to?"

He looked down at her. "Just to meet someone. Another copper."

"But it's Christmas."

"Yep. And we haven't had our Christmas kiss."

Intake of breath on her part. "What Christmas—?"

"This one." He kissed her.

The kiss was not terribly long, or terribly hard. There have been longer, harder kisses in this world, but it was longer, perhaps, and harder than need be.

Carole-anne was knocked for a loop. "Super!" She staggered back to look at him, probably in much the same way Cinderella had looked at the coach and footmen. Then, rearranging a sleeve and a curl (which needed none), she said, "I'll still be here New Year's, in case you didn't know."

Jury laughed.

She went upstairs and he went down.

FIFTY-SEVEN

By now he was late and Mickey was probably already waiting for him at the Croft house, so he knew he shouldn't be stopping at the bridge, but he did anyway. He wanted to check on Benny. He parked his car along the Embankment and went down the steps.

There was a small cluster of people there, warming themselves at a small stove.

"Benny around?" asked Jury.

"Wasn't you 'ere before, mate?"

Jury recognized the man in the greatcoat. Tonight he was wearing an olive green soldier's cap. "I was, yes. I'm a friend."

The soldier snorted. "You're the Filth's, what I say."

The woman called Mags, blanketed in sweaters and shawls, was there, too. "Benny'll be back. He went off after Sparky. That dog o' his. You want t' leave a message?"

Jury smiled. A night of missed meetings and messages. "No, except you can tell him Happy Christmas for me."

"Right-o. Who's 'me'?"

"The Filth."

She chortled.

*　　*　　*

Before he got into his car, he looked over his shoulder at Waterloo Bridge. The old bridge had been a granite thing with columns and arches, wrought iron and black lamps. It had been so romantic—the black Thames, the night, the fog. Even the war was made out to be romantic. He imagined Vivien Leigh looking into the dark water. Robert Taylor with that hint of a smile playing around his lips, smoking a cigarette. Myra and Roy. What a lie.

As he entered the forecourt, the car caught Mickey in its headlights, making him look vulnerable and unprotected. He was standing out on the dock, smoking. Certainly, Mickey *was* vulnerable and unprotected. Jury wondered how he himself would take the verdict that he was going to die. Not well. Who would? "Mickey!" he called and walked through the forecourt out onto the pier.

Mickey took the cigarette from his mouth and flicked it into the water. He said, "Always love doing that, Rich. Flick the butts away, watch them arc and fall." He dug his hands deeper into the pockets of his overcoat.

Jury smiled. "You're worse than I am, seeing cigarettes in such a romantic light. How was Christmas, Mickey?"

"Terrific. Exhausting." He laughed a little.

That Mickey was exhausted was evident. "Sorry I'm late. I stopped at Waterloo Bridge to check on Benny."

"He holes up there, doesn't he? That kid. God."

"He does. But I think somehow he's making it." Jury paused. "You look pretty tired."

"Yeah. I am." He nodded toward the boat farther out. "I was just looking at that boat, thinking about Gemma Trimm." He smiled. "Some kids those two are."

Jury nodded. "So are yours."

"Don't I know it. What gets to me more than anything is that they probably won't have the opportunity to find that out."

"But they will."

Mickey shook his head. "Not without the right schools. Not without Oxford."

"Come on, Mickey. Is this what you dragged me away from my Christmas dinner for?"

"Sorry. No, of course not. Waterloo Bridge." Mickey sighed, as if the same nostalgia that had rushed Jury were rushing him, too. "I was sure you must've caught on at the Liberty Bounds that night."

"'Caught on'?" Jury frowned, started to say something else, but didn't because he didn't know what he was responding to. Then it came to him. "You know who killed Simon Croft."

Mickey watched the water, nodded. "I did."

Jury stepped back. Plant's message hit him right between the eyes. The grocer. The one person Masaccio knew he could trust. Mickey was the person he had known he could trust. In another moment of standing there, staring at Mickey, Jury felt something leave him. It could have been courage; it could have been reason, or rationality, or sanity; it could have been faith. He didn't think it was any of those things. He thought it was hope. And it was gone for good. If he lived, something that looked like it would come back: a poor imitation, a shadow, but not the real thing. He thought all of this in exactly three seconds.

And why wouldn't he live?

Mickey took a few steps back from Jury. He had always been so fluid in his movements that Jury didn't see the gun until it was in Mickey's hand.

"What in hell are you doing, Mickey?"

"I'm really sorry, Rich. Sounds meaningless, but I really am."

"For Christ's sake, you're pointing that at *me*!" Jury took three furious steps toward Mickey. The shot spun him around, but it had only raked his shoulder. His other hand flew to the place. Blood, but not much. Mickey was one of the best shots in the City police. He hadn't tried to kill him. That time. "What . . . *Why*?"

"Because you'd sort it, Rich. You'd work it out. I'm surprised you haven't. But that's only because you're my friend."

He said this in a tone of such demonic innocence, Jury wanted to weep. "Mickey, look—" When an answer comes, there is no orderly procession of facts—first this, then this caused this, then this . . . Jury thought it was more like one of those kaleidoscopes he remembered as a kid, where all the little bits of colored glass or plastic fly together in a pattern. The vanishing point. When you see it, it's too late; it's gone.

Mickey said, "You only had one more step to take, and you were about to. Elizabeth Woburn. They named her after the aunt."

Liza, thought Jury. My God, *Liza. We were all orphans . . .*

He had said it aloud without realizing it. Mickey said, "When you started all of that stuff about the film—I mean, *Waterloo Bridge*—I was sure you knew. Myra and Roy. How much Alexandra looked like Vivien Leigh, and how much Liza did. I thought you were trying to warn me off. To do what, I don't know—" Mickey shrugged, almost absently.

The waters of the Thames undulated as a speedboat rushed by. The dock swayed.

"Can you reason for a minute, Mickey? If I found out Liza was Tynedale's granddaughter, what possible harm could it do? If I told Tynedale, the man would be ecstatic!"

"Oh, that's why I got you on the case. I don't know how long I've got; I needed you to carry on. It would be even more convincing coming from you. Except you worked out a little too much. If Tynedale discovered Francis Croft was the father, no, he wouldn't be ecstatic. You know it. Do you really think he'd welcome Liza into the family knowing that? It would be the ultimate betrayal."

"I don't think so. Tynedale's an unusual man. I don't think he has a strong impulse toward revenge."

"Could I take the chance? Liza will come into millions."

"Does she know?"

"Of course not." Mickey laughed. "But she will. I've left documents with our solicitor."

"Simon Croft knew."

Mickey nodded. "I had to take the laptop, the manuscript—"

"To make it look as if he were killed because of the book. Croft wasn't paranoid." Jury felt lightheaded; he was still bleeding, could feel the blood slick beneath his hand. "You made it look like an amateur trying to make it look like a robbery. That was very clever, very subtle. You'll never get away with this, Mickey. Think."

"Thinking is all I've been doing for six months. I'll get away with it."

The second shot slammed into Jury's side as if he'd had a head-on collision with a train and drove him to his knees. The impact pushed him back, driving everything in its path, flesh bone tissue. It jerked him sideways, knocking him against the pilings, cutting his head. The third shot threw him back as if the train he'd just hit kept right on going. He saw his own blood for a second burst upward and fall like rain. More blood in a sea of it. The fourth shot hadn't been aimed at him, wasn't meant for him. He heard the thud, felt the dock shudder. He couldn't see because he couldn't raise himself.

Moments passed. He waited. For what?

Had somebody come? Here was hope in its cheap new clothes again. Jesus, he thought, we're weak. We'll hang on to whatever old lies we want to just as long as we can go on living. Why didn't whoever had come speak? He felt himself being lifted a little way off the dock; it must be a stretcher they'd put him on. He felt something—a sheet? A blanket?—lowered to cover him. He kept his eyes closed because blood from a cut on his forehead trickled into them. He was glad he was on the stretcher under a cover, even if it was so thin he could barely feel it. Thin as air it was. Then he thought: no, it would take two people to carry the stretcher. His forehead no longer felt blood wet and so it was safe to open his eyes. Strange how the night sky was exactly as he'd left it. The stillness was implacable. He couldn't even hear the water lapping against the pilings. He wondered how much blood he'd lost. The pain had lessened or become at least less acute, as if it had liquefied.

He was unyieldingly sleepy, but he must stay awake. Could be concussion, after all. It was taking the police a long time. Who would have called them to come? Mickey would have; Mickey wouldn't, in the end, have left him to die here. No. Mickey was dead.

He heard a voice.

Mr. Jury, Mr. Jury!

"Benny?" Where was he? "Benny?"

And a clicking sound, nails tapping against the dock. Sparky?

But what had been close, the voice, the nails tapping, now receded into the indifferent distance. No one was near; no one had been. *Death holds no surprises. Hold on to that notion, Superintendent.*

A star fell. He thought about Stratford-upon-Avon and the little park near the church where Shakespeare was buried. There had been several of them, school-children smoking in the darkness of a small, colonnaded building, their words flung into the night like the bright coal ends of their cigarettes.

My God. He wanted to laugh aloud. Bleeding his life away and he was thinking about a smoke. But then they had always been more than just cigarettes, hadn't they? He remembered the schoolgirl flicking hers away into the darkness—(*Always loved doing that, Rich . . . watch them arc and fall*)—and the arc it made, sparking like a star shower. *Brightness falls from the air.* The things of this world, he thought. In the distance, through the frosty Christmas air, he heard a dog bark.

Sparky.

Melrose Plant looked around the rather grim environs of the Grave Maurice and wondered if it was patronized by the staff of the Royal College of Surgeons up the street. Apparently it did serve as some sort of stopping-off point for them, for Melrose recognized one of the doctors standing at the farther end of the long bar.

As Melrose stood there inside the door, the doctor emptied his half-pint, gathered up his coat and turned to leave. He passed Melrose on his way out of the pub and gave him a distracted nod and a vague smile, as if he were trying to place him.

Melrose stepped up to the place the doctor had left, filling the vacuum. He was looking at the woman close by, one of surpassing beauty—glossy dark hair, high cheekbones, eyes whose color he couldn't see without staring but which were large and widely spaced. She was talking to another woman, hair a darkish blond, whose back was turned to Melrose and who drank a pale drink, probably a Chardonnay, whose ubiquity, together with the wine bars that loved to serve it up, Melrose couldn't understand. The dark-haired one was drinking stout. Good for her. The bartender, a bearded Indian, posed an indecipherable query that Melrose could only suppose was a variant of "What will it be, mate?" The operative term was either "grog" or "dog," as in "Want a bit o' grog?" or "Walkin' yer dog?" Having no dog, Melrose ordered an Old Peculier.

The Grave Maurice had its foot in the door of "hovel-like." Melrose looked all around and made his assessment, pleased. For some reason, he could always appreciate a hovel; he felt quite at home. The incomprehensible barman, the patched window, the broken table leg, the streaked mirror, the clientele. The two women near him were a cut above the other customers. They were well dressed, the dark-haired one quite fashionably, in a well-cut black suit and understated jewelry. The blond one, whose profile Melrose glimpsed, appeared to know the barman (even to understand the barman) with his raffishly wound turban. After he returned, smilingly, with the refills and Melrose's fresh drink and then took himself off, the dark-haired woman picked up their conversation again. The blonde was doing the listening.

They were talking about someone named Ryder, which immediately made Melrose prick up his ears, as this was the name of the doctor who had just departed and whom, he supposed, the one woman must have recognized. But he was rather surprised to hear him further referred to as "poor sod." The second woman, whose voice was distinct while at the same time being low and unobtrusive, asked the dark-haired one what she meant.

Melrose waited for the answer.

Unfortunately, the details were getting lost in the woman's lowered voice, but he did catch the word *disappeared*. The dark-haired woman dipped her head to her glass and said something else that Melrose couldn't catch.

But then he heard, "His daughter. It was in the papers."

The blonde seemed appalled. "When was that?"

"Nearly two years ago, but it doesn't get any—"

Melrose lost the rest of the comment.

The one who had made it shrugged slightly, not a dismissive shrug, but a weary one. Weary, perhaps, of misfortune. If she was a doctor too, Melrose could understand the weariness.

Then she said, "... brother was my ... killed ..."

The blonde made a sound of sympathy and said, "How awful. Did—"

If only they'd stop talking clearly on the one hand and whispering on the other! Melrose, who kept telling himself he couldn't help overhearing this conversation, could, of course, have taken his beer to a table, and he supposed he would if his presence so close beside them got to be a little too noticeable. But he wanted to hear whatever he could about this doctor's daughter—it sounded fascinating. He thought the phrase *poor sod* suggested some unhappy tale and he was always up for one of those. Sort of thing that makes you glad you're you and not them. How morbid.

He then heard something about insurance and the dark-haired woman was going on about South America and warmer climate.

She appeared to be planning a trip. He didn't care about this; he wanted to hear more about the person who had disappeared. The blonde occasionally turned to retrieve her cigarette, and then Melrose could pick up the drift.

"—this doctor's daughter?"

The woman facing Melrose nodded. "So it never ends for him ... closure."

"I hate that word," said the blonde, with a little laugh. (Melrose was ready to marry her on the spot. Inwardly, he applauded. He hated the word too.)

"All it means is that something's unended, unfinished. Why not just say that?"

The blonde was not in the mood for a semantic argument. "There never is, anyway," she said, slipping from the stool.

"What?" The dark-haired woman was puzzled.

"Closure. Everything remains unfinished."

The dark-haired woman sighed. "Perhaps. Poor Roger."

Roger Ryder, thought Melrose. When the blonde caught Melrose looking and listening she gave him a rueful half smile. He pretended not to notice, though it would be difficult not to notice that mouth, that hair. Melrose paid for his beer and slid off the stool.

His daughter. Two years ago something had happened to her, and it hadn't been death. Death would have closed it. The girl had disappeared. Had something happened in South America? No, he thought, that must be another story altogether. On the other hand, Ryder's daughter's disappearance—*that* had been in the papers. But Melrose wouldn't have to search the *Times*.

Roger Ryder was Richard Jury's surgeon.